Denise Ryan was born in C
her early years. She then
various countries. She studi
had some bizarre jobs, incl
and a translator and speech
Her hobbies include reading, chocolate, writing fiction, and
confiding intimate secrets to her Dear Diary. She is married and
works as a freelance translator.

Also by Denise Ryan

The Hit
Dead Keen

Betrayed

Denise Ryan

PIATKUS

Copyright © 2002 by Denise Ryan

First published in Great Britain in 2002 by
Judy Piatkus (Publishers) Ltd of
5 Windmill Street, London W1T 2JA
email: info@piatkus.co.uk

This edition published 2002

The moral right of the author has been asserted

A catalogue record for this book is available from the British Library

ISBN 0 7499 3319 4

Set in Times by
Action Publishing Technoloy Ltd, Gloucester

Printed and bound in Great Britain by
Bookmarque Ltd, Croydon, Surrey

To Peter, Mum, Michael
With love and thanks

Also to David, Nuria, Marc and Martin

and to other family and friends
(they know who they are!)

Acknowledgements

I would like to thank the Friends of Williamson's Tunnels Society (FOWT) whose excellent website and quarterly publication, *The Mole*, provided me with much fascinating information and inspiration for this novel.

Good luck and best wishes from member 969.

Thanks also to Mr Bill Douglas of FOWT, for his kind help with a query.

I don't agree with Saddam Hussein that gratitude is a sickness for dogs, therefore I'm grateful to Kerith Biggs of the Darley Anderson Agency and Gillian Green, Senior Fiction Editor at Piatkus Books.

'A strange place it was. Vaulted passages cut out of solid rock; arches thrown up by craftsmen's hands, beautiful in proportion and elegant in form, but supporting nothing. Tunnels formed here – deep pit there. Here the work is finished off, as if the mason had laboured with consummate skill to complete his work, so that all the world might see and admire, although no human eyes save those of his master would ever be set upon it. Here lies the ponderous stone as it fell after the upheaving blast had dislodged it from its bed; and there vaulted over is a gulf that makes the brain dizzy and strikes us with terror as we look down into it. Now we see an arch, fit to bridge a mountain torrent; and in another step or two we meet another only fit to span a simple brook. Tiers of passages are met with, as dangerous to enter as they are strange to look at.'

Charles Hand, describing his exploration of Joseph Williamson's (1769–1840) underground labyrinth in 1907

Prologue

'You don't have a voice,' he said. 'You're nothing. Move.'

He jammed the gun into the girl's ribs. She imagined a bullet burning a charred hole in her mac and the skimpy red silk dress beneath. A hole in her heart through which blood would gush on to the cracked pavement. Her thin legs were bare and she couldn't stop shivering. Her face was bruised, her nose bleeding.

Chill mist swirled and darkness was closing fast. Car headlights glowed yellow on sloping Grinfield Street. Further up was the Bay Horse pub and across the road a big square building with a neon sign: Merseyside Police, Smithdown Lane. She had lost her terror of arrest and deportation. The police and immigration authorities now seemed like merciful angels who could rescue her and fly her home.

Three girls walked up the hill towards the Williamson Student Village on the corner of Mason Street. Their laughter reminded her of how it felt to be free. Not stripped of her clothes, identity, control over her own body. Her life belonged to him now.

He held her tight and they stood close together, like lovers. Two of her long, purple-painted nails were split and bleeding, but she felt no pain. Only terror.

'Give me back my passport,' she begged, staring up at his grim profile, the mouth that no longer smiled. 'I've

1

worked so hard – I'm finished. I promise, I'll never talk!'

'What d'you expect?' he asked. 'A Business Class ticket back to Bucuresti?' He pressed the gun against the pulsing artery in her throat. 'You disobeyed me. I warned you.'

'No! Don't hurt me,' she sobbed, struggling in his arms. 'Please!'

He dragged her along Smithdown Lane past derelict houses, fenced-off yards and deserted workshops. New residential developments were spreading all over Edge Hill, the great sandstone ridge two miles east of the city centre. He had grown up here, travelled the globe and come back to find developers had taken over. Joseph Williamson was long gone, had shuffled off his mortal coil in 1840, aged seventy. But the Mad Mole's legacy, his spirit, lived on.

He recalled the day he had walked down Mason Street to find the dusty cream sandstone walls of Joseph's house fenced off with steel, holes in the floor that gave access to the labyrinth protected by padlocked steel hatches numbered with yellow chalk. Fortunately other entrances were dotted around Edge Hill; entrances that he alone knew of. The ground shook as a train to Lime Street rumbled through the cutting. They reached the Lord Mayor's stable yard with its tumbledown buildings. Scattered bricks, broken window frames and heaps of old tyres littered the cobblestones.

'What is this place? Why do you bring me here?' She had expected a sordid flat where she would be raped repeatedly by several men and beaten, like last time. Did he mean to kill her? She lashed out at him in panic, forgetting the gun. The result was a punch in the face. She sagged moaning in his arms. Behind trees and brushes loomed a big double arch built of brick.

Thorns and sharp stones cut into her knees. He pulled the torch from his coat pocket. The entrance was partially blocked by undergrowth and rubble, sheets of rusted corrugated iron. Cold dampness engulfed them, filling their lungs. He used the belt of the mac to tie her hands. Blood

2

trickled from her nose and she felt dizzy.

He dragged her along a narrow passage, the low ceiling brushing his head. They emerged into a cavern with sandstone walls and soaring brick arches. Tunnels branched off in every direction. Two centuries of rubble lay all around, and the walls bore the pick marks of Joseph's workmen. Pools of concrete showed disturbing evidence of developers' activity. Several tunnels in the area had collapsed recently.

Her escape attempt could have cost him everything. It was a betrayal. A personal insult. She flinched as he touched her left breast, felt her wildly beating heart.

She was twenty, had been fired with ambition to make a new life in a rich country. Saw herself flying home laden with gifts. She had dreamed of her daughter's smile.

He flashed the torch to his right, sensing a movement. A grey rat scurried away.

'I don't want to die,' she sobbed. 'Please! Let me go home to my daughter.'

He stroked her long, black, silky hair. 'You made the wrong choices.'

He saw the dark forest, stunted trees against a crimson sky. The trees slowly turned to crucifixes dripping blood. He thought of Proverbs 16:25. The words haunted him more than the nightmare.

'"There is a way that seemeth right unto a man,"' he quoted softly, gazing into her terrified, glittering eyes, '"but the end thereof are the ways of death."'

He pulled her against him as if to embrace her.

Then he locked both arms around her neck.

Part One

Chapter One

'The bastard! How could he *do* this to me?'

The answer to that question, of course, was 'Easily'. Carmel Devine laid her case notes aside, sat back in her armchair and looked sympathetically at the tearful, auburn-haired woman in black sweatshirt and frayed blue jeans who was perched on the edge of the sofa working her way through a box of man-size tissues. All she could do at this stage was listen and empathise, help Nicole over her crisis as quickly as possible.

'So, Nicole – your ex-boyfriend beat you up, stole your money and stripped your house of valuables before he left. This after you discovered he'd lied about being a car salesman and that he actually made his money from dealing drugs. He threatened to beat you up again if you tried to find him or reported him to the police.'

The misty October afternoon was darkening, and a lavender-scented candle burned in a glass holder on the coffee table. The desk and floor lamps were switched on. Carmel glanced out of her office window on the third floor of the cavernous old building by the Pier Head, with its view of dockland and new leisure and residential developments. The latest plan or proposal was for a sixty million pound, thirty-one storey hotel in the business district. Twenty-first century Liverpool was a city in redevelopment. Soon the place would be unrecognisable.

'It's the second time some sod's ripped me off and done a runner,' Nicole wept. 'I really thought Steve was different. Oh, God, how thick am I?'

'You're not thick. People do nasty, stupid, cruel things all the time because they're fallible, screwed-up human beings.' Carmel paused. 'That's not your fault, is it?'

'Okay, but I feel awful! Devastated. It was bad enough the first time, but now I feel so stupid and useless. Such a loser. That's why I took the Valium.' Nicole raised her flushed, tear-stained face and stared at Carmel. 'I didn't really want to kill myself – because of the kids, you know?' Carmel nodded. 'I just felt so much pain, so betrayed. Thought I was going mental. I wanted to be out of it. Maybe I am mental. I'm twenty-eight, for God's sake!' she said bitterly. 'You'd think I'd have learned sense by now, wouldn't you? I don't give a toss about myself any more, but I've got three kids to think about. That's why I left hospital early – and agreed to this rational emotive therapy stuff.'

'Nicole ...' Carmel leaned forward. 'The way you feel right now is perfectly normal and understandable. You're not mental.' She smiled slightly. 'Practically anyone would agree that your boyfriend treated you very badly. To feel guilty and blame yourself for his actions won't help. You don't control his behaviour. You're not responsible.'

'Maybe not,' Nicole sniffed. She didn't sound entirely convinced, but at least she was calmer now. 'He was lovely at first,' she sighed, wiping her eyes. 'Such a laugh, so caring. Great with the kids. How was I supposed to guess what he was really like? Once he'd got his dirty great feet under the table he turned into a total bastard.'

'Remember at the start of our session I explained the ABC model of emotional disturbance to you?' Carmel asked. 'How A stands for the activating event – in your case, what your boyfriend did to you – B for your beliefs about that event, and C for the consequences arising from those beliefs, namely, your guilt feelings ...'

8

'I know what you're going to say,' Nicole interrupted. 'I've heard about this therapy crap. It's down to me, right? Brought it all on myself, didn't I, because I'm a stupid cow? I've got – what do you call it – faulty cognitions.' She sat back, angry but pleased with herself.

'Sounds painful. Didn't I just say it wouldn't help to feel guilty and responsible?'

'Okay. But—'

'You can try to score points, Nicole, if that's what you want.' Time to lay it on the line. 'We can sit here and argue whether or not rational emotive behaviour therapy is crap. But even if you win the argument, you also lose it.'

'How's that?' Nicole looked sulky.

'Nothing will change. You'll continue to suffer from the problems that brought you here. Is that what you want?' Carmel shrugged. 'Seems pointless to me. A waste of your valuable time. And mine.' Nicole was silent, wrestling with her thoughts.

'Excuse me.' Carmel got up as the buzzer sounded in the outer office. Jane, her part-time secretary, didn't come in on Fridays.

'That'll be my mum.' Nicole also stood up. 'She said she'd meet me. Okay,' she said, slinging her bag over her shoulder, 'you're right. I do want to change my life. I'll give this a go.'

'Great,' Carmel smiled. 'I'm so glad. Let's fix another appointment,' she said, hurrying to answer the door. 'How about next Tuesday at two? That'll leave you plenty of time to pick up the kids from school.'

Nicole would be all right, she thought. There was no history of mental disturbance and the Valium overdose was not a real suicide attempt. The hospital psychiatrist recommended intensive psychotherapy, a stress reduction programme and the teaching of coping skills. With time and effort, Nicole could develop a more positive self-image and become less desperate to please the kind of men who were only out for what they could get. Not easy. But possible.

9

Carmel put away the case notes and glanced at her watch. The next client was five minutes late.

She took the coffee cups into the tiny kitchen, yawned and stretched as she raked her fingers through her long, wavy, corn-blonde hair. It felt slightly dry and the split ends were frizzy; conditioning and ruthless cutting was the remedy. Trouble was, she hated hairdressers even more than supermarkets. The buzzer sounded again.

'About time,' Carmel murmured. She opened the door. 'Oh!' She grinned at the tall, dark-haired man who stood there. 'It's you, is it?'

'Wow, what a welcome!' He grinned back. 'Just came to check you're not falling apart on your birthday.'

'Physically or psychologically?'

'Both.' He stepped forward and kissed her. 'Thirty-three. Same age as Jesus, eh?'

'Well, hopefully I'm not about to be crucified. But never mind me,' Carmel laughed. 'You're only three years off the big forty, the hill of no enchantment. How do I know you won't buy a Harley-Davidson and start lusting after pubescent girls?'

'Because I've got you to lust after.' He shut the door and followed her into the office. 'Hey, listen. I'm sorry about this morning.'

Carmel turned. 'I'm sorry, too, Sean! I'm glad you came round.' Her voice was soft. 'I couldn't reach you on your mobile, so I phoned the office. Anthony told me you were out.'

'Yep. A meeting with a client, followed by lunch.' Sean opened his black cashmere coat. 'Cold out there.' He wore a charcoal grey suit and white shirt, but drew the line at a tie. Carmel looked into his blue-grey eyes and touched a finger to the crease between his dark, straight brows. His black hair had strands of grey at the temples.

'I felt mean and guilty all day,' she whispered.

'Not very rationally emotive of you.' Sean smiled lazily. 'Look – we both know our respective metabolisms can't crank themselves up before ten in the morning, not even with chocolate croissants and a litre of espresso to kick start us.'

'I was running late, and couldn't find that damn client file. After you'd gone Lisa refused point blank to eat any breakfast, and she took ages to get ready for school.'

'Bad hair day again, was it?'

'With knobs on. Then she suddenly decides she hates cheese sandwiches and wants a green apple instead of a red one. She *hates* green apples.' Carmel shook her head, amused. 'If she's like this at five, imagine when she's a terrible teen?'

'Better not. We'll fall off that bridge when we come to it.' Sean picked a stray blonde hair off her shoulder and let it fall. 'You're moulting.'

'Right,' she smiled. 'Falling apart before your very eyes.'

'Oh, I don't know.' Sean studied her slim figure in the black, close-fitting trouser suit with the stretchy turquoise top beneath, her low-heeled, snakeskin-print ankle boots. He thought it was sexy the way Carmel's mascara was slightly smudged, and her mouth painted with the red lipstick she loved. He stroked her cheek and gazed into her cobalt-blue eyes. 'I wouldn't say that exactly.' He slid one arm around her waist. There was a faint smell of incense-like perfume. 'What time will you be home?'

'Around six.' Lights were appearing all over dockland, hazy in the mist which had hung over Liverpool for the past two days. Carmel had recently gone into practice on her own, and Sean's import-export business was doing well. They had talked about moving out of the city, but could not decide where to go. And they liked the shabby Georgian splendour of Falkner Square. 'Why?' she asked, giving him a curious look. 'What have you got planned?'

Sean grinned. 'I'm saying nothing. You'll have to wait and wonder.'

He had arranged a surprise birthday party at home. The

caterers were there now and Jackie, his mother-in-law, was keeping an eye on Lisa. Lisa would be in the kitchen or her bedroom, snacking on her favourite smoky bacon crisps and barbecued chicken wings, drawing angel pictures, playing with her Pokémon cards or trying to communicate with the Furby.

'Oh, go on,' Carmel begged. 'Tell me.'

'No way,' Sean laughed. He let go of her and strolled to the window. 'Great view you've got from here. If you like docks and cranes. Which I know you do.'

'Okay, I give up. How's your friend and business partner these days?' she asked suddenly. 'I only spoke to him briefly.'

Sean's smile faded. 'Oh, Anthony's fine,' he said casually.

'I just wondered. Haven't seen him for – how long? Must be nearly two months.'

'No, well . . .' Sean fingered the waxy, glossy leaves of a gardenia. 'He's been busy. Spent a lot of time abroad. He just got back from another trip. Prague this time. Before that it was Amsterdam and Kiev, some eastern European countries. The antique and classic car market is booming,' he said. 'We've done well with those security products too.'

'That's good. I told Anthony he should come round for dinner one evening next week so that we can catch up. Bring his latest girlfriend if he wanted. He said he'd like that very much, but he'll come alone as there's no girlfriend just now. You could fix a date with him on Monday.'

'Yeah.' Sean drummed his fingers on the windowsill. 'Right. I'll do that.'

'I haven't seen his new house yet either.' Carmel grinned. 'Wouldn't mind an early nineteenth-century mansion with a view of the Mersey and the distant Welsh hills myself! I'll try and persuade him to throw a house-warming party soon.'

'Yeah. Whatever.' Sean stared out the window. He jumped as Carmel's arms encircled his waist.

'You seem preoccupied,' she said. 'Tense. Is everything all right?'

'Everything's fine.' He turned to her. 'I've had work on my mind more than usual recently, that's all. Things are pretty hectic. Lots of stuff to think about.'

Carmel stared up at him. 'There's nothing else?'

'No. Of course not.' He bent his head and they kissed, clinging together. 'I'll be home before you,' he murmured. 'Run you a bath, shall I?' He kissed and nibbled her earlobe. 'Pour us a glass of champagne. Maybe we can grab some time alone – hyperactive five-year-old permitting!'

'Sounds good to me.' Carmel closed her eyes, relaxing in his arms. 'Oh, sod!' She pulled a face as the buzzer went. 'I was starting to hope she might not turn up. I want to go home with you.' She hugged him. 'This minute.'

'I'm not going straight home. Got to make a detour first, pick up something.' Sean let go of her and moved away. 'I just remembered. Shouldn't take long.'

'Oh, right.' Carmel blew him a kiss. 'See you soon, then.'

'You bet.' Sean paused in the doorway, his eyes locked on hers. He hesitated and Carmel thought he was about to say something, but he seemed to change his mind. He turned and strode out of the office, nodded briefly to the woman who walked in. She stopped and stared after him.

'Hi, Sharon.' Carmel smiled. 'How are you?'

'Not too bad today, actually. Hey, you look a bit flushed.' Sharon wore her barrister's uniform of dusty black suit and white shirt, and her fine straight hair was twisted into a bun. 'I haven't had a panic attack for nearly a month now. Is that guy another of your bewildered clients?' she asked. 'Although he looks anything but. It's probably contrary to your code of professional ethics, but would you consider introducing us one fine day?'

'You must be joking, Your Honour.' Carmel closed the door. 'That's right, it is against the rules.'

13

'Can't you just tell me who he is?'

'That's no client, that's my husband.'

'Really? You don't look married. How long?'

'Seven years.'

'Wow!' Sharon walked into Carmel's office, dropped her briefcase and sank on to the sofa, stretching out her thin legs. 'No wonder you're flushed.' She looked at Carmel and grinned. 'You won't get the seven-year itch with *him* around.'

'Coffee?' Carmel suddenly experienced an unprofessional desire to tell Sharon to pull herself together and get on with earning ridiculously large amounts of money. She felt bored and restless at the thought of the hour ahead. And she was worried.

What had Sean wanted to say before he changed his mind? Why was he preoccupied? Was it really just work? Behave, she chided herself. Don't look for trouble that doesn't exist. Typical Carmel, sorting out every head except her own. But she could not dismiss the uneasy feeling.

Carmel longed to go home with Sean. Right now.

Chapter Two

'I killed her.' His voice was hushed.

The chill mist had thickened to fog and the warehouse was dark and silent. Only the office lights were on upstairs, the door ajar. Outside, the Mersey was sluggish, water slapping against the quay. A foghorn sounded close by, and the lights of a ferry crossing to Birkenhead were dimly visible from the office windows.

'Don't worry,' he said, in answer to the woman's look of alarm. She was about forty, with straight, chin-length bleached hair, sharp brown eyes, a pale, unhealthy complexion and prominent cheekbones. 'No one will find the body.'

'You sure about that, love?' Diane Lennox spoke with a flat, Mancunian accent. If she told someone they had won twelve million in the lottery it would sound boring.

He hated her long black leather coat with the fur collar, the purple satin jeans and high-heeled gold leather mules. Heavy black eyeliner gave her a tired look, and pink lipstick never did a thing for yellow teeth. Diane owned several houses in Manchester and Liverpool, each one filled with terrified illegal aliens, young females whose sexual services earned her a fortune.

'The body's hidden in a place only I know about. Me – and a man from another century.'

Diane looked mystified. 'What are you on about?'

15

He shook his head. 'Never mind.'

He meant Joseph Williamson, of course. The Mad Mole, the King of Edge Hill. Born in Warrington in 1769, died 1 May 1840 in his house on Mason Street. Went to work for Richard Tate's tobacco firm as a young man, married the boss's daughter and took over. On his wedding day in 1802 he turned up at church in hunting pink and went off with the Liverpool hunt right after the ceremony. Got gangs of unemployed soldiers at a loose end after the Napoleonic Wars to dig tunnels, vaults and caverns beneath his house and the other houses he owned in Mason Street. The labyrinth, many parts of which remained undiscovered, stretched for mile after pitch-dark mile beneath the streets of Liverpool.

He loved the place. The thought that those tunnels, caverns and passageways had existed for nearly two hundred years, a silent, secret, perfectly preserved subterranean world beneath the bustling, ever-changing city streets, had thrilled him since boyhood. Even the rubble heaps down there, which consisted largely of the remains of demolished Victorian houses, were fascinating. He had a collection of old wine bottles, pottery and coins discovered during his underground expeditions. And there was his most amazing find to date, just ten days ago. The letter and map which had led to his search for the Australian gold, an incredible treasure hunt straight out of some *Boy's Own* annual. According to the map, the gold lay in a previously unexplored section of tunnels which he hoped had not collapsed or been demolished – or discovered by anyone else. He was so preoccupied by Joseph's labyrinth and its secrets that he sometimes found it hard to focus on other more pressing matters.

'I didn't want to kill her,' he shrugged. 'Goes against my Buddhist principles.'

Diane looked at him in disbelief, then laughed coarsely. 'Oh, yeah. Right, love.'

'Seriously,' he grinned. 'I don't even like to swat a wasp.'

'And I suppose you're into veggie-ism, yoga and meditation?'

'I wouldn't go that far. I do a bit of yoga sometimes.'

She laughed again and touched the lapels of his coat. He wore an expensive dark suit underneath. 'You don't exactly look the yoga type!'

Wouldn't mind a night of passion with him, Diane thought, as she did every time she met this man. Unfortunately for her he preferred them young, although he himself was in his mid-thirties. He was a sucker for that I'm-such-a-vulnerable-little-crushed-petal look. Besides, he might be tall and tough-looking with sexy, thick black hair carelessly combed, flinty eyes the colour of gunmetal that seemed to know the secrets of your soul, and a really tasty body, but the guy was a bit scary. 'Want to withdraw from life, do you, love?' she teased.

'The goal is to transcend life, not withdraw from it. But that's enough of my personal philosophy. Show me your filthy lucre.' He glanced around and sniffed.

'Something wrong?' Diane asked nervously. It was creepy the way he sniffed the air, like some feral animal scenting danger.

'No. Well, I am exhausted,' he confessed. Her perfume stank, nauseated him like some noxious gas. It should be banned under the Chemical Weapons Convention. Of course this wasn't the moment to voice his opinion. 'It's been a day from hell.'

'Sorry to hear that, love.' Diane picked up an aluminium briefcase and dumped it on the desk. 'Maybe this'll make you feel better.'

On the desk next to his .22-calibre Ruger Mark II was a computer and printer, a phone and a tall ficus with pointy green leaves. There was also a complete, up-to-date list of the cars they had for sale, foreign and domestic. Year, make, model, body. Colour, number of miles. Their web page was newly updated – not by him, of course. He had no time for that shit. Diane clicked open the briefcase locks.

17

'Sixty grand,' she said. 'As agreed.'

He regarded the bundles of notes with a detached, faintly distasteful air. The cash was payment for his latest consignment, three beautiful Thai teenagers bought by him and sold to Diane for a nice profit.

'They'll be working near the Chinatown area of Manchester,' Diane said. 'I've got a new place there. Twelve-hour sessions, seven days a week.' She smiled with satisfaction. 'I'll make sure the bitches earn their keep.'

'They won't stay beautiful long under those conditions. Still, that's your problem as of now. I'll hang on to the passports and travel documents,' he said. 'They might come in handy.'

'Okay by me, love.'

Each girl had to pay off £7,500 for being brought to the UK, plus £450 a week for meals and board. After that they would be allowed to keep a fraction of their earnings. They would not be allowed to leave the house until they were too terrified to even think of escape, and then they would be accompanied by a minder. The occasional slapping, personally administered by Diane, would keep them firmly focused on the job.

Trafficking in female flesh brought higher profits than drugs these days, and had much less risk. He had never intended to get into it, it had just happened. It was nothing personal. He did not hate women. Most women were commodities, one way or another. It was their history. Their fate.

'Looks fine,' he said, nodding at the money. He snapped the briefcase locks shut. 'Good to do business with you again.'

'My pleasure, love. Fancy a drink to celebrate?'

'No time. Sorry.'

His big worry now was his business partner. After their row this morning the tension between them had escalated to open hostility. If the bastard continued to dig there was no telling what he might uncover. It was becoming impossible

18

to allay his suspicions. He was still angered and shaken by the discovery that the accountants had been brought in. Of course they wouldn't find anything; he wasn't stupid enough to involve the business, although he wanted to do that one of these days. An import-export company was the perfect cover. He was also irritated by his partner's fastidious reluctance to flog used medical equipment, CAT scanners and old X-ray machines. Sick of not being able to run things the way he wanted. It was time for a change.

His old friend had slipped away from him, repudiated their friendship, become the proverbial thorn in the flesh. He had not mentioned the toxic nature of their relationship to anyone. He had to think of a way to deal with this situation before it blew up in his face.

'You're sure they won't find that dead bitch?' Diane nibbled at a garish pink talon. 'Sorry, love, but I'm worried. What if . . .?'

He frowned at this interruption to his flow of thought. 'That's the second time you've questioned my word,' he said softly, darting her a look.

'I wasn't!' Diane lowered her eyes and glanced nervously away. 'I just . . .'

'Shut up!' He tensed, swung round to face the door.

A draught of cold air swirled around his ankles, and there was a sound like a click in the dark silent space beneath their feet. The men had gone home, and he had locked the warehouse door after he let Diane in. But somebody was down there. *Who?* He froze.

'What's up?' Diane whispered, staring at him in alarm. He held up one hand, touched a finger to his lips. Picked up the gun and moved swiftly and silently behind the partially open door. Listened, barely breathing. He was conscious of his heartbeat. There was a scuffle and a bad-tempered yowl as Tiger, the warehouse cat, dashed up the worn stone staircase and into the office. He let out his breath and swore with relief, grinned as Diane gave a startled cry.

'I can't stand bloody cats! Ugh, don't come near me,

you . . .' She jumped back. 'I hate the way they push themselves against your legs.'

'He's on rat patrol. You scared the hell out of us, you little bastard,' he murmured, stooping to stroke the head of the crouching ginger tom. The cat's tail was waving wildly. Then he heard the footfall.

He leapt to his feet, causing the startled cat to hiss, stepped forward and flung the office door wide open. He snapped several switches. Light flooded the big space below.

His problem partner stood on the stairs, one white-knuckled hand gripping the iron rail. Neither man spoke nor moved a muscle. They stared at one another in shock. He looked into his eyes, saw the horror and disbelief there. And something else. Contempt.

His mouth went dry. He knows, he thought. He's heard bloody everything.

He got the feeling he hated, a terrifying, gut-churning sensation that events were running away with him, spiralling beyond his control. A shockwave of panic surged through him. Strange how you really did feel sick and go weak at the knees.

'Now there's a coincidence,' he heard himself say. 'I was just thinking about you.'

The man's handsome face turned pale when he saw the gun. His eyes darkened.

'No,' he whispered, shaking his head. 'What's going on, what the hell are you doing? You can't just . . . for Christ's sake, let's talk about this!'

'Sorry, mate.' His hands were cold and slippery with sweat, and he was shaking, almost as terrified as the man he was pointing the gun at. 'Too late for talk. Way too late.' He was surprised at how calm his voice sounded.

'No! Don't—'

His finger brushed the trigger and squeezed. There was silence. It seemed to go on for a long time.

He fired.

Chapter Three

'No one by the name of Sean Devine has been admitted tonight, or treated as an outpatient. I can't help you any further, I'm afraid.' The smartly dressed, middle-aged Accident and Emergency receptionist looked sympathetically at Carmel. 'I'm very sorry.'

Carmel nodded. 'Well, thanks for your time.' She turned to her sister, Rosa, and two friends, Daniel and Natalie. 'That's every hospital in Liverpool we've tried,' she said, biting her lip. 'I have to contact the police now. Where's the nearest nick to Falkner Square? Or maybe I should go to Canning Place.'

'How about going home?' Daniel suggested, his dark brown eyes anxious as he looked at her. He pushed back his dark, tangled hair. 'It's nearly ten, and I think you've had enough. Sean might be back by now.' He got out his mobile. 'I'll check.'

Carmel pulled her cream wool coat around her, shivering with cold and fear. She wore a tight, sleeveless black dress underneath, and had exchanged her spike heels for black, knee-high boots before abandoning the birthday party that never was.

Panic was building, a weight on her neck and shoulders, a rock in her stomach. She couldn't believe this nightmare was happening. Her life before this moment suddenly seemed perfect. She thought how much she loved Sean.

21

How Lisa loved him. She had left her daughter sulking over the cancelled party, asking unanswerable questions about why Daddy didn't come home. The buffet in the dining room was untouched and wilting, and bottles of champagne were everywhere, crates of them stacked in the kitchen and pantry. Carmel wondered stupidly if Sean had bought the champagne on a sale or return basis. Her mind felt like it did not want to get to the point.

'Okay,' Daniel was saying. 'Thanks, Jackie. No, Sean's not in any hospital around here. Yeah, see you soon.' He stuck the mobile back in his pocket. 'Sorry,' he grimaced. 'Your mother says he hasn't shown up yet. Or phoned.'

The lump in Carmel's throat almost stopped her speaking. 'I'll go and report him missing,' she managed to say. 'Oh, God!' she breathed, her eyes filling with tears. 'Where the hell is he? I just can't think what ...!' Her voice trailed off.

She felt Rosa's silky light brown curls brush her face as her sister hugged her, and caught a whiff of her flowery perfume. Daniel and Natalie glanced at one another helplessly. They longed to comfort Carmel but Sean was seriously late now, five hours. They and everyone else had just about run out of platitudes. They walked into the dark hospital car park and got into Daniel's BMW.

Carmel was taken aback by the bleakness of the police station, or was it because she was in a state bordering on panic? Her face felt hot and her hands icy. The desk officer told them to wait. Fifteen minutes later she was summoned to a small interview room. Only Rosa was allowed to accompany her.

'What happens now?' Carmel asked as the young, uniformed female officer wrote down Sean's name and address, physical description, place of work and where Carmel had last seen him. The woman's handwriting slanted to the left.

'Well, actually, it's a bit soon to be filing a missing person's report.' She shrugged. 'Most people show up

22

within twenty-four to forty-eight hours.' She tapped her blue biro on the table and looked speculatively at Carmel. 'Any marital problems? Did you have a row with your husband recently?'

'No!' Carmel felt a shock of insult. 'Our marriage is fine,' she said stiffly. 'Sean and I are very happy. We have the occasional argument, like most couples. Nothing remotely serious.'

'Sorry, but I have to ask. Is your husband having an affair? Are you?'

'*No!*' Her eyes filled with tears again. 'Absolutely not. I told you, our marriage is fine.'

Rosa grabbed Carmel's hand and squeezed it. 'Are you sure this is necessary?' Her gentle voice was indignant. 'My sister's upset enough as it is.'

'I'm sorry,' the policewoman repeated. 'But yes, it is. Standard procedure. Have you or Sean got financial troubles?' she went on. 'Does Sean have enemies – someone with a grudge, maybe? Has he had a row with any friend, colleague, personal or business acquaintance? Fired an employee during the past few weeks or months?'

'He hasn't had a row with anyone, not that I know of. And Sean's hired rather than fired.' Carmel wiped her eyes. 'His business is doing great.'

'Does he have a drinking problem? Drugs? Mental illness?'

'No, he doesn't. He's never had any of those things.'

'Has a doctor prescribed him any medication?'

'No. I can't remember the last time Sean saw a doctor.'

'For God's sake!' Rosa shook her head despairingly. She could not begin to imagine what Carmel must be going through. It made her own worries – dead end job in a call centre, indifferent boyfriend – seem trivial.

When the interview was over the officer gathered up the papers. 'We'll file a missing person's report.' She scraped back her chair and stood up. 'If your husband remains missing for more than forty-eight hours we'll launch an investigation. An officer will be assigned to liaise with you and the family, keep you informed of any developments.'

'That's it?' Carmel stared at her in disbelief. 'You do nothing for forty-eight hours?'

'Not unless we have good reason to take action sooner.'

'Look,' Carmel said desperately, 'we haven't had a row, we've got no financial problems, Sean's not mental or a drug addict, or off his face on something his GP prescribed, and neither of us is having an affair. That's the truth. We spend nearly every evening and weekend together. It's my birthday and he organised a party for me. Sean would never be this late – especially not tonight – unless something was seriously wrong. It's totally unlike him.' She glanced at Rosa. 'Isn't it?' Rosa nodded. 'Won't you please start searching for him now?' Carmel begged, clenching her hands. 'Sean might have had an accident – he could be hurt, he might be in some kind of danger – God knows!' A tear rolled down and dripped off her chin.

'If your husband had had an accident I'm sure you'd have heard by now. Besides, you told me you'd checked all the hospitals around here.'

'Well, yes. But—'

'I'm sorry, Mrs Devine.' The police officer moved to the door and opened it. 'I'm afraid there's nothing more we can do at this early stage. As I said, we will investigate if he doesn't show up within forty-eight hours. Look, try not to worry too much,' she said, her voice softening. 'We get a lot of cases like this, and most people turn up large as life within a day or two. Honestly, I'm not just saying that. Go home,' she advised. 'That's the best place for you right now.'

'I can't believe they won't do anything for that length of time,' Natalie said as they walked to the car. 'Useless bastards!' She pulled her cigarettes and lighter out of her jacket pocket, smoothed a crease in her long, close-fitting embroidered skirt. Her thick, straight brown hair swung around her oval face. 'I'll give my boss a call,' she announced. 'Maybe he can help.'

24

'I don't think there's anything a family law solicitor could do in this situation.' Rosa looked doubtful. 'I don't imagine he'll be delighted if you phone him at home late on a Friday evening either.'

'Listen, I'm his office manager, although he likes to label me a secretary so he can pay me less.' Natalie's lighter flared and she drew hungrily on her cigarette. 'I run that damn place for him. He knows he has to keep me sweet.'

Natalie had planned to confide in Carmel about the affair she had started with her married boss once the party got underway, and ask her advice. But poor Carmel was in shock now, out of her mind with panic about Sean's weird and inexplicable disappearance. Something terrible must have happened, Natalie thought grimly. If it's not an accident maybe he's been attacked – murdered even. Of course she wouldn't say that; Carmel must be torturing herself thinking the same thing.

'Why didn't I ask Sean what he had to pick up?' Carmel got in beside Daniel and fastened her seat belt. 'I might have some clue then. He said it wouldn't take long, and that he'd be home before I was. Daniel . . .' She glanced across at him. 'Your garage serviced his Audi last week. Was everything all right?'

'Fine.' Daniel nodded gravely. 'No problems. I did the work myself. Sean has to have that car kept in perfect nick, what with all the driving he does.' He stuck the key in the ignition.

'I wish I could reach Anthony,' she sighed.

'Anthony Maskey, Sean's business partner?'

'Right. He's the one I really need to talk to. But his mobile's down, and he doesn't seem to be home or at the warehouse. Strange that he didn't turn up for the party either. Then again, he often comes late.'

Daniel handed her his phone. 'Want to try again?' Lisa had accidentally, or so she said, dropped Carmel's mobile down the toilet the other day, ruining it. Carmel had been annoyed at first, then laughed about it. Daniel wondered when he would hear her laugh again. He had a very bad feeling about all this.

'Thanks.' Carmel took the phone and dialled the three numbers in turn, let them ring a long time. She shook her head. 'Nothing.'

She swallowed hard and choked back a sob of panicked despair. They were silent for the rest of the journey. Daniel sped through the city centre, up the hill past the Anglican cathedral and turned sharply into Falkner Square with its elegant Georgian terraced houses and small park surrounded by iron railings. The trees and streetlamps were wreathed in mist, and the long line of parked cars covered with water droplets. A few leaves drifted down. Carmel held her breath, desperate to see Sean's Audi parked outside the house. Her heart sank at the sight of the silver Ford Cortina parked in Sean's space.

Over the years she had started to worry whenever Sean was more than fifteen minutes late, had imagined death, car crash, collapse due to sudden fatal illness. Murder by strangers, although she knew how rare that was. Fear and horrible imaginings were always short-lived, however, instantly banished by the sound of his key in the door. She would pour a glass of wine and berate herself for panicking, swear never to do it again. She always did. Tonight she had reason to panic.

Her mother, Jackie, flung open the front door. Jackie had not changed for the party, and was still in the dark brown pencil skirt and baby blue angora sweater she had worn to her part-time medical secretary job that day. Her greying blonde hair was done up in a bun. Carmel's father, Frank Graham, hovered in the long, high-ceilinged hall. He had taken off his tie and undone the top two buttons of his shirt. His grey hair was disordered and his face flushed. He was drinking Scotch.

'I've read Lisa a couple of stories, but I can't get her off to sleep,' Jackie said in a hushed voice as Carmel hurried into the cloakroom, dropped her bag and hung up her coat. 'She's waiting for you. Keeps asking about her daddy. Oh, my God!' she whispered, one hand to her mouth. 'What on earth's happened to him? Where can Sean *be*?'

Carmel glanced at her mother and shook her head, not trusting herself to speak. She ran upstairs and went into her daughter's room. Lisa lay in bed surrounded by books and the two watercolours of angels she had painted while waiting for the party to start. The gold and silver glitter on their wings sparkled in the lamplight. Lisa wore her pink, T-shirt nightdress and her long blonde hair was loose around her shoulders. The Furby sat silently on the bedside table, its thickly lashed eyes closed. Normally such toys were cute, but when this one's staring eyes were open they reminded Carmel of photos she'd seen of serial killers.

'Hi there, Lisa babe!' She sat on the bed and gathered her daughter in her arms. 'I'm back.' She kissed the child's forehead. 'I want you to go to sleep now, okay?'

Lisa twisted round in her arms and stared up at her. 'Is Daddy home?' She looked unhappy, her blue eyes full of bewilderment.

'No.' Carmel hugged her, fighting back tears. 'No, darling. Not yet, I'm afraid.'

'When will he be back?' Lisa demanded. 'Why did he miss your party?'

Carmel hesitated. 'I'm not sure. There must have been something very important he had to do. Something he'd forgotten about.'

'Because of your party, you mean?'

'Yes. Probably. He'll be back soon though.'

My God, she thought. I shouldn't say that. But what could she say? How could any parent explain something like this to their child?

'Maybe Daddy had to go on a trip,' Lisa persisted. 'Suddenly. But he promised to take me to the Maritime Museum tomorrow.' She loved the Maritime Museum and the Museum of Liverpool Life, as well as the sweet shop in the Albert Dock colonnades with its mouthwatering selection of exotic-flavoured fudge.

'We'll talk about that in the morning. Lisa, go to sleep now.' Carmel tried to sound firm. 'It's very late.'

Lisa grabbed the Furby and thrust it at her. 'Say something.'

'*Sayonara*, baby!' Carmel scratched at its rough black fur, and the eyes flew open.

'Party time!' it chuckled harshly. 'Me *like* tickle. Hoh!'

'Hoh! yourself,' she said, startled. 'I thought its battery had run out.'

Lisa giggled and lay back in her arms. Sean's all right, Carmel thought, stroking the child's silky hair. He has to be. There's some perfectly innocent explanation for this. He'll come home soon. He knows I'm suffering the tortures of the damned.

A little sigh and the sudden heaviness of Lisa's small blonde head against her shoulder told Carmel her daughter had dropped off to sleep. She laid her down gently, took the books and pictures off the bed and put them on the floor by the window. She tucked Lisa in, kissed her and switched off the red-and-white spotted toadstool lamp, tiptoed out and closed the door.

Come home, Sean! she prayed silently. *Please*. I can't stand much more of this. Carmel went into their bedroom, walked to the long windows and parted the curtains. Falkner Square was dark and silent. Sean was out there somewhere. Was he hurt, in danger? Had somebody attacked him? She couldn't bear to think of that. She went into the adjoining bathroom and dressing room, touched Sean's suits, shirts and sweaters, picked up his bottle of men's cologne and sniffed the delicious fresh citrus scent. She opened his bedside drawer; it contained a bunch of spare house and office keys, two red biros, his passport and an old chequebook full of stubs. Carmel took off her party dress and changed into black jeans and a grey sweatshirt with a hood. She had a feeling it was going to be a long night.

The sense of impending doom weighed heavier on her. What more could she do? She had phoned all their friends and acquaintances, most of whom had been invited to her party. Checked all the local A&E wards. The morgues! Talked to the police, for all the good that had done. There was nothing to do now except wait. Carmel sat on the bed and buried her head in her hands, made herself take slow, deep breaths. I mustn't lose it, she thought. I have to be strong for Lisa. Whatever happens.

The doorbell rang, loud and urgent. She gasped and jumped to her feet. Her heart raced. On the stairs she stumbled and almost feel headlong. She grabbed at the polished oak banister which was slightly too low, having been built for shorter eighteenth-century people. Rosa hurried to answer the door, Daniel, Natalie and her parents close behind. She had taken off her coat to reveal a strappy red silk party dress, tight across her hips and bust.

'Carmel!' she called anxiously. 'Watch it. Take your time.' She opened the front door wide, shivering as a draught of cold autumn air whirled in.

'Hi there,' a man's voice said. 'You're Carmel's sister, aren't you? Rosa. Sorry to barge in like this, but I really need to speak to Sean.'

Rosa stepped back and shot a worried glance at Carmel. 'Sean's not here.'

Anthony Maskey strode into the hall and stopped, his cold blue-grey eyes on Carmel as she descended the stairs. His nose, mouth and chin, and the front of his blue shirt, were stained with blood. His eyelids were puffed and reddened, the whites bloodshot. Carmel stared in astonishment, glad that Lisa was safely tucked up in bed and couldn't be frightened by the alarming spectacle this normally well-dressed, handsome man presented. Anthony clutched a clump of bloodied tissues in his right hand, and more bloody tissues protruded from one pocket of his black overcoat.

'Not here?' he echoed. 'Where is he then? I need to speak to Sean urgently.'

'You're not the only one.' Daniel's voice was grim. Anthony glanced sharply at him, taking in the shoulder-length, tangled dark brown hair and watchful brown eyes, Daniel's powerful shoulders beneath the thin blue cotton sweater, the dark hairs on the backs of his hands.

'Anthony!' Another tidal wave of panic crashed over Carmel, leaving her weak. 'Sean hasn't come home,' she gasped, one hand to her throat. 'I've no idea where he is and I'm worried sick. I've been trying to reach you, I hoped you might know. He didn't turn up for the party.'

Anthony looked blank. 'What party?'

'Sean organised a surprise birthday party for Carmel, didn't you know?' Rosa looked at him in amazement. 'We took it for granted that he'd invited you.'

'He didn't. He said nothing to me about it.'

'I don't understand,' Carmel whispered. 'Anthony, do you know where Sean might have gone? He told me he had to pick up something.'

'I don't know where he went.' Anthony hesitated. 'He was at the warehouse earlier.'

'When, exactly?'

'Between six-thirty and seven. I can't be sure.'

'But I phoned. Four or five times. I also tried Sean's mobile, and yours, but there was no answer.'

'I don't know. I went downstairs, so that must be why I didn't hear the office phone. My mobile was switched off, I left it on my desk.'

'But there's a phone downstairs too, isn't there?'

'Well, yes. Listen, the truth is ...' He looked Carmel in the eye. 'Sean and I had a fight.'

'You *what*?'

Anthony cleared his throat. 'We had a fight,' he repeated. He glanced around at their shocked faces and pointed to his bloody nose. 'Sean did this. I'm prone to nosebleeds, as you know, Carmel. This was a bad one. I had to drive to the Accident and Emergency department at the Royal. They've only just discharged me.'

30

'But what happened?' Carmel stared at him, horrified. 'You and Sean are friends as well as business partners. I can't believe he'd do something like this!'

'I came back to the warehouse to collect some paperwork from the office and lock up. I thought Sean had gone home early again—'

'What do you mean, early *again*?' Carmel interrupted, feeling suffocated with shock.

'Well, he's been leaving early quite a lot recently.'

'When you say recently . . .?'

'The past few weeks. Some days he leaves the office around four, four-thirty.'

Carmel gasped again. 'But Sean never gets back here until around seven. He told me today how busy he's been. That things were hectic, that he had lots of stuff to think about.'

'Oh. Right.' Anthony looked awkward. 'I knew it was your birthday, even though I didn't know about the party,' he went on. 'Although I forgot to wish you "Many Happy Returns" when we spoke earlier. When I walked in this evening Sean was in his office on the phone – his mobile. I didn't hear what he was saying, I wasn't listening. But he sounded angry, very agitated. Then he saw me. I had the impression he thought I'd heard something I shouldn't have. He got aggressive, started shouting about how I didn't know the whole story and it wasn't as bad as it sounded. That it was all my fault because he was sick of my interference.'

'What on earth did he mean?' Carmel was trembling, felt like she was going to faint all over the polished, parquet hall floor.

Anthony shrugged. 'I didn't know what he was on about and I said so, but Sean wasn't having it. Sorry. Excuse me.' They waited while he wiped his nose with the bloody tissues. 'I've never seen Sean like that before.' Anthony sniffed and shook his head sorrowfully. 'I was shocked. I still am.' He stared at the big cordyline plant by the long wall mirror, its sword-shaped, dark auburn leaves brushing the white wall and the polished, walnut telephone table. 'It wasn't him, it was totally out of character. I didn't – *don't* – know what to think.' He looked at Carmel again. 'I hoped he might have calmed down by now, that we could talk and get things straightened out. We've had a few arguments about the business lately. I want him to tell me why he's been acting so weird.'

'Weird? In what way?'

'Tense. Edgy. Secretive. Wouldn't talk to me any more. Like I said, Sean just isn't himself.'

'Tense' struck an ominous chord with Carmel. She tried to think back further than that afternoon, remember any warning signs that Sean might have displayed. She couldn't recall any, but at this moment it was impossible to think straight.

'Anthony?' Rosa hugged her younger sister protectively. 'How did this fight start?'

Anthony looked into her blue eyes, the same cobalt blue as Carmel's. 'I tried to calm Sean, but it was no use. Then he ... I ...' He paused, pressed one hand to his forehead and staggered slightly. Daniel stepped forward and took his arm.

'You all right, mate?'

'Feel a bit faint,' Anthony mumbled. 'I lost about half a pint of blood.'

'That's a lot. Come in here and sit down. Take the weight off.' Daniel guided him into the large, high-ceilinged front sitting room and steered him towards a sofa, Carmel and the others following. Anthony collapsed on the sofa and leaned his head back, closing his eyes briefly. He was white-faced, his forehead shiny with sweat.

'Would you like a drink?' Jackie asked anxiously.

'Cognac would be good, thanks. Or hot sweet tea.' He opened his eyes. 'I think Carmel needs a drink more than I do.'

Carmel looked at her mother. 'I don't want anything.'

'Are you sure, love? Daniel, could you get Anthony a cognac? I'll make some tea as well.' Jackie hurried out of the room, brushing away tears, glad of something to do. She felt terrified for Carmel and Lisa, and could not believe what she was hearing about her kind, handsome, humorous son-in-law who seemed to love his wife and young daughter so much. She had a terrible sense of foreboding.

'Sean ran downstairs and I followed,' Anthony resumed, after taking a gulp of the large cognac Daniel handed him. 'He was in a terrible state. I couldn't let him go like that, I was afraid of what might happen.' He grimaced. 'Not only to Sean, but to anyone who got in his way! I grabbed his arm and he started beating me. Kicking, punching. He landed one right on my nose, and that caused the bleed. Then he ran outside and drove off.' He looked at Carmel's stricken expression. 'I'm sorry, Carmel. I did my best to stop him, but ...' His voice tailed off and he shook his head. He took another gulp of cognac.

'This is crazy!' Daniel frowned. 'What the hell is going on?'

'It doesn't make sense! Sean seemed fine when I saw him.' Carmel stared at Anthony, barely able to take in what he was saying. 'Okay, he was a bit tense and preoccupied. I asked him what was on his mind, if everything was all right. He said things were fine. I just can't imagine him shouting – attacking you, beating you up. My God!' she cried. 'Where's he gone? What's wrong with him?'

She imagined Sean in danger, alone in some dark place. Needing help that did not come. Thinking of her. Of Lisa. Nightmare becoming reality. It was unbearable, but she had to bear it. Rosa's arms tightened around her.

'It'll be all right, Carmel,' she whispered. 'We'll sort this. I promise you.'

'I wouldn't be surprised if that suave bugger's up to something,' Frank said belligerently, waving his glass of Scotch at them. 'He always was a dark horse.'

'Frank, for God's sake!' Jackie, coming in with a cup of

33

tea, glared at her husband. 'Nobody knows what's happened yet – don't go spitting venom at Sean when he isn't here to defend himself.' Frank had always been jealous of Sean, she thought, calling him the blue-eyed boy. It was ridiculous the way he took against people for no good reason. Especially people *she* liked. She handed the tea to Anthony. His face had more colour now, and he looked better. She went to Carmel and put one arm around her trembling shoulders.

'Don't take any notice of your dad, love. He's had a few too many and he's just being bloody-minded. Rosa's right, we'll sort this out. Everything will be fine.'

'Will it?' Carmel could not control herself any longer. She bowed her head and burst into floods of panicked tears. Rosa and Jackie hugged her, distraught at her suffering. Rosa's eyes were wet.

'Anthony,' Carmel sobbed. 'Please help me find Sean! I went to the police, but they won't do anything. You work with him, you're his friend, maybe you can think of something.'

She could not go on. Anthony got up and put the cup and his glass of cognac on the coffee table. He moved towards her and stood close, so close that Carmel could smell his sweat and the expensive cologne he used, mixed with a faint metallic whiff of blood and the Casualty department odour of formaldehyde. His bloodshot eyes gazed down at her.

'I promise you, Carmel.' He laid one hand on her shoulder. 'I'll do whatever it takes.'

Chapter Four

'Don't go out tonight, Gem, please! Don't do this any more,' Kathy Geraghty begged as her twenty-two-year old daughter fluffed and backcombed her long auburn hair in front of the hall mirror, trying to make the shaggy perm as wild and windswept as possible. Ash dropped from the cigarette that dangled between her pale pink lips.

Gemma wore a black lycra crop top, minimal black velvet skirt that showed her lacy stocking tops, and a short, purple leather jacket. The heels of her black leather boots were so high that Kathy wondered how she could stand up straight in them, let alone walk. Or run if she had to.

'You'll get raped,' she warned, her voice loud with anxiety. 'Or worse. I can't stand much more of this! I'm worn out with the worry. I went down the doctor's yesterday about me chest pains. He says it's stress, that I should take it easy. Fat chance.'

'You just shut that mega gob of yours, Mam, and look after the kids.' Gemma stubbed out her cigarette in a white china ashtray with a drawing of Blackpool Tower on it. 'And keep your voice down, for Christ's sake!' she hissed, glancing up the dark stairs. 'I don't want them waking up before I go out.'

'There's so many nut jobs walking them streets.' Kathy twisted her hands together as compensation for not being able to talk in decibels. 'Suppose you meet one? You won't

35

stand a chance! You can't run in them boots, you'll fall flat on your gob. What would the kids do if anything happened to you?' Her eyes filled with tears. 'What would I do?'

Gemma sighed theatrically and dropped her pink comb on the yellow telephone directory. She pouted her thin lips and batted her false eyelashes. 'Where's me drink?' she asked impatiently. Kathy picked up a half-pint glass of vodka-and-tonic and handed it to her, watched as Gemma took two big gulps in quick succession.

'What you looking at me like that for?' Gemma belched as she thumped the glass down on the telephone directory. 'Piss off and watch telly,' she ordered. 'Always on about rape and nutters – never give it a rest, do you? No wonder me dad moved in with that scrubber after his liver transplant.' She looked contemptuously at the small, scrawny woman with her sparse grey hair and reddened hazel eyes. Kathy wore old blue jeans, cheap trainers from the market and her saddest lilac jumper, a Marks and Sparks original.

'I only want to help, love! You can't go on doing this, it's too dangerous. Remember that poor girl who got strangled and cut up near the Dock Road a few months ago? She wasn't even a . . .' Kathy paused. 'She was a student who'd been out clubbing with her mates.'

'Deserved it then, didn't she? Don't know which way's up, that lot. Anyway, they arrested the fella who did it. Picked him up practically five minutes later.'

'But there's been other murders over the years. Unsolved. You're in terrible danger,' Kathy went on. 'Every minute you're out there.'

'Shut up!' The last thing Gemma wanted to be reminded of was the danger. If she thought about that she wouldn't go out the door. One of her mates had got beaten up the other night, had her face slashed. Fifty stitches didn't look cool. Sandra wouldn't be able to work again for weeks, maybe longer. Even if she had the bottle. She was a nervous wreck now, crying non-stop and too frightened to leave her house.

'Why don't you get yourself a proper job? You know I'll look after the kids for you.'

'What's a proper job then?' Gemma mocked. 'Cleaning bogs, like you? Taking crap from behind a supermarket checkout? Getting headaches and sore eyes from a computer in some boring bloody office where the fellas think they're so tasty they should get it for free? I'd go mental.' She glared at her mother. 'I earn hundreds of quid a week,' she boasted. 'Tax free. I'm cool.'

'So cool you can't leave this house without a belly full of vodka!'

'Right.' Gemma's pretty face turned pale beneath the makeup. 'I'm out of here.' She drained her glass and grabbed a small black quilted handbag with a gilt chain. The bag contained strawberry and banana-flavoured condoms, cigarettes and lighter, wallet, lipstick and a tube of lube. 'I've had enough of you for one night.'

Kathy stepped forward and grabbed her arm. 'Don't go out!'

'Sod off!' Gemma wrenched her arm free. 'The only nut job round here is you!'

She slammed the front door and clumped down the long, narrow street of terraced houses. On the main road she paused to zip her jacket. She shivered in the cold night air, lit a cigarette and drew the smoke deep into her lungs. Thought of the hours ahead.

'Stupid cow,' Gemma murmured. Her mother would have a coronary if she knew the half of what the punters asked her daughter to do. Handcuffs, dildoes, golden showers, erotic punishment. Erotic, that was a laugh. Would she do it without a condom, did she have a little sister or mate? Was she into SM, bondage? Okay, she was missing good money by saying no. But Gemma couldn't stomach that sort of thing. She liked to be in control as much as possible, and she certainly wasn't into pain. Besides, sometimes the punters went too far and really injured girls. She stood smoking and looking around for a cab to take her into town.

A Fiat Uno stopped alongside and the driver leaned across and wound down the passenger window. He was fat and middle-aged, with grey hair and a scruffy beard, wearing a pale-coloured, padded jacket. His cold mean little eyes raked her up and down, trying to guess if she was worth his dirty money. He looked horrible, but harmless enough. Gemma prided herself on her psycho-spotting powers. She would never get caught like poor Sand.

'D'you want business, luv?' she called. He nodded. She dropped the cigarette and crushed it beneath her heel, pasted a big happy smile on her face. The punters liked happy, wanted to think you enjoyed it. 'I was just looking for a cab,' she laughed as she got into the car and slammed the door. She unzipped her jacket and thrust her lycra-ed tits in his face. 'Your lucky night, innit? I'm Gemma,' she said airily.

He didn't give his name and she didn't ask. That was against her rules. No names, no personal questions. Sometimes punters told her their names and talked about their sad, boring lives; Gemma didn't give a flying toss either way. When they talked her mind sometimes drifted back to school Biology lessons about the Life History of the Cockroach. Cockroaches were dirty, scavenging, disease-carriers that liked dry, warm hiding places. Just like the punters really. Although a lot of people might call *her* a dirty disease-carrier.

The car stank of chips and burgers and he had a spot of ketchup on his cheek. His thin lips were greasy. Could be a lot worse though. Imagine being married to him, in the ugly sod's bed every night, expected to perform for free? Gemma shuddered, keeping the wide smile plastered on her face.

She was thick and she had to laugh at herself, but every time she went out Gemma couldn't help wishing she could meet some really tasty bloke – loaded, of course – who would fall for her and treat her like gold. Buy her designer clothes, a luxury apartment, a white villa in Spain with a blue swimming pool. It was a crazy fantasy. But dreams sometimes came true. Why not hers? Stranger things had happened. She might just get lucky.

When would it be her lucky night?

Yesterday's mist had lifted, but now the night sky above the city was heavy with clouds pouring rain. If Carmel had wondered what it felt like when the man you loved didn't come home, she knew now. She had read about people whose loved ones disappeared, watched television programmes about them, and felt briefly horrified before turning back to her own safe, happy life. Now she was one of those people who spent their days and nights desperate for news but also dreading it. Hoping, praying, having a panic attack every time the phone or doorbell rang. Endlessly wondering what, how, *why*?

Her stomach felt hollow, but she was too frantic to eat or drink. It was late, but there was no way she could sleep. She wiped her flowing tears. She had started crying last night and hadn't stopped.

'Your heart rate is quite rapid.' The doctor straightened up and put the stethoscope back in her bag. 'But I'd expect that, given the circumstances. I'll leave you a prescription for some tranquillisers.' She scribbled on her pad.

'I don't want tranquillisers.' Carmel lay back on the sofa and smoothed her khaki cotton trousers. She had pulled on the trousers and an old black top that morning, not bothering to shower or wash her hair. Doing normal everyday things seemed out of the question. 'Not with my daughter to take care of.'

'Of course it's up to you,' the doctor shrugged. 'But they'll help you get a good night's sleep, which you could certainly do with.' She looked critically at Carmel's pale face and swollen, reddened eyes. 'You're exhausted.'

I don't need a doctor to tell me that, Carmel felt like snapping. The front door slammed and Rosa came back into the sitting room. The jeans and purple sweater she had

39

borrowed from Carmel were strained across her hips and bust. She picked up the mugs from the coffee table.

'I thought the police were supposed to be helpful and liaise with us, not ask you the same questions all over again.' The gold-rimmed bone china mugs clinked alarmingly as she strung them on her fingers by the handles. 'They'll have to launch an investigation now,' she said. 'It's more than twenty-four hours since Sean—' She stopped, biting her lip as she saw her sister's anguished expression. The doctor tore the prescription off her pad and handed it to Carmel.

'These will tide you over for a couple of weeks,' she said.

'A couple of weeks!' Carmel took the paper and folded it. 'I don't know how I'm going to get through this evening.' Her voice trembled.

'Where is your daughter now?' The doctor pulled on her brown coat.

'At my parents in Southport. Staying the night. It upsets her to see me crying my eyes out non-stop.' Carmel clenched her hands. 'I'm useless to her like this.'

'Don't be so hard on yourself. You're going through a very rough time. Try to get some rest if you can.' The GP glanced at her watch. 'Well, I've got another call to make.' She walked to the door and paused. 'I hope you get some good news soon.'

'Thank you. So do I. Goodnight.'

Rosa showed the doctor out and came back. 'Carmel, why don't you go to bed?'

'I don't want to. Rosa, what did you call her for?'

'Give me a break! You won't eat, sleep, not even rest. I'm worried sick about you.'

'I don't want doctors nosing around. Probably be social workers next, wondering if I'm too hysterical to look after Lisa. They might take her away from me.'

'Rubbish! Don't even think about that.' Rosa held out her hand for the prescription. 'What's medicine woman given you?'

'I don't know, I can't make it out. Doesn't matter, because I'm not taking it.'

Rosa frowned as she scanned the doctor's scrawl. 'It's a wonder people don't croak it right, left and centre from being given the wrong drugs.'

'Maybe they do. Why the hell didn't Sean tell me he was rowing with Anthony?' Carmel's lower lip trembled. 'I told him to fix a dinner date with Anthony for next week and he said okay. That was the perfect moment to tell me they weren't exactly best mates any more. But he didn't say a word.'

'Maybe he didn't want to worry you.'

'I wouldn't have been as worried as I am now. Sean loves Lisa and me. He wouldn't walk out on us. He wouldn't do anything to hurt us.'

'I know.' Rosa sat on the sofa and hugged her. 'Nobody's suggested Sean's walked out on you, have they? Except the police, and I'm afraid you've got to expect that rubbish from them.'

'People think it though, don't they? Daniel, Natalie. Dad. Even Mum.'

'Carmel, listen to me.' Rosa's voice was firm. 'They don't understand, that's all. Any more than you do. They're not jumping to conclusions. Dad just had a bit too much to drink. He was agitated, upset about you and Lisa. You know how he dotes on her. He didn't mean what he said about Sean.'

Rosa did not tell her sister what their mother said. Jackie was terrified Sean had been killed in an accident or murdered, and that his body would be discovered any time soon. Daniel and Natalie, like Rosa herself, didn't know what to think.

'Sean can't have had a mental breakdown,' Carmel went on. 'There would have been symptoms, warning signs. That sort of thing doesn't happen overnight. Maybe he had an accident and lost his memory.' She wiped her tears. 'That happens to a lot of people. Not just in films and soaps.'

'Carmel, we've been over this. If Sean had suffered memory loss and was in hospital you'd know by now. You reported him missing. The hospital staff would have contacted the police, his identity would have been established.'

'We can't be sure. And he may not be in hospital. He could be wandering around. Confused. Needing help.' Her voice broke. 'And I'm not there to help him!'

'Oh Carmel, please don't do this to yourself!' Rosa plucked several tissues from the box on the coffee table and gently wiped her sister's tears. 'Even if that were true, somebody would help him.'

'Would they? If we saw a man wandering around in a confused state we'd think he was drunk or on drugs. That he was a dosser.'

'Not necessarily.' There was a silence. Carmel looked at her.

'Sean might be dead, Rosa!' A tear rolled down her cheek. 'I have to face that.'

'You don't have to face anything until you know the truth.' Rosa hugged her again. 'And at the moment we know sod-all. Sean isn't dead, I'm sure of it. You're worried in case other people jump to wild conclusions – don't do that yourself.'

'I know you're right.' Carmel hesitated. 'There's something else I don't want to face, because I'm terrified it might *not* be a wild conclusion.'

Rosa nodded sadly. 'You wonder where Sean went those times Anthony said he left work early. What he did.'

'Maybe he's lying to me, Rosa! I don't want to believe that, but what am I supposed to think? And why did he attack Anthony, run off and leave him bleeding? It's driving me mental! I can't stand not knowing.' Carmel burst into tears again.

'Carmel ...' Rosa held her close. 'Of course you're freaked out! There's all these crazy jigsaw pieces that don't fit. But there's bound to be news of Sean soon.'

'Is there? Lots of people who disappear are never heard of again.'

'And a lot of them come home safe. You can't think like that. You just can't.'

Carmel raised her flushed, tearstained face. 'Rosa, will you stay with me until ... well, for a while?'

'Of course I will,' Rosa said fervently. 'I'm not going to leave you alone now, am I?'

'You can easily get to the call centre from here. It's nearer, actually. Of course Ian might not like you staying, I realise that.'

'Why, because he'd have to get his own dinner? I told him to move out a few days ago.' Rosa's blue eyes were sombre. 'I've had enough of him, Carmel. Boring, lazy git. He's gone back to his dear old mum now, living like a teenager again at thirty-six. I was going to tell you last night.'

Carmel leaned back. 'Well, I never liked him much. You can do a lot better than that.' She smiled suddenly. 'Sean said he was a wanker.'

'He got that right,' Rosa laughed. 'He'll be glad when he finds out we've split up. As to the call centre – I'm owed favours. Might even scrounge a couple of days off.' She yawned. 'That satellite phone we flog is so expensive only the Mafia, criminals and diverse terrorist groups can afford it. We all expect our jobs to fold any day now. I don't care. I'm sick of asking whingeing gits around Europe if they're standing near a window or if their weather's cloudy. Even my toilet breaks are timed.'

Carmel nodded. 'I don't know how you stand it. A laboratory rat has more fun.' She sighed. 'There is no way I can go back to work on Monday.'

'Of course not. I'll pop over to Newsham Park tomorrow and pack a bag.' Rosa stood up and stretched. 'More tea? Or even better, a great big cognac? Might help you sleep.'

'No, thanks.' Carmel sat up and swung her legs to the ground. 'You have one. Think I'll check the e-mail again,' she said. 'Then go upstairs for a bit.'

There were no e-mails. In the dark bedroom she parted the curtains and stared out of the window, hoping against hope that Sean might drive up and get out of the Audi, see her at the window and wave as if nothing had happened. The sense of unreality persisted. It felt like time lost through illness, or being trapped in a nightmare from which she could wake herself if she just tried hard enough.

It was dark and the rain was coming down hard. Wind stirred the trees. A slight movement by the park gates caught her eye, and she moved quickly behind the curtain. Drug addicts and dossers sometimes gathered in the park at night around the graffiti-covered pagoda in the centre where the four paths merged. Some of the visitors left used needles and broken bottles for local kids to find next morning. She peered out of the window again.

A shadow, a tall, dark figure in a long coat. Male. The face was in shadow, as the street lamp was a good few yards away. The man stepped forward and stood motion-less. He seemed to be staring at the house. Carmel gasped. Seconds later he turned abruptly and vanished into the park.

'Oh, my God!' she whispered. 'Oh God.' She whirled round, pushed her bare feet into trainers, and raced down-stairs. Rosa hurried out of the sitting room.

'Carmel?' She dumped her glass of cognac on the hall table. 'What's up?'

'I saw Sean in the park!' Carmel shouted. Her blue eyes glittered with tears and excitement. She flung open the front door and a chill wind blew in. 'He's alive, he's okay. He's come home to me!' She raced down the narrow brick garden path and across the street to the park gates.

'Sean!' she yelled. 'Sean, where are you? It's Carmel.'

The park was silent except for the patter of rain on leaves and bushes, tree branches creaking in the wind. She sprinted along the muddy path to the pagoda.

'Sean!' she yelled again. 'Where are you?'

Darkness and silence close by, a siren wailing in the

distance. Carmel stopped by the pagoda, heart pounding, her breath coming in gasps. Through the waving trees she could see the big houses all around, most of their windows lit. Her own house. The front door stood wide open, giving it an abandoned look.

'Sean!' she shouted desperately, staring into the darkness. She began to sob.

'Carmel, come back! It's freezing.' Rosa ran up to her and grabbed her arm. 'You didn't see Sean, you can't have!' Her eyes were full of concern. 'He wouldn't stand out here staring at his own house,' she panted. 'That's crazy!'

'So what?' Carmel's voice cracked. 'This whole situation is crazy!'

'You *think* you saw him, but you couldn't have, it's too dark. Come inside,' Rosa urged. 'We'll get soaked and catch our deaths.'

'What's up?' a man called. It was Andy, a neighbour, taking Vegas, his golden retriever, for a bedtime stroll. He carried an umbrella and his cigarette glowed red in the dark. 'Evening, ladies,' he said, recognising them. 'Rotten night. What you doing in the park this late?' He chuckled. 'Or is that a delicate question?'

'We fancied the fresh air,' Rosa said tersely. She nudged Carmel. 'Maybe it was him you saw.'

'Do me a favour! He's at least five inches too short and twice as broad.'

Rosa was almost dragging her. 'I'm going to take that damn prescription and find a late-night chemist.'

'Don't bother.' Carmel shook wet strands of hair out of her eyes.

'Well, you're bloody well going to bed, even if you don't sleep. Hurry up, before that guy thinks of another witty remark.' Andy dropped his cigarette and trod on it, staring at the two women as they crossed the road and went back into the house. Something weird was going on there, he thought. Definitely. Vegas sniffed the cigarette butt.

45

Several hours later Carmel woke up in the darkness, hot and dry-mouthed, her heart racing. She lay fully clothed beneath the quilt. She rolled over in bed, felt Sean's heart-breakingly empty space, and started to cry. Stupid to have refused the tranquillisers. She needed something chemical to dull the fear and agony. She glanced at the clock. Two-fifteen am. I'll go down and get a cognac, she thought.

Had the lashing rain woken her, or some other noise impinging on her subconscious? She caught her breath and sat up as the strange scratching sound intensified. It seemed to come from downstairs. She realised it was a key being turned and twisted in the two front door locks. Then a muffled thud as the door was shoved and met the resistance of bolts and chain.

'Sean! Oh, my God!' She threw off the quilt and leapt up, steadying herself on the bedside table as a wave of dizziness hit her. Rosa must have bolted the door before going to bed, and put the chain on. Silly! She should have realised Sean might come back during the night. Now he couldn't get in.

'I'm coming!' Carmel called, stumbling towards the door. Joy and relief flooded her. She didn't give a damn where Sean had been or what he had done, or what mystery lay behind his disappearance. She loved him and he was back. Nothing else mattered. There was another thud as she ran across the landing. Then silence. She stumbled down-stairs, snapped on the hall light and undid the bolts and chain, her hands shaking. Pulled open the door, ready to fling herself into Sean's arms. Rain blew in her face, making her shiver. But Sean wasn't there. Nobody stood there.

'What the *hell* . . .?' Hugging herself for warmth, Carmel stared in disbelief, crushed by terrible anti-climax. The night air cleared her head. She took a couple of steps forward, ran down the path and out into the square, looked frantically up and down the street. Rain soaked her hair and mingled with her tears.

'Sean!' she shouted. She clenched her hands. 'Are you there? I don't understand!' She waited, shivering as she paced to and fro. She hadn't imagined hearing his key because the door was unlocked; all she'd had to do was unbolt and unchain it. Why didn't he wait? Ring the bell? No, not that, he'd think Lisa was home and he wouldn't want to wake her. Carmel turned and walked slowly back up the path towards the front door, head bowed and shoulders hunched as she sobbed despairingly. She passed the dripping laurel bushes on either side of the front door and stopped abruptly. The hall was in darkness. I switched the light on! she thought. Didn't I? Or am I losing it completely now? Fear gripped her. She moved forward slowly.

Carmel stopped again and gasped in shock as she made out the shape of a tall man some yards away down the hall, motionless and menacing. He was the same height and build as Sean, but Carmel knew it wasn't her husband. He looked like the man she'd spotted by the park gates earlier, the man who had stared at the house and then vanished. She stood there frozen with terror.

'Who are you?' she managed to whisper. 'What do you—?' She raised one arm, groping for the light switch, but someone grabbed her from behind and pinioned her arms before she could reach it. The front door slammed. Some sort of soft cloth slithered across her eyes, was pulled around her head and knotted tightly. There were three of them, Carmel thought, the tall man and two others. She screamed and struggled violently as her wrists were bound painfully tight.

'Carmel, what's happening?' Rosa called fearfully from the top of the stairs.

'Rosa!' she screamed, jerking and struggling in the men's arms. 'Call the police!'

She heard one of them pound upstairs and Rosa cry out. The man swore and there was a struggle. Her sister's cries faded as she was dragged away. A door slammed. Carmel was wrestled to the floor and held down.

'Don't hurt my sister!' she cried. 'Don't—' Thank God Lisa wasn't here.

'Shut it, bitch,' a voice growled in her ear. 'All right, where's your fella?'

'I don't know, I don't know!' She kicked out frantically, futilely. 'How did you get keys to this house, why—?'

'I'll ask the questions, you cow! I *said*, where's your fella?'

The tall dark man wasn't saying anything. He walked forward and stood between her legs, kicking them apart. Carmel sobbed with terror as he knelt and unzipped her trousers then pushed up her top. She felt his cold, dry hands on her breasts and belly, slowly stroking. Oh Christ! she thought. They're going to rape me. Something cold and hard pressed against her left breast, just over her wildly beating heart, and she knew it was a gun.

'Right,' the voice in her ear growled again. Why didn't the other man talk? 'If you don't tell us where he is – *now!* – we'll kill you. After we've fucked you, of course. Then we'll do the other bitch.'

'I don't know where Sean is!' she sobbed, struggling helplessly. Tears poured from her eyes beneath the blindfold. 'I wish I did, but I don't. I don't bloody know anything. That's the truth, I swear!' She thought of Lisa, her parents bringing her daughter home to find her mother and sister shot dead, lying in pools of dark, sticky blood.

The man was stroking her left breast with the cold gun muzzle, circling the nipple, his other hand flat against her belly. Carmel thought she would die of terror before he could do anything to her. She could smell his cologne or aftershave, musky and woody. Amber, like her great-grandmother's beads. The gun was jammed painfully against her racing heart again, then suddenly withdrawn. Her clothes were rearranged and she was dragged to her feet. Her legs trembled so much that she could barely stand. Finally the man spoke.

'Useless.' His voice was a barely discernible whisper. 'Useless bitch.'

He swung his arm and Carmel dropped like a stone as the gun butt caught her on the side of her head.

Chapter Five

It definitely was her lucky night.

Gemma smiled greedily at the five hundred notes. It reminded her of when the Drugs Squad and Operational Support Division had ripped apart her boyfriend's house in a dawn raid eighteen months ago, and found a stash of thirty grand in a kid's shoe box in the airing cupboard. 'That's where I keep my savings,' one of the cocky bastards had joked as she stared, bleary-eyed and coffee-less in furious disbelief, amazed that even Terry could be that thick. 'Can't trust banks, can you?'

Terry was banged up now, getting meals, light, heating and gym facilities at taxpayers' expense. The stupid sod even wrote poetry on a word processor. He was pathetic, no use to her and the kids any more. I'm not dragging myself, Darren and Saskia to visit him again, Gemma thought. I've had it with losers. She pouted as the money disappeared into the glove compartment.

'Thought you told me you didn't smoke,' she said flirtatiously. 'How come you've got matches in there?'

The man looked at her, his eyes brooding. Must be a dealer, she thought. Someone big, judging by his posh suit and coat, this car with the gorgeous, soft, pale-coloured leather seats. It was an unusual make, she wasn't sure what kind. Gemma only knew it must have cost a fortune. She giggled nervously, feeling the vodka. She was warm and cosy in the car, protected from the lashing rain. Radio City played softly, the latest Madonna. Gemma was dying for a cig. She looked out of the window at the great forbidding bulk of the Anglican cathedral, its walls illuminated by spotlights. Orange streetlight slanted across her thin, black-stockinged thighs, and the gilt handbag chain gleamed.

Murder in the cathedral, he thought. Soaring arches, light, memorials to soldiers, sailors and airmen of both world wars, and countless other wars. Stone pillars and balconies, vast, cold echoing spaces. The place was locked, of course. Vandalism had turned the ancient tradition of sanctuary into a wistful, long-lost ideal.

'Don't talk much, do you?' Gemma commented, resenting his silence and the five hundred quid that wasn't hers. Yet. 'D'you want business?' she asked.

He was good looking and sexy, not the type who had to pay for it. He didn't seem weird either. She wondered how old he was; mid-thirties, probably. His eyes beneath dark straight brows looked into her soul. She saw no greed or laughter, no contempt, anger or fear. Only calm and control. 'I can't make you out,' she said, puzzled. He did not reply. 'D'you want business or *what*?' she repeated impatiently. He seemed lost in a dream.

'Sorry.' He smiled suddenly, revealing sharp, white teeth. 'Yes, I do.' He started the car. 'I'd like to do it in the cathedral,' he said, making her giggle again. 'On the altar. But I'm not in the mood to break in. We'll go for a drive.'

'Cool.' Gemma relaxed, reassured by his smile. 'What's your name?' she asked, breaking her rule. 'What d'you do?'

'I don't have a name. I don't have problems, only challenges.' His smile broadened. 'I'm a multi-millionaire who's just waiting for the money to be deposited in my bank account.'

'Aren't we all!' Gemma laughed, but she had a feeling he wasn't joking. She shrugged and sighed, longed for that cigarette. He started the engine and drove off. They cruised

51

through town, past pubs and clubs with groups of people outside, down Lime Street past the Empire Theatre and St George's Hall. She loved being in this posh car with him, it made her feel important. She dreamed about being someone else, having a different life. Tonight could be the start of it, she thought. If I play me cards right.

She was stupidly disappointed when they ended up in a dark, deserted yard on the Dock Road, with high brick walls and the Mersey sloshing somewhere out of sight. The engine died and they sat in silence for a minute. Gemma gazed at the outline of his face in the darkness. The smile still hovered around his lips. This was the point where she normally took charge. But she was suddenly nervous, unsure of herself.

She smelled and would taste of stale cigarettes. Nasty, sweet perfume that clung like an invisible noxious gas. Her teased hair was dried out by harsh chemicals. She would serve a purpose, sacrifice her mean little soul for his greater good. He reached beneath the driver's seat.

'Will you put these on for me?'

'What? No way, mate!' Gemma nearly panicked at the sight of the handcuffs. 'I don't do that,' she cried, sitting up straight. 'I'm not into bondage or SM or any of that stuff. I bloody knew you were too good to be true,' she said bitterly.

'Listen, it's nothing heavy. I promise. Makes things more exciting, that's all. I thought you liked me. Trusted me. I like you, Gemma. We could be friends. Don't forget.' He paused, nodded towards the glove compartment. 'Five hundred.'

Gemma struggled with greed and fear and doubt. She hated the idea of handcuffs. She was alone with a punter in this pitch-dark bloody dockyard. But this guy really didn't seem like a psycho. If he wanted to hurt her he would have done it by now. She smelled the car's leather seats and his posh aftershave, thought of the clothes she could buy with five hundred notes. Darren and Saskia wanted a PlayStation.

'Forget it,' he said suddenly. He dropped the handcuffs and started the engine. 'Where do you want to go?' he asked. 'Somewhere in town? I'll drop you.' He made a snap decision. If Gemma made the right choice now he would let her go and find another victim. A shiver of excitement prickled his scalp. He was already wound up enough tonight.

'No!' she gasped. 'I'll do it. I'll wear them.'

'It doesn't matter.' He looked at her and smiled. 'I can see you're not comfortable with my idea. I don't want to push you into anything.'

'You're not. Go on, let me wear them,' Gemma begged, almost crying with frustration at the thought of losing his friendship and his money. 'I want to!'

The engine died again. 'Are you sure?' He was amused by the dilemma he had created for her. Not that she was much of a challenge.

'Yeah.' Gemma held up her hands, offering them to him. Offering herself.

'Not like that. Behind you.'

He cuffed her wrists, grabbed a handful of dry, permed hair and pulled her head back.

'Ow!' she gasped. 'Watch it, mate. That hurts.'

'Good. You've had your fun,' he whispered in her ear. 'Worshipped false gods, made the wrong choices. Sacrificed yourself for greed. I would have let you go. But now it's time to pay.'

'What are you on about?' Gemma cried, not daring to wriggle in case he pulled her hair tighter. 'Look, mate, stop it, will you? You're hurting me. You can keep your sodding money, all right? Just let me out of here.'

'Too late for that, I'm afraid.' He let go of her hair and clamped one hand over her mouth, felt angry as she started to struggle fiercely. His excitement mounted. She was completely in his power.

'Don't worry,' he whispered. 'I don't want to fuck a dirty sad little slag like you.'

53

The dark forest flashed into his mind, the stunted black tree branches against the crimson sky. He thought of the dead girl lying in that corner of Joseph's labyrinth, her broken body concealed by the rubble of demolished Victorian houses. She would never be found. But he wanted this one to be found, oh yes. A sharp pain in his hand startled him.

'Bitch!' he shouted, enraged. She had sunk her teeth in, drawn blood.

Stifled, Gemma tried to turn her head away and scream. She thought she was so clever, could handle herself and spot psychos a mile off. This guy was a grade A, twenty-four carat. She didn't feel clever now, only terrified. He began to punch her around the face and head and she whimpered at the force of the blows, the agonising pain in her jaw and cheekbones. She could take a few slaps, but he wasn't going to leave it at that.

'I want to go home,' she whispered, dazed. Blood trickled from her nose and the corner of her mouth. 'I want me mum. I want to see me kids.' Sometimes punters got all soppy about mums and kids. Not this one though.

'Out!' He opened the passenger door and shoved her. Gemma fell in a heap on the unforgiving concrete. Cold rain poured down. Her mouth was filling with blood and her jaw felt strange, like it was broken or dislocated. She couldn't speak. He got out and dragged her up, flung her against the brick wall. Gemma collapsed, cracking her head as she fell. He went back to the car for his gun and the plastic envelope containing the sheet of papèr.

'Better luck in your next cycle of existence.' He grinned as he touched the gun to her right temple. 'You might make secretary.'

Gemma's body jerked like a puppet's as the bullets ripped into her head and chest. The gun's noise was muffled by the suppressor – which most people mistakenly referred to as a silencer – but still sounded loud enough, like a great thick book being slammed on a table. The

54

'silent' gun did not exist. He stopped and checked for a non-existent pulse, glanced up at the sky. Bloody rain, he thought.

His anger was gone now, and he felt perfectly calm. He unlocked the handcuffs, put them and the gun away, and shoved her tacky little handbag in the glove compartment to keep as a souvenir. The bite mark hurt like hell. Should he worry about that? A prostitute could have picked up all kinds of sexually transmitted horrors. He wiped the blood on his trousers.

He took a can of petrol from the boot and doused her with it, the smell strong in his nostrils. He struck a match, tossed it and jumped back. A whoosh of flame engulfed the body. He wanted to watch the cleansing flames consume her corrupt corpse, but he had to get away before some drunk staggering out of a pub noticed the funeral pyre. He unfolded the paper, lit a match and let it burn for a couple of seconds. Then he blew out the hungry flame and let the charred pieces scatter. He screwed up the half-burned paper and lodged it beneath a couple of broken bricks a few inches from Gemma's outstretched left hand, protecting it from the wind and rain. It looked as if she could have stuck it there herself, perhaps during a struggle. A minute later he was back in the Jag, racing along the Dock Road towards the city centre.

His hands trembled on the wheel, and he was sweating. He thought about killing and killers, as he often did. The overwhelming majority were stupid, boring, sad bastards, nicked more easily and quickly than a clumsy shoplifter or speeding motorist. They were controlled and swept along by their unfortunate natures, came from abused, unloved backgrounds. To him that was ridiculously, terrifyingly simplistic. Killing was always a choice. Why couldn't people face the truth?

Look at him. He hadn't been abused, although his parents had never been particularly enthusiastic about child rearing. If they'd had the intelligence to use contraception properly he would never have happened. Despite that he had turned out intelligent, educated, good looking, had made his own life. All along, though, something indefinable had been lurking, biding its time, waiting for the right – or wrong – circumstances to flush it out. He had known that since childhood, felt he was different somehow.

He had started dealing when he returned from his global adventures, just to make some extra cash. One thing led to another. Now there was his trade in female flesh. He did not hate women, did not possess the mother fixation beloved of psychiatrists. He had to admit; dominating, controlling and selling female bodies like commodities or livestock, sometimes killing them, gave him a tremendous joy and satisfaction that went beyond money or sex. It gave him power, filled him with strength and purpose. The money was great. But secondary.

Manipulating people, gaining their trust and friendship, even their love, fulfilled a basic need in him. He thought of Carmel. And his partner. They had fallen under his spell, although the spell was broken now as far as the man was concerned. That made him uneasy and frightened, challenged his self-belief. His partner had got in his way, and for that reason alone he had to be destroyed. He would destroy Carmel too, if necessary. He smiled. Poor Carmel, desperate for her knight in shining armour, the shoulder to cry on. That was what women loved, what they never stopped looking for.

His mobile rang and he pulled into a parking spot near the brightly lit Cunard Building. Gemma's bite stung and throbbed. He should get home quickly and wash the wound in hot, soapy water, put some disinfectant and a dressing on it. He wondered if he should get a HIV test.

He was nervous, could not stop shivering and sweating, but he told himself it was just a reaction. He had had it before. Killing another human being – even a lowlife like Gemma – was not nothing. He picked up the phone.

'Yep? What's going on there now?' He wound down the

window a few inches, smelled the rainy air and the river.

'The sister's back from hospital,' a man said. 'Alone. They must have kept the missis in for the night. There was a police car outside the house for a while, but that's gone now.'

He leaned his head back and closed his eyes. He suddenly felt sick and exhausted, plunged into depression. And fear. It wasn't supposed to have happened like that, Carmel getting hurt. He had counted on a quick in and out job while she and her sister were asleep, probably doped up on tranquillisers, hadn't expected them to have bolted and chained the front door because he assumed they would be hoping the man of the house might return at any time. Still, look on the bright side; if Carmel hadn't opened the door and run out into the square they would have had to go round the back and break in, and that could have proved even more messy. It had all been a bloody waste of time anyway. He hadn't found the stolen money. Or anything else.

'Keep me posted,' he ordered. 'Anyone goes in or out, I want to know. Make sure you don't get spotted.'

'No worries. It's all quiet now.'

'All quiet?' He hung up, started the engine and drove off into the rainy night. 'Not for long.'

Chapter Six

'What's the purpose of your visit to the UK, Ms Tarnu?'

The bored immigration officer stared at the girl in front of him. Her dazzling smile was like a beacon, lighting up her beautiful heart-shaped face which until that moment had looked tired and unhappy. She had long, straight black hair and rosy skin, full red lips and perfect white teeth.

'Tourism. And family visit. I am going to stay with my sister, Maria.' Simona smoothed the shiny black mane that reached almost to her waist. 'For three weeks.' She remembered what Mr Ionescu in Bucharest had told her: Say you're a tourist, a backpacker. 'My sister works as a secretary in a lawyer's office.' Simona's expressive dark eyes were nervous, hopeful. 'In Liverpool.'

'And you come from Bucharest?'

'Yes, that's correct.'

'I see.' He bent his head and studied her passport again. Simona had a number the immigration officer could call if he wanted to investigate further. But she had been assured there would be no checks. She wished it really was Maria's phone number scrawled on the piece of paper in her wallet, and not the number of the people she would be working for. What were they like, she wondered again? What kind of restaurant was it? She had to wear a uniform, which was why she had had to tell Mr Ionescu her measurements a few weeks ago: it would be ready and waiting for her. Simona was over-qualified for waitressing, given that she could use a word processor, and do all kinds of office work. But it was a start. She had more chance here than back home, and she could certainly earn better money. What a pity she had not been able to get in touch with Maria and tell her she was following her to England.

Simona waited, her heart beating uncomfortably as the immigration officer's grey head stayed bent over her passport for what seemed a long time. Hurry up, she prayed. Suddenly he stamped it and handed it back to her with a smile. 'That's fine. Enjoy your stay, Ms Tarnu. 'Bye!'

'Thank you, goodbye,' she replied, flashing a smile of relief. She took the passport, slipped it into her rucksack and walked quickly on into Manchester airport's arrivals hall for domestic and European flights, anxiously scanning faces in the waiting crowd. It was hot, crowded and brightly lit and she was sweating slightly. She wiped her hands on her jeans. She wanted to take off her heavy black jacket, but it would be cold once she got outside.

If only Maria were meeting her! Simona looked around, suddenly overwhelmed, feeling the sadness and loneliness of the foreigner in a strange new land. The alien English language was loud in her ears; her English was good, she had studied it for years, but she could barely understand much of what she heard. Did they speak a kind of dialect here? She watched longingly as people talked and laughed, greeted and hugged one another in the universal language of welcoming loved ones home. Simona's eyes flooded, and she had to restrain herself from bursting into tears.

You're not alone, she reminded herself. She sniffed hard and wiped her eyes. Maria is here, living and working in Liverpool, just a few kilometres away. I'll get settled in my new job then I'll look for her. We'll be together again. She hasn't forgotten her family, she's just busy working and enjoying her new life. British working hours are the longest in Europe. It's only a few months since she left Romania, and she never was great at keeping in touch. She will be so happy to see me, so pleased when she sees my photos of Lily. She must miss her daughter so much. Maybe that was why Maria never called – it was too painful for her to hear Lily's voice over the phone, but not to be able to cuddle and kiss her beautiful, affectionate lively toddler.

Maria had sobbed her heart out saying goodbye to Lily at the airport. Simona recalled her sister's anguished, tear-streaked face, her dark eyes full of the pain of parting. When the flight was called she practically had to prise Lily out of her mother's arms. Lily had howled and clung to Maria too. It was heartbreaking for all of them.

Simona realised she was staring at a placard with her name scrawled on it in thick blue marker, held by a young woman with long blonde hair. The woman was casually dressed, wearing jeans and a sheepskin-lined denim jacket, and smoking a cigarette. Simona slipped the heavy rucksack from her aching shoulders, went up to the woman and held out her hand.

'Hello!' She smiled. 'I am Simona Tarnu. You are from the restaurant?'

'You what?' The woman stared at her, ignoring her outstretched hand. 'Look,' she said, dropping her cigarette. 'I was just told to pick you up and drive you to Liverpool. Don't ask me about any restaurant, okay?' She glanced at the rucksack. 'That all your stuff?'

'My . . .?' Simona looked at her, puzzled. She found this flat, nasal dialect hard to understand, but no doubt she would quickly get used to it.

'Your stuff – your things.' The woman ground out the cigarette with the heel of her brown calfskin boot. 'Baggage,' she said loudly.

'Oh! Yes. This is all I have.'

'Right. Come on then.' The woman turned and marched off.

It had been a long day. First the flight from Bucharest to Amsterdam and after that a boring few hours hanging around Schiphol airport. After that the nerve-rackingly bumpy flight to Manchester, so turbulent that the captain had told the cabin crew as well as the passengers to stay buckled up, and no food or drinks had been served. Simona would have liked to sit down and relax, slowly sip a cup of strong, sweet coffee and eat a sandwich or some other snack. There was a café at one end of the arrivals hall, and she could smell hot food. But the woman was obviously in a hurry, and it was not a good time to ask. Surely she would get something to eat when they arrived in Liverpool?

Simona followed the woman out of the arrivals hall and they took the lift to level three of the short stay car park, squeezing in between departing and arriving passengers and the trolleys piled with their bags and suitcases. The woman looked bored, impatient. Simona thought it rude of her not to introduce herself or say a few words of welcome.

'What is your name?' she inquired tentatively. The woman did not answer until they were out of the lift and she had paused to light another cigarette.

'Yvonne.' They stopped at a white transit van in which a young man with a beard sat smoking and listening to the radio. Simona could hear the rock music as they approached. She was taken aback by the insolent way the man stared at her, looking her up and down as if he could see through her clothes. She felt herself blushing angrily. Whoever he was, she knew already that she didn't like him. His eyes were pale and cruel-looking, like a wolf she had once seen in the forest.

'How old are you, love?' he asked, grinning.

'Eighteen.' Simona hesitated. 'Are you from the restaurant where I will be working?'

'Jesus!' Yvonne rolled her eyes and shook her head.

'That's right.' His grin broadened. 'I'm the sous chef. We specialise in the finest, cutting-edge fusion cuisine. East meets West. You'll love it.' He tossed away his cigarette and wound up the window.

Yvonne pulled open the van doors. 'Get in,' she ordered.

Simona was surprised to see four other girls in the back

of the van, two of them Asian. The Asian girls looked about her own age but the others were older, in their early twenties. They all looked exhausted, sullen and dishevelled. She got in and sat down on the dusty seat, clutching her rucksack.

'Right.' Yvonne glared at them. 'No talking, you lot.'

The doors slammed before Simona could protest. Why on earth should they not talk, she wondered, get to know one another? Especially if they were going to be working together.

'She has no right to speak to us like that,' she said indignantly. She looked at each girl in turn, waiting for some kind of response. There was none. Her nervousness increased. 'What is your name?' she asked the girl next to her. She wore frayed jeans, dirty trainers and a pale-coloured mock leather jacket. Her dark hair was long and tangled. 'Where are you from?'

The girl shrugged and did not reply. She leaned her head back and closed her eyes. The engine started. Simona fell on her hands and knees as the van lurched forward. She picked herself up, sat back and stared out of the small rear window, her unease mounting.

Why did they treat her this way? Was there some mistake? Mr Ionescu from the employment agency in Bucharest had got her this job, paid her air fare and arranged her passport, tourist visa and AIDS test, just as he had done for Maria a few months ago. Simona had wondered about the AIDS test, but Mr Ionescu said that was quite normal, standard requirement for entry to many countries. British immigration authorities were particularly prejudiced against people from eastern Europe, he said, and often tried to stop them entering their country to work. Everything had to be in order. The best way was to pretend to be a backpacker. Simona intended to work very hard, so that she could pay off her debt to Mr Ionescu as soon as possible. Once that was done, she could keep all her earnings. She would look for a flat of her own, find Maria.

Maybe she and Maria could share a home. That would be wonderful.

It was too dark and rainy to see much of north-west England. They were driving alarmingly fast down a motorway now, pitch-black fields on either side. There was a smell of petrol fumes and cigarette smoke, and Simona could hear the jangle of the radio. She longed to feel happy and optimistic at the prospect of a new life, at being reunited with her sister, who she missed very much. She felt only exhaustion, hunger and homesickness. And fear. Something was wrong, she thought. Why wouldn't the other girls talk to her? Two of them had fallen asleep. Simona bowed her head and started to sob quietly. Eventually she also fell asleep.

She awoke with a start when the van jerked to a halt. The doors were flung open.

'Come on,' Yvonne called. 'Move it! All of you. Lazy bitches,' she said angrily. Simona grabbed her rucksack and hurriedly climbed out, too dazed to protest at the woman's outrageous rudeness. Her limbs felt stiff and heavy. She shivered with cold and fear.

They were in a wide, tree-lined city street of old houses, although they were not as old and tumbledown as some of the houses in Bucharest. Music boomed and lights blazed from a house across the road where people, mostly men, stood laughing and talking on the front steps. They sounded drunk. Simona flinched as an unseen woman screamed and burst into wild laughter. She heard glass breaking.

'Come on, we haven't got all night.' Yvonne shoved her. 'Get up them steps.'

'Don't push me!' Anger gave Simona courage. Who did this woman think she was? 'I've come here to work,' she protested. 'I will earn money. You have no right to—'

'D'you want a smack or what?' Yvonne screamed, making her jump with fright. 'Don't talk to me about your rights, you stupid little cow! I knew we'd have trouble with this one,' she said to the dark-haired, bearded man. 'Is the boss coming over?'

'Not tonight, he's busy. It'll be tomorrow sometime. Come on, darlin'.' He grabbed Simona around the waist. 'Let's you and me go inside and get to know each other a bit better, eh? Check out your cv.'

'No! Don't touch me!' Simona did not want to go in that house, although she had no idea where else she could go. Before she realised what was happening she was being dragged up the steps and hustled down a long, narrow hall, up a dimly lit flight of stairs. The house smelled damp and musty. The other girls disappeared. They shoved her into a dark room and snapped on the single lightbulb.

Simona looked around, blinking. The large room was bare, with rough floorboards and a spreading damp patch on one wall, faded flowered wallpaper peeling. The sash window had thin black cloth tacked over it. A stained mattress lay on the floor. She clutched her rucksack and backed trembling into a corner near the old-fashioned fireplace, too frightened to speak. The empty grate was black and rusted, the cracked brown hearth tiles littered with burnt matches and cigarette butts. Yvonne crossed the room, pulled the rucksack away from Simona and began hitting her around the head. Simona tried to fend off the blows. The man grabbed her, pinioned her arms and dragged off her jacket.

'What are you doing?' she cried. 'Why have you brought me here? This is a mistake! My name is Simona Tarnu, I have come to England to work as a waitress.'

'You'll work, all right, darlin',' the man laughed. He stank of sweat. 'Don't worry about that. Just won't be exactly the job you had in mind, that's all.'

'This is a mistake!' Simona repeated frantically. Tears filled her eyes. 'Let me go, please. I will go to the police.'

'Listen to it, will you?' Yvonne slapped her across the face. 'Stupid bitch!' She went out of the room and came back with three scruffily dressed men.

Simona looked at them and began to wail in panic. She struggled violently and managed to free one arm, hit out at the man holding her and raked his face with her long fingernails. He shouted and swore, punched her in the stomach. Simona fell on her knees, the breath knocked out of her.

The men came nearer. She saw filthy trainers, ragged denim jeans, leather trousers neatly stitched. She smelled their alcohol-laden breath, cigarettes, their sweat and her own terror. Thought of her parents and her little niece, Lily, thousands of kilometres away in Romania, safe in their village. And Maria? Where was she?

The men dragged Simona to her feet and stripped off her clothes. Yvonne leaned against the damp wall, folded her arms and watched. Simona stared at her, her desperate eyes pleading. She could not believe another woman would stand by and witness her terror and humiliation, do nothing to help. When Yvonne smiled for the first time, she knew she was doomed.

'This is the bit I like best.' Yvonne lit another cigarette.

Naked and shivering in the cold, dirty room, Simona's hands were tied behind her back and she was thrown on to the mattress. She was sobbing and shaking with terror, pleading even though she knew they would not listen. Plaster flaked from the grey ceiling with its long, meandering cracks. The lightbulb was too bright for her tired, sore eyes.

'Don't hurt me, please!' she begged. 'Please let me go.' She stared up at their cruel, smiling faces. They gathered around, their eyes intense as they studied her naked body. 'I am a virgin,' she cried. Yvonne burst out laughing and nearly choked on a mouthful of cigarette smoke.

'Hold up. I get first bite at the cherry.' The bearded man knelt over Simona, his eyes spiteful and angry. She saw the red marks on his face where she had scratched him. She was going to have to pay for that now. 'Hold her legs,' he ordered.

'No!' Simona screamed and thrashed helplessly. '*Please* don't!'

'Shut it!' He hit her across the face, then unzipped his jeans. 'We've seen your cv,' he leered, staring down at her. 'Now here's your job description.' The others laughed.

The pain and humiliation was unendurable, but Simona had to endure it. She prayed that her ordeal would be over quickly, but it seemed to go on and on. After each man had raped her in turn, she felt the pressure and sharp sting of a needle in her left thigh.

Simona passed out.

Chapter Seven

'Somebody's looking for Sean,' Carmel stated. 'And I don't mean the police.'

'But *who*?' Daniel put down his mug of coffee. 'And why?' He frowned and shook his head. 'This gets more and more crazy. You've no ideas?'

'All I have is questions.' Carmel leaned her elbows on the kitchen table and rubbed her eyes. 'Unanswered questions. And a bloody great headache after getting whacked with a gun butt last night. Apart from the shock of what happened. I was never so terrified in my life! Neither was Rosa.'

'You should go to bed.' Rosa dumped a cup of coffee in front of her. 'You've just got out of hospital, and you hardly slept there.'

'Well, it was a bit difficult with all the coming and going in the ward. People talking, crying, throwing up, going into cardiac arrest. And they don't design those beds to five star hotel standards. Anyway, never mind me, Rosa!' Carmel looked worriedly at her sister. 'You were threatened too, held at gunpoint in your room and you didn't know what the hell was happening to me. You must be feeling terrible.'

'Worry about yourself, not me. I'm fine.'

'You can't be fine. Three men burst in, attacked us—'

'Carmel, I swear, I'm all right. Now, how about some breakfast?'

Carmel shook her head. 'I'm not hungry.' She pulled a face. 'The smell of that bacon and those sausages makes me feel sick.'

'That's because your stomach's empty.' Rosa frowned and turned back to the grill and frying pan. She had been shaken to the core after last night, but she wasn't going to let her sister know. She was determined to look out for Carmel and Lisa.

'Carmel, don't take this the wrong way, but—' Daniel hesitated. 'Do you think Sean could have been – I don't know – blackmailed? Involved in something?'

'Something dodgy, you mean?' Carmel looked at him. 'No, Daniel,' she said slowly. 'I don't. And I can't imagine anyone wanting to blackmail him. Is that why you think the police asked for a few hairs out of his comb so they could get a DNA profile? I don't like the idea of that, but they said it was standard procedure. It doesn't mean they think he's committed a crime.'

Daniel flushed. 'I'm sorry. Look, don't get me wrong – I don't mean to imply this situation is his own fault,' he said hastily. 'Maybe he was targeted for some reason. Tricked.' He shrugged helplessly. 'Jesus! I don't know.'

Carmel's eyes glittered with tears. 'I can't stop thinking how I should have made Sean tell me what was wrong when I saw him on Friday. I wish I'd cancelled that client and left with him. I wanted to. But for God's sake, I thought I'd see him at home just over an hour later.' She ran her fingers through her hair. 'I feel so guilty,' she whispered. 'Maybe I could have prevented whatever happened to him.'

'Do me a bloody favour,' Daniel said, startled. 'You're not to blame for any of this.'

'I could have helped Sean. Done something ... I don't know. Oh God!' Carmel groaned as she massaged her temples. 'My head's killing me.'

'Head injuries can make you feel exhausted, and you were exhausted before that bastard hit you. Drink your coffee.' Rosa nodded at Carmel's untouched cup. 'Let me make you some breakfast. Then go upstairs and sleep for a few hours.'

'Rosa's right.' Daniel watched as Carmel picked up the cup and took a sip. Her blonde hair hung limp around her pale face, partially concealing the large blue-black bruise on her left temple. She wore yesterday's black top and khaki cotton trousers. Her blue eyes were frantic, filled with despair. He reached across the table and held her cold hand. 'What do the police say?'

'Well, they no longer think I'm a nagging wife whose henpecked hubbie did a runner. They're searching for Sean – and those men who forced their way in. Rosa gave a description of the man who held her at gunpoint. But she didn't see the other two – neither did I except for one guy's outline in the dark just before the other grabbed and blind-folded me. He was the same guy I saw in the park and mistook for Sean – I'm certain. How the hell did they come to have keys to this house, that's what I can't figure out! Unless maybe they stole them from Sean. But how could they if they didn't know where he was?' She brushed away tears. 'I thought they were going to rape and murder us. Thank goodness Lisa wasn't here.'

'I know.' Daniel squeezed her hand and then leaned across and gave her a hug.

'What did Anthony say when you phoned him?' Rosa's pretty face was grim as she tipped grilled bacon and pork-and-leek sausages on to a platter.

'He wanted to come round right away, but I told him not to. He's shocked about what happened to us. He was wondering if he should contact the police himself, because they haven't interviewed him yet. Although they're bound to do that soon.'

'What will happen to the business if Sean—' Daniel flushed again, quickly corrected himself. 'As long as Sean remains missing?'

'Anthony will take care of things. Why?'

Daniel shrugged. 'No reason. I wondered if anyone

stands to benefit from Sean's disappearance.'

'Well, not me. I don't have a big fat life insurance policy on him.'

Daniel grimaced. 'I wasn't thinking of you, for Christ's sake.'

'No one springs to mind. Not so far.'

'Anthony seems to have had a lot of hassle these past weeks, doesn't he?'

Carmel looked at him, puzzled. 'You mean with Sean?'

'Well ... yeah. I suppose.' Daniel frowned. 'This fight he and Sean had – maybe Anthony misunderstood, got the wrong end of the stick about something.'

'Such as what?' Carmel's spoon clattered on the table. 'I don't see how. Daniel, what are you saying?'

'I don't really know. Only that Sean's not here to give his side of the story.'

'Do you think Anthony's lying?' Panic rose in her. 'There's absolutely no reason why he'd do that! Certainly none I can think of. Sean's disappearance is major hassle for him – apart from the fact that he's worried sick about his friend. Look, I know we've only got Anthony's word for what happened. I've thought about that a lot, but I just can't—'

'Hey, forget it, okay? I'm sorry.' Daniel patted her hand. 'I don't mean to give you more grief. I'm just clutching at straws,' he sighed. 'Dealing in clichés because I don't know what else to think right now. Of course I don't think Anthony's lying. I hardly know the guy. It's just that I'd really like to get Sean's side of this story.'

Carmel clenched her hands. 'So would I.'

Rosa sat at the table and divided bacon, sausages and scrambled eggs between three plates. 'Suppose those men come back?' She jumped in fright as the toast popped up. 'They had guns. They weren't messing about.'

'I shouldn't think they'll be back.' Daniel looked at her trembling hands. 'Not now that they realise you don't know anything about Sean's disappearance.'

'Oh yes,' Carmel said slowly, thinking of the cold gun muzzle lodged against her left breast. 'They're certain I don't know anything!' She blinked in the ray of sunlight that touched her forehead. 'Everybody's talking about a stranger. A stranger who lies to, rows with and beats up his business partner, who's disappeared and is being pursued by God knows who. They're talking about Sean, my husband. It feels like I don't know him any more.' Tears rolled down her cheeks and fell into the coffee. 'I feel so stupid,' she whispered. 'So bloody helpless. Maybe they want to kill Sean. *Why?* And what the hell can I do about it?'

She shivered and hugged herself, fighting shock and fear, exhaustion and paralysing misery. Sunlight streamed into the warm, coffee and bacon-scented kitchen and distant church bells rang out over the city. Daniel let go of her hand.

'We don't know they – whoever they are – want to kill him,' he said gently.

'Well, they don't want to place an order for a classic car or a security product!'

'Carmel.' Rosa looked at her plate. 'Try and eat something.'

Carmel obediently forced down a few mouthfuls of buttery scrambled eggs. 'I'll have more coffee,' she said. 'And a piece of toast. I can't manage the rest.'

'When will Lisa be back?' Daniel speared a sausage.

'Later this afternoon. About five. Mum and Dad are taking her for a walk to the beach this morning, seeing as the weather's sunny.'

'Have you told them about . . .?'

'No! Don't want to scare the hell out of them. Or Lisa.'

A pang of guilt shot through Carmel as she thought of her daughter. Never mind herself, how would Lisa deal with this nightmare? Her hopes would be building right now as she ran about on the Southport sands, longing for her father to be there when she got home. And Sean would not be there. Children often thought they were to blame in situations like this. Did Lisa wonder if she had done something bad to make her father leave? Not yet, maybe. But if time went on and Sean didn't come home? What then?

Carmel got up, walked to the sink and looked out at the long, narrow back yard with its high red-brick walls. There was a cherry tree, a slender silver birch, and three large terracotta pots of green plants. A swing seat, soaked with last night's rain. The strong wooden door in the wall that led to the alley was bolted and padlocked.

She turned and opened the fridge; it was crammed with bottles of champagne and unappetising remains of party buffet food. She took out a bottle of raspberry and orange fruit juice and strolled into the adjoining larder. Crates of Krug champagne were stacked against the walls beneath the wooden shelves, and Carmel knew that the big white cardboard box on the marble pastry slab contained her untouched birthday cake.

She hesitated, then lifted the lid and steeled herself to look at it. Pristine white icing, peach-coloured, fondant roses and green silk leaves. 'Happy Birthday Carmel' in elegant, swirling, peach-coloured letters. The cake smelled intensely of sweetness. She dropped the lid, went back into the kitchen and poured herself a glass of juice, held the chilled glass to her throbbing forehead.

'It's so quiet,' she said, pacing back and forth. 'Without Sean and Lisa.' Rosa and Daniel looked up from their plates; they weren't eating much either. 'This time last week I would have loved the thought of a few hours on my own. I could have written up case notes, read *Psychology Today*, got into a new novel. Listened to music. Now I don't care if I never have another minute to myself as long as I live.' She coughed. Her throat was dry. She drank the juice thirstily.

'Carmel, please go and rest,' Rosa said, her eyes anxious. 'You've got a good few hours before Lisa gets back.'

'All these cliché stories about vanished husbands keep running through my mind,' Carmel went on. 'I just can't stop the horrible thoughts. It's because I don't have a clue. The wife's always the last to know, isn't she?' She clutched the glass. 'You can't win.'

Her voice was bitter. 'If you trust your husband, you're a fool. If you don't, you're an evil, cynical, undermining bitch.'

Rosa stood up. 'Sean hasn't got some secret life – he wouldn't walk out on you and Lisa.' My God, she thought, shaken. I hope I'm right.

'I only wish it was that simple!' Carmel turned, her eyes brilliant with more unshed tears. 'At least then I'd know he was safe. I can't take much more of this,' she cried. The glass slid from her fingers and smashed on the floor. 'How long will it go on? Suppose I never find out what happened? Where is he, why doesn't he come home to me?' She burst into tears.

Rosa put an arm around her shoulders. 'I'm going to tuck you into bed and you can get some sleep before Lisa comes home. You don't want her to see you like this.'

'It's so unfair on Lisa,' Carmel sobbed. 'She doesn't deserve this. And you didn't deserve what happened last night.'

Rosa brushed away a tear. 'Neither did you, sweetheart!'

Carmel paused by the door. 'Daniel, could you do me one more favour and take away that birthday cake?' She wiped her streaming eyes on her sleeve. 'Give some to Ellie's kids – share it with the guys who work for you. Whatever.'

'Sure,' Daniel said quietly. This was not the moment to tell Carmel he had just split up with his girlfriend of two years. He kissed her on the cheek. 'Take care of yourself, love. I'll see you later.'

In the cool bedroom she lay down. Rosa pulled the quilt over her and drew the curtains. Carmel closed her eyes, feeling the dead weight of her body. Her limbs were so heavy that she felt she could sink through the mattress and the floor beneath. Rosa disconnected the phone and went out, closing the door softly.

A gossamer blanket of oblivion floated over Carmel's exhausted mind and settled. She opened her eyes and looked at the eggshell blue ceiling with its white plaster mouldings. Turned her head and looked at Sean's pillow. The anguish of his shocking, heartbreaking absence swept over her with renewed force, and she felt a terrible inconsolable sense of loss.

'I love you,' she whispered, her tears making dark spots on the blue quilt. 'Come home. Please, please don't leave me with this pain.'

She wanted to get up and run downstairs, go out and drive around the city looking for Sean. Talk to Anthony again. How could she sleep when there was so much to do? She stirred and shifted towards the edge of the bed. She had to get up. It was no use. Her body felt too heavy.

Carmel sighed, closed her eyes and drifted into unconsciousness.

Simona awoke dry-mouthed and shivering with cold in the damp bare room, her head throbbing painfully. She was still naked, although at some point someone had thrown a smelly, scratchy, worn grey blanket over her. Bright daylight filtered through the black cloth tacked over the window. It looked as though the sun was shining. The street was silent.

She slowly raised herself on one elbow and looked around, groaning at the pain that gripped her head in a vice. She felt sick, dizzy and disorientated, could scarcely believe she was in this terrible place. Her rucksack was gone, as were the clothes they had stripped off her last night. She remembered the sting of the needle and examined her left thigh; there was a raised, red bump where the woman called Yvonne had brutally plunged it in. Simona was sore and hurting all over, especially between her legs.

The filthy mattress was stained with her blood.

She began to cry as scenes from last night's rape flashed into her mind, remembering the pain and humiliation, the jeering laughter and brutality of the men. Her pathetic, useless pleas. Her helplessness. That was the worst feeling of all, even worse than the pain. To be at someone's mercy, to know there was nothing you could do to stop them hurting you. The knowledge that they wanted to hurt you. That was what could break your spirit.

'My spirit is not broken,' she whispered, brushing away tears. She touched a finger to her bruised and swollen lips. Dark, dried blood flaked off. She wrapped the disgusting blanket around herself, got slowly and painfully to her feet, staggered to the door and rattled the handle.

The door was locked, of course. 'Jesus, help me!' Simona staggered back and collapsed sobbing on to the mattress.

How long would they keep her prisoner here? Naked, dirty, caged like an animal? Without food, water, clothing? She needed the toilet. She was also desperate to bathe or shower away the men's filth, scrub herself from head to toe. Would they come back and rape her again? What had Yvonne injected her with to make her feel so ill? Panic gripped her. She had to escape and find help. Could she climb out of the window? Go into the street with only a blanket to cover her? Simona trembled at the thought of that. But she had to try something. If she stayed here she was doomed.

She froze and gasped with fear as a key turned in the lock and the door opened. A tall, dark man walked in and set down the chair he was carrying. He closed the door and re-locked it behind him. Sat on the chair and stretched out his long legs, his calm, blue-grey eyes studying her. He smelled clean, of soap and subtle, expensive cologne, making Simona even more conscious of her tangled hair, bruised, bloodstained face and the deep shame and horror of her violated, unwashed body. She had no idea why she should feel ashamed; she was an innocent victim. But she knew she would never tell her parents about this. Maybe not even Maria. She caught her breath as a shocking thought flashed into her mind. When would she see her family again? These evil people, whoever they were, might imprison her indefinitely. They might kill her! She bowed her head and sobbed, shaking with terror.

If she had seen this man on the street, in a café or at the Otelinox steel factory where she had worked as secretary to one of the technical directors, Simona's first thought would have been how handsome he was. Now she only wondered if he was going to hurt her. She drew up her knees and huddled shivering on the mattress, the blanket wrapped tightly around her.

'I want you to stop crying,' he said. 'I need to talk to you.'

She was surprised at how gentle his voice sounded. She looked up at him and flinched with terror as he shifted the chair closer to the mattress.

'It's okay.' He sat back and relaxed again. 'I won't hurt you, I promise.' He was silent, his eyes brooding as he looked her over.

Simona hesitated, then displayed the needle mark on her thigh. 'The woman with blonde hair injected me with something,' she whispered. 'It hurt very much.'

'That'll soon fade,' he said. 'We'll put some cream or disinfectant on for you.'

'Why do you talk like a doctor when you only want to hurt me?' she cried.

'I don't want to hurt you. What's your name?' he asked.

'Simona,' she gulped. 'Simona Tarnu.'

'Simona. That's beautiful. And you speak good English.' He did not tell her his name. But she remembered the others last night talking about the boss, saying he would be here today. This must be him.

'I came here to improve my English and—'

'What, to Liverpool?' He laughed.

'My sister lives here. I came to find my sister and work in a restaurant. Why am I here?' Simona started to cry again. 'Give me back my clothes and passport, my money. Let me out of here,' she begged. 'I will not go to the police. I will say nothing about this house. Or what those men did to me.' Of course she would go straight to the police.

He looked amused. 'You've got forty quid in your wallet. How far d'you think that's going to get you?'

He had searched her rucksack! Simona tried to think. 'I will go to . . . youth hostel.'

'Listen to me.' He stopped smiling and leaned forward, his hands loosely clasped. His nails were manicured, the fingers long and elegant. 'You're an intelligent girl and this is the situation. You entered this country on false pretences,' he said. 'Lied about being a backpacker. You realise what that means?'

'But I was told it was necessary because—'

'It means you're an illegal alien,' he interrupted. 'A criminal. If the police catch you, you'll go to prison for a long time. It'll be years before you see your family again.'

'No, no!' Simona stared at him, horrified. 'I am not criminal, I am innocent, please . . .'

A flicker of anger crossed his handsome face. 'Don't argue with me, you bitch!' He reached down, grabbed her by the hair and pulled her towards him. Simona yelped in pain and fear. 'Just listen! You owe me money.' His fingers dug into her scalp, pulling tighter, and the blanket fell, exposing her breasts. 'Thousands of pounds it cost me to bring you here. There is no restaurant. I bought you – I own you now. You'll earn back every penny you cost. And more.'

He let go of her hair and shoved her. Simona fell back sobbing. She pulled up the blanket and covered her breasts, rubbed her fiery scalp with one hand.

'You'll stay here until you agree to co-operate,' he said calmly. 'You'll get a lot worse than last night. If you don't co-operate I'll kill you. That means I'll have wasted my money. So your family will have to be killed. Mr Ionescu knows all about your family, doesn't he?'

'Please!' Simona groaned with terror and despair. 'Not my family, no, please, please!' Maria! Had this happened to her? Was that why she hadn't phoned home in six months?

'Their safety depends on you.' He knelt beside her, stroking her hair now, caressing her bare shoulder. Simona tried not to flinch beneath his touch; she already knew that would make him furious. 'You're beautiful,' he said, his voice gentle again. 'You can make me a lot of money.' His hand slid down and cupped her right breast. She closed her eyes, not daring to resist. 'As long as I'm happy, you and your family stay safe.' He paused. 'Are you ready to obey me?'

'Yes,' Simona whispered, her body rigid with cold and fright. What choice did she have? She did not want to die, and could not bear the thought of her family being harmed. Tears slid from beneath her closed eyelids. 'I will do what you want.'

'Good girl. I knew you'd see sense. You can have some coffee and food now, a nice hot shower. Rest for today. Tomorrow you start work.'

'What work?' she asked dully. But Simona knew, had known since last night. There was no waitress job. No wonder Yvonne had laughed at her, called her a stupid bitch. She had been tricked. Bought and sold like any other commodity, treated like livestock. No, that was not true. Livestock got better treatment. Now this man believed she was his property. Body and soul.

In the twenty-first century, the state of slavery was alive and flourishing.

Chapter Eight

He stopped and gasped as a large brown rat scuttled from a hole in the wall and darted across the passage, its long tail flicking the tips of his boots. He could never get used to the rats down here; the sight of one made him feel as if there was an icy finger with a broken nail stroking the nape of his neck.

He moved on, flashing his torch along intricate brick walls and over skilfully crafted bull-nosed edgings on steps that led down to the second and third tiers of tunnels in this part of the labyrinth. Many of Joseph Williamson's workers had been craftsmen. There was a niche in one of the walls where they had placed candles to light their work, the scorch marks still visible.

He had played in the tunnels as a child, mostly alone. He preferred it that way. It was dangerous; he might have gone in one day and never come out, and his parents would never have known – or cared – what happened to him. People had wandered into the labyrinth over the years, and disappeared for ever. Some had been murdered there or committed suicide, others had drowned in pits of dirty water. There was little interest in Joseph Williamson and his mysterious, largely undiscovered labyrinth then, only half-remembered tales of old people and the occasional article in a local newspaper.

Things were different now. More tunnels, caves and

passages were being discovered. Some of his favourite entrances around Edge Hill had been closed off and appropriated by developers, the city council, private land owners, or the two societies dedicated to the preservation of the labyrinth. They wanted to restore it and eventually open it to the public, the thought of which horrified him.

After two weeks of digging, clearing and searching he still could not locate the undiscovered tunnel, although he had to be close to it according to the old map. There was so much rubble everywhere, great heaps of it in places. Heavy machinery was needed to shift it, and all he had was a spade, pickaxe and sledgehammer. Despite that, he believed he would succeed. The deeper and further he went into the labyrinth, the less rubble there was.

He came to the keyhole-shaped tunnel, and the entrance to another tunnel shaped like a bishop's mitre. A row of walled-up arches, probably hidden entrances to other tunnels. He walked slowly along a narrow passage with an arched roof; a few yards further on the roof suddenly levelled out. Cold, dank air swirled around, making him shiver. The roof arched again, suddenly and dramatically opened into a huge cave known as the Banqueting Hall. The awesome sight never failed to impress him.

There was the story of Joseph's famous 'beanfeast', when he had invited guests for dinner and provided poor man's fare of beans and bacon, whereupon some of the gentlemen had walked out in disgust. Joseph had ushered the remaining guests – his true friends, as he called them – upstairs, where the real feast was laid out. He liked that story. He would have done the same thing himself.

What were the police doing now? he wondered. Sod all, probably. They must have found the half-burned paper by Gemma's charred corpse. What was taking them so long?

He was right under Joseph Williamson's house now, or what remained of it. Not far from the playground of his old school, Archbishop Blanche. He walked slowly out of the huge hall and down a narrow gap. Other tunnel entrances were concealed beneath the rubble. One tunnel, deeper in the labyrinth, with an incredible secret.

Of course he had to face the fact that he might never find the gold. The tunnel could have collapsed or been filled in, might be buried beneath piles of rubble. He was optimistic though. The old map showed tunnels he had not seen on any more recent maps of the labyrinth, in parts undiscovered but still accessible, he hoped, not filled in, collapsed or destroyed by heavy-handed developers. He paused, wiped his forehead and glanced at his watch. It was getting late; too late to go any further this evening. He would study the map again and return in a day or so.

He retraced his steps, flashing the torch to left and right as he walked, looking out for rats. He went down narrow and wide passages, down one level and up another, sometimes clambering over heaps of rubble, until he reached the small narrow tunnel and sandstone steps which led up into the cellar of his parents' old house in Highgate Street. His boots and overalls were covered with dust, his hands blackened. He could not see his face, but knew it was streaked with dirt. He was tired and sweating heavily, coughing from the damp, musty air.

He had kept the house on since his mother's death three months ago. He could not live in it, of course; it was much too cramped and poky, and Edge Hill was no longer quite the upmarket area of Joseph Williamson's day. The house also brought back depressing childhood memories of his father reading aloud alternately boring or terrifying Bible passages, sitting there like some poker-faced sixteenth-century Puritan. His mother, maniacally crocheting garishly coloured cushion covers, tea cosies and patchwork quilts. She had spent her life creating pointless woolly objects.

Why did doctors talk bullshit about people living longer if they kept their brains active? His mother, Sheila, had singlehandedly blasted that one out of the water, having done nothing but crochet crap and drink strong tea until she expired from a stroke at eighty-six. 'Put money in thy

81

purse,' she would whisper slyly to her only son, whenever she noticed him. 'That's *my* favourite Bible quote!' The childish swearing: 'Bloody in the Bible, bloody in the Book, if you don't believe me take a bloody look!' Her tiny gesture of defiance against her domineering, self-important husband and the oppression of life in general. It was enough to make anyone top themselves. Religious belief had kept her going, a maddeningly credulous conviction that there was a point to all the pointlessness.

After his mother's death he had had the mid-Victorian house renovated in preparation for selling it. Some parts of Britain might look like a Victorian theme park, but not many people wanted to live in Victorian conditions. Refurbishing work on pipes in the cellar had uncovered the tiny tunnel with its sandstone steps leading downwards. Joseph Williamson had built many of the houses on Mason Street during the 1800s–1840s, starting with his own. The houses had warrens of underground cellars and strange features such as indoor walls with windows, and rooms with no doors. Highgate Street adjoined Mason Street, therefore it was not surprising to discover a tunnel beneath his parents' house that led down into the greater part of the labyrinth. An older property had previously stood on the site.

He pretended indifference in front of the workmen and said he would have the tunnel filled in, although he had barely been able to contain his excitement at finding his own private entrance to the labyrinth. He cancelled the renovation work and took the house off the market. He told a few nosy neighbours that he was considering renting the property to students, enjoying the horror with which that announcement was greeted.

He pulled off his dust-covered boots and overalls and dumped them on the cellar floor ready for next time. He wore black Mexx trousers and a dark blue sweater underneath. He put on his shoes and black jacket, double-locked the cellar door and strode down the hall towards the front door. He would take a shower when he got back; he never had the slightest desire to linger here.

A flash of red, green and yellow caught his eye, a crocheted circle of wool draped over the back of his mother's ancient armchair. He stopped and closed his eyes for a second, shook his head at the memory of it all. 'Imbeciles,' he whispered.

He locked the house, got into his Jaguar and drove off down the narrow street. It was quiet at this time of the evening. Large television screens flickered behind lace curtains or Venetian blinds. It was cold and clear with a touch of autumnal woodsmoke in the air. October already; the year had flown. His mobile jangled the current tune he had programmed, 'Waltzing Mathilda', as he drove through town past Central Station and down Paradise Street.

'Where were you?' Yvonne sounded pissed off. 'I've been trying to reach you.'

Of course mobiles did not work underground. 'What's happening?' he asked.

'You wanted an update. That bitch Simona is quiet now. Crying a lot, but not giving any trouble.'

'Good. How about the others?'

'We're sending them on to Dublin tomorrow. What d'you want done with Dracula's Daughter?' Yvonne asked. 'You didn't say.'

He thought of Simona's smooth, shapely young body, her lovely breasts and sensitive mouth, the long black hair that was like silk. She was respectable, well brought up, probably Catholic, had been a virgin until last night. Her big dark eyes, filled with pain and tears, hovered before him. He smiled.

'Teach her to dance,' he said. 'She can work in the club and pleasure individual clients upstairs afterwards. She'll enjoy that.' He loved the thought of Simona's humiliation as she danced naked in front of a bunch of glassy-eyed, yelling drunks. She was terrified of him, already learning fast. He loved her fear, needed to feed off it. He also wanted that beautiful body. It had been a while since he'd fancied a girl. There was something special about Simona, something that attracted him deeply. Maybe it would be different with her. He might keep her for himself after all.

Fifteen minutes later he pulled into the tree-lined drive of a large, early nineteenth-century house. In the silent drawing room with its blue walls and white period ceiling he dropped his keys on the polished Victorian sideboard and poured himself a cognac. He went upstairs and showered. Downstairs again, he poured more cognac and took the glass into his study. He sank into the comfortable leather chair behind the antique cherrywood desk, and clicked on the lamp.

He leaned back and closed his eyes, let tiredness wash over him. He felt drained by Gemma's murder. And the other stuff. He needed to feel safe again, back in control. All this crap had blown up out of nowhere. Life's twists and turns seemed to demand of him an equally twisted sense of humour, a degree of irony that he did not possess. It was incredible and disturbing how a single thought or some simple, trivial act could change someone's life. He felt jittery and out of his depth, felt that he had to continually realign his life as if it were a rocket on course for Mars or Venus. He should have seen this trouble coming, dealt with it before it became a problem. The universe had presented him with another lesson to learn. He glanced at his watch. He still had a few minutes.

He got up, opened the wall safe and took out the ancient leather holdall which he had discovered beneath loose bricks and rubble in the tiny tunnel behind the cellar wall in his parents' house. The holdall was cracked and mildewed with a dull, scratched brass lock which he had had to force. It gave him a thrill to think no other living soul knew about the contents. The great secret of Joseph's labyrinth. A secret he intended to keep entirely to himself.

He sat down again and carefully drew out the bundle of papers with deep crease marks, very gently spread them over the desk. Got the familiar fluttery feeling in his stomach. He smiled and picked up the glass of cognac, took another sip. He felt better now.

I should have studied archaeology, he thought, become a historian or scientist of some kind, instead of wasting my twenties and early thirties drifting the globe. A paleobiologist, maybe. Imagine meeting a woman at a party: 'Hi! I search for the fossils of extinct life forms.' There was a conversation stopper.

He unfolded the map and papers. A sailing bill from 1854 advertising the celebrated clipper ships of the original White Star Line of British and Australian Ex-Royal Mail packets. Thomas H. Ismay bought the White Star Line flag several years later when he founded the company which became notorious for the 'practically' unsinkable ship that ended its maiden voyage at the bottom of the icy North Atlantic. There were White Star Line sailings on the first and twentieth of each month between Liverpool and Melbourne, forwarding passengers to Geelong, Sydney, Adelaide and Launceston. The line had taken off when the Australian goldfields opened in 1851.

He picked up another paper, the cargo manifest of the *Shalimar*. Port of loading, Melbourne. Port of discharge, Liverpool. Sailing date, 20 January. Arrival date, 10 April 1852. Delayed by storms around the Cape of Good Hope. A name was scrawled in faded brown ink: Mr Henry Miles, Gentleman, of Mason Street, Edge Hill. 'Gentleman' was heavily underlined. The *Shalimar*'s cargo consisted mainly of gold, tons and tons of it, fortunes made in the goldfields of Western Australia. Henry Miles had written a letter.

Ballarat, 20 December 1851

Darling Alice,
It is my great joy to write and inform you that our long and tedious separation will shortly be at an end. I have returned to Melbourne and will sail for Liverpool on the

85

*twentieth of next month. Time is pressing and there are
many matters to which I must attend. I pray for a safe
voyage, and the preservation of the fortune which will
ensure our future happiness and well-being. Pray for my
safe return, darling Alice, and kiss little Daisy for me.
Your loving Henry*

Hardly worth writing the letter, as Alice might not have
received it until after her husband's return. Alice's letter to
her sister, three years later:

*Mason Street, Edge Hill
21 May 1854*

*Dearest Helen,
Henry passed away in the early hours of this morning,
with Daisy and me at his bedside. The doctor arrived too
late, but assured me there was nothing he could have
done. I am distraught, as is Daisy.*

*To add to my troubles, Mr Simmons, Henry's lawyer,
has behaved very dishonourably towards me again,
pressing me to reveal the whereabouts of the remainder
of the gold, so that it may be taken into what he terms his
'safekeeping'. If I continue to refuse this and his other
demand that I become his mistress, he threatens to voice
certain suspicions to the police. He tells me, incredibly,
that the cook and Daisy's nurse both fear I was less than
devoted in my care of Henry during his illness, and that
my friendship with Mr John Merritt has aroused malicious gossip in the town. I was not aware that there was
any cause for gossip!*

*I am so frightened of this man, Helen! and have been
for a long time. He oppresses me constantly, and I know
he means to steal Henry's property and leave me desti-
tute – or worse – if I do not accede to his demands. He
has power and many influential friends. Late tonight,
when Daisy and our treacherous servants are asleep, I*

will secretly move the chest and its contents down into the warren of tunnels which run beneath these streets, and conceal the gold there for the present. Heavy work, but with God's help I will succeed.

I am afraid for my life. If I am harmed, please come to my aid. I enclose a map of the late Mr Joseph Williamson's tunnels and passageways, showing the whereabouts of the gold. Henry obtained it from a friend some years ago, but looked on it as nothing more than an amusement.

Simmons will never lay his hands upon Henry's fortune. I grieve for Henry; he was so afraid of leaving Daisy and myself without protection. I am certain that such constant anxiety hastened his tragic demise. Pray for me, Sister, that all will be well.
Your loving Alice

Shame the Mason Street address had no house number, although not surprising. Statutory house numbering only began to spread outside London by the 1840s, and letter boxes did not become common until the 1890s, when the post office aimed to achieve delivery to every address in England. It was unusual for old records to specify house numbers.

Alice's letter to her sister had never been posted. Why not? All he knew was that a Mrs Alice Miles had been hanged at Walton Jail in October 1854 for the murder of her husband, Henry. Arsenic poisoning, one of the favourite methods of the day. Alice's young daughter, Daisy, had been sent to live with her Aunt Helen in the Cheshire countryside. Daisy's nurse and Henry's friend and lawyer, Algernon Simmons, a frequent visitor to the house, spoke at length of child neglect and unsuitable friendships. There was arsenic in the house, but arsenic had many non-criminal uses in Victorian times. He was certain that Simmons had murdered his friend, coveting Henry's fortune from the goldfields. And Henry's wife. He wondered what Alice Miles, distraught heroine, had looked like.

Alice must have hidden the gold. Otherwise the holdall would not have been there. But why had Alice left it in the tunnel? It had to have been her. That, like so many things, would remain a mystery. He studied the original map again. It was complicated, a warren of tunnels and passages on different levels, and some of the writing was too small and cramped to decipher even with a magnifying glass.

The labyrinth had altered since then. Collapsed tunnels and passages, blocked up or walled off, filled with rubble. But he felt sure the small tunnel was still there.

'Alice,' he murmured, leaning back in his chair, 'where's your old man's gold? And what's it like? Nuggets, roughly mined? Minted sovereigns? Melted into bars?'

Henry must have brought back a hell of a lot if he still had some in a chest three years later. Why had he not deposited it in a bank? Maybe he didn't trust banks; some things never changed. Was 'distraught' goody-two-shoes Alice really as innocent and sinned against as she appeared? He smiled. Of course he was a cynical git. The phone rang as he was finishing his cognac.

'You're late, sweetie,' a sharp female voice said. 'Appropriating my girlie privilege.'

'Sorry.' He stood up and stretched. 'I'm on my way. Be with you in ten minutes.'

'You'd better! This isn't my kind of place. I'm getting looks.'

He strode out of the study, whistling. The drink and the look at the papers had done him good. He felt better, was getting his second wind. In the state-of-the-art kitchen which he used only for making tea, coffee, toast and microwaved dinners, he dumped his glass in the sink.

'Time is pressing,' he murmured, quoting Henry, 'and there are many matters to which I must attend.'

'Terrible about that young girl, isn't it?' Frank Graham

strolled to the front sitting room windows and looked out at dark Falkner Square.

'What girl?' Jackie sipped the white wine she so badly needed. She hoped Frank would limit himself to one Scotch, seeing as he had to drive back to Southport soon.

'That murdered prostitute. Gemma something.' Frank turned. 'Body was burned to a crisp,' he said with relish. 'Took dental records to identify her. Still . . .' He paused to gulp the rest of his Scotch. 'If you choose that line of work you can't expect to meet the kind of people you'd want to form lifelong friendships with, can you?'

'I wouldn't call it *choice* when a girl or woman becomes a prostitute because she can't find a better way to earn a living wage,' Jackie said, irritation rising in her. 'Choice implies the existence of at least two or more options. Anyway, don't you think we've got enough to worry about?' She glanced around as the door opened and Rosa walked in. 'Did you get Lisa off to sleep?' she asked, her voice hushed.

'Eventually.' Rosa grimaced and flopped on the sofa, stretching out her legs. 'It's awful, Mum,' she said, wiping away a tear. 'The poor little thing's completely bewildered. She just can't understand why her daddy doesn't come home.'

'Well, I'm not too old to give him the hiding of his life when I get my hands on him!' Frank banged his empty glass down on the coffee table.

'Oh, shut up!' Jackie hissed. 'I've had enough of this macho rubbish about giving him a hiding. Sean hasn't done anything criminal and he hasn't left Carmel and Lisa, so just give it a rest, will you? And don't you dare talk about Sean like this in front of Carmel again, or I'll—'

'You'll what?' Frank sneered. 'Pack your cardigans and bugger off in my Merc when you haven't even got a driving licence?'

'Dad, lower your voice, will you?' Rosa looked at him with dislike. 'You'll wake Carmel.' Thank goodness they hadn't told him about last night. She sat up, reached for the wine bottle and poured herself a glass. 'She's still out for the count,' she said to her mother. 'Think I'd better leave her. I hope she'll sleep through the night. She was exhausted.'

'I'm not surprised. Poor love!' Jackie blinked back tears. 'How she's going to cope with this, I just don't know. We have to give her all the support we can.' She looked meaningfully at Frank, who was at the sideboard helping himself to more Scotch. Rosa sighed and got to her feet as the doorbell rang. She was back a couple of minutes later.

'Two of the neighbours,' she explained, sinking back on to the sofa. 'Nikki and Joyce. They said they wouldn't come in and just to give Carmel their love. They said to let them know how they can help. Natalie phoned, and so did a couple of other people. Natalie came round at lunchtime, but Carmel was asleep.'

Jackie nodded. 'That's nice.' She was wondering whether or not to get herself a refill when the doorbell rang again. They all groaned.

'Getting a bit bloody late for well wishers!' Frank glanced at his watch. 'It's gone ten. We'd better be off,' he said to his wife. 'You've got work in the morning. Dr Cameron'll have your guts for garters if his precious receptionist is late.'

'I'll just see who that is.' Jackie got up and hurried out of the sitting room. Rosa took a gulp of cool, flowery wine and stood up, restless again despite her tiredness. She hoped whoever was calling would not want to come in and talk. There was nothing left to say right now. It was a huge strain having to keep quiet about last night, especially when the terror of it was so fresh in her mind. She had had terrifying flashbacks all day, seeing herself huddled in her room with the gun trained on her, hearing Carmel's screams from downstairs and fearing the worst. Rosa hated being so jumpy and frightened, losing that *it can't happen to me* feeling. Or, more accurately, *well, it can but it won't*.

Fortunately Jackie and Frank didn't seem to have noticed. She hoped the police found those men soon – or Sean – because neither she nor Carmel would feel safe again until that happened.

She looked out of the window and froze. The fear and dread she had carried with her all day escalated to stark terror again. My God! she thought. This is it. We'll know now. She thought of Carmel asleep upstairs, getting the first hours of peace she'd had in days. That fragile peace was about to be brutally shattered. She felt desperately sorry for her sister and her little niece. Frank shoved the cork back into the single malt bottle and turned, saw his daughter's stricken expression.

'What's up?' he asked, alarmed. 'Who's out there?' He joined her at the window, saw the flashing blue light of the police car. 'Oh!' he said stiffly, gripping the glass. 'Oh, bloody hell. Those buggers don't look too happy, do they? This is all we need. Don't wake Carmel,' he said. 'Or the little one. Let them sleep until the morning. Bad news can always wait.'

'Dad . . .' Rosa looked at her father. She suddenly felt like a little girl again, wanted him to protect her. 'I'm so frightened!'

Chapter Nine

'The deputy chief constable said I could go right to the top on the fast track, so I let him put his hand up my skirt. But I don't tolerate crap unless I have to. They've only got to say, "I like your perfume" and I stick my nose in the air and say, "I'm *afraid* I think that's an inappropriate comment." You should see them squirm.' Olivia Crane studied the naked blonde girl gyrating on stage. 'Call me ageing and jealous, but I don't think silicone tits are remotely sexy,' she remarked. 'I heard you lose sensation in the nipples after a tit job, too. Still, as long as the guys are happy, eh?' She glanced irritably around the dark, smoky club and turned back to Anthony. 'Why do you always want to meet in dives like this?'

'It's more compromising, of course, Detective Inspector,' he grinned. 'No, seriously, this place is perfect. Everyone's too busy to take any notice of us. And it's so *not you*.' Anthony looked at Olivia's pale, freckled skin, thick, dark red hair twisted into a French knot, the elegant pinstripe trouser suit – Italian, of course – and her eyes, which in daylight were grey-green. She wore a tiny pair of spectacles perched on the end of her nose. 'How are things with your husband and son?' he asked, knowing how Olivia loved to moan about her personal life.

'Alex started his grand tour gap year in Australia. Arrived in Sydney three weeks ago and he's already running up credit card bills like you wouldn't believe.' Olivia gulped her red wine and grimaced. 'God, that's foul! Should have known better than to order it here.'

'Would you rather try the house white?' Anthony joked.

'I'd rather try something strong and colourless. Whatever you're drinking.' Anthony signalled to the barman and ordered two large vodka and tonics.

'And I no longer have a husband,' Olivia continued. 'The decree absolute finally came through. I wanted to get shut of him, as you know, but it was still an ordeal. End of an era. Etcetera.'

'Yeah.' Anthony took her hand and squeezed it. 'I'm sorry.'

'A swinging single at forty-three!' she sighed. 'How sad is *that*?'

'Less sad than being a swinging single at fifty-three.' Anthony smiled. 'Come on, Olivia! You're beautiful, bright, strong. You'll be fighting them off.'

'Will I? Us bright, beautiful, strong girlies aren't allowed to be lucky in love *and* have a career. People are made up now that my personal life's in shreds,' Olivia said bitterly. 'They can feel sorry for me at last, and don't they bloody love it! Dishing out gleeful lectures about how you can't have it all. What they mean is *they* can't, and they don't bloody well want anyone else to. You wouldn't believe what I had to pay Adrian in the settlement,' she went on. 'Being a teacher, of course, he's always had a crap salary.' She lowered her voice. 'It'd be a hell of a lot cheaper to have him – you know?' She nodded meaningfully as Anthony raised his eyebrows. 'But I couldn't because of Alex. He'd be devastated if anything happened to his father.' She picked up her vodka and tonic and swallowed half of it in one go, crunched on the clear, melting ice cubes. 'And of course it might not be a great career move.'

'True. So life's very expensive for you right now? This should help with the credit card bills.' Anthony slid the buff envelope towards her under the table. 'Keep your ex in bog roll and Belgian beer.'

'Not only him. He moved in with his girlfriend. Thirty-eight, she is, and still a student. Spent years sponging off the taxpayer. Bloody hippie.' Olivia quickly slipped the ten thousand into her bag. 'Thanks.' She finished her drink. 'You'll be careful, won't you?' Her almond-shaped eyes were wary. She licked her crimson lips. 'I could get ten years for what I just told you.'

'About thinking up creative ways to avoid divorce settlements?'

'Ha-bloody-ha! You know what I mean.'

Olivia meant warning Anthony if any of his contacts were at risk of arrest, about details of plans police forces were drawing up to combat the trafficking of women and young girls for the sex trade, about European routes which would soon no longer be safe to use. Which customs and immigration officers would turn a blind eye in exchange for supplements to their monthly pay packets. Etcetera.

Of course Olivia Crane should not have been caught dead in a club like this, drinking with someone to whom she had sold various interesting pieces of strictly confidential information over the past couple of years, and turned a blind eye when necessary. But Olivia was lonely, not getting any younger, pissed off with life in general. Bitter about the sexism she had encountered during her years as a copper, although when it suited her she could be more blokeish than the blokes. Ruthless pragmatism ensured her survival.

Anthony thought back to the frosty November night almost two years ago when he had met her at a Rotary Club dinner. Olivia's marriage was starting its descent, on final approach to the family law solicitors and divorce court. They had a brief affair because he wanted a cop on the payroll, and this was the perfect opportunity. He made sure they stayed friends after it ended. Anthony knew Olivia thought of him as one of her best friends. Not that she had many.

'Discretion is my middle name,' he smiled. 'You know that. Another drink?'

'Sure. Let me get these.' Olivia waved to the barman. 'Hey!' she exclaimed. 'What happened to your hand?'

Anthony lightly touched the plaster. He had dabbed disinfectant on the wound and changed the dressing several times, but the bite mark still hurt. He was trying to push thoughts of hepatitis and HIV out of his mind. 'It's nothing,' he said idly. 'Tiger scratched me, that's all.'

'Tiger? Who's that, one of your silicone-titted bimbos?'

'He's our bloody-minded warehouse cat.'

Olivia laughed. 'So,' she said, picking up her fresh drink, 'weird about your missing mate, isn't it? This Sean Devine person.'

'He's not exactly my mate.' Anthony frowned. 'Business partner, that's all.' He had been waiting for Olivia to get to that. 'I was going to ask if you'd heard anything. I know the—' He stopped. He had nearly referred to Carmel Devine as 'the widow'. Perhaps that was the correct term for her. If only he could be sure. His mind flashed back to the night of Sean's disappearance. His panic, his fury at what had happened.

In the split second he fired at Sean, Sean had dived for his legs and brought him down in a rugby tackle. They had ended up fighting on the office floor, the gun skittering this way and that. Diane dodged around them and ran out, useless bitch. But it wasn't her business and she didn't want to know. Sean lost his mobile, wallet, diary, and house keys in the struggle. He had left his car keys swinging in the ignition because he had only returned to collect Carmel's main birthday present, the small, gold-beribboned package that had lain in his desk drawer for the past two days. On such stunningly trivial events did capricious fate twist and dance.

Anthony was frightened and furious that Sean had over-heard him confess to what most people would describe as murder. Sean was already a bloody great thorn in his side;

trouble had been on the cards for a while. Anthony had spent some time thinking about the best way to dispose of Sean, but now the decision had been literally thrust upon him. He managed to fight Sean off, grab the gun and was struggling to his feet when the phone rang, distracting him for one vital second.

Sean seized his chance and flung the dirty great ficus in his face, the heavy plant in its terracotta pot catching him agonisingly on the bridge of his nose. He staggered back, blinded by soil and tears, blood gushing from his nose. He dropped the gun, too far away for Sean to reach in time. Sean grabbed the briefcase containing the sixty grand instead and threw himself down the stairs, managing to dodge another bullet that should have embedded itself in his brain. Accurate shooting was hard enough without being half-blinded and panicked, your fingers slippery with blood.

'You're fucking dead meat!' Anthony could hear himself screaming. 'Dead meat, Sean! Don't go near the police or your wife and kid will be too.' He had fired again twice and got lucky, wounding Sean seriously. Trouble was, Anthony didn't know how seriously; the bastard had managed to stagger to his car, fall in and drive off before he could finish the job. The rain washed away the trail of blood, which pooled at the spot where Sean had collapsed into the car.

Where the hell had Sean gone? Was he dead, or holed up somewhere? Carmel Devine certainly didn't know anything. Anthony visualised his hand pressing down on her smooth, flat belly, nuzzling her left nipple with the gun. Carmel had almost died of fright. Although he thought she was more terrified for her sister. And her precious Sean, of course. He would stick close in case Sean contacted her. Anthony was certain he would, sooner or later – if he was alive. But hopefully he had done the decent thing and bled to death somewhere quiet. Anthony had covered himself, whatever happened. But he couldn't feel safe and in control again until he knew for certain that Sean Devine was dead. If Sean wasn't dead, he had to find him as soon as possible. Then kill him.

'I know his wife,' he said. 'She's in a right state.'

'No kidding.' Olivia laughed, her eyes sparkling with malice. 'Well, if you think she's got her tits in a tangle now, wait until she finds out we want to question her darling husband about a murder.'

'*Murder?*' The tiredness was creeping back and it was hard for Anthony to act shocked. 'What murder?' he asked, striving for authentic incredulity.

'That scrubber, Gemma Geraghty. Don't tell me you haven't heard?' Olivia looked at him in surprise. 'The local hacks can't believe their luck. Makes a nice change from nightclub stabbings, dodgy councillors and local author signing sessions.'

'Of course I've heard about it, but . . .' Anthony laughed disbelievingly. 'What the hell makes you think Sean Devine's got anything to do with that?' At last they were getting their act together, he thought. If Sean turned up alive and couldn't be killed immediately, he would find himself under arrest for the murder of a prostitute. Who would believe a word he said then? 'Is this a wind-up?'

'No wind-up,' Olivia smiled. 'Of course I shouldn't discuss this with you, you being his partner. You might even be implicated, for all I know.'

'Yeah, right!' Anthony's heart jumped. 'So that's why your minions asked me how I spent the other evening,' he said casually. 'I had dinner with a couple of clients and we went to a club afterwards. Didn't get home until around two a.m. I realise that doesn't exactly give me a watertight alibi – should I need one.' He paused, his fingers sliding up and down the chilled glass. 'You are joking, aren't you?' He tried to conceal his unease. 'Since when do I need to go out raping and murdering scrubbers?' he asked, knowing that Gemma hadn't been raped. Not by him, anyway.

'We don't think she was . . . well, never mind. But no.'

Olivia shook her head and drank more vodka. 'I know that's not your style. I wouldn't want a mutually beneficial relationship with a psycho. The point is, do you think it's Sean Devine's style?'

'No way!' Anthony breathed again. 'There has to be the mother and father of all fuck-ups here! Sean Devine wouldn't murder anyone. I admit he was acting weird these past few weeks, and the other night ... well, I told your little helpers what happened then. But he's a good guy. He's happily married, he ...'

'Aren't they bloody always. If he's so good and happy, why disappear like that?'

'Who knows?' Anthony stared at her. 'You're telling me you think it's because he murdered that girl? What the hell makes you think Sean did it?'

Olivia finished her drink and waved the empty glass at the beleaguered barman. 'He was very careful not to leave any evidence behind, more than most murderers are. But not careful enough. And we think Gemma may have got the better of him.'

'What d'you mean?' Anthony was delighted at his success. Shame he couldn't share it with someone, indulge in a bit of boasting.

'There was a struggle and she managed to get something off him without his noticing. We *think*. A crumpled piece of paper that must have been in one of his pockets, or maybe somewhere in his car. There were a couple of hairs too – black. We were damned lucky, the paper nearly got burned. She must have had it screwed up in her hand, then let go and managed to push it under a brick. We asked the fragrant Mrs Devine for a couple of her husband's hairs, so we could check the DNA with the crime sample. And guess what?' Olivia looked at him triumphantly. 'They match.'

'Jesus! But what's the paper, and how does that link Sean to the ...?'

'It's headed writing paper with your firm's logo. Confirmation of an order for a car, signed by him. We still have to make sure it's his signature, but that's not—'

'How do you know Sean didn't post the order confirmation?' Anthony interrupted. 'Whoever he sent it to could be the murderer.'

'Not when the guy to whom it was addressed was in the Seychelles getting married in front of half his family and a dozen friends! He swears he didn't receive it, and we've no reason not to believe him. Said he told Sean he was going on holiday and there was no hurry. Sean must have had the paper on him. How else could Gemma have got hold of it? And like I told you, the DNA matches. That's the main thing.'

'I'm stunned!' Anthony shook his head sorrowfully. 'I can't believe this. It's just not Sean. Murder . . . a prostitute! He couldn't *do* anything like that.'

'How would you know? You're only his partner.' Olivia touched his arm. 'Of course you think you know someone after you've worked with them for years,' she said softly. 'It comes as a shock to find you don't. I understand how you feel.'

'Hold on a minute – surely you can't always convict somebody purely by DNA?' Anthony argued, wanting to be sure. 'I mean, it's possible for an innocent person's DNA to match a crime sample, isn't it? Unlikely, but possible. And the test results aren't always conclusive. There's a myriad of fuck-ups that can happen.'

'You're so right, handsome! But there's more – icing on the cake. Me and the lads couldn't believe it when that witness came forward.' Olivia sniggered drunkenly. 'In this city you practically have to kidnap your witnesses.'

Anthony lifted his glass and put it down again. No, he thought. There can't be a witness. Olivia's miserable, tired. Pissed. She's got it wrong. Stay calm. Nothing to worry about. He played with his gold cufflinks while music pounded in his ears. The blonde girl hurried off stage to whoops and catcalls, and another immediately took her place.

'Some woman taking a leak.' Olivia added a splash of

tonic to her vodka, the ice cubes clinking as she stirred the drink vigorously. 'Like I'll have to do in a mo.'

Anthony broke out in a cold sweat. He clenched his hands under the table. 'But I heard on the local news that the murder happened in a dockyard,' he said, trying desperately to think straight. 'Women don't take leaks! I mean, not . . .'

'Not in public.' Olivia nodded. 'Our redoubtable heroine had to improvise. I really shouldn't be telling you this,' she laughed. 'But what the hell? It's not like it'd be worth another ten grand stuffed down my gel bra.'

No, Anthony thought. Much more than that. My life! He felt sick with fear.

'She was driving home after singing in some tacky social club,' Olivia explained. 'Swore she'd only had one glass of wine all night because of having to sing and drive, but she'd drunk loads of tonic water and orange juice. Got caught short. So she parks the car, walks along until she finds this pitch-dark dockyard. Tippy-toes in, lifts her dress, pulls her knickers down – and gets the fright of her life!' Olivia rocked with drunken laughter. The laughter turned to coughing and wheezing, and she had to put down her drink and reach for her inhaler. 'God, the smoke in here's getting to me,' she gasped. She stuck the inhaler in her mouth, took two short puffs and shoved it back in her bag. 'That's better. Feathers and ciggy smoke,' she said. 'The bane of my life.'

'Feathers?' Anthony repeated mechanically, still trying to get his head around the shock of the lady witness taking a leak.

'Yeah. Can't go to a hotel or stay over at anyone's place without finding feather pillows and quilts on the bed. Makes me wheeze like hell, gets worse and worse. My face and neck goes all blotchy. Too much exposure to goose-down and my bronchioles, or whatever they're called, would be so seized up I'd asphyxiate. You'd think feather bloody pillows would have died out with Queen Victoria.'

She stood up, grasping her bag. 'Right,' she said, 'I'm off to powder my nose. Back in a sec.'

Anthony watched as Olivia weaved her way through the crowd of glassy-eyed men, attracting stares from the few not mesmerised by the red-haired girl on stage who was performing creative acts with an empty beer bottle. He sat back, his mouth dry and his stomach churning. He wiped his sweating palms on his trousers.

A witness. It was bizarre, unreal. He drained his vodka and signalled to the barman again. The man nodded politely and immediately brought fresh drinks to the table. This can be dealt with, Anthony thought, fighting shock and fear. It's just another challenge, an obstacle that has to be removed. You can handle it. Don't panic. He longed to walk out of the club and drive home so that he could think in peace. But first he needed to know more.

Olivia returned and sat down heavily. 'Ah,' she breathed, spotting her new drink. 'Thank you, kind sir. This'll improve my driving no end.' She clutched her bag with its valuable contents.

'So what were you saying about the singing witness?' Anthony asked, trying not to sound too interested.

'Oh, yeah.' Olivia sniggered again. 'Calls herself an amateur artist as well as a singer,' she said. 'Does oil paintings of Liverpool landmarks. The Liver Buildings at dawn, that sort of crap.'

'Very nice.' Anthony felt like strangling Olivia. Elizabeth Tate, the wife of Joseph Williamson, had been an artist. She had died in 1822, aged fifty-six. It was rumoured that Joseph spent more time burrowing underground after her death, digging deeper and deeper in an attempt to assuage his grief. Anthony did not believe that. The pair had had a stormy marriage, by all accounts. Joseph's labyrinth was his life's work. He would have carried on regardless.

'What makes me sneeze and wheeze, apart from feathers?' Olivia murmured. She tapped her nose. 'Pepper!' she said. 'Paula Pepper. Heard of her?'

Anthony thought. 'The name doesn't ring a bell.'

'That's her stage name. In real life she's Mrs Les Higginbottom, would you believe? She was in shock after what she'd seen. Babbling on – they couldn't shut her up. She said it was dark and she hadn't noticed the murderer's car until the door opened and he pushed the girl out. Said it was a funny sort of car. Distinctive. Sean Devine drives an Audi,' she said, not noticing Anthony flinch. 'Nice, but not all that distinctive. Of course he could have used another motor.' She nudged him. 'Paula gave a good description of our mutual friend.'

Anthony felt lightheaded. 'How could she do that if it was so dark?'

'She got a good look at him when he torched Gemma and the flames flared up. Imagine it,' Olivia breathed. 'Crouched by the wall, knickers round her ankles. That'll give the jury a right laugh. Bet she peed all over her shoes.' She leaned closer. 'Did Sean Devine happen to know anything about . . . you know?' she whispered.

'About our mutually beneficial relationship and my private business interests?' Anthony shook his head. 'No way. Absolutely not.' He took a deep breath. 'Listen, I'm sorry to be a bore, but are you sure about all this? Sean Devine wasn't the type to murder anyone.'

'You reckon?' Olivia looked annoyed. 'Who's detective inspector here?'

'Okay. But he only seemed interested in his wife and kid.' If it hadn't been for the shock of the witness, Anthony would have enjoyed this conversation. 'If you saw his wife, you'd understand why.'

'A looker, is she?'

'Well, a lot would think so.' Anthony shrugged. 'But she's not my type.'

'Oh, right,' Olivia laughed. 'We know your type, don't we? Fragile, helpless little flowers yearning only for *lurve*, too young and stupid to know better. They get a rude awakening when they fall into your arms! I sometimes wonder why you had an affair with me,' she said moodily. 'Business, was it?'

'I won't deny I think we've got the perfect relationship. We also happen to like each other. You're a friend, Olivia.' Anthony's expression was serious. 'You mean a lot to me. You're going through a tough time, and I'm here for you. Don't forget that.' The words made him want to gag. But he had to keep her sweet.

'Go on, say all the right things,' she sighed. 'You're good at that.'

'I mean it.' Anthony hoped she was not getting any crazy ideas about rekindling their affair, now that she was cast adrift on the meat market at her age. He thought of Simona's beautiful face and fresh, firm young body, and experienced a surge of desire. Simona was terrified of him, and that was good. But he also wanted her to like him. Maybe even love him.

'It's tragic, isn't it?' he said, determined to distract Olivia from her yo-yo emotions.

'What is, you handsome devil?'

'Sean. What's happened to him.'

Olivia leaned back and stretched, a ceiling spotlight picking up golden glints in her auburn hair. 'You think he's dead then?'

'Dead?' Anthony echoed, startled. 'No! Why the hell would I think that?'

She leaned forward again and smiled, revealing small white teeth stained with lipstick. Her eyes shone. Anthony jumped as he felt her hand slide up his thigh and press into his crotch. Her strong, flowery perfume floated on the smoke-laden air. 'Darling . . .' She nibbled his left earlobe. 'You keep talking about the guy in the past tense!'

'Carmel, wake up! The police are here.'

Her mind drifted, rising reluctantly through layers of consciousness. She did not want to wake up because something was bad, something was terribly wrong and she could not

103

bear to face it. But she had to. Carmel opened her eyes and registered Rosa's frightened face, one hand shaking her shoulder, the bedroom light hurting her eyes, and outside the windows tree branches waving against a dark sky. Knowledge flooded back and she sat up, cold with fear.

'The police? What do they want?' she whispered. 'Have they found Sean?' She glanced around the bedroom. 'Where's Lisa? How long have I been asleep?'

'Hours. They won't say anything except that they need to speak to you.' Rosa hugged her tightly. 'And Lisa's fine. Fast asleep. Mum and Dad are downstairs. It's ten-past ten.'

'Ten past *ten*?' Carmel flung off the hot, heavy quilt and got to her feet. She looked at herself in the dressing table mirror, pushing back her hair. The police would not call at this time of night to inform her of something else they couldn't do. She steeled herself, and turned to face Rosa. Her hands were shaking. 'Ready.'

'Carmel, are you . . .?'

'No, I'm not all right. But I'll manage. Have to, won't I?' She followed her sister out of the room and downstairs. Don't let Sean be dead! she prayed. Please. I can't lose him. Lisa can't lose her father. But these things happened. Why not to her?

It was the same two officers who had called the day before, the blonde uniformed constable whose patronising sympathy and unauthorised use of her first name Carmel resented, and the young, red-haired man in the dark suit and grey mac. She had forgotten their names and couldn't have cared less. Frank and Jackie sat on one of the sofas, silent and wary. Carmel was surprised to see that her parents were holding hands. She walked to the mantelpiece and looked at the police officers, trying to read their expressions.

'How are you feeling, Carmel?' The woman smiled, her light brown eyes gleaming with curiosity. It was such a stupid question that Carmel did not bother to reply.

'Sorry,' the woman said. 'This must be very difficult for you. It's usually you who asks other people that question, isn't it?'

'Actually, no.' Carmel folded her arms. 'Tell me what's happened.' She felt sick and faint. 'Is there news of Sean?'

It seemed that they couldn't stop staring around the room, at the cream walls and the ceiling with its decorative plasterwork, at the dark green leather sofas, the coffee table, the empty fireplace and the family photographs on the tall mantelpiece. Carmel and Sean's favourite photo was of Lisa, aged two: she wore a red suit and her blue eyes were bright and crinkling with laughter as she clutched a rag doll, soft blonde baby hair curling around her happy, flushed face. Sean had taken the picture one sunny December afternoon, laughingly complained that he couldn't get Lisa to sit still for a minute. The rag doll and a couple of jellybabies did the trick.

'There's something we'd like to show you,' the man said gravely. 'All right if I sit down?' Carmel nodded. He reached into his briefcase and drew out a clear plastic bag sealed with blue tape, leaned forward and handed it to Carmel. 'Do you recognise this item, Mrs Devine?' He took out a pen and notepad.

'Well, it's a half-burned piece of headed notepaper from my husband's company,' Carmel said, bewildered and full of foreboding. 'Confirmation of an order for a car, signed by him.'

He nodded. 'You can confirm that it is your husband's signature?'

'Yes, of course I can. Where did you find this paper? What's going on?'

He didn't answer.

'What's going on?' she repeated. 'Is Sean hurt? Is he—' She couldn't go on. Jackie got up and hugged her daughter.

'Tell us, for goodness sake!' She was on the verge of tears.

'We don't know where your husband is, Mrs Devine.'

The detective looked her in the eye. 'If he's alive or dead now. But we believe he left this paper at a crime scene. A young girl, a prostitute named Gemma Geraghty, was murdered the other night. Shot several times in the head and chest, her body doused with petrol and set alight. Maybe you've heard,' he said. 'It's been on the news and in the papers.'

He paused to let his words sink in. Carmel Devine's reaction told him she had not heard. Unless she was one of the great undiscovered acting talents of the millennium. He dispassionately noted her shocked, terrified, utterly bewildered expression, the intense blue of her eyes contrasting with her ashen skin. The shake of her head and inarticulate cry of horror, of denial, as her lips parted to scream the word '*No!*' over and over.

'Mrs Devine—' He had to raise his voice to make himself heard. 'We have evidence to indicate your husband committed this murder.'

Chapter Ten

'I take it you don't want me to do the second set?'

'You're right there, love! Your agent told me you were a class act. Or did he say he was on Class A drugs?' The tall, skinny, mournful-looking manager of Holy Trinity Social Club resentfully handed over a roll of grimy, creased, ten-pound notes. He wore evening dress, the white shirt none too clean, and his balding dome shone beneath the weak dressing room lightbulb. 'I know people'll laugh at me for having these crazy expectations,' he went on, blowing out camel dung cigar smoke, 'but when I hire an artiste I expect her to be able to remember the words of the bloody song she's supposed to be delivering with the appropriate power, passion and panache.' He paused, waiting for a reaction. None came. 'Is Pepper your real name?' he asked, needling.

'No, love. I got it from that seventies police series with Angie Dickinson.' Paula Pepper, alias Mrs Leslie George Higginbottom, sank on to the cracked, fake leather dressing table stool and looked sadly at her glittery reflection in the greasy mirror. Big hair, tinted her favourite shade of chestnut brown, a diamanté collar around her slim, tanned, wrinkled neck, sequinned blue strapless evening gown, tits pushed up by the built-in, underwired bra. Brown and gold shadow on heavy, tired-looking eyelids, dark blusher and 'face shaper' that now looked like two smudges of dirt.

Glossy red lipstick that strayed over the thickly pencilled lip liner, like a river meandering into little tributaries.

'You're right,' she sighed, despondent and consequently vulnerable. Normally she would have given a cheeky bastard like this a right earful. 'I sang like crap tonight. Muffing the words to "Crystal Chandeliers" was certainly a first.'

'And last, as far as this club's concerned,' the manager said brutally. 'You were rubbish. You should pay me, not the other way round. I've got a reputation to keep up – you've made me look a right dickhead.'

That's enough, Paula thought, summoning her last reserves of dignity. I might have sung like crap, but I don't have to take this from the likes of him. 'You can look a dickhead all by yourself, love,' she remarked. 'Smell like one as well!' She turned, sniffing disgustedly. 'I didn't realise you could still buy Brut. Or that there was anyone out there sad enough to wear it.'

'Don't give up the day job, will you?' he sneered. 'That's if anyone's sad enough to employ a clapped-out, miserable old cow like you.' He went out and slammed the door, leaving a trail of acrid cigar smoke in his wake.

Paula wiped away a tear. If the manager had been nicer and more understanding she might have handed back most of her fee and kept just enough for expenses. Be fair, though, it wasn't his problem. She was a professional, supposed to be able to walk out on stage, give them the chat and put a song across, regardless of how rotten she might feel. She was lucky the audience had only booed, not pelted her with bottles, glasses and filthy ashtrays. Paula sighed again, picked up her bag and rooted in it for her mobile.

'It's me,' she said when Les answered. 'How's your flu, love?'

'I'm at the blowing-out-green-snot-like-an-alien stage,' he replied disconsolately, his voice muffled. Paula listened while he did just that. 'Made meself a cup of tea and added a drop of Jamesons. I'm in bed now, watching telly. How did it go tonight?' Les asked, sniffing vigorously.

'I was a mess.' Paula's eyes filled with tears. 'The manager didn't want to pay me, and I can't blame him. I even forgot the words at one point, just stood there like a bloody idiot. They booed me – it was a nightmare, I thought I was going to die! It's no use, Les,' she whispered. 'I'm a nervous wreck since that terrible night.'

'Well, of course you are!' Les's catarrh-muffled voice was indignant. 'You don't witness a young girl get murdered – and like *that* – then pop home for a good night's kip and forget all about it. I told you, Paula, you need a break. Give yourself time to get over the shock. You're not doing yourself any favours, love, trying to carry on as though nothing's happened.'

Paula sniffed and wiped her eyes. 'I thought that was the best way.'

'Not always it isn't.'

'Anyway,' she said, 'I'm not doing the second act. I'll get me stuff together and come home right now.'

'Good idea. That's more like it. You can have an early night and a nice relaxing day tomorrow doing your painting. You'll soon be your old self again. Let's see, what day is it? Tuesday. I'll cancel that pub date in Birkenhead this coming Friday, think up some excuse.'

Paula smiled. 'You can tell them I caught your flu.'

'No, that's tempting fate. You're bound to catch it then. I'll think of something else.'

Paula's heart lightened. 'Thanks, Les. You always make me feel better, love. I just wish I hadn't gone to the police,' she sighed. 'But I was so shocked, so terrified when I saw what the evil bastard did to that poor girl. I had to tell them what I'd seen. Now I'm wondering what the hell I've gone and let meself in for.'

'For God's sake, love, don't start that again! We've been through all this. You did the right thing. Imagine if people went around ignoring brutal murders committed under their noses? We'd all be in for it then, wouldn't we? Sooner or later. Remember that poem about people who stand by and do sod-all and in the end it's their turn for the chop?'

'True. I just hate the idea of going to court, Les. Frightens the life out of me. And some snotty, claret-swigging barrister's going to make me look a right moron. They always try to discredit witnesses, and in my case they'll think Christmas has come early. Caught short with me knickers down!'

'It's a bit previous to worry about that, love. The police haven't even arrested the murderer yet.'

'Les, that fella who they say murdered her ... he's missing. Suppose he finds out about me?' Paula glanced back at the door and lowered her voice. 'I'm scared.'

'There's nothing to be scared of,' Les said stolidly. 'This isn't some gangland murder where they try to nobble the jury and intimidate witnesses. You'd have to worry then, yeah. But there's no way this fella can get to you. He doesn't know your name or anything about you. Besides, you couldn't even identify that photo the police showed you. You said it wasn't the murderer.'

'No. Looked a bit like him though. Same hair, and the features were similar. They could be brothers or cousins. But it wasn't the same fella. The one in the photo looked human, for starters. Lovely warm eyes. The police say they've got evidence he did it, and they're annoyed with me for throwing a spanner in the works. But I can't help it. He's not the murderer.' She shuddered. 'I'd know *that* face again anywhere.'

'Look, you've done your best, love, and that's all anyone can expect of you. Now stop chuntering on that mobile,' Les ordered, 'and get yourself home presto pronto. I'll stagger downstairs and put the kettle on.'

'All right.' Paula smiled. 'Thanks, darlin'. I'll see you soon.'

'The roads are slippery,' Les warned. 'Weather forecast says there's a storm brewing. Take care driving.'

'I will. Ta-ra, love.'

Paula shoved the mobile back in her bag and gathered up the rest of her stuff. She thought of her warm, cosy, terraced house and comfortable bed. Les waiting for her, sitting at the kitchen table in his old plaid dressing gown. The kettle boiling. How delicious the tea would taste, drunk from one of her mother's old bone china, non-dishwasher-proof Wedgwood cups. Paula did not keep the Wedgwood in a cabinet gathering dust, like her mother had done, scarcely daring to breathe on it. She liked to use and enjoy the china every day. That meant the occasional breakage, of course, especially when Les did the washing up. She smiled. Poor old Mum would have been horrified.

She stuck the roll of notes in her purse. They really were filthy, she thought disgustedly. The manager must have kept them specially to palm off on her.

'Miserable sod,' she muttered. She wrapped herself in the long camel coat that Les said she needed for coming out of pubs and clubs on chilly nights like this one, pulled off her diamanté earrings and slipped them in a pocket. Then she took them out and put them on again. Sod it! Show some front. She fluffed her voluminous hair and took a last glance in the mirror.

'You haven't lost it, babe,' she whispered. 'You can still kick ass.'

Or would be able to once she managed to force these horrible murder scenes out of her head. It was impossible to forget, of course, especially after such a short time. But surely the flashbacks would gradually become less intrusive, less disturbing. She would calm down, stop feeling so frightened, insecure and unhappy. Get back the all-important power, passion and panache.

Paula slung her bag over her shoulder and paused, one hand on the door knob. She thought of the murderer's face lit by the flames of his victim's funeral pyre. What really frightened her was that he had looked so calm and controlled. So *normal*. Perhaps murder was normal to him. He was also a real looker. She couldn't get over that. Why

111

should a man like him bother with prostitutes? Then again, what the hell did she know? He might be a pimp. Or have kinky tastes that his wife or girlfriend didn't share and refused to indulge him in. Well, obviously he did have kinky tastes. And why shouldn't he look calm? He probably believed he could get away with his crime. How thick was it to expect a murderer to look ugly, evil, twisted and furtive?

He's out there, Paula thought. He might do it again. At the same time she dreaded his arrest because she was terrified of giving evidence in court, knowing those calm eyes would be watching her, noting every detail. Maybe her evidence would put him away. Men hardly ever seemed to get heavy sentences for murder, especially if the victim was their wife or girlfriend, or a prostitute. Suppose he was banged up, and ordered some criminal contact on the outside to hurt her? A hit man, maybe? It was possible. Suppose he got out of jail after two or three years and came looking for revenge? She would have forgotten all about him and be getting on with her life, then one day . . .

'Stop it!' Paula said aloud. 'You'll drive yourself mental!' She opened the door and left the dingy dressing room.

No one took any notice of her as she walked through the noisy, crowded bar and pushed through swing doors to the beer- and disinfectant-smelling entrance hall with its black-and-white vinyl floor tiles. Two men came in and walked past, glanced dismissively at her because she wasn't exactly twenty-five any more. Paula resented the way they looked at her, as if they thought she had no right to exist. A lot of men looked at you like that. She shrugged. Sod them. Paula knew she would cheer up as soon as she got home to Les.

Les was her rock. They were happy together, had their health, good friends, money in the bank. She couldn't ask for more. This ghastly murder she had been unlucky enough to witness was the only cloud on her horizon. She could not allow that cloud to billow and boil up until it blotted out the clear blue sky. No way. And she wouldn't have counselling, like that police officer had suggested. They meant well, of course, but Paula didn't think talking about the murder was such a good idea. She had the feeling it would entrench things in her mind and consequently make the trauma worse. It would be harrowing enough giving evidence in court when the time came.

Paula paused at the club entrance and pulled out the keys to the BMW before braving the cold, dark car park. She always kept her keys handy. She hated those silly films where the dippy heroine only started to mess about looking for her keys when she reached her car or front door, giving plenty of time for the rapist, mugger or murderer to strike. It made her squirm with irritation. Life wasn't like that. Most women had more sense, especially nowadays.

The club's car park was crowded, and she had been obliged to park in a corner beneath overhanging trees, where light from the streetlamps barely penetrated. Branches dipped low, brushing the car roof, and Paula tutted as she noticed a pale splash of seagull or pigeon crap on the bonnet. That was a job for Les tomorrow; he always joked about how ladies should not be required to remove bird crap from cars. She started and glanced around, thinking she had heard footsteps or a click. The between-the-shoulder-blades feeling hit her with full force. But there was nobody about, not even some drunk peeing against a wall or tree trunk.

'Get a grip,' she whispered. 'You're frightened of your own shadow, woman!'

Shivering and spooked, she unlocked the car door and tossed her bag on the passenger seat. Got in and quickly locked the doors. She took a long, shuddering breath and stuck the key in the ignition. Only when Paula glanced in the rearview mirror did she notice the man's eyes, calm and controlled, silently regarding her.

She froze, paralysed with shock. She had to be imagining this, didn't she? It couldn't be real. Trauma and stress played terrible tricks on your brain. This was stupid. Okay, she'd had a shock. But it wouldn't do to let it get to her like this. She had a life to live. She would start the engine, drive home to Les and her cup of tea. Her warm, soft bed.

Paula blinked and stared in the mirror, waiting for the murderer's image to dissolve. It didn't. He smiled at her. Warm, friendly. It was impossible to believe he meant her any harm. Then Paula remembered the thud of the gunshots as they smacked into the poor, helpless young girl. Saw his face in the flames that burned her body. Watching. Calm.

'*No!*'

Something cold slipped around her neck and tightened instantly, choking the terrified scream that rose in her throat. The diamanté collar was ripped off. Paula kicked out and struggled frantically, her mouth wide open as she tried desperately to catch a breath. She put up her hands and scrabbled helplessly at the strangling leather strap. She arched her back, her body writhing.

'I watched your act.' His voice was soft against her ear, his warm breath caressing. He smelled of mints. 'You weren't very good tonight. We both know you've got other things on your mind.' He twisted the strap tighter and wrenched it mercilessly. 'Don't we, Paula?'

If she could just take a breath! Gain a few seconds, fight him off. The car rocked with her desperate, panicked struggles. Why didn't somebody come to her rescue? Paula's right knee banged against the dashboard and her glittery dress rode up over her thighs. The earrings fell off.

'Good legs, Paula,' he whispered. 'Legs are always the last to go, aren't they?'

It felt as though her eyeballs would pop out of her head. She choked and gagged, frantically twisting her body from side to side, her legs flailing. Her left shoe came off. She felt warm urine stream down, soaking her knickers and dress, the seat beneath. Paula had not wet herself since she was five years old. It had happened at school one sunny autumn morning in assembly during her first term. She had cried with shame and humiliation, although the teachers had been kind.

Paula heard a strange noise, a terrifying wheeze or gurgle, almost a whistle. It was like something out of a horror film. She realised she was making that noise.

She was fighting so hard, trying to get that breath. But it wouldn't come. It was no use. He was too strong. Les, she thought. I love you. Help me, somebody help me! Her heart pounded in her chest and she couldn't see. Everything was black, blacker than the darkness.

This is it, Paula thought, just before she passed out. Death. Here, like this.

He got me.

Chapter Eleven

'Carmel, wait!' The little reporter girl with the blonde bob and virulent red lipstick shoved forward, almost forcing her way into the hall. She wore black jeans, high-heeled black boots and a short, purple leather coat. 'Don't slam the door on me.'

'I can't, can I?' Carmel's expression was grim. 'Your foot's stuck in the way.' She turned, shielding her face from flashbulbs and freezing rain. 'Get out of here and leave me alone,' she cried. 'I've got nothing to say. Except that I want privacy for myself and my daughter.' Fat chance. This was a feeding frenzy and she was bait.

'Listen,' the reporter argued, 'we're going to do the piece anyway. You should grab this chance to give your side of the story. What was your marriage like, Carmel? Will your work as a counsellor help you cope with your missing husband being wanted for the murder of a prostitute?'

'My husband hasn't murdered anyone! And I'm not a counsellor – I'm a qualified psychologist who specialises in rational emotive behaviour therapy. Now, go away. Please!' Carmel tried and failed to shut the front door.

'Did your husband murder Paula Pepper because she identified him as Gemma Geraghty's murderer?'

Carmel froze. 'I told you, he hasn't murdered anyone. And that woman didn't identify my husband as the

116

murderer. Get your facts straight. Whoever she described, it wasn't him.'

'The police believe Sean's guilty, though. Carmel, where do you think he's hiding?'

'He's not – I don't know where he is. Leave me alone!'

'How's your little girl coping? What have you told her?'

'Go *away*!' Desperate, Carmel kicked at the girl's foot and felt savage satisfaction as the reporter cried out and jumped back, her face creased with pain. Let her sue for assault if she wanted. She slammed the front door, locked it and put the chain on. The bell immediately rang several times. 'Fuck off!' she whispered. Anxiety coursed through her, tightening her chest and constricting breathing. She walked to the foot of the stairs, paused and looked up. She was trembling all over.

'Lisa?' she called, trying to keep her voice steady. 'Breakfast.'

She hurried down the hall and into the kitchen, dashed to the cooker and turned the gas lower just in time to stop the two poaching eggs frothing everywhere. She plucked two slices of charcoal from the toaster; the bloody thing either charred the bread or barely coloured it. Carmel dropped the pieces in the bin and swore again as the phone rang. It might be another reporter. Or someone she actually wanted to speak to. She lifted the receiver, ready to slam it down again if necessary.

'Carmel? Good morning. It's Anthony.'

'Oh, hi!' She closed her eyes in relief. 'I'm sorry I couldn't talk to you the last couple of days. Rosa told me you phoned a few times, but I was so . . .'

'It's all right, don't worry.' His voice was gentle. 'I understand. It's bad enough that Sean's disappeared, but for the police to say he's wanted for murder now . . . it's the most bizarre thing I ever heard. They've really screwed up on this one.' He paused. 'How are you feeling after the other night? How's your head?'

'Oh, still aching. But it's not too bad. And I'm exhausted.'

'Of course you are. Have you heard anything from the police about those men who burst in and assaulted you and Rosa?'

'No,' she sighed. 'I don't think they'll find out who did it, even if they bother to try. All they care about is putting Sean in the frame for a murder he didn't commit. And—' Carmel hesitated, biting her lip. 'There's something else.'

'What?' Anthony prompted. 'Tell me.'

'I think the house is being watched.'

Anthony closed his eyes and cursed silently. Those stupid bastards! He'd warned them to make sure they weren't spotted. He was surprised, nevertheless, that Carmel Devine had noticed them, the state she was in. She wasn't falling apart quite as dramatically as he would have liked.

'Are you sure about that?' he asked quietly.

'Well, not entirely. I was standing at the bedroom window around three this morning – couldn't sleep, of course – and I saw two men in a BMW squeezed into a space across the road by the park gates. I got suspicious.'

'I can understand that,' Anthony remarked. 'And maybe they were up to no good. But it wasn't necessarily anything to do with you.'

'Except that they drove off at speed the minute they noticed me. So fast I couldn't even get the number. The car headlights were off.'

Anthony breathed a silent sigh of relief. 'D'you think they were the same men who—'

'I don't know. I didn't see them, remember? But they must be connected with whoever's looking for Sean. That's why I think ... hope ... he's alive.' Her voice shook.

'Did you tell the police?'

'Yes. They weren't interested. They think I'm paranoid. Or a liar. Trying to distract their attention from Sean, giving them false leads. Whatever.'

'That's a shame.' Anthony decided it was time to change the subject. 'I hope you're not taking any notice of all that bullshit in the papers?'

'You mean about Carmel the New Age, crystal-crazy counsellor and her dodgy businessman husband with the penchant for murdering prostitutes? And of course they don't neglect to mention that I'm *blonde* – which just about says it all.'

'I know it's easy for me to dish out advice, but you've got to try and ignore it.'

'Yes, but ... Anthony, what they write is stories.' Carmel's voice rose an octave. 'Pure invention. They quote me on things I didn't even say. I never used to sympathise with people who complained that lies were written about them,' she went on. 'They'd say, "I was misquoted" or, "I never said that", and I'd think yeah, right. But now I understand exactly how it works.'

'It stinks. So,' Anthony said, feeling pleased, 'clearly things aren't too good with you right now.'

'Terrible,' Carmel whispered, her eyes wet. 'Basically.'

'I'm sorry.' He cleared his throat. 'I'm also sorry to bother you this early,' he said, sounding awkward, 'but apart from wanting to know how you are, I wondered if we could possibly meet sometime today? There's a few things we need to discuss.'

'Sure,' Carmel said. 'It'd be good to see you.' She paused. 'What things?' She glanced around as Lisa walked into the kitchen and dumped her canvas rucksack on a chair. 'Listen, I'm sorry, but I have to go now,' she said. 'I'm working this morning then meeting a friend for lunch. I'm free for the rest of the day after that. Is it okay if I come to the warehouse around two?'

'That's fine,' he said. 'See you then.'

Carmel hung up and turned to her daughter. 'Lisa, there's no way you can go to school with your hair like that.'

'You look nice, Mummy.' Lisa slouched in her chair and

picked up her glass of raspberry-and-orange juice. She wore her dark blue school uniform with the yellow stripe, and her blonde hair hung loose, sticky with the glittery gel of tiny gold and silver stars. Lisa usually reserved the gel for wilder moments, but Carmel had no need to ask what had got into her lately. 'I like your black trouser suit. And that perfume. Are you going back to work today?'

'Just for this morning.' Carmel took a slotted spoon and lifted the poached eggs out of the pan. 'Did you hear what I said?' She gave her daughter a warning look. 'The hair has to go. This is Liverpool, not Beverly Hills. You've got school, not a party.'

'I like my hair this way,' Lisa pouted. 'It's cool.'

'Not for school. Hey, that rhymes.' Carmel pressed the 'cancel' button on the toaster and the bread popped up, perfectly browned. She spread butter on it. 'Eat your breakfast then I'll comb out that muck and tie it back. Have to be a ponytail today, there's no time for a plait.'

She served Lisa her breakfast, reached for her green-and-gold coffee mug and sipped, savouring the dark, sweet liquid. Coffee had become the fuel that kept her going. The other fuel was hope. Hope that somehow this nightmare would resolve, Sean would come back safe and they would live happily ever after. But that only happened to characters in Lisa's bedtime stories. Carmel banged the mug down on the draining board, suddenly feeling as though she might choke on the coffee.

Sean wanted for murder – murder of a prostitute! And now this nightclub singer, the only witness to that murder, was dead. The description Paula Pepper had given the police sounded very like Sean. But Paula Pepper had not identified Sean from his photograph. Carmel turned away and stared out at the rainwashed back yard, her hands clenched. Tears filled her eyes and she started to tremble again.

'Are you all right, Mummy?' she heard Lisa ask. She took a deep breath, swallowed hard and turned, forcing herself to smile.

'I'm fine, darling. Honestly.' She looked at Lisa's plate. 'Eat your breakfast.'

Lisa had hardly mentioned her father these past few days. Carmel watched her poke at the eggs with her fork, a sulky expression on her face. It was as if mother and daughter were protecting one another, each trying to shield the other from yet more hurt and fear. Now a barrier had risen between them. Carmel could not tell Lisa her feelings, any more than Lisa dared reveal hers. It was heartbreaking. What can I do, Carmel wondered again? Sean didn't commit those murders, he can't have. But who's after him? Why? Where is he? Where do I start? The unanswerable questions whirled around her brain until she felt she would go crazy.

'I don't want this puke,' Lisa protested, shoving her plate away. She got up, went into the pantry, and came back clutching the tartan tin of all-butter shortbread.

'It isn't puke.' Carmel sighed. 'It's scary the way you sometimes seem to hardly eat anything, and then when you do it's only stuff like biscuits, crisps and cake,' she remarked. 'You make me feel like an unfit mother. Your eating habits used to drive me mad when you were a toddler too.'

She remembered her anguish at the screams and tears when her daughter had stubbornly rejected one meal after another, food flying everywhere except into her mouth. Sean had tried to comfort her, saying Lisa would eat when she felt like it and that young children didn't deliberately starve themselves.

'You're fit, Mummy, not unfit.' Lisa snapped off a triangular-shaped wedge of shortbread and popped it into her mouth, eating with a satisfaction she would never get from salad, fresh fruit or vegetables, not even her favourite peas.

'Here's your lunch,' Carmel held up the Pokémon lunchbox. 'Cheese sandwiches, a *red* apple, and a curly-wurly. Don't eat just the curly-wurly.' She pushed the box into Lisa's rucksack and gasped as she drew out a silver-framed photograph. 'Oh, Lisa! I've been looking for this. I didn't know you had it.'

Carmel had taken the photograph of Lisa and Sean in July, on a day out to the Lake District. They sat on a moss-covered rock, Sean laughing as he cuddled Lisa in his arms. The sun shone and the wind whipped their hair. Lisa had her rucksack on her knee, heavy with the stones and pebbles she loved to collect. She looked happy, safe, secure in her father's arms. Secure in his love. What did Sean's little girl have to feel secure about now?

'You can't take this to school,' Carmel said. 'It might get broken. Or lost.'

'No! It won't, Mummy.' Lisa's lower lip stuck out in the familiar gesture that spelled displeasure and imminent rebellion. 'I'll look after it, I promise. I want it with me, please, please!'

'Oh, all right.' If the photograph did get lost there would be more tears and trauma, but she did not have the heart to deny Lisa. 'Just make sure you don't . . .'

They jumped in fright at a sudden pounding on the front door. The bell rang three times, loud and urgent. Lisa stared up at her, blue eyes wide with shock.

'Carmel Devine!' a man's voice shouted. 'Open up. Police!'

'What do they want, Mummy?' Lisa ran to Carmel and flung her arms around her mother's legs, clinging for dear life. 'Have they found Daddy? He didn't really kill that Gemma woman, did he?' Her confident, little girl's voice shrank to a frightened, baby-like whisper.

'No! Of course he didn't.' Carmel hated the fact that she could not protect Lisa from rubbish in newspapers that other children at school repeated to her, faithfully regurgitating their parents ill-informed opinions and speculation. 'Daddy wouldn't hurt anyone. We both know that, don't we?'

'Yes.' Lisa pressed closer. 'Mummy, I'm scared!' She had tears in her eyes.

'Open up!' the man shouted again. 'Police!'

If she didn't answer the door they would probably break it down. 'It's all right, babe.' Carmel picked up Lisa and hugged her. 'Don't be scared.' She was trembling as she walked down the hall.

'I want Daddy,' Lisa cried, arms tight around her neck.

'So do I, darling,' Carmel whispered. 'So do I.'

She unlocked and unchained the door and opened it a fraction. A group of plain-clothed police officers burst in and shoved her aside, making Lisa scream in terror. The tall, young, red-haired detective thrust a piece of paper in her face.

'I'm DS Davie. Your husband, Sean Devine, is wanted for questioning in connection with two murders,' he said, his voice loud and threatening. 'We have a warrant to search these premises.'

'How many more times do I have to tell you my husband is innocent?' I sound like some convict's wife, Carmel thought. Yeah, right, of course he's innocent. Aren't they all? She hugged Lisa tightly, smoothing her daughter's sticky hair with one hand. The child's face was hidden in her neck and she could feel her small body shaking.

'Do you have to do this in front of my daughter?' she asked, struggling to keep calm. 'Makes your day, does it, frightening children? She's five years old.'

The officer stared at her for a second, his pale brown eyes angry and embarrassed. But he was not going to be put off. The men were pouring into every room, shouting at one another to search here, there, look for this or that. Carmel gasped as something crashed to the floor in the kitchen. A uniformed woman constable walked into the hall and took her arm.

'Let's go in here, shall we, love?' She pointed to the sitting room.

'You can't do this,' Carmel cried. 'This is our house. It's private. You've no right.'

'We've got every right. Now let's go in here and sit down. Nice and calm, eh?'

'Don't talk to me like that!' Carmel tried to shake off the female officer's grasp. She didn't want to break down in front of them. She had to be strong for Lisa. But the tears were welling up, spilling over, and she was trembling with shock and fright. DS Davie strode down the hall then stopped and turned abruptly.

'Are there any firearms on the premises?' he barked.

'What a *fucking* morning!' Olivia Crane slammed her office door and leaned against it, breathing hard. 'That's the last time anyone sends me to liaise with those woolly-backs,' she muttered, dumping the cup of steaming coffee on her desk. 'Especially when I'm supposed to be working on a murder case. And the weather! I was knee-deep in mud and sheep crap.' She slipped off her mac and pulled a white paper bag from one of the pockets, opened her desk drawer and took out the two-kilogramme box of chocolates she had brought back from a weekend in Antwerp. 'Find anything at Sean Devine's house?' she asked Neil Davie, who had followed her in. She untied the green-and-gold ribbon on the chocolate box.

'Nope. No murder weapon, nothing to connect Devine with Paula Pepper. No sign of Gemma's missing handbag or Paula's earring either. Place was clean. We took away some papers and stuff. The computer and floppy discs. Can't think how Sean Devine found out about Paula,' Neil said, frowning. 'It's bugging the hell out of me.'

'Yeah.' Olivia glanced away. It was bugging the hell out of her too. Big time. She had woken that morning with another hangover, horrified to think she had passed on confidential information which might have resulted in the woman's murder. She didn't know that for sure, of course, shouldn't allow herself to panic. But it was one hell of a coincidence that the murder had happened just twenty-four hours after she had shot her mouth off to Anthony Maskey.

Anthony might know more than he let on, might even be in contact with Sean Devine, for all she knew. He could have tipped him off about the witness. But why would Anthony do that? It didn't make sense. Well, of course it didn't. Nothing made sense when you didn't know the facts.

Olivia was worried sick. Paula Pepper's murder was gruesome, but she had witnessed enough gruesome sights in her time. If she was incredibly unlucky and someone found out she had passed on this information, she was finished. Goodbye career and hello prison. She would go down for years.

'What's this?' Neil Davie peered into the paper bag and looked at the yellow chocolate box with its silky ribbon. He grinned. 'Thought you were trying to eat sensibly so that your immune system doesn't get compromised by the traumatic life event of divorce?'

'I never said that. You don't half talk some bollocks, Neil.'

He gave her one of his long, meaningful – or meaningless – looks. 'Well, maybe *I* meant I think you should eat sensibly.'

'Stuff it.' Olivia took out a mirror and fluffed her hair. 'I'm Gemini and Mercury my ruler is retrograde and this rain never bloody lets up and I've spent the morning with woolly-backs. Or *rural dwellers*, to be politically correct. So I need chocolate doughnuts and Belgian bonbons.'

Neil laughed. 'Most people go to Belgium for booze and fags. You go to buy chocolate.'

'And why not? Like most things, it's a damn sight better and cheaper than the crap you get in this bloody country.'

Neil moved to the window and stared out. 'Maybe all this rain is the end of the world,' he said dreamily. 'It's going to keep on raining until the flood waters rise to engulf all birds, beasts and humans. And this time there won't be a Noah's Ark.'

'Bugger off and get a life.' Olivia tore a fluffy, sticky doughnut in half and bit into it hungrily. 'Mmm,' she said, 'that's hitting the spot already. Now, if you don't mind,' she said pointedly, 'I've got a very private call to make.'

'Have fun.' Neil went out and shut the door. Olivia leaned back in her chair, opened the bottom drawer of her desk and took out a bottle of Smirnoff Blue. She had to try to reach Anthony again, but what she really wanted was to get rid of Neil so she could have a quick slurp. She poured a generous tot of vodka into the hot coffee, sipped it and sighed. Popped a praline into her mouth and savoured the smooth rich taste. The chocolate melted on her tongue.

Vodka, choccie doughnuts and bonbons, what a lunch! Alex, with his carefully balanced meals of pasta, fish and salad, would be horrified. She heard his voice: 'You've got to look after yourself, Mum. Eat properly. Cut down on the booze.'

Olivia sipped the hot, vodka-laced coffee and drummed her fingers on the table. Alex had left Australia and was backpacking around Thailand now, had phoned her in the small hours from some island, the name of which sounded like the eff-word. Suppose he was robbed or had an accident, hung out with morons who got him into trouble? Young males were more at risk from violent crime than females, contrary to what most people believed. There were so many things that could go horribly wrong, if you thought about it. Olivia took another gulp of coffee. So better not think about it. She picked up her mobile and put it down. Ran her fingers through her auburn mane, took off her specs and closed her eyes for a few seconds.

The question repeated itself in her head: how could Sean Devine have got to Paula Pepper? There was no one else who would want to murder the bloody woman. Only herself and several other officers had known about Paula before her death – apart from Anthony. Of course it could be just terrible coincidence, some stray nut job out for his sick buzz. Olivia found that hard to credit though.

A sudden sickening thought struck. Could Anthony Maskey have murdered the woman? No, that was crazy!

And impossible – if Anthony had murdered her, he must have murdered Gemma Geraghty too. And he couldn't have, because they had evidence to indicate Sean Devine had done that, despite Paula's irritating refusal to identify him as the murderer. Olivia breathed again. Anthony was no angel, and that was putting it mildly, but he would never do something like this. It wasn't his style and didn't make sense. Just to imagine it gave her a burning hot flush of pure horror. If Anthony was guilty, it meant she had got herself hooked up with a psycho whom she couldn't shop because he had her exactly where he wanted her. And she wasn't that bloody stupid, was she? No way!

Olivia took another swig of vodka-coffee. There was a piece of the jigsaw missing, that was all. It would turn up, as it nearly always did. She just had to be patient. She swore as someone knocked at the door. She needed privacy, time and space to get her head round all this.

Neil again. 'Les Higginbottom's here, Boss. Jacko's out for the afternoon, so that leaves you next in line. Reckons he's remembered something that could be vital to solving his wife's murder.'

'You don't say. Neil, the last thing I need is some bloody Sherlock Holmes on the case.' Olivia scrunched the paper bag and lobbed it at the waste bin. It missed. 'Tell Mr Higginbottom to go home and grieve and keep out of my big hair. I've got more important things to do.' Like talk to Anthony. Surely he hadn't told anyone about their intimate conversation of the other night? He would be angry when she asked him. But she had to know.

'But Boss, suppose it's important?' Neil lingered, nervously fingering his horrible red-and-blue striped tie. 'You never know. If it is, and you don't pick up on it, you could end up in the shit.'

Olivia flinched and stared at him. She had to admit she was less than careful at times. And this was one time when she needed to be ultra-careful. She looked down at her smooth, elegant hands, the long, crimson nails.

'Okay.' She reached for her drink and gulped the rest of it. 'Show the old git in then.' She felt a bit better; the vodka was working its restorative magic.

'Good afternoon, Mr Higginbottom.' Olivia stood up and held out her hand as the short, grey-haired, bespectacled man walked into the office. He wore a black suit and tie, and over that a padded grey anorak with a white stripe down the sleeves. He looked completely sad and inoffensive. Olivia was bored rigid already. But charm and sympathy were desirable in the circumstances. She didn't want this old bastard lodging a complaint about police insensitivity.

'I'm Inspector Olivia Crane, how do you do? I'm terribly sorry about your wife,' she said, gazing into his reddened eyes behind the thick glasses and holding on to his rough, cold hand. 'Please allow me to offer you my condolences. I assure you, we're doing everything possible to find the man who . . .'

'Murdered my lovely Paula!' Les Higginbottom finished, his eyes wet. 'Thanks, love,' he said gruffly. His voice was nasal and full of cold. 'You sound like you really mean that.' His moon face was pale, and he looked crushed, shrunken with grief.

'Please sit down, won't you?' Olivia was slightly taken aback. Neil pulled up a chair for him. 'Can I offer you some tea or coffee?' she inquired. 'A glass of water?'

'No, ta. I've drunk enough tea to sink a battleship. Me friends and neighbours, you know. They're being very good.'

'I'm so glad to hear that.' Olivia sat down and clasped her hands. 'I believe you wanted to speak to the officer in charge of the investigation into your wife's murder,' she began, 'but unfortunately he's not available this afternoon. So, if you could just tell me what this is about?' Make it quick, she thought. I'm not in the mood for rambling monologues about how gutted you are.

'This is my fault,' Les Higginbottom said, his voice

breaking. 'Paula was a lovely woman, she was so precious to me. I don't know what I'm going to do without her. This murder – it's all my bloody stupid fault.'

Olivia's eyebrows shot up, and she glanced sharply at Neil. 'What exactly do you mean, Mr Higginbottom?' Don't tell me he did it, she thought. It won't be a piece missing then, it'll be the whole bloody jigsaw.

'I went everywhere with Paula, I drove her to all her engagements.' Les took off his glasses, pulled out a big white handkerchief and wiped his eyes. 'But that night I stayed in because I had flu. I've been blaming meself ever since. If I'd gone with her she'd still be alive. It's all my fault.'

Neil patted him on the shoulder. 'Mr Higginbottom, you're not to blame.'

'I should have protected her. She was in a right state after witnessing that murder.' Les blew his nose and raised his tearstained face. 'She was terrified, you know.' He looked at them both. 'Thought the murderer might go after her. I told her she had nothing to worry about, and I believed that. I can't think how the bastard found out her name and where she lived and that she was a singer. But he did.'

Olivia was silent. She watched as Les took a white envelope from his anorak pocket and laid it gently on the desk. 'I was too upset before,' he said. 'The shock, you know. But now I've remembered this. And—'

'What is it?' Olivia picked up the envelope. It contained a tiny cassette tape.

'Our answering machine tape,' Les replied. 'There was a funny hang-up call the night before Paula—' He stopped. 'I mean strange. Not funny, ha-ha.'

'I see.' Olivia held the tape out to Neil. 'Neil, can you arrange . . .?'

'Sure.' He went out, leaving the door open. A cold draught whirled in.

Olivia stood up and stretched, stared out of the window.

She felt nervous, terribly restless. And frightened. The rain was still coming down hard, and she really fancied another shot of Smirnoff Blue. Neil came back and stuck the tiny cassette tape in a machine, rewound it and switched it on.

'He didn't say anything,' Les explained. 'Must have just listened to the message and hung up. I didn't think anything of it at the time, but it seems odd when I look back. There's some sort of background noise on it.'

'Okay.' Olivia nodded, trying to conceal her impatience. 'Let's have a listen.'

Neil pressed the play button and the tape whirred. Someone named Grace, asking Les and Paula round for a meal one evening. Mexican Chicken, one of her specials. Of course Grace wasn't to know that Paula would be stiffed out on a mortuary slab by the date she suggested. A jolly soul named Harry wanted to know if Les fancied a pint and a game of snooker. The tape whirred and squeaked as Neil pressed fast forward.

'Stop!' Les said urgently. 'Here!'

'This is Les Higginbottom and Paula Pepper. Les is Paula's agent, so if you're interested in booking Paula for a singing engagement, please leave a message after the beep.' Silence, as if someone was listening. The 'funny noises' emerging from the background roar. Then hang-up. Beep-beep-beep.

'What's that noise?' Neil looked puzzled. 'A car horn? Don't know what the other is. Sounds like one of those tapes of so-called ghost noises,' he said irritably.

'Don't be daft, lad!' Les looked at him indignantly. 'That's a foghorn by the river. And a cat yowling.'

'How many people have cats?' Bored, Neil glanced at Olivia and mouthed 'crap!' behind Les's back. Olivia grasped a pencil and looked down at her notepad to hide the blush that burned her face and neck. She was sweating.

'When Paula got in her car and drove off to the club,' Les continued, 'this other car followed. I was at the sitting room window. I didn't think anything of it at the time.'

'What kind of car?' Neil asked.

'Dunno, didn't really see. Something flash. The driver was a fella.' Les wiped his eyes. 'Dark hair, dark overcoat. Smart. Well built, from what I could see. Good looking. Mid-thirties, I'd say. Now I wonder if he was following Paula? If he was the—' Les choked on the words. 'I could have stopped him!' he burst out. 'When I get me hands on that bastard, I'll kill him!' He staggered to his feet, shaking his fist. 'I'll show him what it feels like to have the life throttled out of you!'

'Come on, Mr Higginbottom.' Neil took his arm and gently steered him out of the small office. 'Let's get you a cup of tea.'

'I don't want any more bloody tea! I want justice for my Paula!'

The vodka-coffee, pralines and choccie doughnuts were burning a hole in Olivia's stomach lining. She was getting too old to tolerate that kind of diet. Blood rushed to her face again and drained away. She began to shiver, despite the burning radiator behind her under the window. Terror gripped her. She stretched out a shaking hand and pressed the play button one more time.

A foghorn. The river. Anthony's office was in an old warehouse by the river. And the faint mewing or yowling was indeed a cat: Tiger, the bad-tempered warehouse moggy who had lashed out and given Anthony that nasty scratch on his hand. A smart, good-looking, dark-haired man in his mid-thirties, driving a flash car.

More coincidence.

Chapter Twelve

'What were the police looking for?'

Anthony was glad to hear they had searched Sean and Carmel's house. Even if Sean was alive and reappeared soon, who would believe a murderous psycho with a para-noid wife capable of telling any lie that she imagined might help him? But Anthony couldn't be really happy until he knew Sean was dead.

'The murdered prostitute's handbag is missing, accord-ing to her mother and the newspapers. So naturally they assumed Sean had grabbed it as a grisly souvenir of his alleged dark deed.' Carmel put down her coffee cup with a clatter and stared out of the Tate Gallery café window, the waters of the Albert Dock reflected in her blue eyes. 'They were also searching for firearms. Every respectable murderer has his own illegal gun collection, doesn't he? Complete with baby names for each weapon!' Her voice was low and furious. She tossed back her blonde hair and studied her long, manicured fingernails. 'Thanks for coming here.' She looked at him gratefully. 'I just couldn't stay in the warehouse, seeing Sean's office and his stuff lying around. It was as if he'd nipped out and would be back any second. I wish!' she muttered. Her eyes filled with tears.

It was good to see Anthony again and his presence comforted her, although his slight resemblance to Sean made her heart ache more. He even wore similar clothes to Sean, a dark suit and long black overcoat. The only difference was that Anthony liked ties. Today's was plain silk, Venetian gold.

'Yeah.' Anthony nodded sombrely. 'It feels really weird without Sean there. I miss him like hell.'

He was silent for a minute, letting the chatter, clatter and savoury food odours of the busy café wash over him. He especially enjoyed the smell of fresh ground coffee. 'Did they take anything?' he asked. Anything that might provide a useful hint as to Sean Devine's whereabouts; he could check it out himself or get Olivia Crane to do it. Sean seemed to have disappeared off the face of the planet.

'They took our computer, the floppies, lots of papers belonging to Sean and me. Personal as well as business.' Carmel wiped her eyes with a tissue. 'I'm sure they'll have a great laugh reading my diary.'

'I didn't know you kept a diary,' Anthony said, surprised. He wondered what she had written about him. She must have mentioned him here and there.

'I started it when I was fifteen. I don't write it every day, just a couple of times a month.' Carmel screwed up the damp tissue and dropped it on her saucer. 'I never expected that some copper would be grubbing through my private, intimate thoughts, probably as we speak.' She glanced out at the dock waters again. 'Still, if that's what floats their boats, let them get on with it. They're obviously sadder than I'll ever be. Despite everything.'

'You're right.' Carmel Devine's tear-washed face looked a mess, but the blonde hair and her slim figure in the tight-fitting black trouser suit were attracting some interest from male customers. Anthony glared at one man at a nearby table who seemed to have forgotten his coffee and lemon gâteau, and turned back to her. 'I wish there was something I could do to help,' he murmured.

'You are! I mean, just being able to talk to you helps a lot. You're a friend – my friend as well as Sean's. You

133

understand.' Carmel sniffed back more tears. 'I just wish he'd confided in one of us. I feel such a failure. Why didn't my own husband think he could talk to me about whatever was going on? Sean must have been desperate – and I didn't pick up on that, I thought things were fine. What does that say about me? About our marriage?'

Anthony was desperate himself. 'Sean probably didn't want to worry you,' he said, realising how feeble that sounded.

'Rosa said that. But what does Sean think I am now?' Her voice rose. '*Worry* doesn't even begin to cover it.'

'I know.' Anthony reached across the table and took her hand. 'What did you do with Lisa while the police were turning your house upside down?'

'They made us stay in the sitting room with this grim WPC. I wasn't allowed to take her to school, or do anything while they were swarming around. I took her after they'd gone. She was really upset, of course, didn't want to go, but I thought it might calm her and take her mind off things a bit. Provide some much-needed semblance of normality.' Carmel sighed and picked up her coffee cup. 'I'd planned to go back to work this morning, but of course that didn't happen. I've already lost four clients, and a consultant at the Royal just decided not to refer a patient of his to me. Can't blame him really, I suppose, although his telephone manner could have been less brusque. Anyway, it doesn't seem important right now.'

'Of course it's important, Carmel. This is your career, your livelihood.' Anthony was pleased about the lost clients. The lower Carmel sank, the more desperate she would become, the more she would turn to him. Sean had to contact her soon, if he was alive. He couldn't stay away much longer. Anthony had a nasty feeling the bastard was still alive, although God knew how! And how had he managed to stay hidden, when any hospital would have contacted the police about someone who staggered into Accident and Emergency with a gunshot wound or two? It was a mystery. But if Sean was dead, surely someone would have discovered his decaying corpse by now?

'Quarter to three,' Carmel murmured, glancing at her watch. 'I have to go and pick up Lisa soon.' She looked at Anthony and grimaced. 'I'm sorry, I completely forgot you wanted to discuss some things. What are they?'

'Well ...' Anthony pressed her cool hand, felt the softness of the skin. 'Nothing pleasant, I'm afraid.' Time to pile on more pressure. He felt excited by the thought that he might even be able to turn Carmel against her own husband. 'I know I should have told you this earlier, but there was so much going on and you were too—'

'I know.' Carmel stiffened. 'Go ahead. What is it?' she asked fearfully, suddenly dreading what Anthony was going to say. 'Something about Sean?'

'Yes. I didn't think you were ready to hear this before.' Anthony hesitated. 'I'm not too sure you are now either.' He let go of her hand.

'Anthony, please!' Carmel turned pale and her eyes were filled with anxiety. 'It can't be worse than anything I've heard so far.'

'I don't know about that,' he said. 'Okay. First of all, I'm not sure what to do about the business now that Sean's – well – absent.'

'Is that it? God, I thought ... I don't know what I thought!' Carmel let out a breath and stared at him in disbelief. 'If there's too much work for one person, can't you just get some help until ...' She swallowed. 'Until Sean comes back.' She felt annoyed with Anthony for frightening her like this. 'Hire a secretary. I don't know why you both didn't do that ages ago.'

'I don't mean I need a secretary. I can handle the work, no problem.'

'Okay. Then what *is* it? Anthony, please get to the point.'

'All right.' Anthony leaned across the table, so close that she could smell the expensive aftershave he wore,

135

something subtle but distinctive, with woody, musk and amber notes. She suddenly sniffed, puzzled and disturbed. Where had she smelled that before? Anthony's next words wiped the question out of her mind. 'To be honest with you, Carmel,' he said quietly, 'I don't believe Sean will be back. Ever.'

'*What?*' she gasped. 'What the hell are you talking about?' She went cold. 'Of course he will! I don't know where he's gone, or why, exactly, but he hasn't left me – certainly not for ever! Somebody's after him for some reason. Maybe he thinks he'll put me and Lisa in danger if he comes home now. But he will come home.' She clenched her hands, fighting the panic that rose in her. 'He has to!'

Time to drop the bombshell. 'Carmel, two weeks before he disappeared, Sean said he wanted me to buy him out. He told me he was finished with the business, that he wanted to go abroad and make a new start.'

'*What?*' She leapt up, knocking over her chair. People stared. 'No!' she gasped. 'No way. It's not true!'

'I'm afraid it is.'

'No! If it was you would have told me sooner. I don't understand. Sean would never leave me and Lisa, he—' She stopped. She felt sick.

'Please, Carmel.' Anthony got up and moved swiftly around the table, set the chair upright and took her arm. She was shaking. 'Sit down,' he murmured. 'I know this is really difficult for you. But just hear me out, okay? Please.'

Carmel collapsed on to the chair, her face white. No, she thought again. Sean wouldn't leave me! But didn't she sometimes wonder during the frantic, panic-filled days and long sleepless nights if her husband hadn't done exactly that? If he was alive! She stared at Anthony in shock, could not think of anything to say.

'I already told you Sean had been acting strangely.' Anthony wondered how much more she could take, he didn't want her fainting on him. 'I know you really don't want to hear this,' he said slowly, 'and I'm very sorry. But

I also believe Sean was involved with another woman. A girl, actually,' he added, twisting the knife.

Carmel could barely breathe, and there was a hissing in her ears. 'No!' The word came out as a groan. She shook her head. 'He wouldn't . . .'

'I saw her a couple of times,' Anthony went on. 'In his car. They were kissing.'

Carmel flinched and gave a little sob. 'She couldn't have been more than nineteen or twenty. She was beautiful, she had dark eyes and long black hair. I think Sean used to go off during the day to meet her. It'd certainly explain his frequent absences. I don't know her name or anything about her. Sean had long since stopped confiding in me. Don't get me wrong,' Anthony added hastily. 'I don't believe for one second that Sean murdered that prostitute. Or the other woman, the nightclub singer. The police have got their wires well crossed there. I don't care what evidence they say there is. And I don't believe Sean meant to disappear when he did. He wanted to wait until we'd sorted out the business. He knew it'd take a while for the paperwork and the money to come through. Maybe he intended to tell you he was leaving, I don't know. I was worried about you, in a dilemma about whether or not to interfere. I knew Sean wouldn't thank me for it. But the night he disappeared – when I'd heard him raving on the phone and he attacked me—' Anthony paused and shrugged. 'I don't know what he was involved in, but something must have gone seriously wrong.'

Carmel was silent as she struggled to take in what Anthony was saying and keep a grip on herself at the same time. She tried to picture Sean with the dark-haired girl. Kissing her, making love with her. I don't want to live any more, she thought. I can't go on, I can't take any more pain. If it wasn't for Lisa . . .

Carmel experienced another feeling – deep humiliation. I wasn't good enough, she thought. Not attractive, sexy, interesting, exciting enough. Obviously not young enough either. Sean had found someone better. There was always someone better. She fought the doubt and insecurity that threatened to overwhelm her, make her feel totally vulnerable. Had she been living in a fantasy world, stupidly believing a disintegrating marriage to be fine? Too preoccupied with sorting out other people's heads to think about her own? Was she really that blind? Carmel suddenly decided that no, she wasn't. There was something terribly wrong with what Anthony said. She knew her husband. And this wasn't Sean's style. Any of it.

'Are you okay?' Anthony asked, worried by her long silence. 'Would you like another cup of coffee?'

'No thanks.' She looked at him. 'So what you're saying is that all this is really nothing more than the sad, old cliché of husband dumping wife and running off with younger model?' Carmel had a sudden horrible feeling that Anthony was enjoying – no, more than that – relishing the shock and pain he'd caused her.

'Well, of course, it's not quite that uncomplicated.' His steely eyes studied her, measuring her reactions. 'But, basically ... yes. I'm very sorry,' he repeated.

'You've spoken to the police. Did you tell them what you've just told me?'

'No.'

'Why not? Surely it's information vital to Sean's case? You could get into serious trouble for withholding it.'

He shrugged, smiled slightly. 'I don't care about the police, Carmel.'

'But you care about *me*, don't you?' Her voice rose, along with her doubts about Anthony. 'You know how freaked out I was that night Sean disappeared. How freaked I still am. I was terrified he might be dead! How the hell could you let me think that – go on thinking it – if you knew it wasn't true? You can't possibly have believed I'd be more upset to know Sean had left me for some girl rather than to think he'd been murdered or killed in an accident!'

Anthony's jaw tightened. Some women would, he felt like saying.

'Now, hold on a minute, Carmel!' He tried to conceal his anger at the hectoring tone of her raised voice, the accusing look in her sparking eyes. This wasn't going the way he'd hoped. 'When I promised you I'd do all it took to find Sean, I meant what I said.' He kept his voice low. 'I thought I could look for him, maybe find him quickly, get the situation sorted before it got worse.'

'How do you mean, *sorted*?' Carmel's eyes were wet. 'Persuade him not to run off with his nineteen-year-old beauty?' she asked sarcastically.

'Well, yes, as a matter of fact. I thought I could find him, talk some sense into him and help him get out of whatever trouble he was in. But unfortunately things didn't work out that way. Sean disappeared, and I was just too bloody late.'

'So why didn't you tell me – and the police – then?'

'I still hoped I could sort it. And I wanted to spare you.'

'You didn't spare me,' she cried. 'I thought Sean was dead!' She gave a sob. 'He could be dead, for all I know. For all *you* know – you don't have a clue what happened to him after he disappeared, do you?'

'No.' That was true. 'I've handled this badly,' Anthony confessed. 'But I honestly thought I was doing the right thing. As to the police – a couple of detectives turned up at the warehouse, took a quick look around Sean's office and asked me a few questions. I didn't tell them anything because I was afraid Sean was in trouble – not the kind they could help with – and that they'd stop searching for him if I said he'd disappeared of his own accord. You don't want me to tell the police Sean was having an affair, do you?' he asked, his voice gentle. 'Things will only look worse for him. I want him found, Carmel, I want to know he's safe. So do you. But we have to face the fact that Sean doesn't want to be found.' He paused. 'It's time to move on.'

Carmel grabbed her bag and stood up. 'I can't listen to

any more,' she said abruptly. 'I need time to think about all this, try to take it in. Get myself together.'

'Of course. Are you okay to drive?' he asked. 'Let me give you a lift.'

'No, I'll be fine. I have to collect Lisa, anyway.'

Anthony got up and helped her on with her short, floaty black mac. His hands on her slender shoulders felt heavy, weighing her down. Carmel shuddered at his touch and moved away. She couldn't breathe, had to get out of here. She had the feeling Anthony wasn't her friend after all. That he wasn't Sean's friend either, never had been. But maybe what he said was the truth. And maybe she didn't want to face it.

'I need to know – when you're ready to discuss this—' Anthony was pleased to note how stricken she looked, how the fight had gone out of her. Like most women, she was credulous and had no guts. 'What to do about the business. Might be easier for you if I just take it off your hands. Sean and I did have a firm verbal agreement. That counts for something in law.'

'*What?*' Carmel whirled round and stared at him, shocked again. 'I can't discuss law and verbal agreements just now, I'm afraid,' she whispered. Was he crazy?

'Sorry.' Anthony flushed. 'I did say when you were ready. I'm just trying to help make things easier for you. Think of practical things that you haven't been able to consider – in the circumstances.'

'I see.' But she didn't. Carmel backed away.

'You'll be in touch?' he asked, his voice urgent.

She did not reply. They walked out of the café. Her legs felt weak and she had to concentrate on taking small, careful steps on the slippery, rain-washed cobbles.

Carmel could not believe that Sean had left her for another woman, had not even bothered to tell her that their marriage was over. Okay, a lot of men did exactly that, and the wife was often the last to know. It was a joke – to other people. I can't think now, she told herself. Or freak out. I

140

have to collect Lisa from school. Drive her home, cook her tea, talk to her, sit with her later while she has her bath. Read her a bedtime story. Losing it is a luxury I can't afford.

'Take care of yourself, Carmel.' She felt Anthony's warm lips on her cheek as he hugged and kissed her goodbye. She nodded, in a daze, barely able to respond. She felt his eyes on her as she walked away. It was a very uncomfortable sensation.

Carmel didn't know how she got to the Landcruiser and drove off without killing herself or someone else, negotiated the city streets until she reached Lisa's school. Fifteen minutes early, she sat in the car staring out at people with safe, secure happy lives. She felt numb. All she could think of was Anthony talking about law and verbal agreements.

When Carmel walked through the school gates she noticed that several of the waiting parents ignored her or gave her wary looks. Yesterday she would have been upset. Today she didn't care. She entered the building and headed down the corridor, pushing through hordes of shouting children delighted at their release. Lisa was nowhere to be seen.

Oh Christ! Carmel thought. Where is she? Panic rose in her as she looked helplessly around. Someone tapped her on the arm and she gasped with shock.

'Mrs Devine, hello. Sorry I scared you.' It was Mrs Mackay, Lisa's teacher. Carmel could not remember the woman's first name. 'Lisa's with the headmistress,' Mrs Mackay said. 'We tried to get in touch, but we couldn't reach you at home or at your office.'

'What's happened?' Carmel asked wildly.

Mrs Mackay's mild brown eyes were sympathetic, as if she knew Carmel was at the end of her tether. 'I'm sorry to have to tell you this,' she said. 'Things must be difficult enough for you just now. But I'm afraid Lisa got into a nasty fight with another child.' Carmel groaned, one hand pressed to her forehead.

'One of her classmates, a girl named Raquel Lynch. Raquel got the worst of it. We had to send her home.' The teacher pursed her thin lips. 'Luckily, her mother was in.'

'Luckily. How did this fight start?' But Carmel knew. I shouldn't have sent Lisa to school, she thought. I should have kept her with me. Can't I get anything right?

Mrs Mackay glanced around and lowered her voice. 'Lisa says Raquel made some unfortunate remarks about her father.'

'You mean cruel and nasty remarks, I presume. What were they?'

'Well, she said . . . she called Lisa's father a murderer.'

'Oh, my God!'

'A serial murderer. Who would be put to death by lethal injection if he lived in America. To be precise. Lisa punched her in the face and stomach. Raquel's nose was bleeding.' Mrs Mackay's lips pursed again. 'I'm afraid we can't tolerate that kind of behaviour here.'

'I agree. I wouldn't let someone get away with calling my father a murderer.'

'That's not at all what I meant, Mrs Devine. You're not being very helpful. No matter what the provocation, a violent response is never justified. We'd prefer it if Lisa stayed away from school for a while.'

Carmel suddenly remembered the musky, amber smell again. It hit her as strongly as if someone had just sprayed it in her face. She flinched and felt the gun press against her naked breast, its muzzle circle her nipple. The unknown man's whisper: 'Useless bitch.' But he wasn't unknown after all.

That man was Anthony Maskey.

'Not coming for a bevvie with us then, Boss?'

'How many more times do I have to tell you?' Olivia snapped. 'I'm not in the mood. It's dark and cold, pissing with rain again and I'm knackered. I just want to drive home, soak in a hot bath perfumed with essential oil of lavender, then watch telly.'

'Bloody hell, you're really losing it!' Neil Davie grinned down at her. Olivia sat at her cluttered desk fidgeting with the sleeves of her sharp trouser suit, her makeup and long, thick, dark auburn hair immaculate. 'Can't you tell me what's up?' he asked. 'You've been in a right state this past day or so.'

Olivia shrugged. 'I'm not in a state,' she said sullenly. 'Nothing's wrong.' She had lost all desire to speak to Anthony Maskey. She felt terrified of him now. This was her worst nightmare.

'You're not still worried about Alex, are you?' Neil's grin broadened. 'Come on, Olivia! He's got his head screwed on, you said so yourself. And he's a damn sight safer in Phuket than he would be in clubland on a Saturday night.'

'Yeah.' She stood up and stretched, pushing back her chair. 'Okay. I'm off home.'

'Shame about that tape.' Neil looked thoughtful. 'Of course good old Les didn't think to dial 1471 at the time he got that hang-up call. Or get the number of that car. We don't even know if the call was from the murderer anyway,' he said. 'But the description Les gave of that driver sounds a lot like Sean Devine.'

'Yes.' Olivia looked at him. 'It does, doesn't it?'

'Still can't think how he got to her. It's doing my head in. And no sign of him yet.'

'Well . . .' Olivia opened her desk drawer and pretended to root amongst the pens and papers. The box of chocolates was down to its last layer. If she didn't watch herself she would balloon like a body builder on steroids. She hadn't been to the gym lately either, and membership was costing her a fortune. 'As Scarlett O'Hara said, tomorrow is another day.'

'Yeah.' Neil sighed. 'Can't tempt you for that drink then? You're usually the life and soul of the party.'

'I'll be life and soul some other time, Neil.'

'Okay. See you tomorrow. Thank God it's Friday!'

He went out, whistling, and Olivia pulled on her mac and took her black leather bag from the coat stand. She switched off the desk lamp and walked out, jingling her car keys. Neil was right when he said Les's description of the mystery car driver sounded like Sean Devine. It also sounded like Anthony Maskey, but of course Neil had no reason to suspect him. She had to make sure he didn't find one. For her own safety.

Olivia trembled with fear as she walked to her car, head bent against the wind and rain, and stuck the key in the lock. What did it feel like to be strangled? To know you were being murdered? She never wanted to set eyes on Anthony again.

At home she went straight to the kitchen, got the Smirnoff Blue from the freezer and poured herself a huge measure. She added a splash of tonic and gulped the drink down, poured another. There was fresh tagliatelle and a tub of bolognese sauce in the fridge, but no way did she feel like dinner. She went into the living room to check the answering machine. No messages, thank God. She threw off her mac and dropped her mobile on the sofa. It had been switched off for two days. Olivia was about to go upstairs and run her bath when the phone on the little table beside the sofa rang.

She froze. What if this was Anthony? She couldn't talk to him, she just couldn't! She stood there, clutching her glass and staring at the phone as it continued to ring. Then she swore. Of course it wasn't Anthony! Apart from the fact that he would never wait this long, they only spoke to each other on their mobiles. It was the safest way. What was she thinking? Fear was turning her brain soft. She snatched up the receiver.

'Olivia? It's Adrian. I still haven't received the cheque for my share of the house.'

'I only wrote it the other day,' Olivia snapped. She liked

the spacious thirties house and didn't see why she should sell it because of the divorce; of course that had meant buying Adrian out, even though she'd paid most of the mortgage over the years. 'It should clear the account by the end of the week.'

'Better had, or I'll be on to the solicitors. Have you heard from Alex lately?' Adrian asked. 'How is he?'

'He's fine. In Thailand now. Said he's sent you a post-card.'

'That's good. And how are you, Olivia? Who's the unlucky bloke handcuffed to your bedposts tonight? Hope I'm not interrupting anything.'

'Not at all. You could come round for a civilised post-divorce visit,' she said sweetly. 'I'll do you a delicious deathcap mushroom omelette.'

'I'll bet you would and all, you old witch.'

'I feel so much happier these days,' Olivia went on. 'Really making up for lost time. I never understood why you got so hot and bothered about my little flings.'

'D'you know something?' he laughed. 'Neither do I.'

'I mean, it wasn't as if you had anything left to offer,' she said, stung. 'Does your sad old scrubber tell you size doesn't matter and never mind if you can't manage it every night or even once a week, *darling*?'

She crashed the phone down before Adrian could call her a sad old scrubber. 'Arsehole,' she whispered. 'Don't sodding phone *me* and ask about cheques!'

She went upstairs, taking glass and vodka bottle, and ran her lavender-perfumed bath. The drink and the hot, oiled water relaxed her tired and aching body, but not her mind. Olivia winced, horrified as she thought of all the incriminating stuff Anthony Maskey had on her. She had even confessed to him that she had considered having Adrian stiffed. How thick was *that*?

She shuddered as she remembered herself the other night, nibbling Anthony's earlobe and sliding her hand up his thigh, thinking maybe she could end up in bed with him.

I must have been desperate, she thought, her face burning. Certainly arseholed! It wasn't great the first time around. Anthony might be tasty to look at, but he wasn't exactly a thrill between the sheets. Not much enthusiasm and even less technique. Sometimes he had hurt her. That was the only part he really enjoyed.

Anthony trafficked girls and women for the sex trade, turned them into slaves. Her information – for which he paid her handsomely – helped him. But Olivia could not reveal Anthony as a twenty-first-century slave trafficker or the murderer of Gemma Geraghty and Paula Pepper without putting her own life at risk. And for what?

She could prove Anthony was a slave trafficker, but not a murderer. He would get off with a light sentence. Dealing in drugs got you sent down for years, but it was more than okay to buy and sell women. Governments and police forces didn't want the hassle, and Olivia did not blame them. It was easier to declare the victims illegal aliens and deport them, or criminalise them some other way. And let's face it, a lot of the silly bitches knew what they were letting themselves in for.

Anthony could have put Sean Devine in the frame; it would have been easy enough to whip a couple of stray hairs out of his partner's comb and plant them at the crime scene. No other DNA had been found, although if a sample was taken from Anthony they might get something. But Sean Devine's innocence could not come to light. His wife must never know the truth. Maybe Anthony wanted to murder Sean – if the guy wasn't already dead. Sean's death was the best solution all round. Olivia had to protect herself. Especially now that she knew what Anthony was capable of.

What was Anthony's motive? Greed? Fear? Did he suffer from some psychosis, a personality disorder? A lot of criminals were mentally ill, if not legally insane. It didn't matter. Olivia would stand by and let him get on with whatever he felt he had to do. Stand by, that is, as long as she wasn't next in line. She had to disassociate herself from him as of now. And Anthony might not understand that. Or be happy about it.

It did not suit her to imagine the misery and desperation of Sean Devine's wife and young daughter, or the suffering of the vulnerable trafficked girls, imprisoned and beaten by pimps and forced to work as sex slaves. It was a cold, cruel world, and there were only winners or losers. Olivia knew what she intended to be.

She got out of the bath, wrapped herself in a warm towelling robe and went downstairs. She bolted, chained and double-locked the front and back doors, poured more vodka and lay on the sofa, her head whirling.

'Saint Rita,' she whispered, praying to her patron saint, 'let me stay cool!'

She really had been stupid enough to get mixed up with a psycho! It was agonising, didn't bear thinking about. But she had to think. How could she get away from Anthony Maskey without arousing his undoubtably paranoid suspicions and endangering her life? It was the most desperate of desperate dilemmas.

The phone rang again, and she sighed. Adrian, wanting to trade more insults? Or her mother fancying a cosy chat? She sat up and grabbed the receiver.

'Olivia!' Anthony said, a smile in his voice. 'At last. Where have you been hiding? I was beginning to think you weren't speaking to me any more.'

Chapter Thirteen

'Liverpool bloody city council's not going to tell *me* I can't shave my pubes!'

Simona sat trembling in the smelly dressing room as she waited to go on stage, and listened to two girls argue about restrictions the council was thinking of imposing on sex clubs in the city. They were bold, seemed happy even. Simona could not believe any woman would choose to dance naked for a living, but it seemed these two had. They worked in other clubs as well as this one, were free to move around as they wished. They did not speak to her, on the manager's instructions. They were lucky enough to get paid, even if they had to hand over part of their wages to the manager and the bouncers. Every penny she earned belonged to Anthony.

Simona tried hard to rise above her sordid, terrifying existence, keep hope alive. But she wondered if she would ever be free again. Or reunited with Maria. She imagined her parents horror at her fate. She was trying to find out about Maria, but it was very difficult because no one in the house or at the club ever talked to her.

'Come on, you dozy bitch!' Yvonne appeared and shook her roughly by the shoulder. 'Get your useless arse out there!'

Simona flinched and stood up. She hated Yvonne, who was more cruel and sadistic than any of the male minders.

She walked forward and stepped into the world beyond the curtain. The bump-grind music pounded in her ears and vibrated through her body. The noise, shouts, laughter, cigarette smoke, stink of beer and male sweat. Blue lights flashed in her eyes.

Simona switched off as she had quickly learned to do, whipping away her feathered bra and G-string, kneeling, shaking back her long hair, submissively spreading her legs. Turning and wriggling her behind. She smiled at the dark, anonymous mass of faces, stroked her breasts, grabbed the pole and ground her pelvis against it. Maria, she thought. Where are you? Did they make you do this too?

Simona was jerked out of her trance when a drunk threw a beer bottle, which skidded across the stage towards her. Cold lager splashed her legs as she kicked it away. The man was dragged off by bouncers. More whoops and jeering laughter. Simona's great fear was that one night the crowd of men would surge forward and overrun the stage, grab her and tear her apart. She knew she would die then.

Her act finished, she ran back to the dressing room and covered herself with a threadbare blue cotton robe, tying the belt tightly around her slim waist. She had to perform twice more, then it was time to go to one of the small, dimly lit rooms above the club and wait for clients, lying naked on a bed.

Simona studied her body in the long wall mirror. Yvonne and the other minders gave her plenty to eat, but it was very bad food. No fresh fruit or vegetables. They didn't eat good food themselves and never cooked, just bought hamburgers, chips, curries. Simona had never tasted curry before. She got Coca-Cola, fizzy orange and heavily chlorinated tap water to drink. The coffee they drank was horrible, and they gave her tea with sugar and milk added. Only the British put milk in tea. She would have liked to buy herself a bottle of multivitamins to try to safeguard her health, but she had no money and was not allowed to leave

149

the house except when they drove her to the club. She had
no freedom or dignity, she was nothing but a slave. A sex
slave. Tears rose to her eyes and she carefully wiped them,
trying not to smear the thick eyeliner and mascara they
made her wear. If she cried they would hit her – somewhere she wouldn't bruise, or not too badly. A lot of clients
didn't mind the odd bruise; sometimes they liked to cause
them. She had to smile for the clients, pretend not to have a
thought in her head except how to satisfy their desires.
Their pleasure was all-important.

The door opened and Anthony walked in, wearing a suit
and his long black coat. The smell of his cologne floated on
the stale air; a beautiful smell on an evil man. Simona
gasped with terror and cowered on the bed, trying to cover
her nakedness. Would he be cruel or gentle? She never
knew. Whatever his mood, it could change like lightning
and for no apparent reason. What was he doing here now?
She normally had to work until three or four in the
morning.

Stop behaving like a frightened animal! she thought
suddenly. She was not entirely helpless – there was one
card she could play. Anthony was ruthless and without
compassion, but he was interested in her, attracted to her.
She had to exploit that attraction and turn it to her advantage. It was her only chance. Every day she thought about
escape, but she was too closely guarded. Even if she did
escape, where would she go? She didn't want to be caught
by the police or immigration authorities and rot in jail for
the next ten years. Or be deported before she found Maria.
And she was afraid for her family. But she could warn them
and they would tell the police back home. They would be
safe then, surely. If she was to escape from Anthony's
clutches, find Maria and get out of Britain she would need
to get back her passport – or a passport. She needed money
too. This bastard had both.

'Don't hide yourself from me,' Anthony said, sitting on
the bed. 'You're beautiful. You don't need to hide. Come

here.' He leaned over and kissed her thigh. Simona willed herself not to flinch. 'Your skin's like satin,' he murmured. He cupped her breast, squeezing the nipple slightly. She gave a little gasp of fear.

'Don't be afraid, Simona. I won't hurt you, I promise. I watched you tonight,' he said. 'You were very good.' He smiled. 'So good that I can't resist you any longer.' He pulled her against him. 'You're really special. You're the most beautiful creature I've ever laid eyes on. I knew all along you existed. I dreamed about you.'

Creature. That's all she was to him. A thing, a commodity that could be bought, sold, raped and abused, caged like an animal, either left alone for hours by her jailers or tormented by them when they got bored. Anthony laid her down and kissed her, stroking her breasts, his tongue probing between her lips. Simona forced herself to endure his embrace, every nerve in her body screaming. This means nothing, she told herself. He can possess my body because this is the physical world. But not my soul. That thought did not help. Anthony could hurt her body, cause her a lot of pain. He could injure her soul too, even if he could never own it.

'Your eyes,' Anthony murmured, kissing her cheeks and forehead, 'they're like black jade. You're an angel.' He smoothed her hair. 'My angel.' He took off his coat and wrapped it around her, the silk lining soft and warm against her skin.

'I'm taking you home with me, Simona. You can see my house. We'll lie in bed and drink vintage champagne. Would you like that?'

'Yes,' she lied, her voice barely a whisper. What else could she say?

He frowned, and her heart skipped a beat. 'Say my name.'

'Anthony. Yes, Anthony. I would like that.'

'Good. We'll spend the night together. Maybe more than one night.' He stood up and lifted her, cradling her in his arms. Her bare feet dangled. 'You're going to be mine,' he said, kissing her again. 'Really mine.'

Simona looked into his eyes. They were bright and full of lust. The fatal spark of madness. Her stomach churned and her heart raced with fear.

Why did she have a feeling that this coming night was going to be even worse than the night those men had raped her?

Carmel awoke, terrified, her eyes straining to make out the shape of the dark form she felt certain was standing in the bedroom silently observing her, some evil presence. Outside in Falkner Square a full moon sailed above the tree tops, its pale light slanting across the dressing table and one corner of the bed. Carmel snapped on the bedside lamp and stared around the big, cold room, her heart pounding. There was nobody. It must have been a nightmare. But it seemed so real.

She got out of bed, pulled on her robe and looked nervously at the closed door, feeling reluctant to brave the dark landing beyond. Had she heard a noise? Was somebody out there? Don't be ridiculous, she told herself. She glanced at the clock: two-forty am. She had to check on Lisa. She opened the door, stared fearfully into the blackness and crept forward, feeling her way until her eyes became accustomed to the darkness. She couldn't put the light on and risk waking Lisa. She gripped the smooth, low banister, making sure not to trip on the three steps that led down to her daughter's bedroom.

Lisa was curled up fast asleep, clutching the photo of herself and her father in the Lake District. The Furby sat on the bedside table next to the toadstool lamp, its thickly lashed eyes closed. Carmel crouched and listened to the child's soft, regular breathing, gently lifted a long strand of hair that had fallen across Lisa's forehead, and smoothed it back.

Of course she could not condone Lisa's violent response

to Raquel Lynch's taunts, but Carmel nevertheless did not blame her daughter. She blamed herself. Ridiculous that Lisa was in trouble for fighting back, but not Raquel for causing deeper and longer-lasting wounds with her cruel words. Raquel's mother, Laura, was an unfriendly woman who had always blanked Carmel even before Sean's disappearance and the awful press coverage and police harassment. Raquel had only repeated her mother's words to Lisa. People could be so callous, so stupid and unthinking. Carmel kissed Lisa, feeling fiercely protective of her, tiptoed out of the bedroom and started to go downstairs. Rosa's bedroom door opened a fraction.

'Hey,' she whispered. 'What's up?'

'Nothing.' Carmel turned. 'Get back to bed – you've got to be up and out of here again in about four hours.'

'I'm awake now. I fancy some hot chocolate.'

They went downstairs. Carmel had not told Rosa, or anyone, what Anthony had said to her yesterday afternoon. What she was thinking about him. She had dealt with Lisa, keeping the terrible things on hold at the back of her mind. Waiting until she could process them.

She had tidied up a bit after the police had left, but the house was still a demoralising mess. And now that Sean, her and Lisa's private space had been violated, it didn't feel like home any more. They went into the kitchen and Carmel stood still, feeling her fear and the hollowness in her stomach. She looked at her face in the mirror. It was pinched and pale. Her eyes looked bigger.

'I'll make the chocolate,' she said.

'Fine by me.' Rosa smiled, pushing back her mass of light brown curls. 'You make it slowly and with reverence, and the result is always much more delicious than my lumpy gunge.' She pulled her red wool dressing gown around her and tied the belt.

'You don't get lumps when you use a whisk.' Carmel thought about Sean and Anthony while she heated full cream milk in a saucepan, whisked in four heaped spoonfuls of designer cocoa powder and two spoonfuls of granulated sugar, snapped off six pieces of 75 per cent cocoa solids chocolate and added those. The mixture frothed and bubbled, the rich, soothing chocolate smell filling the kitchen. She poured it into two mugs and they sat down at the table.

'Mmm,' Rosa breathed. 'That smells gorgeous. Fancy a shortbread?' she asked, getting up. 'That's if Princess Lisa hasn't polished off the lot.'

'No thanks.' Carmel waited until Rosa had sat down again and was munching a sugary, fork-pricked triangle. 'I saw Anthony this afternoon,' she said. 'Well, yesterday afternoon now. He told me—' She stopped and looked down at the steaming chocolate. 'Some things.'

'So what were they?' Rosa swallowed a mouthful of buttery shortbread. 'I thought you were even more quiet than usual last night. What things, Carmel?'

'Maybe it's arrogance, stupidity, or a pathetic inability to face painful reality,' Carmel began, 'but I just can't bring myself to believe that Sean's run off abroad with a nineteen-year-old girl who he's been screwing for weeks or months. During office hours, so as not to alert the missis.'

'*What?*' Rosa gasped, dropping her biscuit. It broke, scattering crumbs on the table.

'Or that he was involved in some criminal activity that backfired on him, which is why he's now on the run – if he's still alive. That he wanted to sell Anthony his share of the business, and he won't be back because he doesn't want to be found. Ever.'

'My God, Carmel!' Rosa stared at her in jaw-dropping shock. 'But why on earth didn't he tell you – and the police – before now? That's vital information, he had no right to withhold it.'

'My question exactly. He said he hoped he could find Sean and sort things out, that he thought I was too freaked to deal with it. I think that's bullshit. Apart from the fact that he was taking a hell of a lot upon himself, it didn't seem to occur to him that I'd be slightly less freaked to at least know Sean was alive. Anthony says now it's time to move on. I'm supposed to take a deep breath, pull myself together, and sensibly sell off my husband's share of the business to him.'

'But that sounds crazy!'

'They had a verbal agreement, apparently, and that counts for something in law.' Carmel's voice hardened. 'Anthony's trying to relieve me of all these tedious practical matters that I'm too hysterical to get my fluffy little head round. Isn't that kind of him? What a friend.'

'But this is incredible!' Rosa gaped at her. 'And how the hell could he mention law and verbal agreements when he'd just told you . . .?'

'That's what I thought,' Carmel said grimly.

Rosa shook her head in disbelief. 'I don't know what to say – what to *think*. My God!' she breathed, staring at her sister's pale face. 'You don't – do you think it's true? I can't believe Sean would have an affair with some girl behind your back, lie to you for weeks or maybe months, then walk out and leave you in this terrible suspense. Leave *Lisa*. I just can't imagine him being that cruel and deceitful.'

'Neither can I.' Carmel picked up her mug of hot chocolate and cradled it to warm her hands. 'Maybe Anthony's the one who's lying,' she said slowly. 'About Sean. About everything.'

Rosa was silent for a few seconds. 'But why would Anthony lie?'

'That's what I keep asking myself.' Carmel put the mug down and raked her fingers through her hair. 'I've only got Anthony's word for what happened between him and Sean that night, haven't I? And before. Okay, I had no reason to doubt him. Anthony's been his business partner and trusted friend for several years now. I thought he was almost as desperate as me to find Sean.' Carmel paused. 'Suddenly he isn't any more.'

155

'How could he talk about moving on?' Rosa breathed. 'It's unbelievably crass.'

Carmel looked at her sister. 'When I listened to him yesterday afternoon it was like watching a mask slide off. It was as if he derived sadistic pleasure from telling me about Sean and this beautiful girl. Okay, I admit, I don't want to believe it. But what freaked me most of all ... the aftershave or cologne Anthony wore ... the man who held the gun to my breast that night, who never spoke – he had the same smell. I think that man was Anthony. He stole Sean's keys. He's lied about everything.'

'Oh, God! But again ... *why*?'

'Look at it from a different angle.' Carmel drummed her fingers on the table. 'What if Sean was having problems with Anthony, not the other way round?'

'But you two have always been so close. Why wouldn't Sean tell you?'

'I don't know,' Carmel whispered. 'Maybe he didn't realise what was going on at first, or how serious it was. Then, that night, things suddenly got very serious. Maybe Sean stumbled on some terrible secret about Anthony. Anthony tried to hurt him – kill him even, and that's why Sean's disappeared.' She twisted her hands together. 'This could all be down to Anthony. Remember what Daniel said about who stands to benefit? If Anthony gets Sean's share of the business, he'll certainly benefit.'

Rosa frowned. 'It still doesn't add up. Surely there's plenty for both of them? Anthony's doing fine,' she said. 'Would he really be that greedy? From what I've heard, he seems to have more cash on the hip than you and Sean put together.'

'Yes.' Carmel nodded thoughtfully. 'Doesn't he just!'

'What d'you mean?'

'Anthony implies Sean was involved in criminal activity.' Carmel paused. 'What if Anthony's the criminal, has been all along?'

'Okay. Suppose he's running some scam, maybe creaming

156

off company profits, and Sean found out. Anthony would be ticked off big time, but he'd hardly be motivated to kill Sean. That's an excessive response by anyone's standards.'

'Not necessarily Anthony's.'

'And it's got sod-all to do with the murder of that prostitute and the nightclub singer.'

'Not if Anthony murdered those women,' Carmel said breathlessly. 'Fitted Sean up. Who else but Anthony would want to hurt Sean? *That* makes sense. And when our Ant found out about the witness he had to stiff her too.'

Rosa turned pale. 'Hold up, Carmel! That's one hell of a leap, from running a scam to committing two murders. Why would Anthony want to murder a prostitute anyway? Surely not just to fit Sean up?'

'Who knows? And whatever he's up to could be more than a scam. Might be something really big, with a lot at stake.'

'Such as what?'

'I don't know, do I? Drugs, weapons . . . anything.'

'And how could Anthony have known about that witness? Her name didn't appear in the papers until after she got strangled. Who knew about her before she died?'

'Only the police, I presume. He probably pays some corrupt cop for tip-offs.'

'Oh, brilliant!' Rosa paled again. 'That opens up a whole new realm of horrific possibilities.'

Carmel jumped up and began to pace. 'I don't know if I'm right about any of this. But Rosa, you should have seen Anthony when he was talking to me. His eyes, his voice. He was so cold-blooded, so matter-of-fact. I couldn't believe it was the man I knew. Thought I knew,' she added grimly.

'I liked Anthony. I once had a secret crush on him,' Rosa confessed, blushing.

'Think yourself lucky it didn't come to anything. A real friend would be loyal, go on running things,' Carmel argued. 'But it's barely two weeks since Sean disappeared, and his so-called friend is already trying to muscle in on his share of the business.' She shivered and gave a choked sob. 'What if Anthony did kill Sean? Maybe that's why he's so certain Sean will never come home.'

'So why would he bother to fit Sean up for murder? No!' Rosa leapt up, skirted the table and flung her arms around her sister. 'Sean's still alive, Carmel!' she cried, hugging her. 'You've got to believe that.'

'But where did he go? What's happened to him?' Carmel's body shook with sobs. 'I keep thinking Anthony could have murdered him by now, buried his body somewhere. That I'll never see him again. Lisa will have to grow up without her father, and her life will be ruined.'

'Carmel, don't torture yourself like this! That won't happen.' Rosa trembled with fright as she recalled the gruesome murders of Gemma Geraghty and Paula Pepper. If Anthony was responsible, they had a real live psycho on their hands. 'D'you think the house is still being watched?' she asked.

'I don't know,' Carmel moaned. 'I haven't seen those men or that car again.'

'Because if so, it means Sean's alive. You said that yourself. Let's see if we can spot them,' Rosa suggested, desperate to do something.

Carmel wiped her eyes on her sleeve. 'There's a pair of binoculars in one of the attic rooms – unless the bloody police confiscated them.'

'Good. Come on.'

The pair of Second World War field glasses that had belonged to their Great Uncle James were in their dusty, scratched leather case, nestling in a box of Lisa's baby clothes. Carmel took them, went down to her bedroom and switched off the lamp. She scanned the square, Rosa standing anxiously by her side. A minute later she lowered the binoculars and stepped back.

'Look!' She handed the glasses to Rosa. 'The BMW

down the street to your right. Parked further away this time. Between the Ford Mondeo and that Astra. Can't tell if it's the same two thugs as before.'

'What's that old guy in the light-coloured anorak doing?' Rosa murmured. 'He must be drunk or something.'

'Never mind him. Look at them,' Carmel breathed. 'Shaven-headed and smoking, of course. Overweight from all the sitting. I don't believe this! They obviously have no sense of irony. I bet they watch gangster movies so as to know how to behave. Keep back,' she hissed. 'Don't let them see you.'

Rosa lowered the binoculars. 'Shall we call the police?' she asked nervously.

'I already did, remember? But yes, I will again. I wish I could see that BMW's number plate.' Carmel turned. 'Let's check the alley.'

They crept back down to the kitchen, unlocked and unbolted the door and went into the yard, shivering in the cold night air. Carmel unlocked the door in the wall.

'Be careful,' Rosa whispered, clutching her arm.

Carmel looked up and down the moonlit alley, empty except for the wheelie bins placed at intervals. A black cat sat on top of one bin, vigorously carrying out its toilette. It stopped licking its private parts and looked at her as if to say, do you mind? She jumped back, startled, as she saw two dark figures lurking at one end of the alley. Their cigarettes glowed red. She closed the door softly and slid the bolts.

Back in the kitchen, Carmel locked and bolted the door and hung the key on a hook inside one of the cupboards. She looked at Rosa.

'Don't you think you should get back to bed? You'll be knackered in the morning. Talking gibberish to all your mafia and terrorist satellite phone clients.'

'I'll wait until you've called the police. So,' Rosa said, hugging herself and shivering, 'those men wouldn't be out there if Sean was dead. They probably think he'll come back here – or try to contact you some other way.'

Carmel trembled with cold and nerves. 'For God's sake, don't breathe a word of this to Mum and Dad – to anyone.' Her blue eyes were frightened. 'If you see or speak to Anthony, be as normal and friendly as possible. He mustn't think we suspect him. Maybe I shouldn't have said anything to you. I don't want to put you in danger.'

'Joking, aren't you?' Rosa said indignantly. 'Sisters are for ever, there is no friend like a sister, etc. Now pick up that phone and call the officers of the law.'

'What's the point?' Carmel frowned. 'Those bastards will be out of here the minute they spot a cop car. Even if the police catch them, what then? They probably won't get anything out of them. I can't prove Anthony committed those murders, or that he's responsible for Sean's disappearance. I don't even know if I'm right. Maybe I should try to find out what he's up to.'

'You're crazy, sister dear!' Rosa looked horrified. 'Much safer to tell the police your suspicions and let them investigate. That's their job, isn't it? And Anthony won't know you suspect him, because whatever you tell the police will be confidential.'

'You mean like Paula Pepper the vital witness was confidential? Until she ended up strangled behind the wheel of her own car.'

'Oh, God! Look, suppose you do discover Anthony's a murderer and God knows what else? You can't arrest him yourself. You'll have to tell the police at some point. I'd tell everybody,' Rosa cried. 'The more people know you suspect Anthony, the safer you'll be. Let him defend himself. Let *him* be pushed into a corner!'

'Rosa, if Anthony's what I think he might be, pushing him into a corner would turn him into a frightened rat. And we all know what they do.'

'You can't go after Anthony all by yourself. Think of Lisa. She can't lose her mother as well as her father—' Rosa stopped as Carmel flinched and turned pale. 'Sorry,' she whispered. 'I didn't mean . . .'

160

'I know. It's okay. You're right,' Carmel sighed after a minute. 'I will tell the police. I can still try to find Sean. But I'm being watched. How do I find him without leading them straight to . . .?'

Carmel didn't get to finish her sentence. She was interrupted by the crash of shattering glass.

Part Two

Chapter Fourteen

'Are you serious about pressing criminal damage charges against Mr Higginbottom?' Olivia asked, her gaze cold as it rested on Carmel Devine. The woman was a few years younger than herself, and Anthony was right about her being a looker, although she didn't take much care of her appearance. The blonde hair was a mess, but a lot of men would find that sexy. Olivia could not have squeezed into the tight black Armani jeans and baby blue angora sweater Carmel wore. The sister sat tensely beside her on the sofa, wearing baggy, shiny black sweatpants and a grey sweatshirt. The sitting room light was on because of the boarded-up windows.

'Yes, I'm serious.' Carmel nodded, hands clenched in her lap. 'As I told the officer who arrested him in the early hours of this morning. How come it's taken you this long to get here?' she asked angrily. 'It's nearly five, I've been home all day waiting.'

Olivia ignored the question. Carmel Devine wasn't in a position to make demands. 'You won't consider dropping the charges?' she persisted. 'Mr Higginbottom's state of mind is somewhat deranged at the moment.' Bloody old fool, she thought. 'He's devastated by his wife's murder, and he'd read some stuff in the papers . . .'

'You mean inflammatory speculation printed about my husband which obviously incited this man to get drunk, turn up here at four in the morning and smash my sitting room windows? He was screaming threats and obscenities. A few neighbours turned out to cheer him on – I thought there was going to be a lynch mob.' Carmel looked at Olivia, her eyes sparking with anger. 'My daughter was terrified!' Her voice shook. 'She's been through enough lately, and this is the last thing she needs.' As if on cue, the door opened and Lisa walked in.

'Hi there!' Cute, Olivia thought, smiling at the child. Lisa wore jeans and a pink sweatshirt with a teddy bear in the middle. Her long blonde hair was tied in a ponytail and secured with a stretchy, glittery pink band. 'I'm Olivia and this is Neil,' she explained. 'We're just here to have a chat with your mum.'

'About last night?'

'Lisa ...' Carmel glanced round and smiled. 'We're talking,' she said gently.

'Grown-up talk?' Lisa pouted. 'I hate that. It's so boring!'

'Yes, it is.' Rosa got up. 'So why don't we get a packet of crisps and some juice?' She glanced at her watch. 'Hey, it's nearly time for Pingu.' She and Carmel liked the wacky little penguin almost as much as Lisa. 'Come on.'

Lisa looked at Carmel, her blue eyes pleading. 'Are you coming to watch Pingu, Mummy?'

'Not just now, darling.'

'When?'

'Soon. I promise. See you later, okay?' Rosa took Lisa's hand and they went out. Carmel turned back to Olivia. Why did they always come in twos? she wondered, looking at silent Neil Davie loitering by the boarded-up windows. Deaths and sundry other disasters come in threes, police officers in twos.

'It won't look too good,' Olivia pushed her specs further up her nose, 'you pressing charges against a man whose wife your husband is suspected of murdering. I'm just giving you some friendly advice.'

166

'That's very kind. But I've had enough.' Carmel stood up and walked to the mantelpiece. 'Last night was the final straw. I'm very sorry Mr Higginbottom's wife was murdered, but it wasn't my husband who killed her. And I won't tolerate my daughter being frightened like that. Dropping the charges would be as good as saying I deserved what happened. I didn't.' She paused. 'My husband was set up.'

She flushed angrily as Neil Davie smirked and turned away. Olivia looked startled, however, shocked. She sat up straight and uncrossed her legs. She wore an elegant black pinstriped trouser suit, and her auburn hair was done up in a French twist. 'Have you got any evidence to support that theory, Mrs Devine?' she demanded.

'Unfortunately not,' Carmel admitted sullenly. 'Only suspicions.'

'And who do you suspect fitted your husband up?'

Oh God! Carmel thought. I hope I'm doing the right thing. 'His business partner,' she said slowly. 'Anthony Maskey. I believe he murdered Gemma Geraghty and planted that paper and Sean's hairs at the crime scene. When he found out Paula Pepper was a witness he murdered her too. Paula's description of Gemma's murderer sounds like Sean – but she couldn't identify him from his photo and said he wasn't the murderer. It also sounds a lot like Anthony Maskey.' Carmel stared at them. 'What if he's the man she described? I've already told you this house is being watched,' she went on. 'I haven't seen anyone today, but I'm sure they're around. I think Anthony Maskey's behind it. And that night Rosa and I were threatened – he was behind that too. He stole Sean's keys, that's how he got in here. It was him who held that gun against me.' She trembled at the memory of it.

Neil stopped smirking. 'Neither of you saw Maskey. How can you possibly know he was one of those men? That it was him who threatened you?'

'His smell . . . his aftershave. When I saw him yesterday

I smelled it again. It *was* him!' Olivia looked at Neil and rolled her eyes.

'Okay, I know that's not enough. But I think Sean is still alive.' Carmel wished desperately that they would take her seriously. 'And that Anthony wants to kill him. But I don't know why. Maybe Sean found out something about him.'

Olivia looked startled again. Then she frowned. 'Such as?'

'I don't know. Anthony implied Sean was involved in something criminal,' Carmel said. 'I think he's lying. I think he's the criminal, not Sean.'

'Well, you would, wouldn't you?' Neil said rudely.

'I've only got Anthony's word for what happened the night Sean disappeared.' Carmel looked at Olivia. 'Don't you think you should investigate him?'

'We've already questioned Anthony Maskey,' Olivia said stiffly. 'There's no reason to investigate him further.'

'He said Sean isn't coming back, and that he wanted me to sell his share of the business to him. He said Sean had been having an affair. Okay, I know you'll think I don't want to believe that. But you could at least ask him why he wasted your time by withholding what would be vital information. He says he wanted to protect me. That's crap. Anthony Maskey's the only one who stands to benefit from Sean's disappearance,' Carmel said tensely. 'Or so he imagines.'

'You can't prove he murdered Gemma Geraghty. And there's no motive.'

'The motive was to set Sean up.'

'I doubt that. And even if Anthony Maskey's guilty, how do you suppose he found out there was a witness?' Neil asked, his expression grim.

'That's something else that scares the hell out of me,' Carmel replied. 'I imagine only a few police officers knew about her – until she was murdered. Is that correct?' Neil nodded. 'Well, one of them could have tipped him off.'

'Do you realise what you're saying here, Mrs Devine?'

Neil's voice was icy. He looked at Olivia, who did not meet his gaze. 'That's a very serious allegation.'

'I'm aware of that. I wasn't sure whether or not to tell you my suspicions. If Anthony Maskey finds out I think he's a double murderer, I could be in terrible danger.'

'Excuse me.' Olivia Crane's face turned scarlet as she started to cough and wheeze. She quickly felt in both her jacket pockets and pulled out an inhaler. The coughing grew worse and she leaned forward, her shoulders hunched. Neil took an uncertain step forward and glanced helplessly at Carmel.

'She's an asthmatic,' he said unnecessarily.

'I'd never have guessed if you hadn't told me.' Carmel went to Olivia and laid one hand on her shoulder. 'Sit back,' she said. 'Try to relax and focus your breathing so that it slows down. I'll get you a glass of water.' She patted her shoulder. 'Be all right. You'll feel better in a minute.'

Olivia nodded. 'Thanks,' she gasped, her eyes streaming. She felt comforted by Carmel's care and obvious concern, despite the way she and Neil had treated her. Sean Devine's wife was a nice woman. The little girl was sweet too, a real cutie. Olivia had always wanted a daughter. Guilt suddenly filled her soul. What must Carmel and her child be going through? Hounded by press, the police, and now that stupid old sod Les Higginbottom. But there was nothing she could do to help. Everything Carmel said confirmed her own suspicions about Anthony Maskey. Come on! Olivia thought, coughing into her handkerchief. Life's a bitch and then you die, remember? Don't go all soppy just because someone's nice to you. How sad is *that*?

In the kitchen Carmel poured Olivia a glass of mineral water and quickly made her a small cup of tea, thinking she might like that as well. She didn't bother about herself or DI Crane's colleague. She put the tea and water on a tray, and was about to go back to the sitting room when the phone rang.

'Hi, Carmel. It's Anthony. How are you?'

169

'Not too bad.' Oh God! she thought, closing her eyes. She pressed the button to tape the call; she had a feeling it might be important. 'Someone smashed my front room windows last night,' she said, remembering she had to be friendly and not arouse his suspicions. 'The husband of that murdered singer. He'd been reading a lot of rubbish about Sean in the papers.'

'What did you do?' Anthony asked. He sounded bored, like he felt he had to ask. Of course he wanted to get to the important stuff.

'I called the police and they arrested him.' She gripped the phone. 'I'm going to press criminal damage charges, although no doubt people will think I'm an evil bitch persecuting a bereaved husband. That's what the police think,' she said. 'They're here now, trying to persuade me to change my mind.'

'Well, pressing charges could mean a lot of hassle – for you. No news about Sean?'

'Nothing. Oh, and I have to keep Lisa off school for now. She hit a girl who said Sean was a murderer and would get the death penalty if he lived in the States.'

She hadn't meant that to sound remotely funny but Anthony laughed, an unpleasant laugh. His reactions are all wrong, she thought. How come I didn't spot that before? Now it seems so obvious. 'Shall I call back later if the police are there?' he asked.

'That's okay. I can't talk for long though. What did you want?' Of course she knew.

'Have you thought about the business yet? Decided to sell?'

'No. It's only a day or so since we talked.' Carmel controlled a sudden violent urge to scream at Anthony, shout at him to fuck off because he was evil, a murderer, and she hated him for destroying her life and Sean's, all the while pretending to be their friend. No, she thought. He will not destroy my life. Or Lisa's. I'll find Sean and we'll be together again.

'But it's an easy decision.' Anthony's voice was tense, as if he was having a hard time controlling his anger. 'And I told you, it's what Sean wanted.'

'Even if I agreed to sell, I'm not sure I'd have the authority. I was never involved with the business. I'm not a partner or anything. I've got no say.'

'But suppose you'd got divorced? Or Sean died? I mean—' He stopped. 'What I mean is, you must have made plans in case anything happened to him?'

'I'm afraid there are no contingency plans in the event of Sean's disappearance.' Carmel hoped that didn't sound sarcastic. But what did the bastard expect her to do, reveal the terms of Sean's will? 'I'd prefer to leave things for now,' she said firmly. 'It's way too soon to decide anything. I'm sure you appreciate that.' Like hell.

Anthony was silent, and she imagined him seething with rage. He expected her to believe everything he said, do what he wanted. She wasn't falling into line, and he couldn't handle that. Tough!

'Okay. Fine. But I don't know how much longer I can guarantee you an income from the business.' Anthony's voice was calm again, very controlled. 'Sean's gone, he's stopped earning. Profits are down already. The longer you hold out, the more the value of his share diminishes.'

So it was barely veiled threats now. 'I can't talk any more,' Carmel said, not trusting herself to stay calm. 'The police are waiting. Then I have to take Lisa out for some fresh air. Stock up at the supermarket. We've been home all day.'

'Right. I'll call again soon,' Anthony said sullenly. That sounded like another threat. He hung up without saying goodbye or exhorting her to take care of herself.

Carmel took a deep breath as she replaced the receiver. She was sweating slightly. Anthony's threat made her think about money. She was trying so hard to cope with the shock and trauma of Sean's disappearance and be there for Lisa, that she had not even considered how she was going to

171

manage financially. If Anthony refused to pay Sean's salary and she continued to lose clients hand over fist, she was in big trouble. It was all happening so quickly.

'Oh, Sean!' she whispered, brushing away a tear. 'For God's sake, come home! Or let me find you.' She picked up the tray and went back to the sitting room. Olivia had stopped coughing, but she was still flushed and wheezing.

'Sorry to keep you.' Carmel put the tray on the coffee table, 'Had to answer the phone. Thought you might like some tea,' she said, handling Olivia the cup.

'Oh, that's great,' Olivia breathed. 'Thanks so much.'

'Mrs Devine.' Neil came forward and sat on the edge of the sofa. 'You're a psychologist. Have you ever noticed anything about Anthony Maskey's behaviour that makes you think he might be capable of murder?'

Carmel glanced at him hopefully. Did this mean they were taking her seriously at last? 'You mean narcissistic or antisocial tendencies ... psychoses of any kind?' He nodded. 'I can't say I have,' she admitted. 'But then I was never looking. Anthony's something of a loner, and he never talks about his past. His parents are dead, his father years ago, his mother recently. He never mentions them. He has a lot of girlfriends, but never seems to find anyone special. He's desperate for people to like him, and hates it if they don't. Sometimes I thought he overdid the charm. And my daughter's never taken to him. Not that any of that's necessarily significant, of course. But when I speak to him now, his reactions seem all wrong.' She nodded towards the door. 'That was him on the phone.'

'What did he want?' Neil asked.

'To know if I'm ready to sell off Sean's share of the business. If I hold out, as he puts it, he says the value of Sean's share will diminish, and that he can't guarantee Sean's salary. He's threatening me.'

Neil pulled his hands out of his pockets and raised his eyebrows. He glanced at Olivia, but she seemed to be in a daze. The teacup trembled in her hand.

172

'I taped the call,' Carmel said to Neil. 'Just in case you're interested. What I really hate is ...' She paused. 'Anthony talks about Sean in the past tense. As if he was dead. Or as if he wants him dead.'

Olivia gasped. Carmel noticed that she had turned very pale.

'Fucking *bitch*!' Anthony jumped up and hurled his mug of coffee at the wall where it smashed, splashing dark brown liquid over the white plaster and staining one corner of the calendar with its picture of November's car, a 1964 blue Jaguar XKE. Tiger, who had been peacefully raking his claws up and down the desk leg, gave an indignant miaow and scuttled next door to Sean's empty office.

'Hey, mate! What the bloody hell's all that about?' The customer who had been downstairs looking over some of the cars strolled in, a thin, spotty young man with a shaved head, gold earring and leather coat.

'Oh ... I just talked to my girlfriend.' Anthony turned to him, trying to pull his rage-contorted features into some semblance of a smile. 'She's giving me the runaround.'

'Tart trouble? You wanna get shut of it, mate, that's what I'd do. Listen.' The boy lit a cigarette and scratched his stubbly, spotty chin. 'Nothing personal, like, but how do I know you're not flogging any of them grey import cars?'

'Because all my cars are UK-specified,' Anthony said tightly. He didn't have time for this. 'With a corrosion warranty. They don't have retracting wing mirrors, a narrow radio band, or Japanese stickers clapped all over them. I always confirm specifications and delivery dates. If you think I might shaft you, go somewhere else,' he snapped. 'I don't operate like that. It's more than my reputation's worth.'

Why wouldn't Carmel Devine do what he wanted? He had told her her bloody husband wasn't coming back, but she stubbornly refused to collapse into a gibbering, submissive wreck. Anthony was sickened by the fact that he had to stay polite and friendly with the bitch in case she remembered something important, something that might lead him to Sean. Carmel was devastated, still in shock. But not shocked enough.

He was under so much pressure and yet he had to keep a grip on things. At times he felt he was losing it. He was worried about Olivia Crane too, she had sounded nervous and scared on the phone last night, mumbling pathetic excuses about work overload and her mobile being down. It was what Olivia didn't say that bothered him; she hadn't mentioned Paula Pepper's murder, not even briefly. She seemed desperate to avoid the subject.

Anthony wondered if Olivia had been doing rather more thinking than was good for her. She couldn't do anything more than think, of course, not without landing herself in a pile of excrement. But she was afraid. And frightened people were dangerous, unpredictable. Olivia Crane might become a risk, a liability, and he didn't need that. Especially not now. Anthony became aware that the spotty, earringed boy was staring at him. Cigarette smoke floated towards him and drifted up his nostrils.

'What was that?' Sometimes he seemed to lose track, could not remember what had happened or the things he had done. 'What did you say?' he asked anxiously.

'I said, take it easy, mate.' The boy looked at him, puzzled. 'You okay? Don't let that bloody tart get to you, all right? She's not worth it – none of them are.'

'What tart?'

'Christ!' The boy grinned and puffed out smoke, shaking his head. 'Look, I'll be back tomorrow, all right? Got a couple of other places to check out. See you, mate.' He went down the stone steps and the warehouse door slammed behind him. A car engine started up outside.

Rain was falling again, and the River Mersey was calm. The clock on the wall showed six-twenty, two minutes slower than his watch. Anthony picked up his mobile and dialled.

174

'What's going on there now?'

'Couple of coppers were here earlier. After that she went out with the kid. The park and then Tesco's. They're back home now. The sister went out, probably to work. And some bloke's just gone round there.'

Anthony frowned. 'What bloke?'

'Dark hair, curly. Looks fit. Dressed in overalls.'

'Oh, yeah. I know him.' Anthony remembered Daniel from the night of the party. He smiled. The wolves were already gathering, sniffing and circling the lone, vulnerable prey. 'Right,' he said. 'Keep me posted.' He hung up. Tiger strolled in, leapt gracefully up on the desk and walked towards him, purring like a little motor.

'Talking to me again, are you?' Anthony tickled the cat under the chin and it lifted its head and arched its back as it purred with pleasure, tawny eyes half closed. 'I suppose you want dinner?'

He got up and the cat miaowed and followed him into Sean's office. Anthony had moved its bowl and litter tray in there, as well as a fridge and two boxes of Tiger's favourite cat food. Because Sean would not be back. He opened a can of tuna chunks, took a carton of full cream milk and a packet of smoked salmon from the fridge. Tiger chirruped with excitement and pushed hard against his legs, going crazy at the delicious fishy smell.

'I spoil you, don't I? But you'll still be hungry for mice tonight,' Anthony murmured, watching as the cat attacked its food. Mice and rats made him think of Joseph's dark, silent labyrinth, where he had not been for days now. He needed that world again. Soon, Alice Miles's gold awaited. But so did Simona. At home, in his bed. Naked. Anthony knew he should drive her back to the house and make her earn him more money servicing clients in the club. But he wanted her with him. Needed her.

And Olivia Crane had reluctantly accepted his invitation to dinner. They had a lot to talk about.

It was going to be a very special evening.

Chapter Fifteen

'I wondered about that Anthony the night of your party,' Daniel frowned. 'Of course it's easy with hindsight, but I did think there was something weird about his behaviour. It was like he was acting a role, getting a buzz out of fooling us all.' He shrugged. 'But you knew him—'

'*Thought* I did,' Carmel sighed.

'And when you said he didn't stand to benefit from Sean's disappearance, I stopped thinking about the guy.'

'The world's greatest psychologist, that's me! I'm not even fit to be Carmel the Crystal-Crazy Counsellor.'

'Now don't start beating yourself up again,' Daniel warned. 'There's more than enough bastards around who'll do that for you.'

Carmel sat back on the sofa, folded her arms and crossed her slim legs. Daniel lounged in an armchair by the fire, wearing his dark blue overalls, a mug of coffee in one hand. 'I can't prove anything,' she fretted. 'I might have got it all wrong. Maybe I shouldn't have told the police my suspicions. That's all they are.'

'No, I think you were right to tell them. What happens now?'

'That's anybody's guess. The police had a look round the square, but didn't spot anyone watching the house. Although I know they're out there. And DS Davie said he'd talk to Anthony again.' She grimaced. '*Soon.*'

'You're doing all you can to help Sean.'

'Not enough.' She sighed again, and pushed back her hair. 'Oh God, I need to know what Anthony's up to! If I'm right. Why didn't I suspect him sooner?'

Daniel sat up. 'You had no reason to. Besides, people like that can be dead crafty. They're not described as cunning and manipulative for nothing. But he's only human, despite what he likes to think. He let his guard drop, tried to be too clever – and the minute he did, you saw through him. That name, *Mask*-ey,' Daniel said thoughtfully. 'Prophetic, isn't it? He was wearing a mask all the time.'

Carmel shivered in the warm sitting room. It was not quite dark, but she had already drawn the blinds. Feeling you were being watched took away the pleasure of looking out into the square and park. 'Thanks for getting that guy to put in new windows so quickly,' she said. 'I'm really grateful.'

'No problemo.' Daniel smiled and sipped more coffee.

'How are you getting on?' Carmel asked. 'I mean, without Ellie?'

'Oh . . . coping, you know. I miss her two boys as well,' he said. 'Andrew and Michael. They were great.' He sighed. 'Ellie and I weren't getting on, but it was still a shock when she upped and left. I thought we'd work things out. The teaching job in Edinburgh – she must have planned that months ago. I don't think she even told the boys until the last minute.' He grimaced. 'For security reasons. Anyway, I'll just have to get on with it. Where's Lisa, by the way?' he asked.

'In the back room, glued to kiddie TV. It's *Rotten Ralph* just now, I think. And Rosa's working until eleven.'

'Why don't I take you both out for a curry or pizza or something?' Daniel suggested. 'We could share a bottle of wine with it.'

'That's really sweet of you, Daniel, but—' Carmel hesitated. 'To be honest, I don't feel like dining out. In the circumstances.'

'Yeah. Of course.' Daniel smacked his forehead. 'How thick am I!'

'No! You mean well, and I'm grateful. It's not just that I don't feel like. I'd rather not go out any more than I have to,' she confessed. 'Since that stuff in the papers I'm frightened of Lisa and me being recognised and hassled, maybe even attacked. If we're seen with you in a restaurant, eating and drinking, looking as if we're having fun, some moron might choose to regard that as provocation. Sean's innocent and I've got nothing to be ashamed of. I shouldn't care what people think. But I'm afraid.'

'Sure,' Daniel said quietly. 'I understand. I'll get us a takeaway then, shall I? Or am I being a nuisance? Just tell me if you want me to leave.'

'I don't. And of course you're not a nuisance. A takeaway would be great. Let's ask Lisa what she'd like.' Carmel stood up. 'After that ... Daniel, I'd like your help with something,' she said slowly. 'I don't blame you if you say no. It could be dangerous.'

Daniel looked at her and saw the fear in her eyes. 'Anthony, right?'

She nodded. 'I want to go to the warehouse and search his office, look for some clue as to what he might be involved in. I also want to look round Sean's office. I don't know what I'll find – if anything.' She bit her lip. 'But I have to try.'

'And the problem is, how do you manage that without Ant's henchmen tailing you?'

'Exactly.' Carmel glanced at the partially open door. 'I'm taking Lisa to Mum and Dad's after tea,' she said, lowering her voice. 'She'll spend tonight and tomorrow with them. She loves it there and gets spoilt rotten. It'll be good for her to get away for a bit. Safer too. You could go and get us the takeaway. We'll eat, then after tea you leave. Walk back home, switch the lights on, make it look like you're in for the night. I'll drive off with Lisa, and they'll follow. Give me fifteen minutes. Then you drive to

Southport, park in that road behind my parents' house, and wait for me. I'll sneak out the back. You only live round the corner, so you always come here on foot,' she said. 'They won't recognise your car, they won't even be looking. We'll search the warehouse and you can drop me back at my parents afterwards. Then I drive home. It'll look like I've been at Mum and Dad's all evening.'

'A cunning plan,' Daniel grinned. 'But what if Anthony's at the warehouse? Or worse, walks in and catches us with our sticky fingers in his drawers? If you'll pardon the expression.'

'That's what I mean about dangerous. But no.' Carmel smiled slightly. 'As far as I'm aware, Anthony's not one for working long hours. Sean said he liked to go out on dates or just drive home to his mansion on the Wirral and play lord of the manor. Wouldn't mind a look round there either,' she said. 'But that *would* be pushing it.'

'How will you get into the warehouse?' Daniel asked. 'Break in?'

'No way! I've got Sean's spare keys. Anthony doesn't know they exist.'

Daniel frowned. 'Are you sure?'

'They never bothered to get spare sets, because each thought they could borrow the other's if necessary. You know how you don't get round to doing things. Then Sean finally had a spare set made about two months ago, one Saturday when we were shopping in town. He put them in his bedside drawer and forgot about them. I'm sure he didn't mention the keys to Anthony – they might not have been getting on any more by then – and I certainly didn't. I know how to de-activate and re-set the alarm,' she said. 'Sean showed me once. Fortunately, Anthony wasn't there at the time.'

'Fortunately.' Daniel grinned again and smoothed his tangled curls.

'Daniel, are you sure you want to do this?' Carmel asked anxiously. 'I don't think anything will go wrong, but

179

there's no guarantee. Maybe I shouldn't have asked you.'

'Listen to me, Carmel Devine!' Daniel got up, lightly rested his powerful arms on her shoulders and looked into her eyes. 'I love you,' he said. 'I love Lisa and I love Sean. Once he's safe home and the three of you are together again, he's not going to be well chuffed with his old mate if he finds out I let you walk alone into the lion's den. Is he?' He grinned. 'Especially when my name's Daniel.'

Carmel's eyes filled with tears. 'Thank you,' she whispered.

'No problem.' He hugged her and she breathed in his smell of sweat and oil. She didn't feel so alone now. And she felt better because she was doing something to actively help Sean. That did not take away the fear though.

'Right.' Daniel grinned down at her. 'Let's unglue Lisa from the telly and ask her if she wants curry or pizza.'

'Hm. Not bad for a sad, divorced old slapper! No, you're not *old*. Don't define yourself by the warped standards of the masculist power structure. You know, this talking to yourself is a really bad habit. Comes of being alone, I suppose. Sad, sad!'

Olivia surveyed herself in the bedroom mirror, twisting and turning as she pulled the black dress down over her full hips. Her long, auburn hair swung loose, and she wasn't wearing her specs. 'Oh God,' she sighed, taking another swig of vodka, 'I really don't want to have dinner with a fucking psycho!'

She couldn't back out though. Anthony would be suspicious; she felt he already was. Not a good idea to fuel his paranoia. A surge of nerves gave her a fluttery sensation in her stomach. She sipped more vodka and took a snort of her Ventolin inhaler. On an impulse, she took the Glöck out of her dressing table drawer, checked it and put it in her handbag.

Who was paranoid now? Olivia had never needed to use the gun, bought a year ago from one of her organised crime

contacts, a drug dealer who was an ex-contact as of yesterday. He wasn't too pleased at the sudden break-up of their
mutually beneficial association. But Olivia was terrified
now, losing her bottle along with her taste for the extra-
curricular activities that up to now had supplemented her
salary so nicely. It was no good any more. Because of
Anthony bloody Maskey.

There was nothing to be frightened of, she told herself
yet again. Anthony had no reason to hurt her. Who are you
kidding? Olivia thought. Since when did psychos need
reasons! He probably killed that scrubber for pure pleasure,
as well as the desire to fit up Sean Devine. She imagined
him putting the bullets in Gemma, strangling Paula Pepper.
Gasped and closed her eyes at the horror of it.

'Oh, Christ!' she whispered, gulping more vodka. She
had money, her house, her career. Most important of all,
Alex. Enough was enough. She had had a good run and it
was time to stop. Before good luck, pushed too far, turned
bad.

Olivia decided to sacrifice Carmel Devine to Anthony,
along with her missing husband. Once Anthony knew
Carmel had told the police she suspected him of murder, he
would go ballistic and forget about Olivia, enabling her to
withdraw and eventually end their association. She felt bad
about Carmel, she really did. And that sweet little girl,
what was her name? Lisa. In many parts of the world children her age were forced to give blow jobs to adult men.
Pose for photographs so that the perverts could jack off. As
well as all those girls Anthony trafficked and forced to
work as prostitutes. Olivia had seen it all during her time in
Vice. That was the reality. Not pimps' and tricks' lies about
easy money, flexible working hours, selling a service as
opposed to your body and soul, being smart enough not to
give it away.

Olivia profited from Anthony's buying and selling of
female bodies, from all the misery and exploitation. That
made her a pimp too. It sickened her if she thought about it.

So better not think about it. Let's face it, if she didn't stick up for herself and make her own luck, her own money, who would do it for her? Nobody.

She slipped on a pair of heavy, chunky platform shoes, took her bag and drank the rest of her vodka. She went downstairs, threw on her coat and took her keys, felt the comforting shape of the gun in her bag. She remembered the first time she had handled a gun during firearms training. For some strange reason, it had made her laugh uncontrollably. The instructor said laughter or tears were common reactions.

Olivia glanced at herself in the hall mirror. She looked pale and tired, despite the blusher and bright red lipstick. Frightened. The only person she wanted to see right now was her son, but of course Alex was thousands of miles away sowing wild oats and broadening horizons. She was alone, and she just had to get on with it.

'Life's a bitch and then you die,' she murmured.

'Stay down, just in case. Until we're away.' Daniel wore a black padded jacket zipped up to the chin and had covered his hair with a black woolly hat. He drove slowly down the narrow street crowded with parked cars, and turned left. A minute later they were driving along the dark Southport sea front, the road lit only by cats' eyes. 'Okay,' he said. 'Nobody about. It's a cold night. Most people'll be in the pub or at home watching telly.'

'Sounds good to me.' Carmel pulled herself into a sitting position and fastened her seat belt. 'This isn't your car.' She shook back her hair. 'Where did you find a small, white transit van at such short notice?'

'It belongs to one of the lads who works for me. I've borrowed it before, and he only lives two minutes away. I know it'd be safe to use my car, but this is even better. No one looks twice at a white van.' Daniel grinned. 'Unless it's to make sure they stay clear in case there's a psycho behind the wheel.' His smile faded. 'Sorry!'

'It's okay.' Carmel felt in the pockets of her leather coat. 'I've got the keys to the warehouse and to Sean's desk. I even remembered to bring a torch. I also wrote down the safe combination. Sean had it in his diary from last year. Disguised as the phone number of a fictitious company named San Fed.Con.'

'Very cloak-and-dagger.' Daniel checked the time on the dashboard clock. 'Are you sure we're not too early? It's only just gone eight-thirty.'

'I don't think so. We'll check outside the warehouse first. Oh God!' She shivered. 'I hate this. I'm a rotten coward, so bloody scared! Not the heroic type at all.'

'Good. Heroes are often dickheads with no imagination.' Daniel glanced at her, 'We'd better have a plan in case Maskey walks in on us.'

Carmel nodded. 'I'll just tell the truth – say I wanted to take a look around Sean's office. I mean, I am Sean's wife, I do have a right to be there. Anthony can't object, although he'll hate it. The problem is, what will he think then? He's not stupid. Oh God, I don't know!' She took a strand of hair and twisted it nervously. 'Let's just hope he's got a hot date tonight.'

Daniel grimaced. 'Let's hope.'

Back in Liverpool they cruised through the centre of town and headed for the river. They approached the dark warehouse on the quay, the van bumping over the cobble-stones. The river was calm, a full moon rising above the sluggish water. A few stars glittered. Over the water was Birkenhead, dock cranes outlined against the sky.

'That warehouse looks even more creepy at night,' Carmel whispered, as Daniel parked some distance away. He switched off the headlights, leaving the engine running. 'It's from the eighteenth century, you know. Originally used for storing cotton, tobacco and animal skins.' She paused. 'Maybe they even kept slaves there.'

'Wouldn't be amazed.' Daniel peered at the building. 'Seems dark and deserted enough,' he remarked. 'No cars.

183

Wait here, let me take a look.' He got out of the van, leaving the door partially open, and Carmel watched nervously as he walked towards the warehouse, her heart thudding. He was back after two minutes.

'Yep,' he said in a low voice. 'All clear.' He looked at her. 'Got everything?'

Carmel pulled out the keys and torch. 'Yes.'

'Right.' He squeezed her hand. 'Let's do it.'

Carmel smothered the panic that surged inside her as the warehouse door swung open and cold dankness hit her face. She ran to the alarm and de-activated it within the required thirty seconds. She switched on the torch and they headed up the stone staircase to the offices. They went into Sean's office first. Tiger, curled up on the desk, raised his head and miaowed indignantly at them.

'Look,' Carmel whispered, flashing the torch beam over the litter tray and boxes of cat food. 'He's using Sean's office as the cat's bedroom!' She pulled at the desk drawers. 'Unlocked. I suppose Anthony's searched it. Probably before the police did.'

'What the fuck are you doing?' Daniel gasped as she suddenly left the desk, ran to the door and snapped on the lights. She looked at him calmly.

'If we're interrupted by Anthony, I don't want him to catch us flashing a torch around in the dark. It'll look even more dodgy then. Stupid of me, I didn't think.' Carmel put the torch in her coat pocket and went back to Sean's desk. 'Nothing in here,' she muttered, riffling through papers and old copies of *What Car?* magazine and *Jaguar World*. There was a Mars Bar and two packs of smoky bacon crisps: Sean's idea of lunch. She smiled tenderly. Then pain stabbed at her.

'If there was anything, Anthony or the police probably took it. Come on,' Daniel urged as Carmel lingered, a disconsolate expression on her face, 'let's hurry this up. With all these lights on, I feel like I'm wearing a bloody great sign saying "shoot me".'

They went next door to Anthony's office and saw the

coffee stain and trail of drips on the wall and carpet, the smashed pieces of china. The large ficus was dumped in one corner; the plant was bent and twisted, its pointy leaves shrivelled.

'Looks like he poisoned that thing with weedkiller,' Daniel murmured. 'Creepy. And to just leave it there like that. D'you want to look on his computer?' he asked.

'No time. Besides, Sean told me Anthony isn't really an ICT-person. He hardly uses the thing. I gave him that plant.' Carmel shivered. 'Maybe he'd like to poison me too. I hope his desk isn't locked,' she said. 'I don't want to have to break it open.'

'Look. No worries.' Daniel slid out the top drawer. 'He either forgot or doesn't think he needs to lock it. Maybe he doesn't. Any good stuff will be in the safe.'

'Let's hope so. Looks like just paperwork in here.' They searched the desk and discovered a large buff envelope. 'It's the deeds to a house.' Carmel quickly leafed through the papers inside. 'Highgate Street, Edge Hill. I think that's his mother's place. She died recently. Anthony was brought up there.' She glanced at Daniel questioningly. 'Edge Hill . . . isn't that where all those warrens of old tunnels are?'

'Yeah. Built in the early nineteenth century by Joseph Williamson, the Mad Mole. He lived in Mason Street. Highgate Street's just round the corner. Or parallel.'

'This is weird,' Carmel remarked. 'Here's a letter from the estate agent confirming that the property has been taken off the market in accordance with Mr Maskey's instructions. Why would Anthony do that? I can't imagine he'd want to live there. These must be the keys,' she said, pulling them out. 'That's a lot for one little old terraced house, wouldn't you say?'

'I certainly would.' Daniel took the bunch. 'Let's borrow them, shall we? Could be a spare set. He probably doesn't look in this envelope very often.'

'Okay, but what if they're not and he does?'

'He'll think he's mislaid them. He won't connect their

loss with you, will he? He has you watched, followed everywhere. There's no way you could have nicked them.'

'Right. Anyway,' Carmel said, her blue eyes fierce, 'fuck him!'

'That's what I admire, a lady of spirit.' Daniel glanced around the room. 'Where's the safe? I don't see one.'

'It's in the wall behind that filing cabinet.' They moved the heavy filing cabinet and Carmel took out the safe combination number, scribbled on a pink post-it note. 'I feel like a bank robber,' she said nervously.

Daniel grinned. 'Good, innit? Wow!' he breathed, as the safe door swung open a minute later. 'Wouldn't mind some of *that*.'

'Where the hell did he get all this cash?' Carmel stared at the neat stacks of notes. 'Can't be just from car sales. Most buyers pay by cheque.' She took out a few bundles of notes. 'God knows how much there is! No time to count it. I shouldn't think he'll keep it here long. Maybe just overnight. I bet he's got another safe in his house,' she said, shoving back the money she'd taken out. 'I'd love to get a look in there. Hang on. What . . .?' She grabbed a small square package partially hidden by the bundles of cash. It was wrapped in dark blue paper and tied with thin gold ribbon. A tiny card was attached, sealed inside an envelope.

'Looks like a present,' Daniel murmured. 'And it's got your name on it.'

Carmel hesitated, then tore open the envelope. 'To Carmel,' she read, her voice trembling. 'Happy Birthday. I love you. Sean.' She brushed away sudden tears. 'Sean must have meant to surprise me with this on the night of the party. He'd already given me a dress that morning. This must be extra. Something really special.'

'And why not?' Daniel hugged her. 'The guy loves you. You and only you. There's no way he was screwing around or planning to run off with some tart.'

'I know that. Oh, Sean!' She sniffed and swallowed, fighting back more tears.

'Put it in your pocket,' Daniel said. 'It's yours. I bet Sean had this in his desk and Anthony hid it in here. You can open your present when you get home.'

'No!' Carmel clutched the little package. 'I won't open it until Sean's home.'

'Nice one.' Daniel kissed her on the cheek. 'Now let's check this out.' He reached into the safe, pulled out a large, bulky envelope and shook the contents out on to Anthony's desk.

'What's he doing with four foreign passports?' Carmel slipped Sean's birthday gift into her pocket. 'Young girls,' she whispered, flicking through the documents. 'Eastern European.' They studied the photographs. The girls all had long, dark hair. Dark eyes, full of hope and confident anticipation. The glimmer of smiles.

'Look at the visas and these other papers. They've had AIDS tests. You don't need an AIDS test to enter the UK, certainly not as a tourist. And if these girls are supposed to be tourists,' Daniel said grimly, 'why the hell has our Ant got their passports locked in his safe?' He stared at Carmel, his brown eyes shocked and frightened. 'This means the bastard could be a . . . oh, Christ! What do you think those girls are doing now?'

'Well, I don't imagine they're backpacking.' Carmel gripped the passports as a shudder of horror and revulsion ran through her. 'This is even worse than I expected,' she whispered. 'I thought it might be drugs. Or weapons. But I was wrong. Anthony deals in human beings!'

She felt a surge of hatred for him. He was ruthless, had no respect or compassion. He thought these girls – and how many others – were consumer items to be traded like any other commodity. Deprived of freedom, their lives destroyed. So that he could make a profit. Feed his sad, sick ego. Had Sean found out about Anthony's trade in human beings? Was this why he had disappeared?

'Pimping,' she said, her voice weighted with pure contempt. 'The oldest profession.'

Chapter Sixteen

'I know what you're too frightened to ask me, Olivia.' Anthony sipped his cognac and stretched out on one of the drawing room sofas. He was annoyed by her stricken silence and evasive replies, which had continued throughout a less than cosy dinner. 'Do I know something about the murder of that nightclub singer and, ergo, Gemma the scrubber? I don't. I swear on my mother's life. Or her grave. Whatever.'

'No!' Olivia stared at him, shocked. 'That is ... well, okay. I'll admit I've been sick with worry. It's one hell of a coincidence that Paula Pepper was murdered less than twenty-four hours after I'd told you about her.'

'Life's crammed with coincidence. Why didn't you share your concerns with me?' Anthony paused, studying Olivia's frightened face in the firelight, her shaking hand as she lifted her glass of cognac and took a tiny sip. She had definitely lost her cool. 'What's wrong?' He smiled. 'D'you think I murdered those women? Is that why you've been avoiding me?'

'*No!*' She looked agonised. 'Of course not. And I haven't been avoiding you, I just needed to think. I wondered if maybe someone could have overheard our conversation in that club – or if you'd repeated any of it, for whatever reason.'

'Now you're being really stupid,' he said coldly.

'Don't get angry,' she begged. 'I told you, I've been worried sick. All sorts of things were going through my mind.' She bit her lip and looked at him nervously. 'Anthony ... *did* you have anything to do with those two murders? It doesn't matter. I just need to know. It's important for us to be honest with each other. You can see that, can't you?'

'You haven't been very honest with me lately, Olivia.'

Did she seriously expect him to confess murder – or involvement in murder – to a police officer, even a corrupt cop who took his money? Anthony toyed again with his new and alarming idea. Suppose Olivia had been rumbled by her colleagues or the anti-corruption squad, and offered a deal? She wouldn't hesitate to sacrifice him to try and save herself. His worry about that possibility was growing by the minute.

He thought. There were no listening devices in the house; he had the place regularly checked by a security expert. He never discussed anything important on the phone. But what if Olivia was all wired up beneath that sexy little black number that would look so much better on Simona? Olivia could be careless at times, and she was bound to get caught sooner or later. Anthony knew he wasn't the sum of her extra-curricular activities. He frowned and stared into the flames.

'Any news of my missing business partner?' he asked.

'No,' she answered, too quickly.

She was holding something back. Something important. Yes, Anthony thought. Definitely a liability. All good things come to a bad end.

'I thought *you* might have some news about Sean Devine,' Olivia said suddenly. It was no use, Anthony had rumbled her. Her best chance now was to be frank and try to get as much as possible out of him. Information was power. 'I mean, you want him more than we do. You want to kill him. Don't you? That's if he's not dead already.'

'*What?*' Anthony felt a flash of shock. 'How did you get

that crazy idea into your red little head? Why the hell would I want to kill Sean Devine?'

'He found out something he wasn't supposed to know. You killed Gemma Geraghty and fitted him up so that if he's alive and you don't get him, we will. He's completely discredited – who'll believe anything a murderous psycho says? We're helping you look for Sean – I bet that appeals to your sense of humour. You killed Paula Pepper when you found out she was a witness, thanks to me and my big mouth.' Olivia put down her glass. 'Look, Anthony, none of this matters. If Sean Devine isn't dead and he knows about you, then of course you've got to deal with him. That's in my interests too. For Christ's sake, I'm the last person who'd shop you, aren't I?' She looked at him pleadingly. 'But you have to be straight with me.'

'Fine.' Anthony gripped his cognac glass. Olivia could ruin everything. 'There's just one problem with your brilliant theory, Inspector. It's wrong. I didn't murder those women,' he lied, 'and I don't want to kill Sean Devine if he's still alive. He's the guilty party, not me. I haven't a clue how he got to Paula Pepper.' He smiled. 'For all I know, you could have tipped him off.'

'Now *you're* being really stupid,' she said hotly.

'Am I? You're one busy lady, Olivia. Don't try to tell me I'm the only great white shark in your blue, blue ocean.'

Anthony's mind raced. Penalties for trafficking in women were not heavy and the offence was hard to prove, especially with intimidated girls unwilling to give evidence – that's if they weren't deported as illegal aliens before they could provide it. So it was best for the police to try to do him for the murders of Gemma and Paula. Was the bitch wearing a wire? Trying to get him to confess, throwing him to the wolves, betraying him so that she could secure herself a better deal? Stay cool, Anthony told himself, fighting his anger. He shifted on the sofa, sweating with nerves, the cognac and the heat from the glowing fire.

190

There was only one way to find out.

'Look, why don't we forget Sean Devine and those stiffed ladies? They're all boring the hell out of me. You're looking very sexy tonight,' he said, forcing himself to smile again when he really wanted to snarl and smash his glass in her face.

'Oh, for ...!' Olivia rolled her eyes impatiently. She was not sure which was worse, the stubborn, infuriating denials that insulted her intelligence, or a full and frank admission to double – maybe triple – murder. Either way, Anthony was playing cat and mouse with her. She felt vulnerable, at a disadvantage. It was impossible to guess what the elusive bastard was thinking.

She glanced around the firelit drawing room, at the panelled walls and grotesque, heavy Victorian furniture that was designed to last, oppress people for centuries to come. Olivia loathed anything Victorian. Oil paintings of stags, gloomy windswept grouse moors and hunting scenes laden with bird and animal corpses hung on the walls, each one illuminated by a tacky little light. Candles flickered on the tall mantelpiece. This house and its grounds were a mini Victorian theme park, a cliché that made her cringe. And there was Anthony in his silly evening clothes, sipping cognac and staring into the fire, playing the gentleman. The perfect Victorian gentleman, who bought and sold women, exploited them as chattel.

What a wanker! Olivia thought. He's an idiot, a joke. Not a top shag either. During their affair – oh, God – she had blamed his lack of enthusiasm on her heavy thighs, smallish breasts and stretch marks. She had dreamed up every trick in the book to try to turn him on, all of which failed. Anthony only enjoyed being rough and hurting her. That made sense now of course; sexual dysfunction went with the profile. Shame in a man with Anthony's looks. It was like ripping open a fabulous, expensive box of top quality Belgian chocolates only to find a dog turd inside.

Her handbag with the gun in it lay on the floor, six

inches from her left foot. Olivia picked up her glass of cognac again and took another sip. Time to sacrifice Carmel Devine. She didn't like to do that, but she had to protect herself. She was afraid of Anthony's reaction nevertheless.

'I've got something to tell you.' Her heart thudded unpleasantly. She hesitated. 'You're not going to like it.'

'There's a lot of things I don't like.' Anthony looked at her. 'Go on.'

'There's a problem. Namely, Carmel Devine. She says you murdered Gemma Geraghty and Paula Pepper. That you're responsible for her husband's disappearance. She thinks you want to murder him – if you haven't already.'

'So that's where you got your brilliant theory,' he said quietly. 'From *her*.'

'I need to know the truth, Anthony.'

The silence in the room was broken only by the crackling of the log fire. There was a hiss as several sparks exploded and soared up the chimney. Anthony got up, strolled to the windows and looked out over the moonlit lawn and dark mass of trees and bushes beyond. He struggled for self-control, wrestling with the chaotic emotions that surged inside him. The bitch! he thought. The fucking, betraying bitch. After all I've done for her.

'Who did she tell all this bullshit to?' he asked.

'Me and my sergeant,' Olivia replied nervously. 'Of course I couldn't stop him telling the other CID officers what she'd said. They were all talking about it.'

'I see. And what's the general consensus?' Anthony walked back and stood on the hearthrug. Olivia noticed that his hands were clenched.

'Well, you'll be questioned again and you'll probably have to make a new, more detailed statement. I'm sorry, but there's nothing I can do to get you out of that.'

'Not much use, are you, Olivia?'

Her face burned in the firelight. 'I said I'm sorry, okay?' She didn't like the look in Anthony's eyes. 'I did my best.'

'Your best isn't good enough.'

'The general consensus is that so far there's no evidence to back up Carmel's story.' Olivia cleared her throat. 'But on the other hand, they're not totally dismissing it. They can't connect Sean with the Paula Pepper murder. Of course if anything happened to Carmel now,' she said awkwardly, 'that wouldn't look good.' She could appease her conscience a bit by trying to warn Anthony off, persuade him to leave Carmel alone. For a while at least.

'Wouldn't look good for *me*, you mean? I'd get the blame?'

Olivia jumped in shock as Anthony's cognac glass shattered on the hearth and blue flames hissed and flared. Broken glass sparkled in the firelight.

'I trusted that bitch!' he shouted. 'I thought she trusted me, looked on me as her friend. I was her bloody husband's friend too.' He swung round and glared at Olivia. 'I helped that cheating, lying cow! I supported her. And this is the thanks I get!'

He really believes that, Olivia thought. He's mad! 'You've aroused her suspicions by leaning on her to sell you her husband's share of the business. That was a mistake, Anthony. You should have waited, it's only two weeks since the guy disappeared. And trying to tell her he ran off with some girl – you laid it on a bit too thick. Hey, take it easy,' Olivia pleaded. She was getting more and more frightened.

'Don't tell me to take it easy!' he roared. 'I did the bitch a favour.' Anthony turned on her, breathing hard. 'Why didn't you help me? You could have—' He stopped, remembering the scary possibility that Olivia might have wires taped to her tits beneath the black dress. 'You could have told them she's a mad bitch talking crap!'

'For God's sake! My colleagues have got minds of their own, haven't they? I can't just say, hey, this is crap, back off guys and expect them to obey.' I have to get out of here, Olivia thought. Anthony was wild with rage, out of

193

control. 'We can't control everything and everybody, can we?' she said, trying to be the quiet voice of desperately needed sweet reason. 'Life just isn't like that.'

She shifted on the sofa and her left foot edged closer to her handbag. Anthony was silent, breathing hard, his furious eyes darting everywhere like a trapped animal. Olivia waited, hoping desperately that he would calm down. She tried to think of the most tactful way to get the hell out. She never wanted to see this man again.

'Take your clothes off,' Anthony said suddenly. 'I want to fuck you.'

'Are you crazy?' Carmel gasped, as Daniel shovelled the passports and bundles of notes into a black plastic bin liner. 'We can't take this stuff!'

'Why not?' He grabbed another handful of cash from the safe. 'It's evidence.'

'Yes, but if we take it we can't prove we found it here. Or that the money is profits Anthony made from trafficking women. I need those girls themselves, not just their passports. There's nothing here to prove he murdered Gemma or Paula either. If I take this to the police it'll be obvious I've got keys to the warehouse and know the safe combination. They might think I planted it myself, to put Anthony in the frame and get Sean off the hook. It won't help Sean – it'll make things even worse for him.'

'So what now?' Daniel paused, his forehead damp with sweat. 'Just leave it?'

'We've got no choice. All I can do is try to persuade the police to search this office while Anthony's present. Make them do it before he gets rid of the stuff.'

'And how are you going to manage that?'

'Have another go at DS Davie. But I can't tell him I've been here and found this.'

'Okay.' Daniel sighed. 'Let's put it back. We'll check out his dear old mum's place.'

Highgate Street was quiet, televisions flickering behind

net curtains in the lighted sitting rooms of the small, terraced houses. Including Anthony's mother's house. Except that house had Venetian blinds instead of net curtains.

'Someone's living there,' Carmel said, as Daniel squeezed into a parking spot between a Mini and a silvery Cortina. 'That's why he took the place off the market. He's renting it out. No mystery there. Damn! We've nicked his keys for nothing. Let's nip back and I'll replace them before he realises they're missing.'

'Hold up.' Daniel switched off the van's engine and turned to her. 'Why would he bother to rent out this house?' His dark eyes were thoughtful. 'He's got his mansion, a thriving antique and classic car business, safes crammed with cash and foreign passports. If he's a modern day slave trader he must be making a fortune just from that. Trafficking women makes ballistic profits and there's a lot less risk than with drugs. People who do it hardly ever get nicked and even if they are . . .'

Carmel nodded, her expression grim. 'Deal drugs or pull off a gold bullion robbery and you go down for years, but sell a woman or child into sexual slavery and hey! no big deal. Talk about fucked-up values!' she exclaimed furiously.

'D'you think Anthony wants to keep this place because of his parents' memory? He grew up here.'

'I can't imagine him being all wobbly sentiment about his old childhood home and dear departed mum and dad.'

'Okay. Listen.' Daniel tapped her shoulder. 'There might not be anyone living here. What would you do if you wanted your empty house to look occupied?'

'Stick time-lapse switches in every room,' Carmel said slowly. She unclicked her seat belt. 'Let's ring the bell,' she suggested. 'Make some excuse if anyone answers. Then again . . .' She laughed nervously. 'What if it's the bogeyman? I don't see his flash Jag anywhere, but he does have other cars to choose from.'

'What's the phone number of his big posh house? I'll nip down the road to that call box and check if he's home. Safer than using my mobile.'

'Daniel, a hang-up call would freak a normal person, never mind someone like *him*.'

'So you'd rather take a chance on the bogeyman opening that door to us?'

'No! Okay,' Carmel sighed. 'But be careful.'

'You too. Stay out of sight and keep the doors locked.'

Carmel watched anxiously, huddled in the passenger seat as Daniel strode towards the call box, hands in his jacket pockets. She thought of Lisa, tucked up in bed at her grandparents' by now, Jackie reading her stories. Her father was out, at a golf club dinner. Children Lisa's age were sold into prostitution, Carmel thought. In Europe, Asia, all over the world. By people like Anthony Maskey.

How could anyone describe prostitution as a job like any other, a normal condition for any individual's life? They did not want to see the reality, face the fact that the vast majority of prostitutes in the world were forced into it by homelessness, poverty, hunger, war, race, discrimination and sexual abuse. In most cases, choice did not enter into the equation. Some people talked about the right to be a prostitute. How about the right *not* to be one?

Hatred of Anthony swept over her again. That bastard had been her friend, Sean's friend. Or so they had thought. He had shared food and confidences, gained their trust. How long had he been buying and selling women? Carmel jumped as Daniel opened the van door and slid in beside her.

'The lord of the manor's in residence,' he whispered. 'Let's go.'

They unlocked the front door and entered the house. The television in the sitting room was loud, blaring music, laughter and applause. They explored the downstairs rooms and the old-fashioned kitchen with its stone sink and wooden draining board.

'It's like a time warp,' Daniel exclaimed. 'No fridge or washing machine. Bloody hell, look!' He pointed. 'A mangle and a dolly tub.'

'What are they for?'

'You wash the clothes in the dolly tub and feed them through the mangle. See?' He turned the handle. 'My great-granny had them – lying in the yard after she got herself a washing machine. No pictures or photos on the walls,' he commented. 'No books, just a few Bibles. Look at all those squares and circles of crochet stuff draped everywhere.' He grimaced. 'I'd have ended up a psycho if I'd lived here.'

Carmel gave him a look. 'Not necessarily. I presume this is the cellar door.' She rattled the handle. 'Locked. My God!' she whispered, turning pale. 'Suppose he's got decomposing bodies down there?' She sniffed. 'I can't smell anything.'

'Let's check upstairs,' Daniel said nervously. 'We'll do the cellar last. Bloody hell.' He shivered, hugging himself. 'It's freezing in here.'

The upstairs consisted of two spartan bedrooms and a tiny spare room, all with yellowed walls and stripped beds with stained, lumpy mattresses. The dust was thick everywhere. Another two Bibles were in the master bedroom, lying on small round tables each side of the three-quarter bed. The low watt lightbulb made everything look filthy.

'Surprise, surprise!' Daniel fingered the dusty, red, green, yellow and blue crocheted circle that lay on the table under the thick Bibles.

'Don't touch that,' Carmel said urgently. 'You'll disturb the dust, he'll know someone's been here.'

Daniel quickly withdrew his hand. 'Right. The cellar.' He swallowed and took a deep breath. 'It may be freezing,' he said, 'but I'm sweating cobs now!'

They unlocked and unbolted the cellar door and looked fearfully at the flight of stone steps leading downwards. Daniel switched on the light, a more powerful bulb than any others in the house. He paused and glanced at Carmel.

'You okay?' he asked. 'You look a bit pale. Would you rather wait here?'

'On my own? You're joking! Come on, let's get this over with.'

'Can't see any decomposing bodies,' Daniel said as they went down the stairs and stood in the small, cold space. 'Old plumbing, that's all. Looks like those pipes were being replaced and the job got held up. What's he been doing over there, hacking a hole in the wall?'

'I think it's the entrance to a tunnel.' Carmel stared at the rectangular black gap in the wall. 'Looks like it was bricked up before.' She walked forward and peered inside. 'It's not very high. I'll be okay, but you'll have to stoop.'

'We'll need the torch after all. Look at these boots and overalls. They must be Anthony's. Maybe he discovered the tunnel when these pipes were taken out. Hey!' Daniel's eyes shone with excitement. 'The tunnel could be the reason he changed his mind about selling this place.'

'I'm sure it is.' Carmel looked puzzled. 'Why would a tunnel run from under his house? And I wonder where it leads?'

'No idea. There was probably an older house on the site before this one was built.

Carmel switched on the torch and shone it into the musty blackness. 'Looks creepy,' she remarked. 'Narrow and twisting. Very old brickwork. Hang on!' She turned back to Daniel. 'Joseph Williamson – the Mad Mole, the King of Edge Hill. You said Mason Street's just parallel to here. This could be one of the entrances to his labyrinth. No one knows how many miles of tunnels there are. Anthony's found his own private entrance to the Devil's Kingdom – right here in his mother's house!'

'Yeah, looks like it. But what does he want with—' Daniel stopped. 'What was that noise?' he asked, turning pale. He glanced over his shoulder up the cellar stairs, then back at Carmel. 'Did you hear . . .?'

'It's the front door. Oh, God!' She froze, gripping the torch. 'Someone's coming!'

They stared at one another in horror as the front door slammed and footsteps sounded in the hall.

'Anthony, you don't want me!' Olivia was trembling. 'Not that way, not any more. It was never exactly great, was it? For either of us. Besides, I thought we were discussing what to do about Carmel Devine.'

'Were we?' She was obviously desperate to get him confessing to something on tape. Well, he wasn't that thick. Anthony crossed to the phone and quickly dialled 1471, wondering who the hang-up caller was. That provided no clue. He wasn't in the book, could it have been some imbecile dialling the wrong number and not bothering to apologise? Or did somebody want to check he was home? If so, why? He crashed the receiver down and turned back to Olivia, his anger mounting.

'Forget Carmel Devine,' he said coldly. He would deal with that bitch when he was ready. 'What's wrong?' he asked, staring at Olivia's frightened face. 'You were all over me last time me met. Couldn't keep your hands off. What's changed all of a sudden?'

'Nothing. Honestly.' Olivia shrank at the thought of his hands touching her naked body. His murderous hands. 'Anthony, it's late,' she pleaded. 'You're upset and I'm exhausted. Let's call it a night, shall we?'

'D'you know who that was on the phone?'

'Of course not! How the hell would I?' Olivia reached down for her handbag and gave a cry of shock as Anthony moved swiftly forward and kicked it away, his foot catching her hand painfully.

'Take your clothes off, DI Crane,' he smiled. 'Let's have a nice game of hide-and-seek. You'll enjoy that.' If she was wearing a wire he had to let her go. For now. But she had nothing. All he had confessed to was his anger, his outrage at being betrayed. 'Come on. You know you want to.'

What was his game? Terrified, Olivia unzipped her dress, wriggled it down over her full hips and stepped out of it. She slowly removed her shoes, black tights and lacy knickers. Anthony sighed with relief as she unhooked her push-up gel bra and dropped it on top of the dress. No wire. He was safe. He grabbed her bag and rooted in it, found the gun.

'What's this?' He waved it at her. 'So you think you need to be armed when you come calling on me! That's interesting.'

Shit! Olivia thought. 'I've had that gun for ages. I carry it everywhere.'

'Yeah right. Along with your lipstick and anti-ageing cream. I thought you were wired,' Anthony laughed with relief. 'That you'd been rumbled and they'd offered you a deal if you could get me to confess all.'

'*What?* You're—!' No, Olivia thought. Bad idea to use the word 'crazy'. 'Well, as you see, I'm definitely not wired!' She tossed back her hair. 'There's nowhere else to conceal a microphone.'

'Isn't there? Maybe we should play a little game of gynaecologist and patient.'

'Oh, come off it!' She looked at him defiantly. 'Can I get dressed now?'

His cold eyes flicked over her breasts and round belly. 'Please do.'

'And may I have my gun back?'

'Not just yet.'

Olivia scrambled back into her clothes, not knowing whether to feel relieved or insulted. He didn't want to screw her, he only wanted to make sure his every word hadn't been taped. Talk about paranoid. She was really frightened now.

'Anthony, listen,' she begged. 'Nobody's on to me, I swear. Besides, I'd never grass you up. You've got nothing to worry about. We're in this together. Partners.'

'You're not my partner,' he said contemptuously. 'I used you. That was all.'

200

Olivia didn't care for his choice of the past tense. 'Okay,' she nodded. 'Fine. I'd like to say goodnight now, if that's all right with you.' She stopped and reached for her tights and shoes.

'Leave them,' Anthony ordered. He levelled the gun at her. 'Turn around.'

'Anthony, what are you . . .?'

'Do it!' he screamed, startling the hell out of her. She quickly obeyed. He picked up her tights and stuffed them in his pocket. 'Now, move,' he said, his voice quiet again. 'Out of here and across the hall. Go on.'

Olivia preceded him into the study. I bet he's never opened one of those, she thought, glancing at the gold-tooled, leather-bound volumes of encyclopaedias that lined the walls. What did he have in mind? Some sort of pervy punishment, spreadeagle her across the desk? She shuddered to think that once she would have found that exciting. Then disappointing. Whatever Anthony wanted, she had to endure it, she didn't dare refuse, not with the mood he was in. She could only hope he wouldn't be too rough.

A bottle of single malt stood on the desk. Olivia shivered again, stroking her cold arms. Her bare feet felt cold too. This evening was turning out to be even nastier than she'd anticipated. She wished to God she had kept quite about Carmel Devine. That had really freaked Anthony. Her plan to allay his suspicions and get him off her own case had backfired. She thought she was so bloody clever, always in control. She wasn't, never had been. She had spectacularly underestimated Anthony Maskey from the moment they had met at that dinner.

'Face the wall,' he ordered. 'Arms by your sides. Don't talk.'

Olivia heard the desk drawer open and slam shut. A second later a cold handcuff was clipped around her left wrist.

'No!' she gasped, panicking. 'No, don't!' She couldn't let him tie her hands. She tried to swing round and push him away, but it was too late. Anthony gripped her other wrist and fastened the cuffs.

'You don't listen.' His voice was soft in her ear. 'I told you not to talk.' He dragged her around the desk and flung her into the chair. Picked up the bottle of Dalwhinnie, uncorked it and stood over her, holding it to her lips.

'Drink!' he breathed, his eyes gleaming. 'Go on.'

'Why?' Olivia gasped. 'Anthony, please let me go!' Her heart thudded with terror. 'I told you, you don't need to worry. I'm your friend, I promise. I'm loyal to you.' She suddenly realised she was pleading for her life.

'Loyal? You don't know the meaning of the word. I said, *drink*!' he snarled. 'Or d'you want me to shove a tube down your throat?'

Olivia quickly took several big gulps of Dalwhinnie, coughing and choking as the strong liquid burned her throat. She stopped to breathe, her eyes streaming. Golden liquid dribbled down her chin and under the dress between her breasts. The whisky smell was very strong. Anthony forced her to swallow three-quarters of the bottle's contents before he replaced the cork.

'That'll do,' he said. 'Don't want you chucking it back up, do we? Most non-alcoholics would be by now. I've never told you this, but I hate the way you drink. Makes you even uglier.' He dumped the bottle on the desk, pulled the tights out of his pocket and gagged Olivia, trapping her hair as he wrapped them around her mouth and nose.

No! she thought, dizzy and disorientated. He can't do this. I can't breathe! Anthony pulled her to her feet and dragged her out of the study. Olivia stumbled as she felt the drink go straight to her legs. He began to drag her upstairs.

'Of course I killed that sad scrubber and the stupid old slag who thought she could sing,' he panted. 'And you and Carmel are right about Sean – I want him dead too. I shot him, but I've got a bad feeling he's still alive. He walked in on me when I was conducting some important business, overheard me confess to killing someone you don't know about. The bastard escaped with sixty grand of my money. I'll get him though, and then he'll die. Like you're going to now.'

Olivia struggled against Anthony's painful grip, her mind blank with terror. But the alcohol was doing its work; she was dizzy, her arms and legs weak. And without the heavy platform shoes she couldn't even try to kick him. It was hard enough to draw breath; she felt an asthma attack coming on.

'You're a liability, Olivia.' Anthony grabbed a handful of hair, forcing her head back. 'You know too much. You're not as smart as you think. You didn't see this coming, did you? Your cop mates would have got on to you sooner or later – they're thick, but not that thick. I wasn't going to hang around and wait for you to throw me to the wolves just so you could get a shorter stretch.'

He wrapped his arms around her waist and dragged her to the top of the stairs. 'It's time for you to die a tragic death,' he whispered in her ear. 'A natural death. Sorry it can't be quick. I'm sure you'd prefer a bullet. But it's not all bad news.' He sniggered. 'You'll have time to reflect on your sins and say a last prayer. If you remember any.'

They reached the top of the stairs and she sagged in his arms. He lifted her, carried her towards one of the horrible dark wood-panelled doors, unlocked it and pushed it open.

For a second Olivia thought drink, panic and lack of breath had made her hallucinate. It was snowing inside the room! She blinked, unable to believe her eyes. Then she realised the snowflakes were feathers. Tiny, white, curled feathers. Floating, drifting, swirling and spinning, landing softly on the smooth, polished floorboards and taking off again. The room was empty apart from the feathers, the white walls bare. Thousands of feathers. Millions. She started to shake her head and moan, tried to gather strength to beg him for mercy. But the tights around her nose and mouth gagged her words. She felt the beginnings of a terrible asthma attack . . .

'Thanks for telling me about your allergy.' Anthony carried her into the room and laid her on the floor. Olivia's face and chest were flushed dark crimson, and she sweated as she heaved for breath. She lay there wriggling and staring up at him, her eyes frantic. 'Handcuffs not too tight?' He rolled her over and checked them. 'No. Good. Don't want them leaving imprints. Let's just secure your ankles.' He stooped and pulled off his tie. 'Right,' he said a few seconds later. 'I'll leave you to it.'

He stood up. Red blotches and weals were appearing on Olivia's face, neck and arms. She rolled over on to her back, with difficulty. Her body was racked with smothered coughs, her chest heaving and she wheezed and gulped frantically for air. She watched him walk to the door, stop and look back.

'Can't take off the gag, I'm afraid.' He smiled. 'Don't want any of those nasty little feathers getting into your mouth and throat or up your nose, do we? Whatever would the pathologist think? You're so allergic you'll die from their effects without inhaling them. It'll look like a fatal asthma attack. I've thought of everything.'

The feathers swirled, landing on her face and neck, her bare arms and legs, tickling and itching unbearably. Anthony snapped off the light, went out and shut the door, turned the key in the lock. He was leaving her to slowly suffocate. In the dark. Alone.

Tears filled Olivia's eyes and she would have cried. But she had no breath for sobs. Her lungs felt as though they would burst. She started to choke. Panic-stricken, she suddenly thought of Paula Pepper. Being strangled couldn't be worse than this! At least it was quicker.

But Anthony hadn't thought of everything. The red, raised weals on her skin, which were making her eyes swell and inflaming her nasal passages, would surely look suspicious to a pathologist. Don't let him get away with murder, Olivia prayed. I couldn't bear that. But what was she going to know about it anyway?

Anthony paused outside for a moment, listening, then walked slowly across the landing. He unlocked his bedroom door and went in. Simona lay motionless in the big bed, unconscious from the tranquillisers he'd fed her some hours ago. Her slender arms were stretched above her head, her wrists bound with rope and secured to the bedpost. He lifted the sheet.

Her body was covered with bruises and sore, red welts. Her face was pale and there was dark, dried blood around her swollen lips. The fabulous, shiny dark hair fanned out across the white pillow. He stroked her face and breasts, tickled her smooth, shaved armpits. Simona writhed, groaned and slowly awoke. Dazed, she stared at the ornate ceiling for a few seconds, then turned her head. Her eyes widened when she saw him, and she gave a gasp of terror.

'Hi there!' Anthony smiled. 'Did you miss me?'

He started to pull off his clothes.

Chapter Seventeen

The footsteps halted at the cellar door. Carmel and Daniel stared at one another in horror. No time to hide or escape, unless they wanted to take their chances in the dark, narrow tunnel. But was getting trapped and possibly lost for ever in a labyrinth running for miles beneath Liverpool's streets an option? Carmel's heart pounded with fear.

'We have to try the tunnel,' she gasped. 'He'll kill us! How did he get here so—'

'Anthony?' a woman's voice called. 'Are you there, lad? It's me, Mary.'

'Hello?' Daniel shouted back. 'Just a sec, I'm coming up. Stay here,' he whispered to Carmel. 'Quick, hide under the stairs. I'll try and front this out.'

Carmel crouched in a dark, dusty corner beneath the stairs. Daniel's footsteps sounded overhead and she suppressed a moan of terror as he snapped off the light, plunging her into darkness. She did not dare switch on the torch. Who the hell is that, she wondered? Obviously someone who knew Anthony – and pretty well, if she had keys to his house. Daniel left the cellar door open a crack, and a beam of pale yellow light hit the grey wall. Carmel tried to hear what was being said.

'Hi there!' Daniel grinned at the small, solidly built woman in the dark blue duffel coat, blue jeans and colourful woolly scarf. Her grey hair was short and straight, with a fringe, and she had friendly, curious brown eyes. 'Can I ask who's got spare keys to the house I might be going to rent?' he asked boldly.

'You're going to rent this place?' The woman relaxed. 'Oh, thank God for that!' she laughed. 'Anthony's been winding me up, saying he'd let the place to a couple of students. I knew he was joking though. He planned to sell the house, then changed his mind. Said he couldn't bear to part with it. I'm Mary,' she said, extending her gloved right hand, 'Mary Maddox. I live next door.'

'Pleased to meet you. Ow!' Daniel gasped, flexing his fingers. 'That's a bone-crunching handshake you've got there, Mary!'

'Sorry, luv! Don't know me own strength, everyone says that. Broke one of the bath taps a couple of weeks ago, twisted it too hard when I turned it off. Are you a mate of Anthony?' she asked.

'Er, yeah, you could say that. We do a bit of business now and then. He gave me the keys and said to look round. He couldn't come with me, he's busy tonight.'

'He should have told me you were coming. I'd have let you in and given you a guided tour, made you a cup of tea. I've known Anthony for years. He's a lovely fella, isn't he?' Mary smiled, her eyes shining. 'Always cheers me up, gives me a laugh. He's got a heart of gold as well.'

'Yep,' Daniel said tightly. 'Anthony's one in a million.' He gripped the keys, longing to release Carmel from her dark prison beneath his feet.

'Done great for himself too. He's very good to me. Slips me a few quid every month ... well, more than a few. I keep telling him I don't want it, but he insists. Says I'm all the family he's got left.'

'Are you related to him?' Daniel asked, startled.

'Oh, no. He means I'm *like* family. As good as. Anthony was about fifteen when me and my husband moved here,' Mary said. 'Derek – my husband – died of a heart attack three years ago. We knew Anthony's mum and dad. His

mum was a nice woman, but that father – *well*!' She
frowned and fingered the padlock on the cellar door. 'Is the
work on the cellar walls and pipes finished?' she asked.
'Anthony put this padlock on a few weeks ago, said he
wanted to keep the door locked because it might be dangerous down there with all that stuff lying around. He didn't
give me a key, and I didn't ask. No fear of me going down
those steps, not with my dodgy knees. I get dizzy too,' she
explained. 'High blood pressure. So I don't like going up
and down stairs if I don't have to.'

'I can imagine,' Daniel said sympathetically. So Mary
did not know about the tunnel. 'What did you mean?' he
asked. 'About Anthony's father?'

'That fella was a right swine, luv!' Mary looked indignant. 'Led his wife, Jean, and that poor lad a dog's life.
Worked as a shipping clerk in the Cunard Building, thought
he was the bees knees. Did nothing but read the Bible, not
that it ever did him any good. Wouldn't let poor Jean have
mod cons, thought they were evil. Had a screw loose. Jean
once said he used to belt Anthony when he was little. Of
course he didn't like her being friends with me. We had to
keep that quiet. She never even got a telly until after the
miserable old sod popped his clogs. Had a stroke one
morning on his way back from church. Couldn't take the
modern world's wickedness any longer! Anthony got out
when he was seventeen. Found a room and a job as a
mechanic. The girls were always after him,' she grinned,
'although I got the impression he preferred cars. Then he
went off round the world. He always kept in touch with his
mum after his dad died,' she said, 'but I still think he
blamed her. She was too busy skivvying for that old git to
be much of a mother. I think Anthony thought she should
have stood up for him. But he never talks about her and I
wouldn't pry.'

Daniel glanced at his watch. 'I don't want to be rude,
but—'

'Oh, I'm sorry, luvvie! There I go again, rabbiting on.

What d'you think of the house?' Mary asked eagerly. 'I wouldn't mind having you as a neighbour.'

'Thanks,' Daniel smiled. He shrugged. 'Needs a lot doing to it. That kitchen's from the Dark Ages.'

Mary nodded. '1900, to be exact. That's when these houses were built. A lad like you'll want a microwave for all your pizzas and TV dinners,' she said, her eyes sparkling with mischief, 'and one of them fancy new fridges with a computer that tells you when to get more lager in.'

'Don't know about that. But yeah, there's a few other places I want to check out before I decide. Does Anthony come here often?' Daniel asked.

Mary thought. 'I last saw him about two weeks ago,' she replied. 'But I don't always see him coming and going, and he doesn't always knock on my door. He's a busy lad. Sometimes I only know he's been here because there's an envelope on the mat. I'm mostly in the back room or the kitchen, I keep the front sitting room for visitors. I pop in here a few nights a week to check the place. Anthony's got time-lapse switches in all the rooms, and he likes the telly left on most days and evenings. You can't be too careful, can you, with all these burglars around?'

'No.' Daniel checked his watch again. 'I'll just take a look upstairs before I go.'

'Okay, luv. D'you want to pop next door and I'll make you a cup of tea?'

'Thanks for the offer, but I'm meeting me mates for a pint.'

'Sounds like fun.' She grinned. 'Well, I'll leave you to lock up. Nice to meet you, luv,' she said, backing away. 'Hope I see you again soon.'

'Nice to meet you too, Mary. Take care of yourself.'

'I'll be careful if I can't be good. Ta-ra, luv.'

When Mary had left, Daniel opened the cellar door and switched the light on.

'Did you hear all that?' he asked. Carmel was halfway up the stairs.

209

'God, it was horrible down there on my own! Yes.' Carmel nodded, white-faced. 'Just our luck, isn't it? She's bound to mention you to Anthony now.'

'So what? He won't know it's me.'

'He'll know somebody was here. And wonder how the hell they got the keys. Let's hope he and Mary don't meet for a while, and she forgets to ask him if you're moving in. She obviously thinks the world of him,' Carmel said. 'She doesn't have a clue. Just as well, for her sake.' She laid one hand on her hammering heart. 'Let's get out of here,' she breathed. 'When that front door opened, I thought we were dead!'

'Tell me about it.' Daniel grinned. 'Hang on while I check she's not looking through her front window. If she sees you, we *are* dead.'

Mary's dark green sitting room curtains were safely drawn. They collapsed into the van and Daniel drove off at speed.

'What a night!' He laughed nervously. 'I'll need a long hot shower and half a bottle of brandy when I get home. I suppose we'd better replace those keys now,' he said as they drove down Grinfield Street, heading back towards Liverpool city centre, 'before Ant realises they're missing.'

'Yes. And I'll have to persuade the police to search his office before he gets rid of the cash and passports. I need to prove he murdered Gemma and Paula, and that he's a pimp who sells women into slavery. Of course I realise the latter is incidental, as far as the law's concerned,' she said sarcastically. 'But it'll still help to put him away.'

'Sounds dangerous.' Daniel glanced at her. 'You'll be needing my help again.'

'Daniel, you've done more than enough already! I can't ask—'

'You'd better! No argument. Shall I keep Sean's spare keys for you?' he suggested. 'Might be safer not to have them in your house. You never know.'

'That's a good idea. Thanks, Daniel. I'll give them to

you after we've braved the lion's den a second time.'
Carmel shuddered with dread at the thought of going back
into the warehouse. Her nerves were stretched almost to
breaking point.

'Sure you want to leave Anthony's stuff in the safe?'

'No! But like I said, we can't take it. The police have to
find it themselves.'

'Yeah. I suppose. I just hope it's still there if and when
they look.' They stopped at traffic lights. Daniel smiled,
stretched out one hand and ruffled her hair. 'You were
terrific tonight,' he said softly. 'Sean's bloody lucky to
have you for a wife.'

Carmel smiled back. 'And you for a friend. Oh, my
God!' she gasped suddenly.

'What's wrong?' Daniel jerked the van forward as the
lights turned green, and stalled it. The car behind beeped
impatiently. 'What is it?' he asked, alarmed.

'I just thought of something else,' she said as he restarted
the engine and drove off. 'Sean could be in just as much
trouble if I leave the stuff than if I take it to the police.'

'How's that?'

'Well, even if I can get DS Davie to search Anthony's
office first thing in the morning and he finds the money and
passports – which is a huge *if* – what's to stop Anthony
swearing they belong to Sean?' Carmel turned pale. 'He
might try to tell them he thinks *Sean*'s a trafficker in human
beings as well as a double murderer.'

'Christ! But it'll still look bad for Anthony. How's he
going to explain why he didn't report the stuff, hand it
over? He can't say he didn't know what was in his own
safe.'

'He could easily make some excuse about the money.
And the passports, visas and AIDS test papers were in an
envelope, remember? He could say he never checked the
contents. He might look careless or indifferent, but that's
all.'

'What about fingerprints?' Daniel pointed out, driving

fast along a dual carriageway. 'Sean's won't be on those passports – but Anthony's will.'

'So are yours and mine. Anthony could make sure the police see him handle them. Then even if Sean's prints can't be detected, ours might be. It could look as though you, me and Sean were running a human trafficking business together.' Carmel's voice rose in panic. 'They might even bang *us* up! Oh God, I should never have asked you for help! What would Lisa do without me? And how could I look for Sean then? What would *you* do? I'll never forgive myself if I get you into trouble.'

'Stop it! Just calm down, all right?' Daniel grabbed her hand and squeezed it. 'You're running away with yourself. None of that's going to happen. Bloody hell, what a mess!' He let go of her hand and shook his head, his expression grim. 'Don't suppose you've got any bright ideas? I haven't.'

Carmel took a couple of deep breaths. Then she nodded. 'Actually, I do have an idea,' she said slowly. 'I'm not sure if it's *bright* though.'

It was after midnight when Carmel finally pulled up outside her house in Falkner Square and switched off the Landcruiser's engine. She closed her eyes and leaned her head back for a few seconds, exhausted and trembling. It had been very hard for her to re-enter the warehouse, but she had forced herself to do it. For Sean's sake. Now she felt like she was going to collapse.

Her tired eyes, looking in the driving mirror, picked out the dipped headlights of the black BMW as it sneaked into a parking space on the opposite side of the road by the park gates. She had outsmarted them tonight. Could she do it again?

She dragged the keys out of the ignition, locked the car and walked slowly up the path to her front door. I'll certainly sleep tonight, she thought. I hope I can make it upstairs first. Her legs were leaden with weariness. Rosa opened the door, her broad figure outlined against the hall light. She wore her red dressing gown and her hair was wrapped in a blue towel.

'Mum phoned a couple of times,' she said. 'She's worried. You'd better call back, let her and Dad know you're safe home. Where have you been? What are you doing with that torch?' Rosa stared at her. 'Your hair and clothes are all dusty!'

'I'll explain everything while you make me a cup of tea.' Carmel put her arms around her sister and hugged her. 'God, I'm so tired!' she sighed, resting her head on Rosa's shoulder for a minute. 'Forget the tea,' she said. 'Will you pour me a lovely big iced vodka with orange and raspberry juice?'

'Sure. Listen Carmel, I've got some news for you.' Rosa looked anxiously at her as they drew apart. 'There were a couple of messages on the answering machine,' she said. 'From the CID, leaving a number and asking you to contact them. So I phoned back. They said they sent two officers round this evening, but no one was home.'

'Since when did that deter them?' Carmel's voice was bitter. 'I'm surprised they didn't just barge in like last time. *What* news?' she gasped, trembling with fright as Rosa's words sank in, the familiar hope and dread welling up inside her.

'The police want you to go and see them first thing in the morning. You're to ask for DS Davie. They've found Sean's Audi,' Rosa said.

'Where?' Carmel gasped. Her heart began to beat furiously.

'In an underground hotel car park in the centre of Manchester.'

'And Sean? Was he . . .?' She couldn't go on.

'No.' Rosa shook her head. 'I'm sorry, Carmel. There's no sign of Sean.'

The dead girl was moving, throwing off the bricks and

rubble that covered her, rising from her tomb in the cold, dark, silent labyrinth. A pale hand emerged, a slim arm. She sat up, stretching as if from a long sleep, still wearing the torn, red silk dress. She stood up and walked gracefully out of the tunnel, through the brick arch into the light. Anthony trembled, shouted, tried to run after her. But he could not move.

A second later she was walking through the forest, the forest of his nightmare. Her long, black silky hair swirled around her head, outlined against the crimson sky. He was in front now, blocking her path, but he seemed invisible to her. Her big dark eyes stared beyond him, transfixed as if by some heavenly vision. She was smiling. Each tree she touched turned to a crucifix dripping blood.

'I love my daughter,' she cried joyfully. 'I am going to see my daughter.'

'No!' He was shouting at her, but she didn't hear him. She was in a world of her own and he couldn't reach her, touch her, stop her. 'You're dead,' he screamed. 'You're dead, you can't go anywhere!'

Blood dripped on to her face and her bare white arms. She didn't notice. She paused by one of the crucifixes and looked up. He groaned with terror. Olivia was hanging there, and she wasn't dead either. She was staring at him, and she was laughing. But her red-glowing eyes were filled with hatred.

'There's a gun under that lovely soft feather bed you gave me,' she hissed. 'You'd prefer a bullet, wouldn't you, Anthony? But it can't be that way.'

He was screaming and sobbing now, seized with indescribable terror. The ways of death, he thought. The end. He had failed and he was helpless, all his efforts were for nothing. They were alive and he was dead. They would destroy him, cast him into a black void from which there was no escape. He could hear his own screams, reverberating throughout the forest, being deadened by the stunted trees and low crimson sky. He hated that sky; it was evil and filled with menace. Warm, sticky blood dripped on to his forehead and ran down his face. He could taste it.

Anthony woke up sobbing and drenched with sweat, his mouth wide open in another terrified scream that turned out to be nothing more than a whimper. He reached blindly for Simona, lying rigid beside him, and clutched her to him as he sobbed on her breast, desperate for the warmth and comfort of another human body. Her heartbeat pulsed against his cheek.

'I'm not human,' he cried, his body shaking. 'I'm cursed. Why? Why?'

'Anthony,' she whispered. 'Untie me. Let me comfort you.'

He did as she asked. He felt her arms slide around his shoulders and hold him. She put up a hand and began to stroke his hair, the nape of his neck. Her gentleness soothed him, and his sobs lessened. They lay still, locked together. Moonlight slanted across the rumpled bed.

'Anthony,' Simona whispered again after a minute. 'Do you feel better yet? Shall I bring you something to drink?'

He raised his head, recovering slightly, and stared at her, astonished by this unexpected gesture of kindness from someone he had kidnapped, abused and degraded. She had to be acting, trying to take advantage of the situation. He leaned across and switched on the bedside lamp, breathed a long, shuddering sigh. The sheet and pillow were drenched with his sweat.

'No,' he muttered. 'I'll get it.'

He pushed her down and tied her wrists again, his hands shaking. He looked at her as she lay there, at the bruises and weals that covered her body, the swelling around her mouth. 'Sorry I was a bit rough,' he said suddenly. 'I didn't mean to hurt you that much.'

She shivered. 'I am cold!'

He got out of bed, pulled up the quilt and covered her. Then he put on his robe and walked to the door. She was still a big groggy from the Valium he had made her take so that she would sleep through Olivia's visit. Olivia's last visit! He wondered if Simona would have actually got him a drink, or tried to escape. Anthony didn't feel like giving her the benefit of the doubt. He went down to the study, picked up the bottle of Dalwhinnie that he had forced Olivia to drink from, and poured himself a big measure. He went into the drawing room and sat by the dying fire. Olivia's shoes and handbag lay on the carpet. A silvery lipstick tube had rolled out of the bag.

Was the nightmare a premonition? He had never had one, but he believed in them. Suppose the bitch in the tunnel wasn't dead? What if she really had moved? He had to go back and make sure she had not risen from her grave. First though he had to check on Olivia. He shivered with fear as he remembered her eyes in the dream, redder than the ghastly sky, glowing with hate.

'Come on!' he whispered, gulping whisky. 'Get a grip.' The nightmare didn't mean anything. People frequently dreamed about events that had happened to them or others, as well as things they had said, done or heard, all mixed up. It was the brain's way of sorting the millions of electrical impulses and the jumbled impressions with which it was continually bombarded. Nevertheless, Anthony was suddenly desperate to get back to the labyrinth.

The old nightmare itself was bad enough, the stunted blackened trees turning to crucifixes dripping blood, but this time it had a hideous new twist. What did it mean? Were his victims coming back to haunt him, like in some gothic horror? He stared fearfully around the big, shadowy room.

Over the years Anthony had toyed with the idea of visiting a psychologist to have the childhood nightmare analysed, analysed, he hoped, out of his head for ever. He imagined being able to look forward to a peaceful night's sleep, knowing he wasn't going to wake up in a panic, sweating and whimpering with fear. Thinking of psychologists reminded him of Olivia's final piece of useful information – that Carmel Devine now suspected him of two murders and being responsible for her precious Sean's disappearance.

Anthony started to sweat with fear again. Carmel had no evidence, as far as he knew. But she could cause trouble, especially if the police weren't dismissing her accusations. There was no way he wanted to answer more questions or make a new statement, become the subject of an in-depth investigation if he was really unlucky. Carmel was supposed to lead him to Sean, but so far she had not led him anywhere except up the garden path. The hunt for Sean was going nowhere.

Should he keep quiet, pretend he didn't know Carmel suspected him and behave as if they were still friends? Or have it out with her and try to persuade her he was innocent? Fury swept over him. He longed to silence the betraying bitch once and for all, but he couldn't do that. Not yet. In the meantime, however, he could certainly show her who was boss.

He took the glass and bottle of Dalwhinnie upstairs. Simona lay still, staring at the ornate ceiling. Anthony liked the look of fear which crossed her face as he approached the bed. He poured himself another large measure of single malt and drank half of it. The drink made him feel much better. He took his watch and put it on. It was three-forty a.m.

'Anthony,' Simona whispered, 'please can I ask you something?'

He was about to tell her to shut up, that he had an important job to do, when he suddenly changed his mind.

'What is it?' He looked at her warily. 'You're not going to ask me to let you go?'

'No.' Simona hesitated. 'Do you know my sister?' she asked tentatively. Her dark eyes were pleading, fearful. 'My sister, Maria? She also came to Liverpool – more than six months ago. That man, Ionescu, bought her plane ticket and helped her get the visa. I want to find her, I want to

217

know—' She stopped and gave a nervous little sob. 'Where Maria is. If she is safe.'

'Your *sister*?' The girl in the nightmare flashed back into Anthony's mind as he stared at Simona, seeing her as if for the first time. That hair, the big dark eyes, the curve of her mouth and chin. Light dawned. Of course! he thought. How come I didn't spot the resemblance before now? He nearly laughed.

'Yes, my sister,' Simona said. 'Maria Tarnu.'

Anthony looked into her eyes. 'Never heard of her.' He could tell Simona was unsure whether or not to believe him. He put down his glass, got on the bed and knelt over her. 'You think I'm lying,' he said roughly. 'Don't you?'

'No ... please!' She cried out in pain and shock as he hit her across the face.

Anthony opened his bedside drawer and took out the pack of Valium.

'Time for you to go back to sleep,' he said. 'But first I want to show you something.'

He untied her again, dragged her out of the room and across the landing. He unlocked the door of the room where Olivia was imprisoned, and flicked the light switch. He felt frightened again, thinking of the nightmare. *Was* she dead?

Feathers danced and swirled as the door flew open. Olivia lay sprawled a few feet from where he had left her, her head lolling to one side. Her face was purple, her skin mottled. Simona gasped, then started to scream and struggle frantically in his arms as she realised the feather-covered object was a woman's body.

'This is what happens,' Anthony yelled in her ear, 'to anyone who questions me!'

He dragged her back to his bedroom, tied her wrists again and made her swallow three Valium along with some whisky. She was hysterical, tears pouring down her face, but the tablets would take effect soon.

'You're lucky,' he said. 'You get to stay with me now.' He took a torch from the drawer and fetched a pair of tweezers from the bathroom. He had bought the tweezers some months ago when a sliver of wooden toothpick got lodged between two molars and he didn't want to visit a dentist to have it removed.

He went back to Olivia, knelt over her and put his head to her chest. He took off the handcuffs, felt her neck and wrist for a pulse. Nothing. She was cold and still. Definitely dead. Anthony's face burned as he thought of his terror during the nightmare, the shameful fact that he had turned to Simona for comfort. He got the vacuum cleaner from the cupboard by the stairs and hoovered up every feather in sight, being particularly careful to make sure none remained hidden in Olivia's hair or anywhere on her body. That took a long time, and exhausted him.

He undid the tie around Olivia's ankles and was pleased to note that there were no marks. He had used just the right amount of pressure. He removed the gag and switched on the torch, carefully examined her mouth, nose and throat for any stray feathers that might somehow have got lodged. He couldn't find any.

He got up and laughed as he rested one foot on Olivia's hip, rolling her body back and forth. His pose reminded Anthony of a photograph he had once seen as a boy, in a library book about Nazi atrocities: a black and white photograph of a grinning SS officer, one shiny booted foot resting on the neck of his helpless victim, a concentration camp prisoner in striped clothing who was sprawled on the ground in agony after being strung up with his arms behind his back . . . on a crucifix . . .

Anthony gasped in horror and shut his eyes, trying to shake the image. He could hear Simona's distant wails. He took his foot off Olivia's hip and stared down at her. She looked helpless, he thought. So vulnerable. The tragic bitch had never realised just how vulnerable she was. How expendable.

'Right, Detective Inspector,' he said briskly. 'Let's get you home, shall we?'

Chapter Eighteen

'Have you questioned Anthony Maskey again?' Carmel hurried after DS Davie as he led the way down the corridor and out into the police station yard where Sean's Audi was parked. She had taken Lisa to school and had a long, fraught interview with the headteacher, who had reluctantly agreed to let her daughter return.

Lisa was equally reluctant to go back, but at least her classmates would think twice about picking on her in future. Carmel had put up her hair for the interview and dressed in a severe black suit with a purple sweater beneath, low heels and a black silk mac in an effort to look like a calm, responsible parent who had her life – and her errant daughter – firmly under control.

'Have you questioned him?' she repeated, dodging a WPC carrying a cup of coffee.

'No,' was Neil Davie's abrupt response. He strode on.

'But you said you would. After what I told you. He's threatening me, for God's sake!'

'Wouldn't call it a threat, exactly. Okay, he won't win any diplomacy awards but we can't nail him for that.'

'Why have you changed your mind? Stop!' Carmel pleaded. 'Wait a second, let's talk about this.' It wasn't only Anthony Maskey and what she and Daniel had found in his safe that freaked her; she had spent a sleepless night trying unsuccessfully to psych herself up for the ordeal of having to see Sean's Audi and formally identify it, perhaps search the car for possible clues.

'Look, I'm sorry.' Neil Davie stopped and turned to her, his face pale and strained in the November sunlight. 'The truth is, it's chaos here this morning. My Inspector – DI Crane – didn't turn up for work or answer her phone. I went round to her house.' Neil swallowed hard, his jaw set and his hands bunched in his jacket pockets. 'She was lying on her sitting room sofa. Dead.'

'*What?*' Carmel stared at him in shock, recalling the brusque, confident, unsympathetic Olivia, who had only thawed slightly when Lisa appeared. '*How?*'

'Too soon to say.' Neil swiped at an escaping tear. 'But it looks like a fatal asthma attack. You knew she was asthmatic? That day at your place when she . . .'

'I remember.' Carmel nodded quickly. 'I'm so sorry.' She stared at him. 'This is awful – I can't believe it!'

'Neither can I,' Neil muttered, sniffing hard. They were silent for a few seconds.

'It's a bit strange though, isn't it?' Carmel frowned. 'Her dying alone like that.'

'What d'you mean?'

'Well, during an asthma attack – even a fatal one – the sufferer's condition doesn't usually deteriorate so fast that they don't have time to call for help. Wouldn't DI Crane have been able to do that before things got really bad? And didn't she have her medication with her?'

Neil shrugged and glanced away. 'Dunno.' He wasn't going to tell Carmel that Olivia's body stank like an old alehouse and that she must have boozed to the point where she wouldn't have been able to locate a phone, never mind pick it up and call someone. He would never forget the shock of seeing her lying there in that black dress, her face and lips blue, the normally smooth, pale skin so horribly mottled and cold. Neil also felt guilty, as if he had somehow let Olivia down.

'She got divorced recently,' he said. 'It was finalised just weeks ago. Must have hit her harder than I realised. Stress or shock always made her asthma worse. And her son's away, travelling in Asia. She missed him like hell, and she was worried sick. I'll contact Alex's father and let him break the news,' Neil said glumly. 'It's better if he hears it from his dad. I don't think that's down to me.'

'No, of course not. What d'you mean, the divorce hit her harder than you realised?'

'Well ...' Neil flushed. 'She'd been on the sauce more than usual. But that didn't mean she couldn't do her job. Olivia Crane was a bloody good copper,' he said fiercely. 'Everyone knows that.'

'I'm really sorry,' Carmel repeated. 'It's a shock to me, and I hardly knew her.'

'Yeah. Thanks.' Neil turned away, suddenly brisk and in control again. 'Right, let's take a look at your husband's car. We'd like you to tell us if there's anything missing. Or unusual. You know?'

'Yes.' Carmel drew in her breath as she caught sight of the dark blue Audi, parked in a corner of the yard. She forgot about Olivia Crane's untimely death.

'No one named Sean Devine was registered at that hotel. Or at any other in Manchester. Of course he could have given a false name and address, paid cash.' Neil paused as he noticed Carmel's anguished expression.

'I doubt if Sean would have had enough cash on him to pay for a hotel room. He never carried much. And he hasn't withdrawn money from our account or used his credit cards since he ...' Carmel stopped and looked down.

'The car was locked and the keys gone,' Neil went on. 'We don't know if he abandoned the car or meant to come back to it.' He stopped a few feet away from the Audi. Carmel could not see inside the car because of its tinted windows. 'Any idea why your husband would have gone to Manchester?'

'No.' She shook her head. 'He went there on business occasionally, that's all.' She stared at the car, her eyes filling with tears. 'He didn't know the place very well.'

'You don't think he might have gone to the airport? Piccadilly or Victoria stations?'

'Not the airport. You took Sean's passport,' Carmel reminded him, her voice cold. 'When you and that bunch of yobs turned our house upside down.'

'There's places you can fly to without a passport,' Neil said, ignoring her remark. 'London, for instance. Other Brit cities. Or he could have got a false passport.'

'Sean wouldn't know how to get a false passport any more than I would. Even if he did, how could he pay for it without using cash or a credit card? I'm sure he didn't buy a plane ticket.' Carmel looked at Neil, her eyes wet. 'And he wouldn't risk London. It's too obvious. Besides, Anthony Maskey's got a lot of contacts there. It wouldn't be as comfortingly anonymous as you'd imagine. I bet you haven't found anything to connect Sean with Paula Pepper's murder, have you?' she challenged. 'Hasn't it occurred to you that the paper and those hairs could have been planted at the crime scene? It would have been the easiest thing in the world for Anthony Maskey to take a couple of hairs from Sean's comb. Why don't you get a sample of *his* DNA and re-examine the bodies of those two women?'

Neil looked irritated. 'Don't tell us how to do our job, Mrs Devine. But no,' he admitted, 'we haven't found anything to link your husband to Paula Pepper's murder.'

'Talk to Anthony Maskey again. Even if Sean had murdered Gemma Geraghty – which he didn't – how on earth do you think he could have found out there was a witness, plus her name and address?' Carmel pleaded. 'There's no way! Anthony Maskey could have, though. Especially if he was paying some corrupt police officer to keep him abreast of developments.'

Neil's irritation escalated to anger. 'I warned you about throwing around allegations like that. I understand you're desperate, but—'

'No, you don't! Anthony's got another business besides

security products and classic cars. He buys and sells girls and young women for the sex trade.'

What would she think of next? Neil sighed. 'Got evidence for that, have you?'

Carmel hesitated. 'I'm sure you'll find some if you look hard enough.'

Neil stared at her. 'You said Anthony Maskey murdered Gemma Geraghty and Paula Pepper. That he was the man who entered your house and threatened you with a gun. Now you're saying he's involved in trafficking women. Why didn't you mention this last time we talked to you?'

'Because I was still trying to work it out. Just before he disappeared, Sean said that Anthony had made a lot of trips abroad recently, mostly to eastern Europe. And for months he'd had money to burn. The business was doing great, but he couldn't possibly have got all his money from that. Sean was having problems with Anthony, not the other way round. I think Sean found out what he was up to and Anthony threatened him, maybe tried to murder him. That's why he disappeared – why my house is being watched.' Her cobalt blue eyes stared up at him, pleading and tearful. 'I miss Sean,' she said, her voice breaking. 'I want him back, so does my daughter. He isn't a murderer. He's in terrible danger!'

'All right. Listen.' Neil was full of doubts about all this, at a loss what to think. In shock about Olivia's death. 'I said I'd talk to Maskey again and I will.'

He wished fervently that Olivia was alive and that he could discuss this with her. The sight of her empty office was painful beyond belief. He had to sort through her stuff later too. He felt choked.

'Call me,' Carmel begged. 'Let me know what happens. I realise you're terribly upset about Inspector Crane, and you've got a million and one things to do, but . . .'

'Yeah. I have.' Neil glanced at his watch. 'Just take a look at this car, will you?'

He could not believe he would never see or speak to

Olivia again, hear her complain about her ex-husband or express concern for the son she loved so much. Her death was wrong, stupid, devastating. Everyone in the division was stunned. The daily routine had ground to a halt and there was an air of unreality, of shocked disbelief. People hung around subdued and talking in hushed voices. Or not at all.

'You can identify this car as belonging to your husband, Sean Devine?' he asked.

'Yes.' Carmel wiped her eyes as Neil opened the passenger door for her. She looked inside, gasped and recoiled with shock. The driver's seat and part of the passenger seat were covered with dark, dried bloodstains. She stared in horror. Neil watched. He hadn't mentioned the bloodstains, having wanted to see her reaction.

'I was right!' Carmel whispered. She turned so pale that he stepped forward, afraid she might faint. 'Sean tried to escape and Anthony wounded him. Oh God, he's hurt!' She burst into a storm of panicked tears. 'Where is he, where did he go?' she sobbed. 'Maybe he's dead after all! Oh, Sean!'

'It might not be his blood,' Neil said hastily. 'We don't know your husband's dead.' He wondered whether or not to call a WPC. 'Don't cry.' He touched her arm. 'I'm sorry, I know it's a shock. I should have warned you about the bloodstains.'

'Can I look in the glove compartment?' Carmel turned to him, wiping her streaming eyes, making a supreme effort to control herself. 'My prints and hairs or whatever will be in there. It won't affect your search for evidence – not that you'll find any.'

Neil opened the door wider. 'Go ahead.'

The tiny, somewhat cross-looking teddy bear that Lisa had given Sean swung from the driving mirror. Carmel opened the glove compartment and a Mars Bar wrapper floated out. There was a crumpled white bag spilling green and red chewy snakes mixed with sticky, pink and white teeth-and-lips, revolting confectionery that Lisa loved. The bag was bloodstained.

There was a hollow ache inside Carmel, a terrible longing for Sean and terrible fear for him. Being in his car made her feel close to him. But she wasn't, she had no idea where he was. Sean was hurt, he could be dead! Despair swept over her. Her fingers trembled as she took the neatly folded pile of maps from the glove compartment and peered inside, running her hand around the interior.

'Anything unusual?' Neil asked, leaning over her. 'Missing?'

Carmel pulled a handkerchief from her pocket and wiped more tears. 'I'm not sure ... I don't think so.' She trembled with fear and horror as she imagined Sean collapsing into the car, hurt and bleeding, terrified for his life.

'Okay. The boot now, please.' He opened the boot and came back. 'Mrs Devine?' She sat there crying quietly. Neil suddenly felt very sorry for her.

She looked in the boot. Spare tyre, box of tools, the big red torch. A cardboard box containing several empty carrier bags. The folded tartan blanket that Sean's Auntie Janet had given them last Christmas.

'Nothing,' she whispered. She shook her head, her eyes filled with despair.

Neil thought. Suppose Carmel Devine was right about Anthony Maskey? Vice wasn't his province; he'd have to talk to someone. Olivia would have been the perfect person. And suppose Maskey did have a copper on his payroll? Someone in CID, maybe, working on the murders? A colleague that he liked? *Trusted*.

The thought of that gave Neil a hot flush, followed by an icy chill. Maskey had no form, as far as he knew. But neither did Sean Devine. Why would Sean get to the age of thirty-seven, a popular guy with a thriving business who appeared to be happily married – Carmel Devine seemed to really love her husband – and then suddenly, for no apparent reason, go out one night and murder a prostitute? It didn't make sense. It never had, despite what the DNA seemed to be telling them.

Suppose they had been after the wrong guy all along? Neil knew Olivia would call him a dickhead for thinking this way. He had voiced his concerns to her after the interview with Carmel, and she had contemptuously dismissed them. He heard Olivia's strident voice again: 'She's one of those wives who thinks her husband's God. There's a lot of them around, despite all the whingeing about feminists. She's totally bloody naïve. Ignore her. She should keep the fairy tales for her kid's bedtime.'

'Sorry to rush you.' Neil glanced at his watch again as Carmel stood there looking desolate. 'But I've got to get on. So do you, I imagine. Off to work this morning?'

'I'm going to my office. I won't get any work done.' Carmel touched the Audi's smooth paintwork, her fingers trembling. 'What happens to the car now?'

'It'll be moved to . . .' Neil paused. Someone was shouting at him from across the yard. An urgent phone call.

'You'll have to excuse me,' he said. 'Thanks for coming in. I'll talk to Maskey again and call you.'

Carmel grabbed hold of his arm. 'Promise?'

He looked down at her, his strained features relaxing. 'You sound like my four year old. She's always making me promise. Yes,' he said. 'I *promise*. Now, can I have my arm back, please?'

Carmel watched him sprint between the rows of cars and disappear into the building. The pale November sunlight was gradually warming the frosty air, and she could smell coffee and fried bacon. It made her feel sick. There *is* something, she thought suddenly, staring at the car. Something missing.

But what? It was tantalising, maddening, frustrating. She walked round to the front of the police station, got into the Landcruiser and drove to her office. Heading downtown towards the Mersey, she noticed the black BMW crawling along in the stream of traffic behind her. No doubt this morning's visit to the police station had already been reported to Anthony. Had Anthony looked in his safe yet? She could expect another phone call soon, even a highly unwelcome visit. Carmel suddenly wondered if DS Davie might be Anthony's corrupt cop. Whoever it was, that person would do everything in their power to prevent Sean's innocence coming to light. The odds were stacked against him.

She parked outside the old Pier Head building, went up in the lift to her office and had to unlock the door because there was no sign of her secretary. Only Jane's keys and a sheet of paper with her slanted handwriting, anchored to the desk by a Murano glass boiled sweet with red swirls inside.

Hi Carmel,
Most clients have cancelled their appointments, and more consultants (see list) have called to say they won't be referring patients now. I've found another job and they want me to start immediately. I don't need a reference. Sorry to leave you in the lurch, but I'm sure you understand that I don't want to go on working here. It's creepy and there have been a few weird calls.
Best wishes, Jane

'Nothing like loyalty, is there?' Carmel ripped up the note and tossed the pieces in the bin. 'And it's just as well you don't need a reference.' But she had more important things to think about. Like finding Sean. Please God, she prayed as she walked into her silent office. Don't let him be dead! What kind of wound had caused those bloodstains? A knife? A gun? The same gun Anthony had pushed against her bare breast that night? She shivered with terror as she thought of what she and Daniel had done last night. They had taken a hell of a risk. If Anthony had walked in on them they would be dead now, she had no doubt. What would he do next? He was going to be very upset when he looked in his safe.

She stood at the window gazing out across the sunlit

dockland, at the skeleton of yet another new building under construction, tiny red-clad figures crawling all over it. A giant crane, swinging slowly across the sky, a rusting container dangling from a thick cable or chain. The sparkling River Mersey, the ferries and pilot boat out. She flinched as the phone rang, then turned slowly and crossed to her desk. It was probably Anthony. She dreaded speaking to him.

'Hello?' If she didn't answer, he might come here. Or turn up at the house.

'Carmel? Anthony. I phoned you at home but there was no answer. You're back at work then,' he stated. 'How are things?'

'Not great.' She stared at the crane outlined against the blue sky. Why did he bother to phone her? Hadn't his corrupt copper told him about Sean's car being found in Manchester?

'Any news of Sean?' She heard the excitement and urgency in Anthony's voice.

Maybe the cop hadn't told him yet. Well, she wasn't going to. You bastard! she thought. You don't know how much I hate you. But you'll find out. You won't get away with what you've done.

'No.' She gripped the phone. Did Anthony know she suspected him? What would he do next? He wasn't going ballistic, so obviously he hadn't yet looked in his safe. 'There's no news.'

'Oh.' He sounded crushed. 'Can we meet for lunch?' he asked. 'I'd like to talk.'

'No!' Carmel shuddered violently. 'I'm too busy. I've been away from the office a lot and I need to catch up on things. Then I'm going to see Lisa. She's staying with her grandparents.' As if he didn't know.

'Okay. Soon then.' He paused. 'Have you thought any more about . . .?'

'No.' Carmel tried to control her fury. This man had threatened and hurt, maybe even murdered her husband,

229

and now he wanted Sean's share of the business. She would make damn sure he never got it. 'I have to go,' she said abruptly. 'Goodbye.'

She crashed the phone down and swore. Then she collapsed into her chair, leaned her head on the desk and burst into floods of tears again. It was all too much. Where was Sean? Would she ever see him again? If he was alive, wasn't there some way he could contact her? She felt helpless, confused. Terribly alone.

The tears brought no relief. After a while Carmel got up, went into the tiny kitchen and poured herself a glass of sparkling spring water, wishing it was vodka. She took the drink into her office and stood at the window, slowly sipping. Might as well go home. There was nothing to do here, although she pretended to Anthony she was busy. She couldn't be bothered to phone any consultants and argue with them, or chase up clients. There was no need to look for a new secretary. Everything was falling apart and she didn't even care. She only wanted Sean. Alive and safe.

Why Manchester? she wondered. Because it was the nearest city? The drive would have taken about half an hour. How did Sean manage that if he was injured and bleeding? She was so tired of questions and no answers.

Family, friends, acquaintances, business contacts, places they had been to on holiday, police inquiries, everything had drawn a frustrating, heartbreaking blank. And if Sean was alive, why didn't he withdraw cash from their account or use his credit cards? Only dead people didn't spend money.

She wondered again if someone was hiding him. Someone she hadn't thought of, perhaps not seen in a long time, who was more Sean's friend than hers. It might be someone she had never met. And *what* was missing from the Audi?

The phone rang again. The glass slipped from her nervous fingers and shattered, spilling fizzy water over the woodblock floor. Carmel ignored the mess and stared at the ringing phone, her eyes brilliant with tears. If this was

Anthony again ... she waited, but it went on ringing. Finally she picked up the receiver, steeling herself.

'Carmel?' The man's voice was weak and faint, and the line was bad. But she recognised it none the less. 'It's me ... can you talk? I called before, but ...'

'Sean!' she gasped. Shock jolted through her. 'You're alive!'

Anthony watched, his nervousness mounting as DS Davie and a detective constable moved around his office, sifting through papers, picking up various objects and putting them down again. 'Seen all you want?' he asked aggressively. 'I'm running a legit enterprise here, you know.'

'I never said you weren't.' Neil raised an eyebrow. 'It's your non-legit enterprises that concern me, Mr Maskey.'

Anthony gripped the arms of his chair. 'What the hell's that supposed to mean?'

'Do you believe in treating young girls and women like livestock?' Neil asked, his tone polite and non-committal. 'Buying and selling them just as you would any other consumer item? Some people do, I'm afraid.'

'I don't know what you're talking about!' Anthony went cold with shock. Had Olivia blabbed before he killed her? Carmel Devine suspected him of being responsible for Sean's disappearance, but she knew nothing about the trafficking in girls – she couldn't, there was no way! He just had to deny everything. 'Listen,' he said, his voice rising, 'you've already asked me about those two murdered women. Now this! What are you trying to do, pin all the unsolved crime in Liverpool on me?'

'Mind if I take a look around?' Neil asked.

'I thought that's what you were doing!'

'Maybe we could go to your house later. I can get a search warrant, but that's not necessary, is it? I mean, if you've no idea what this is about, you've got no worries.'

'Don't give me that bullshit! I've got a right not to be stitched up.'

'Of course you have.' Neil looked closely at him. 'So does Sean Devine.'

Anthony jumped up. 'Are you saying I know something about his disappearance?'

'It seems you do. You told his wife he'd run off with another woman and wouldn't be back. Why didn't you tell that to us when we first talked to you?'

'Because I never said it. She's lying.' Anthony cursed Carmel. Why couldn't the bitch keep her mouth shut? Well, she had it coming.

Neil raised his eyebrows. 'Why would she lie?'

'How the hell would I know?'

'You stand to benefit if Sean Devine doesn't reappear. You could take over his share of the business. D'you think his wife will agree to sell, like you want her to?'

'I don't!' Anthony protested furiously. 'I haven't even asked her – I wouldn't do that. It's hardly the right time, is it?'

'That's what I thought when I listened to a tape of a recent phone conversation during which you told Mrs Devine that if she continued to hold out, as you put it, the value of her husband's share would diminish and you couldn't guarantee her an income from the business.'

'She taped the . . .' Anthony smiled suddenly. 'Okay. Look.' He sat down again and shook his head regretfully. 'I'm Carmel's friend. I'm just trying to help. She's in a terrible state . . . what woman in her situation wouldn't be? She's too upset to think of practical problems, like how I'm supposed to go on running this place single-handed.'

'So you thought you'd focus her mind for her.' Neil looked at him with contempt.

'I suppose.' Anthony shrugged. 'Okay, I could have been more tactful. Is that it?'

'Yes. Once we've taken a look round.'

'You've got no reason to! This is harassment.'

'I'm hoping you'll co-operate so the search warrant and

formal interview won't be necessary.' Neil shrugged. 'Up to you.'

Anthony felt trapped and furious. The bastard was playing with him, flaunting his power. Where the hell had that stuff about buying and selling girls come from? If not Olivia, who? *Who?* Things were slipping again, sliding out of control, and it unnerved him. Anthony clenched his hands and stared out of the window at the river.

'Is that a yes?' Neil asked. Was the guy so uncomfortable because he was guilty? Or because he was innocent?

Anthony was silent, mentally going over the contents of his desk and filing cabinet. Nothing incriminating in there. He nodded reluctantly. 'Okay.' He stood back and gestured towards the desk. 'Help yourselves.'

He watched as they riffled through and found nothing. 'Don't you want to check Sean's office?' he asked, trying to distract them. 'Might be something there.'

'Maybe.' Neil glanced around. 'We'll look in the safe first, I think.'

'The safe?' Anthony flinched and broke out in a sweat.

'Yeah. Where is it?'

He hadn't had time to get rid of the cash and the girls' passports. *Shit.* Anthony sweated with fear. No, he thought. Don't panic. You can turn this to your advantage.

'It's in that wall,' he said, dry-mouthed. 'Behind the filing cabinet.'

Neil nodded to the detective constable, a stocky, dark-haired man wearing a grey fleece and blue jeans. The man walked to the filing cabinet and shoved it aside, exposing the scuffed white wall, the safe, and the corpse of a grey mouse.

'Ugh, look at that.' Neil made a face. 'Body fluids everywhere.' He turned to Anthony. 'You all right? You've gone a bit pale.' The detective constable smirked.

'I'm fine.' Anthony nodded. It's Sean's money, he said to himself, swiftly rehearsing his story. Not mine. I don't know where it came from, but I'm sure it's not from the business. Most clients pay by cheque. Sean put it there a few hours before he disappeared. Told me to mind my own business. The envelope? Haven't a clue what's in it. I never looked. His dry lips moved slightly.

'If you've got mice it means there's no rats,' the detective constable said.

'Like to open the safe, please?' That was the last thing Maskey wanted to do, Neil thought. And maybe he had a very good reason for not wanting to open it. Maybe Carmel Devine was right after all. 'Can you remember the combination, or are you one of those people who writes it down disguised as a phone number?'

Anthony swallowed. 'I can remember it.' He slowly recited the combination to calm himself. Flew over his story again. So what if they didn't believe him? They couldn't prove he was lying. They couldn't prove a fucking thing. He heard the lock click.

'Actually,' he began as he swung open the safe door, 'there's something—'

He broke off, staring in shocked disbelief. The safe was empty except for some papers and a few client cheques. The cash, the envelope with the passports – Sean's beautifully wrapped birthday gift to Carmel – were all gone.

'What's that, Mr Maskey?' Neil asked sharply. 'What did you say?'

'Nothing!' Anthony stammered, blanching. He felt sick. 'I . . .'

Only one other person, apart from himself, who knew the safe combination. Who would have taken the gift. Who could have got in here. No, Anthony thought. That's impossible. How could he? I took his keys, and there's no spare set. I shot him! He was bleeding, seriously wounded, I thought he was a dead man. This is crazy! He can't have come back.

Sean Devine.

Payback time?

Chapter Nineteen

'Sean, where the hell *are* you?' Carmel cried. 'I saw the bloodstains in the car, I know you're hurt! Anthony did it, didn't he? He forced you to disappear.'

'Yes. I walked in on him that night and caught him doing a deal with some woman to sell two young girls as sex slaves.' Sean sounded tired and weak. 'I realised what he'd been up to then, how he'd got all that money. I also overheard him confess to murder. He shot me, but I managed to escape. He wants me dead, Carmel.'

'Oh God. I knew it!' She trembled with fright.

'Anthony said he'd kill you and Lisa too, if I went home or to the police. I knew he wasn't joking. That's why I had to stay away. I didn't dare contact you at first in case he got wind of it somehow. When he murdered that prostitute and fitted me up – then the witness, the one person who could have helped me and who I didn't find out about until after her death – I realised I'd have no chance if I came forward.'

'Are you – were you – badly injured?' Carmel held her breath.

'Not as badly as that bastard hoped! No. I was lucky. He winged me a couple of times – the bullets grazed my left arm and hip. I was bleeding, but it looked a lot worse than it was. I'm all right now, love, I swear. Let's not talk about that.'

'But ... two gunshot wounds!' Carmel's eyes filled with tears. 'Oh, Sean! Are you really all right? You don't sound it.'

'I promise you I am,' he said urgently. 'You've got to believe me. I wouldn't be able to call you if I wasn't, would I? How are you?' he asked. 'Stupid bloody question!'

'Anthony tried to tell me you'd run off with some girl and wouldn't be back, that you were involved in something criminal. Of course I didn't believe him. And I knew you hadn't murdered those two women.'

'I'll think twice before I leave a comb lying around again,' Sean said grimly. 'I saw a headline in the paper about that prostitute – couldn't believe it was *me* they wanted.'

'The police can't link you with the second murder, but of course the papers don't print that. Sean, Anthony's having our house watched in case you turn up there.'

'I know he is.'

'You do? But how ...?'

'Carmel, love, I'm sorry but I can't talk long. It's too risky. I couldn't call you at home in case our phone's tapped or bugged, so I kept trying to get you here. This phone's probably safe, but I can't be sure. I just want to tell you I'm okay – or will be. And that I love you. I'll sort this mess and come home as soon as I can.'

'I'm doing everything possible to get the police to investigate Anthony ... well, bang him up and chuck away the key, basically. I think I'm getting somewhere.'

'For Christ's sake, Carmel, be careful. I don't want you putting yourself and Lisa in danger. He mustn't realise you know about him. And don't tell *anyone* about this call. Not even Rosa, Daniel, or your mum. For your own safety. And theirs. Promise me!'

'I promise,' she said reluctantly. 'Sean, I miss you so much. It's terrible without you. Tell me where you are,' she begged, tears rolling down her face. 'I need to see you.'

'I can't tell you where I am. The less you know, the less danger you're in. Carmel, please don't cry. I love you – I love Lisa. I miss you like hell!' His voice was choked. 'But if I come home before I've sorted Anthony and proved my innocence, I'm a dead man. The three of us could end up dead.'

'You can't possibly sort Anthony by yourself. You've got to let me help you.'

'No way. Don't take any risks. What I need is for you to look after yourself and Lisa, to just hang in there. Know that I love you and I'll be coming back. That's the best way you can help me. I've got to go now. I've been on too long already.'

'Sean, wait. Please! I've got so many questions.'

'No time now. I'll call again, let you know I'm okay.'

'I'll buy a new mobile and give you the number. When will you call?'

'Not for another few days at least. Maybe a week. But I will call, I promise.' His voice was choked again. 'I love you! Hug Lisa for me.' The phone went dead.

'Sean, no!' Carmel groaned, gripping the receiver. 'Don't go, please don't go!' She leaned her head on the desk, crying bitterly, the dial tone buzzing in her ear. After a minute she replaced the receiver and sat up, scrubbing at her swollen, reddened eyes with damp tissues. She looked at the phone, picked it up again and listened. She didn't remember hearing any clicks or other strange noises that might indicate a tap; same with the phones at home. And she wasn't going to risk electrocution by taking them apart to look for bugs. She would buy a new mobile today.

Sean wasn't dead, as she had feared, or seriously injured. He was alive, he was okay and he was safe – for now! She had to hold on to that. Pull herself together and find a way to help him. The best way, of course, was to nail Anthony Maskey. How did Sean know Anthony was having the house watched? Carmel wondered as she stood up and began to collect her things. He must be hiding in

Liverpool, or nearby. *Where?* It would be torture waiting for his next call, hoping and praying that he was still safe. But he was alive, thank goodness! She had hope, a real chance now. Carmel decided to go home and think what to do next. She longed to tell Rosa and Daniel about the call. But Sean was right. Safer for them not to know.

She locked her office and left the building, got into the Landcruiser and headed home. The sun was still shining and there was a brisk wind blowing off the Pier Head. This morning I was in despair, she thought. Now, at last, I've got hope.

She parked in Falkner Square and was walking up the path to her house trying to think what could be missing from the Audi – why hadn't she remembered to ask Sean? – when she stopped and gasped. The front door was ajar, the locks broken and wood splintered. For a second she thought the police had been back. Down the long hall broken glass glinted on the floor amid dark, pooling liquid. She could hear water gushing from the kitchen taps. Water also dripped down the stairs. The police would not have done that. She stood there stunned.

Carmel walked slowly into the hall and stopped again, sniffing the air. She smelled gas. Alcohol. The burning of some substance that might once have been coffee. Plug sockets were torn out to expose live wires. Water pooled around her black suede shoes, soaking into them. Broken glass crunched beneath her feet.

In the kitchen the fridge-freezer was wide open, it contents scattered over the floor. Smashed wine bottles and crockery lay all around. The table and chairs were upended. Carmel turned off the taps and burned coffee machine and shut the fridge door, knowing that was useless since the plug had been ripped out of its socket and the flex cut. She quickly turned off the gas and electricity. She stooped, the hem of her black silk mac trailing in wine and cold water, as she noticed some fragments of flowered porcelain; it was her great-grandmother Martha's Dresden sugar bowl.

Carmel gathered the pieces of porcelain and gently laid them on the counter. In the other rooms books had been tumbled off the shelves, trampled and ripped, family photographs smashed and torn. The photograph of Lisa as a baby, laughing and clutching the rag doll, had received special attention; it was ripped into tiny pieces, so tiny that there was no hope of repair. Carmel stared, her heart pierced with grief and shock. It was as if whoever had torn it wanted to hurt Lisa.

'You bastard!' she whispered. This was Anthony's doing, of course. Who else? He must be freaked by the disappearance of the money and passports from his safe, now stowed in Daniel's safe at the garage, to which Daniel alone had access. Sean's wrapped birthday gift was in the small black leather rucksack she wore; Carmel was determined to keep the gift with her at all times. It was like a talisman, a symbol of hope.

Anthony couldn't possibly think she had got into the warehouse and taken the things, not when she had no keys, couldn't de-activate the alarm and didn't know the safe combination – or so he thought – and when he had her followed everywhere. He couldn't blame Sean either, since he'd stolen Sean's keys. Anthony did this because he was desperate; he wanted to terrify her, teach her who was boss, prove he could invade her private space any time he liked. Maybe he thought she knew something.

Upstairs Carmel turned off the shower, sink and bath taps and pulled the plug out of the overflowing bath, soaking her arms. The bathroom reeked of her perfume and Sean's aftershave; the bottles were smashed on the floor, mingling with warm bathwater. 'Cunt' and 'bitch' were scrawled across the steamy mirror in red lipstick and blue and white toothpaste. Not very original, she thought. That did not make it any less frightening.

There was so much mess Carmel did not know where to start. Numb with shock, she picked her way through smashed toys, scattered makeup and toiletries, torn clothes, more spine-cracked books. In her and Sean's bedroom, all the drawers were pulled out and their contents tossed on the floor. Except for the folded newspaper cuttings about the murders of Gemma Geraghty and Paula Pepper, detailing Gemma's lost handbag and its contents, Paula's missing diamanté earring. The cuttings, which Carmel had kept in her bedside drawer, were gone.

The police had not returned confiscated business papers and passports, the computer or her diaries. Otherwise they too would have been stolen or destroyed. The mess and the deadly silence were shocking, heartbreaking, horrifying. It was as if the spirit was gone from the house, trampled and destroyed, replaced by something evil. Carmel stumbled across the landing and down the stairs. She had to get out.

Her shoes, mac and black trousers were soaked; she trembled with cold and shock. Daniel, she thought. I'll call him after I've contacted the police. As she reached the foot of the stairs the phone started to ring. Carmel stopped and looked at it in disbelief, astonished that the intruders had left it intact. She picked up the receiver.

'Mrs Devine? Neil Davie.'

'You've got to help me,' she cried. 'I just got home to find Anthony Maskey's trashed my house! Everything's wrecked, there's live wires – it's too dangerous for me to bring my daughter back now.'

Neil sighed. 'I'll send someone over. I went to Maskey's office and talked to him again,' he said tiredly. 'He let us take a look round, opened the safe. He was very nervous and uncomfortable and – well, basically, I do think there's something in what you say. But I'm afraid we didn't find anything. I can't pull him in for questioning or get a search warrant. Not without a good reason.'

'Oh, I'll give you a reason, no worries!' Carmel shouted, suddenly enraged. 'A bloody good one. I've just about had enough of this! What else has to happen before you do something about that bastard?'

'Mrs Devine, try to stay calm. I'll—'

'Don't tell me to stay calm when you leave a murderer and slave trafficker free to hunt down my husband, who can't come home because he'll either be murdered or banged up for two murders he didn't commit! Threaten me and my daughter, trash our house . . .' Carmel's eyes filled with tears. 'He tore my baby's photograph!'

She hung up and stumbled back down the hall. The phone immediately rang again, but she ignored it. In the kitchen she teetered over broken glass and crockery to reach the pantry and adjoining storeroom. Two five-kilogramme bags of rice and various kinds of pasta had been emptied all over the storeroom floor, and junk spilled from an overturned cardboard box. Carmel stared at the box's scattered contents, at the sweeping, shifting sands of rice. She stooped and picked up a handful, let the grains run through her fingers. She remembered what was missing from Sean's Audi.

'The keys!' she whispered. 'Rice Street.'

Where had she not even thought to look for Sean?

Right under her nose.

'That bastard Devine has to be somewhere around here! He got into the warehouse, didn't he? Of course I'm sure, don't question me. Oh yes, he nicked something. Never mind what, you don't need to know. Don't ask me how he got in – I haven't got a fucking clue. I keep trying to work it out and I can't. No, it's not *her*, I know that much. She was at her parents with the kid, then she drove home alone and went to bed. The guys didn't find anything when they trashed the house – that'll teach her to go blabbing to the police trying to put me in the frame. What? No, for the murders. She doesn't know anything about the other . . . no, I'm sure neither she nor Devine have got spare keys. And she doesn't know the safe combination or how to de-activate the alarm. Even if the bitch did, she'd never have the nerve to . . .'

On and on and on. Anthony was terribly agitated, had been

all day. Simona lay in the bath, her eyes closed as she listened to his angry voice in the adjoining bedroom. It was very late and she was exhausted. Outside the bathroom window, several stars glittered in the clear winter night sky. Anthony had made her take a bath because he said she stank.

Tears squeezed from beneath her eyelids. The hot, lavender-perfumed water soothed her bruised, hurting body, but nothing could shake the image of the dead woman in the room of feathers from her tortured mind. How many days had it been now? Simona was not sure.

Who was the woman? Why had Anthony murdered her? She wondered what he had done with the body. Drug-induced sleep had mercifully numbed Simona's brain, and she had no idea how long Anthony had been away that night. However terrified she was, there was nothing she could do. It was pointless to allow the horrific image to dominate her thoughts and paralyse her with fear; she had to concentrate on her own survival. But she couldn't get it out of her mind. She stiffened as Anthony finally stopped talking and banged the receiver down. A second later he appeared in the doorway, a drink in his hand. He wore black trousers and a rumpled white shirt, no tie. His angry eyes were bloodshot.

'If you carry lavender you see ghosts,' he remarked, sniffing the air. 'That's what my mother used to say. Silly old cow.' He looked at Simona. 'Don't you want to know?'

'Know what?' she whispered, sliding down so that the water covered her breasts.

'About the stiff.'

'Stiff?' she echoed, puzzled.

'The corpse. Dead body. The mystery lady with the purple face lying in the room of feathers, remember? I think you do. You were pretty upset – still are.' Anthony finished his drink and put the glass down. 'Never seen a stiff before?'

'That woman ...' Simona swallowed and shook her head. 'She is not my business.'

'You're right.' Anthony nodded. 'Good answer. You're learning. But aren't you curious?' he persisted.

'No.' She glanced away. 'I am not curious.'

'You're a lying bitch.' He came forward and sat on the edge of the bath. 'She was a police officer,' he said, staring down at Simona's breasts, visible beneath the blue-green water. 'I paid her for information – a lot of money. But in the end she had too much information. That's why I had to kill her.'

'I don't understand. Why are you telling me this?' Simona lay very still, the water gently lapping her aching breasts. The nipples were very sore and tender. She dreaded him hurting her again. She did not try to conceal her terror or suffering at the pain he inflicted on her. It was the only way to satisfy a sadist. Simona hoped she could satisfy Anthony so much that he would not want to murder her before she had a chance to escape. Any existence, even being caught and imprisoned for years by the immigration authorities, was preferable to this.

'I'm telling you because you're special. Don't cry now,' he said. 'I've got something else to tell you. Something that'll make you very happy.'

Was he playing with her again? He liked to torture her mind as well as her body. Simona did not believe Anthony would let her go, especially not after telling her about the woman. Was she really a police officer he had paid for information? She had a feeling Anthony was unable to separate fact from fantasy. For instance, did he really think she could love or even like him after what he had done to her? Simona hated him with all her heart. She wanted to kill him.

'Don't look at me like that, you bitch!' His hand was on her head, shoving her under the water. She kicked out, her feet sliding helplessly along the smooth surface of the bath. She fought him, splashing and wriggling, but he was too strong. Her mouth, ears and nostrils filled with hot, oily water, and she choked and gagged, panicking. Anthony

243

held her under until she thought she would drown. Suddenly he let her up. She clung to the sides of the bath, coughing and retching, gulping for breath, her eyes streaming, sodden hair clinging to her face like strands of seaweed. Anthony pushed her hair out of the way, grabbed her by the throat and looked into her terrified eyes.

'You really shouldn't piss me off like that. I've got a lot on my mind right now. Some very worrying stuff happening.' He let go of her and pushed her back.

'Why don't you kill me?' Simona sobbed. 'I don't want to be a slave, a caged animal tormented by you. I would rather die.' She coughed up more lavender water. It might smell good, but it tasted revolting.

'I'll kill you if and when I'm good and ready. But I think you'll change your mind when you hear what I've got to say. You see, I was thinking about your sister.'

She looked at him and gasped. 'My sister?'

'Yeah. I realised I do know her. She's not round here any more, but I could easily find her. A few phone calls, that's all it would take. Of course, whether or not I do it depends on your attitude. Your willingness to co-operate.'

'Co-operate with what? You're lying,' Simona wailed. 'Why would you help me find Maria? You will never let us be reunited. You only want to imprison and torment me!' She sat up and stared at him, her eyes filled with rage. 'I hate you!' she hissed. 'I would rather die than be here with you in your hell!'

Anthony flinched when she said that. His face crumpled, took on a frightened and hunted look. I don't care any more, Simona thought, leaning back sobbing. She would have jumped out of the bath and thrown herself out of the window, if it had not been double-glazed and locked like all the windows in this horrible isolated house, hemmed in by the oppressive mass of trees. It felt like the end of the world here. Did no one else ever come to this house – except people Anthony wanted to murder? No one came to clean or cook, there was no one she could ask for help. The atmosphere in the house was stifling, stunted, evil. Filled with an incredible sadness and desolation. Like its master.

'You don't believe me.' Anthony got up. 'Okay, fine. I'll prove it to you. Stay there,' he ordered. 'The doors and windows are locked, you can't get out anyway.'

He strode across the wide landing and ran downstairs. Simona sank back and closed her eyes again, feeling her aching body, her heaving breaths, her hunger, exhaustion and desperation. Another night with this sadist. Unless Anthony went out again. Where did he go? To hunt and kidnap more girls and imprison them in that terrible house in the city, force them to work as prostitutes? Did he stroke their hair and breasts, talk to them about debt and bondage and slavery?

Simona sat up and climbed awkwardly out of the bath, trying not to slip or make any splashing sound. She would not stay here. She was trapped in this fortress of a house, but she could still go down to the kitchen, take one of those long, black-handled knives with the gleaming blades that neither Anthony nor anyone else ever used, and stab him with it. Not through the heart, because Anthony had no heart. In the neck, the jugular vein. She would go to prison of course, probably be kept there until she was old. So what? She didn't care any more. Just to watch Anthony's blood flow, to know he was dead and could no longer hurt her. That was enough.

Simona crept out of the bathroom and was halfway across the landing when she stopped and gasped, shivering. Anthony was coming back upstairs already. Courage drained away and stark terror returned. She turned and fled, quickly climbed back into the bath. Why had she said those things to him, was she crazy? He would kill her. She would never escape, never see Maria or her parents or Lily again. Anthony came into the bathroom and grabbed her by her wet hair. Simona gasped in pain.

'I told you to stay in that fucking bath, didn't I?'

He hit her across the face and blood trickled from her

nose. She shrank down in the water, crying and sniffing blood, terrified of what he might do next. Anthony walked back to the door, took something out of his pocket and held it up.

'Maybe this will change your attitude!'

Simona gave a startled cry as he flung it at her. The thing smacked on to the water and floated. She picked it up and opened it, saw the name and photograph. Dark eyes similar to her own looked back at her. That shy, hesitant smile, the curve of the lips. She gasped and clutched the precious document to her breasts, started to wail and sob again.

It was Maria's passport.

Chapter Twenty

The girl's face was mottled by death, her features swollen and puffy, turning blue, black, purple, and covered with chalky dust. Still recognisable, though. The long, dark hair had lost its sheen and was caked with rubble. Her red silk dress was damp and filthy. The sweet, sickly stench of decay floated on the chill air.

Anthony gagged at the sight and stink of the rat-chewed corpse, and broke out in a rush of cold sweat. A violent surge of nausea overwhelmed him. He dropped the torch, staggered backwards and threw up, steadying himself against the rough, sandstone wall of the tunnel. He felt so dizzy he was afraid he might faint. No, he thought. Don't do that here. He imagined himself lying unconscious with the rats scurrying over him, their tails flicking his face, sharp teeth and tiny paws nipping and clawing at his flesh, eating him while he was still alive. He groaned and bent double again, his stomach churning. He held his coat out of the way, and tried to stop vomit splashing on his shoes. Anthony was shamed and surprised by his reaction, but at least one thing was certain. The bitch was dead, not like in his nightmare. She wasn't going anywhere.

He straightened up and leaned against the wall, panting and sweating heavily despite the chill in the dark tunnel. He pulled a white cotton handkerchief from his coat pocket, and wiped his face and hands. He forced himself to pick up the shovel and cover her body with rubble again. How long did it take for a corpse to decompose? Months, years? A lot longer than he'd thought, anyway. He dropped the shovel and paused, weak and shaking. At least there was no one to witness him losing it like this.

When the girl's body was safely covered once more, he picked his way back towards the tunnel entrance, clambering over heaps of rubble, and came out into the lord mayor's stable yard. The stable yard buildings were due to be demolished in the near future, the site having been leased to a housing association. A few protesters objected, saying that some of the Williamson tunnels beneath the site would be lost or destroyed, and that the old stable yard buildings formed an important part of Liverpool's heritage. Planning permission had been granted none the less.

The Joseph Williamson labyrinth was attracting more publicity lately, local and national, and that worried him. If he could just find the gold! The recent newspaper report about the tunnels receiving a European development grant that would enable them to be cleared, fully explored and finally opened to the public did not alarm him too much. Things like that took an eternity to happen, and often did not happen at all. In the meantime, there were plenty of other things to alarm him.

It was driving him insane, trying to work out what was going on. Obviously Sean Devine wasn't dead. And he wanted revenge. For the rest, Anthony could only speculate. Someone must be helping Sean – and that person was most likely to be Carmel. But he knew where she was every second of every day, and she hadn't done anything out of the ordinary. There had to be another set of keys to the warehouse. Where the hell had they come from? He'd had the locks and alarm changed, got a new safe combination, but all that might be too late now that Sean had stolen the fifty grand – on top of the briefcase of cash he'd escaped with on the night he disappeared – and the girls passports. What would he do with the money and passports? Did

Carmel know about all this? She might be in contact with Sean by phone, but wasn't that too risky? They couldn't know who might be listening. Anthony was infuriated and panicked, but at the moment all he could do was wait and freak himself about what might happen next. He did not dare touch Carmel for now, not since the police had questioned him again. Her trashed house would keep her occupied for the moment, anyway. He wanted Sean dead – would Sean try to kill him? Or did Sean have some dickbrain plan to force him to go to the police and confess to murdering Gemma and Paula? What the hell did he want?

Anthony carried a gun everywhere now, his house had CCTV plus the sophisticated alarm system. Sean's house – and his interfering bitch of a wife – were under constant surveillance. Sean would be crazy to try anything. But Anthony was frightened. He had to find the bastard! The frustration was unbelievable.

He came out into Smithdown Lane, walked along and got into his Jaguar, parked near the Merseyside Police building. Smithdown Lane was the traffic headquarters, but they did not seem to mind a bit of illegal parking on their own doorstep. He started the engine and drove up Grinfield Street, blaring the horn and swerving to avoid a couple of drunks who staggered out of the Bay Horse and across the road, holding on to one another and laughing like drains.

'Yeah,' Anthony murmured, 'night in the city! Go out with your mates, get off your face, and play in the traffic.' He shook his head irritably. He kept glancing in the driving mirror to make sure no one was following. That nosy copper, for instance. Neil Davie. Maybe even Sean. Anthony took several quick detours just in case.

There were no drunks in Highgate Street. Everybody seemed to be home watching television as usual, probably eating their tea off trays so as not to miss any vital quiz or cookery programmes. His mother had loved cookery programmes, knew all the names of exotic ingredients she would never dream of buying and using. Anthony favoured

Thai cuisine, but if he wanted the authentic experience he had to go to London. Or preferably Bangkok.

He grabbed the photocopied map of the labyrinth, got out of the car and went into the house. The lights were on, and so was the television. He went down the cellar steps, changed into his overalls and hard hat and picked up the big torch. He glanced around nervously, sniffing the stale air. Was something different? No. He was edgy, and no wonder. There was no way Mary would let anyone into the house, certainly not without first asking his permission.

Anthony looked at the small tunnel entrance then took a moment to study the map again. He had got further last time and come up against what was probably the entrance to more tunnels. This time he would take a clew, the big ball of twine, to guide himself through the labyrinth.

'Labyrinth,' he murmured as he knotted one end of the twine around a hot water pipe, 'a complicated structure with many passages, intricate or tortuous arrangement. Like my bloody life right now.'

More rubble shovelling was in order. Anthony grabbed the spade and pickaxe and stepped inside the tunnel, walking slowly along the narrow passage with its intricate brickwork, unravelling the ball of twine as he went. They did not take this much trouble with building nowadays, did not possess such levels of skill and craftsmanship. Joseph's labyrinth, if left in peace, would last for eternity. Problem was, it would not be left in peace. Anthony flashed the torch to left and right, and gasped as a big grey rat scuttled across his path. That was the only thing he hated down here, the bloody rats. He wished he could exterminate them all.

The recent rain had left pools of water in places. Some tunnels always had water in them; he had to be careful. He came to where the tiny tunnel running from his mother's house branched out into the larger part of the labyrinth. He had had to dig through a heap of rubble at what had initially appeared to be a dead end. Anthony did not go near the

'Wine Bins' room or the Banqueting Hall this time, as his route lay in the opposite direction. He went down one level and up another, crossed a narrow stone arch that spanned a black pit about ten feet below. The pit was filled with water. Rats were not the only terrors that lurked down here.

Sometimes Anthony imagined rounding a corner and bumping into Joseph Williamson himself, dressed in his scruffy clothes and smoking a pipe, his expression childishly obstinate as in the portrait of him that hung in the Walker Art Gallery. There was a story that an acquaintance meeting him in Liverpool had remarked on the sad state of his dress and Joseph replied that it did not matter because everyone knew him there. The man made the same remark on meeting Joseph again in London. 'What does it matter?' Joseph laughed, 'no one knows me here!'

Anthony flashed the torch upwards and saw one of the cast iron grids that had run along Mason Street and other Liverpool streets during Joseph's day, now covered by paving stones. A rusted chain hung from the grid. A few yards further on the thick sandstone walls started to close in on him as the tunnel narrowed again. He went down a flight of steps and along a narrow passage, his shoulders brushing the walls, until he came to the gap where the two tunnels branched off, each one disappearing into pitch darkness. He stopped, breathing hard. He had taken the right-hand tunnel last time and come up against a bricked up arch blocked by a mound of rubble he had had to climb and crawl over to get a look at. According to the map, more tunnels lay behind the arch, some of them leading as far as the city centre. They could have been destroyed by now, of course; Anthony had no way of knowing. This time he would try the left-hand tunnel, where other tunnels were supposed to connect with tunnels behind the bricked-up arch.

He headed down the narrow tunnel, shining the torch into the dense, cold darkness. The walls were rough and uneven, the floor strewn with rubble. He had to walk carefully so as not to trip. Anthony stopped and shone the torch at a niche in the wall, with scorch marks made by a candle. Ahead was a great mound of rubble that almost reached the tunnel's ceiling.

'Shit!' he breathed. He would have to clamber over that lot to find out what lay beyond, and he was already tired and sweating despite the cold. He leaned against the wall, took several deep breaths then approached the mound, the thought of Alice's gold driving him on. His feet slid as he scrabbled and hauled his way to the top, keeping a grip on the torch, spade and pickaxe. Behind him in the darkness he could hear scurrying, scratching sounds as nervous rats ran for cover. Anthony cried out in fright as two tiny red eyes glowed at him in the dark. A tail flicked his left hand.

'Fuck off, you little bastards!' The thick walls and low ceiling stifled his shout and sucked it in, almost forcing it back down his throat and into his lungs. Dust filled his mouth and nose, making him cough. He scrambled to the top of the rubble mound, his head touching the brick ceiling, and paused to get his breath back. Dimly, ahead of him he could see a stone arch, like the entrance to a church, a black gap below it. Anthony smiled in triumph. The arch wasn't walled up! He lifted the torch and shone it ahead, digging in his feet to get a better grip. The rubble gave way beneath him and suddenly he was slipping, sliding forwards and down, fingers scrabbling desperately for something to hold on to.

'No!' he yelled, kicking helplessly. Spade and pickaxe rolled away and he dropped the torch as he flung up his arms, trying to save himself. To his horror, he heard a splash. He landed in icy water up to his neck, and went under. Anthony shut his eyes and mouth to stop the water flooding in, but he could not stop it going up his nose. It was brackish, filled with mud and particles. Terror gripped him. He surfaced, coughing, spitting and gulping for breath. Something bobbed up and bumped him in the face; it was the ball of twine.

'Help me!' he gurgled, thrashing about. 'Help!'

Who the hell would help? He was alone, deep inside this pitch-dark, largely unexplored labyrinth. Nobody knew he was here. Mary did not know he had gone into the house unless she bothered to look out of her front room window and notice his Jag. Even then she might not come in, and she certainly would not go down to the cellar. By the time anyone found him – if they did – he could have drowned alone in the dark. What a bloody fool he was to risk his life for a chest of gold that might not even be there any more! How could he have ever thought this place romantic and fascinating? He was living in a dream world. It was evil, twisted, terrifying. He could be entombed here along with all the other victims the labyrinth had claimed.

How deep was this black pit of muddy water? Did it go down to another level? Part of the tunnel floor must have collapsed. The water might be contaminated by noxious chemicals of rotted Victorian and Edwardian corpses. Something touched his left leg and he screamed. Anthony struggled frantically, trying to swim, but his overalls and heavy boots were dragging him down. He sank and resurfaced, splashing about, groping for a hold and shouting hoarsely, half-choked by panic, darkness and the filthy water. If only he could grab the torch! But it had gone down with its light blazing, like the SS *Titanic*. The darkness was terrifying.

Rough sandstone scraped the backs of his hands and he lunged for the arch, kicking his already half-frozen legs and feet. There was a ledge just below the surface of the water. Anthony clung to it, coughing and choking, his breath coming in sobbing gasps. He had to haul himself out somehow before his body became numb with cold. Above the narrow ledge was a step with bull-nose edgings. He kicked and flailed, reached up and managed to grab it, his arms straining in their sockets. He kicked at the wall beneath the water, searching for a foothold, then made a huge effort and hauled himself out, clinging to the step as he dragged himself up. He had no breath left to groan or swear.

Crouched soaking and shivering on the step, Anthony reached cautiously down and swirled one hand around in the water, trying to create a current that would bring the ball of twine floating towards him. After a minute he sat back; there was no sign of it. He estimated the pit of water was about fifteen feet in diameter. He was shivering violently, his teeth chattering. Panic gradually receded and he tried to think, evaluate the situation. That didn't make him feel any better.

How the hell was he supposed to swim back across the pit and re-scale that treacherous, high rubble heap? He couldn't go back, but he couldn't go on either, and certainly not without the torch. He had no idea what other hazards lay ahead, he might end up seriously injured, trapped down here for ever. Darkness clung to him suffocatingly. Anthony raised one hand and held it close to his face; he couldn't see it. There wasn't even a watery glimmer of torchlight. He was walled up alive in a bloody great tomb.

'No!' he groaned, his eyes filling with tears. '*No!*'

This was worse than his worst nightmare, the crucifixes dripping blood.

Because he wasn't going to wake up. This time it was real.

'You *what*? Don't give me that sh – !' Neil Davie stopped, remembering every word he spoke in the depressing, smoke-filled interview room was being recorded on tape for posterity. Or at least the next thirty years. He glanced at DC Catherine King, sitting calmly beside him in her grey suit, not a straight, fair hair out of place. Nothing seemed to surprise her. 'Are you seriously alleging—?'

'Eh?' The girl lounging opposite him, with pasty, spotty skin, long straight greasy blonde hair, wearing jeans, a black sweater and grubby sheepskin coat, gave him an angry look as she lit her third cigarette in fifteen minutes.

'Speak English, can't yer?' she said nasally, her red-rimmed hazel eyes narrowed as she blew out smoke.

'Are you saying,' Neil repeated, itching to belt her across her impudent face, 'that Detective Inspector Crane took drugs and money from your house when it was searched, then sold the drugs and kept the money? You're lying, aren't you?' he said, trying to keep his voice calm. 'You'd say anything to get off this possession charge.' He leaned his elbows on the table and inhaled a cloud of her cigarette smoke. 'I should warn you that making malicious allegations – telling lies – about a police officer isn't the way to do it. You could get yourself in a lot more trouble than you're in now.'

'I'm not lying!' The girl sat up, enraged. 'Carl, my fella, was there too. He saw her do it. She opened the kitchen cupboard, took the money and stuff out, and shoved them in her bag. It was only the three of us in the room. She just looked at us and gave us a fuck-you grin. Bloody red-haired old bow-wow!'

'Don't talk about Detective Inspector Crane like that!' Neil couldn't stand it any longer. 'If this is supposed to have happened nearly three months ago, why didn't you tell us before now?' he demanded.

'Joking, aren't you, mate?' the girl sneered. She sat back, pleased that she'd needled him. 'Who'd have believed us? I'm only telling you now because you're picking on me again. Got to protect meself, haven't I?' She grinned. 'You'll have to get the anti-corruption branch to check that bitch out. I saw a telly programme about them. One of your mates'll grass her up and he'll have to be a protected witness. Go and ask old bow-wow,' she said aggressively, 'Just watch her try and front it out. I'll sort the bitch this time – I'm not taking any more shit from that bloody old cow!'

'I can't ask DI Crane anything,' Neil folded his arms tightly, 'because she's—' He stood up suddenly and turned away, scraping back his chair.

'Ohh Jesus!' the girl squealed. 'That went right through me!'

'Carry on, will you?' he said to Catherine. He strode out of the room and down the corridor, took the stairs at a run. He slammed the office door and marched to his desk, relieved that for once the room was empty.

He stood gazing out of the window, staring down at the rainwashed car park, at the empty space near the entrance that Olivia had always commandeered. Thought about getting himself some coffee, but couldn't be bothered. He wished he hadn't given up smoking. He swore under his breath as the door opened and swung round, ready to tell whoever it was to piss off. Catherine walked in.

'You okay?' she asked, a look of concern in her pale blue eyes. 'Madam down the stair can stew for a bit. They've given her a cup of tea. Thought I'd get out of that room too, take a break before all her ciggy smoke asphyxiated me.' She closed the door and joined him at the window. 'It's awful about Olivia,' she said quietly. 'You worked very closely with her – you must miss her a lot. That little bitch is probably lying through her teeth. But you know she's right – we do have to check her allegation. Plus those other inconsistencies we've discovered in some of Olivia's cases. That missing evidence. I can understand you don't want to face it,' Catherine went on, 'but she may not have been such a great copper after all.'

'We don't know that,' Neil said sharply. 'Don't you start accusing her as well. Easy when someone's not around to answer back, isn't it?'

'I'm not accusing Olivia. I only said things have to be checked out. Look, I'm sorry, all right? I didn't mean to upset you.' Catherine glanced away, her expression troubled, and they were silent. 'Fancy a coffee?' she asked after a minute.

'Yeah, go on.' Neil shoved his hands in his suit pockets. 'I didn't expect to be this upset,' he confessed. 'I just can't get my head round it. I'm off my food, I have trouble sleeping.' He grimaced. 'Had a few too many last night.'

'You can't let it get to you like this,' Catherine said. 'Olivia would say you were mad. You should take care of yourself, Neil.'

'Yeah. I know.' He missed Olivia's humour and sarcasm, the sharp greenish eyes and mane of red hair against the grey background of the offices. 'Her death just doesn't add up,' he said. 'I thought it did. But it doesn't.'

Carmel Devine's words went round and round in his head: '*Strange, her dying alone like that. Surely DI Crane would have had time to phone for help before things got really bad?*'

'Olivia was well bladdered,' he frowned, 'No argument about that. But so much that she couldn't pick up a phone? I doubt it. Even if she'd passed out, wouldn't she have woken when the asthma attack started? And she always kept her medication handy.'

'She'd been out for the evening, hadn't she?' Catherine said. 'Where? Who with?'

'That's what we don't know. An insomniac neighbour saw a man bring her home about three am. Carry her home, more like! But we don't know who he was and we can't trace him.'

'Any description?'

'Tall and dark, driving a flash car. Could be anybody. Olivia was—.' Neil flushed. 'Well, she'd been playing away from home a lot over the years. That's why her marriage broke up.' He glanced at Catherine. 'What's funny?'

'If a bloke was screwing around you wouldn't go all coy and think it was such a delicate matter. Typical!'

'All right,' he said irritably. 'Point taken.' Neil drummed his fingers on the windowsill, staring down at the empty spot where Olivia's car should have been parked. 'She was really on edge a few days before she died. She was worried about her son, but there was definitely something else – she wouldn't say what. And her asthma was worse. That afternoon at Carmel Devine's, for instance. Carmel Devine said Anthony Maskey had killed Gemma Geraghty and Paula Pepper, not her husband, and that some copper on his payroll could have tipped him off about the witness. Olivia suddenly started wheezing like crazy, coughing her guts up. I thought I'd have to rush her to Casualty.'

Neil went quiet as a bolt of horror shot through him. He glanced away, avoiding Catherine's curious eyes. A colleague, he thought. Someone I know and like. *Trust.* No! he thought. He recalled how Olivia had aggressively dismissed his concerns about the case against Sean Devine. So aggressively that, looking back, it was almost as if she could have been trying to protect someone. Anthony Maskey?

'What's up?' Catherine asked.

He started. 'Nothing.'

'Neil, I ran that check on Anthony Maskey you asked for.' She picked up a paper from her desk and handed it to him. 'There's some old stuff – a minor rap for dealing, and a rather more major one for attempted rape. Years ago. The rape thing was never proved, and he walked. That's it.'

'So Maskey's got form.' Neil stared at the printout.

Catherine watched him. 'When you say something doesn't fit – do you mean you don't think Olivia's death was an accident?'

'I don't know what I mean. I've just got this bad feeling.'

'Was there anything unusual at her house?'

'I couldn't find her mobile. Or her address book. She always had them with her. That was weird.' Neil frowned again. 'Olivia didn't commit suicide, that's for sure. Some guy carries her home at three am and next thing she's dead. Even though she's got medication in her bag beside her on the sofa – and surely would have had time to call a doctor or ambulance. I wish I could find that guy,' he said slowly. 'I'd really like to talk to him.'

'We could have another word with the insomniac neighbour.' Catherine looked thoughtful. 'But the autopsy report does confirm that Olivia died from suffocation – a fatal asthma attack. They couldn't explain those hives though – urticaria, they're called – that were all over her skin. Except that they indicated a massive allergic reaction. Could have been something she ate.'

Neil shook his head impatiently. 'Olivia ate all those foods that are supposed to cause allergies – cheese, eggs, peanuts, chocolate, fish, strawberries, you name it. She never had any trouble. The only thing she was allergic to was feathers.'

'Feathers? A cousin of mine's allergic to feathers,' Catherine remarked. 'He comes out in this terrible, red, itchy rash and he can't breathe properly.'

'Yeah, same with Olivia. Except that her asthma made the allergic reaction even worse. She often said if she was exposed to them for long enough she'd be—' Neil broke off and his eyes widened in shock. Catherine, heading towards the door, did not notice.

'I'll get the coffee,' she called. 'You stay here, relax for a bit. Then we'll go back and finish that bloody interview.' The door closed behind her.

Neil sat down and leaned his elbows on the desk, staring out at the rain. I'm knackered, he thought, rubbing his eyes. I can't handle this now. Olivia didn't know Anthony Maskey and she wasn't murdered! Why would he – or anybody – want to murder her anyway? But wasn't being someone's paid informant always a hazardous game? Their shelf life could be shorter than the average fresh cream cake.

'Stop it,' he said aloud to the empty room. 'This is crazy.'

But the thoughts ran on, one association relentlessly evoking another. Olivia's edginess, fear almost, before she died, her refusal to say what was wrong. Her sudden attack of asthma at Carmel Devine's house the minute Anthony Maskey's name was mentioned. Her angry refusal to believe anyone but Sean Devine could have murdered Gemma Geraghty or Paula Pepper. That was totally unlike Olivia. Normally she had an open mind about each case, was always eager to pursue new lines of inquiry and look at things from every possible angle. But now it seemed there were some big question marks about Olivia Crane's way of doing things. And today, this little cow's allegation about Olivia stealing drugs and cash during a search. Doing it blatantly – as if it wasn't the first time.

Who was the tall, dark, mystery man with the flash car, who had carried her into her house that night? Anthony Maskey was tall and dark. He was certainly mysterious. And he owned a very flash car. Had Olivia known him, tipped him off about Paula Pepper witnessing Gemma's murder? Did he know about Olivia's feather allergy?

'Oh, Jesus!' Neil groaned. 'Olivia, tell me this is all bull-shit. Please!'

Olivia couldn't tell him anything any more. He was on his own. Neil leaned back in his chair and shut his eyes. He felt as if he'd just aged a decade. Catherine came in with two cups of coffee and stopped briefly when she saw his expression.

'Bad news?' She dumped a cup in front of him. 'Neil, what the hell's wrong?'

He sat up straight and stared into her pale blue eyes. 'What if Olivia wasn't just bladdered when that guy carried her into her house?' he asked, choked. 'What if she was already dead?'

Chapter Twenty-one

'Bloody hell, what a mess!' Daniel shook his head as he surveyed the wreckage in the sunlit kitchen, his expression grim. 'There's still a lot of clearing up to be done,' he commented. 'But at least the gas and electrics are safe now, and you're not wading around any more. You can switch on lights and make coffee without blowing yourself up. Those locks and the steel plate in the new front door should stand up to pretty well anything.' He turned back to Carmel. 'Even a police battering ram.'

'I don't know how I would have managed without your help, Daniel. You saved my life. I can't tell you how grateful I am.'

'Hey! No worries.' Daniel smiled at her, although he was seriously worried. Anthony Maskey's cash and passports were burning a hole in his safe at the garage; the longer they stayed there the more frightened he became. Carmel looked frightened too, and no wonder after her house had been trashed like this. Tearing up the photo of Lisa as a baby was a particularly nasty touch. Carmel wore dark denim jeans and a turquoise sweater, no makeup, and her thick, wavy blonde hair was loose, falling over her shoulders. She was pale and exhausted; the trauma of the past weeks had left its mark. Daniel watched her take a quick sip of coffee and put the cup down. She's lost weight, he thought. The buttered toast she'd been making herself when he arrived had been consigned to the kitchen wastebin after just one bite and now an untouched cheese sandwich lay curling up at the edges.

'What do the police say?' he asked. 'I don't suppose there's any proof Maskey did this? Or had it done.'

'Oh no, of course not!' Carmel's voice was bitter. 'DS Davie's sympathetic now, but not much help. The truth is, he's too upset about the death of that inspector.'

'Still got his job to do though, hasn't he?' Daniel was annoyed. 'She's dead and that's very sad, but you're alive and you – and Sean – need help *now*. How long will Lisa stay with her grandparents?' he asked.

'I'm not sure. At least until I've got the house cleared up. I want to redo Lisa's bedroom as well – they made a terrible mess in there. In the meantime, she needs to be somewhere she can feel safe. I really miss her though!' Carmel sighed. 'Dad's taking her with him to the golf club this morning, that'll be a new experience for her. They'll have lunch there too. Mum will be home from work by the time they get back.'

Daniel nudged her and grinned. 'Lisa might turn out to be the new Tiger Woods in about ten years time.' He picked up his mug of coffee. 'So what are you up to today?'

'Well, clearing this place, of course.'

'Not going to the office?'

'No point,' Carmel shrugged. 'No heads to sort out.' And Sean had said he wouldn't call back for at least another few days. Her new mobile lay on the kitchen table. She wished she could tell Daniel about Sean's phone call. And where she was going later. He was entitled to know, after all he'd done to help. But Sean was right, it was too dangerous. Daniel was already taking a big risk keeping Anthony's cash and passports in his safe.

'You've got no patients left at all?' Daniel looked startled.

'Oh, a few. Not enough to go in eight hours a day five days a week for. Let's see, it's Thursday, isn't it? I don't have another appointment until three tomorrow afternoon. Then nothing else until next Tuesday.'

'Bloody hell.' Daniel put down his coffee. 'What will you do for money?'

'Oh, baby, wow!' Carmel laughed suddenly. 'I'll do anything for money.'

'Be serious.' He frowned, digging his hands into his overall pockets.

'If Anthony Maskey refuses to pay Sean's salary and I can't hang on to enough clients, I'll just have to look for some other line of work.' Her smile faded. 'Maybe Anthony could get me a job in a lapdancing club. Although he's not into paying wages, is he? And at thirty-three I suppose I'm knocking on a bit for that lark ... got a few faded stretch marks too, courtesy of Lisa. Then again, there are plenty of necrophiles who lust after decrepit thirty-plussers! But *seriously*,' she said, as Daniel's frown deepened, 'there's some savings, so I'm okay for now. If push comes to shove, I'll sell this house and find something smaller. Or move in with mum and dad until I can get back on my feet. I'm sure they won't let me and Lisa starve. But ...' she paused, blinking back the tears that were never far away, 'I'm hoping Sean will come home long before things get that desperate.'

'Of course he will. God, this is fucking crazy!' Daniel pulled her to him and wrapped his arms around her. They stood still, his chin resting on her hair. She closed her eyes and bit her lip, longing to tell him about Sean's call. And Rice Street.

Carmel had completely forgotten about the garage with the flat above, in the quiet little street near the Anglican cathedral. She had only remembered when she saw the rice grains and the duplicate keys in the storeroom junk box and finally twigged that the original keys, in their dirty little red plastic wallet, had been missing from the Audi. Sean would not have taken them for no reason.

She hadn't been to Rice Street since Lisa was a baby, and

Sean hadn't gone near the place in more than two years. He had considered leasing the garage because he'd lost interest in doing up old cars, and renovating the flat above so he could let that too. But he hadn't got around to doing anything. Carmel couldn't be certain Sean was hiding there – or that Anthony didn't know about the place. Not surprisingly, neither the police nor Anthony's hired help had shown any interest in the rusted, blackened keys. Everyone had sets of old keys lying around. As long as Anthony had her watched, it meant he hadn't got Sean. So Anthony couldn't know about Rice Street. Or hadn't thought of it yet. Carmel prayed fervently that he wouldn't.

She and Daniel drew apart. 'I'll stay a bit longer,' he offered. 'Help you clean up some more.'

'Thanks, Daniel, but I really want you to go to work now. You've taken enough time off to help me, and so has Rosa. I don't want you to lose your business and she her job because of me. We'd all be up the scupper then. I'm fine,' she said. 'Really.'

'You sure? Well, I'll see you later.' Daniel pulled on his jacket, started to walk away then stopped. 'Heard from Natalie lately?' he asked. 'Any of your other friends?'

'Natalie's phoned a few times and we've had lunch. I'm meeting her again soon. Some others have called round.' Carmel shrugged and smiled sadly. 'Some haven't.'

'Hmm. I just wondered. Right,' he said. 'See you.'

Carmel left the Landcruiser parked outside the house, walked around the corner and hailed a cab to take her into town. The cab drove past the university buildings and headed down the long hill towards the city centre, the black BMW trailing them in the stream of traffic, at what the driver obviously considered a discreet distance. The sunshine faded as the cloud layer thickened. A few drops of rain fell.

Carmel stared out of the window, avoiding the driver's eyes in the mirror. Anger rose in her. It was intolerable, invasive, a violation, to be followed around like this and have her house watched twenty-four hours a day. To be separated from her daughter because it wasn't safe for Lisa to be in her own home right now. She pulled the soft leather jacket around her and clutched her bag, playing with the strap.

'Drop me here,' she called as the cab rounded the corner by Lewis's department store. She fumbled in her wallet for coins. The cab lurched to a halt at the traffic lights just past Central Station. Carmel jumped out and joined a bunch of pedestrians hurrying across the busy road, huddled together for safety. Church Street was pedestrianised; the men could not follow her down there, at least not in the BMW.

She glanced back and swore. A man was getting out of the car, which was stuck in traffic further up the street, gesturing urgently to the driver. He was youngish, with a moustache, wore jeans, trainers, a denim jacket and black woolly hat. Unfortunately he looked fit and powerful, like a bodybuilder. He started to sprint after her, mobile clutched in one hand.

Carmel rounded the corner, out of his sight for just seconds. She ran, dodging amongst the crowds of strolling shoppers and schoolchildren playing truant, and disappeared into George Henry Lee's department store. Inside she paused by a counter of leather purses and wallets, and looked through the swing doors. The man was standing in the middle of the street next to a bin overflowing with empty hamburger cartons, glancing around angrily and talking on the mobile. Was he calling for reinforcements? Would he read her mind any second, guess that she'd come in here because there was more than one exit?

She turned and hurried past the leather goods counter and across the store towards the lingerie department, fighting her way through seemingly endless rows of padded, unpadded and underwired bras, silky lace knickers in baby blue, black, or wicked crimson and dangling suspender belts, to reach another exit that came out near St John's Market and the Everyman Theatre. She raced past the theatre and collapsed into a waiting cab.

'Rodney Street, please,' she panted, breathless and sweating. Rice Street was two minutes walk from there; best not to give the exact address. The cab sped up Renshaw Street and turned into Leece Street at St Luke's Place, by the bombed-out church. In Rodney Street Carmel got out and walked past the row of Georgian houses, most of which contained the private practices of dentists or medical specialists. She crossed the road, walked down Pilgrim Street and turned into Rice Street.

Rice Street was tiny and quiet with a sleepy rural air, a refuge from the noise and bustle of the city. Some of the old warehouses were in an advanced state of decay. Carmel stopped and looked around, searching nervously for any sign of the BMW or the bodybuilder in the woolly hat, before she approached Sean's garage on the corner, with the flat above. The windows were dirty, the dark green frames flaking paint, and the place had a deserted, desolate look. She looked up and down the small street again, feeling horribly vulnerable. An invisible dog barked in a nearby back yard, but there was nobody about. She walked round the corner and down the tiny alley, not wanting to go in the front way.

Carmel stuck the key in the big padlock, hoping the yard doors were not bolted on the inside. They were. Shit! Now she had to go in the front way. She ran back around the corner and unlocked the front doors, her mouth dry with fear and her fingers shaking as she fiddled with keys and padlocks. Once inside she quickly relocked the doors, then stood looking around the dark, dusty, silent space, with its brick walls and rough, uneven concrete floor. It smelled musty, damp. Could Sean be here now? Her heart pounded with fearful anticipation.

'Sean?' she called tentatively, her voice tiny in the large, empty space. No answer. She walked to the door in the wall which opened into the passage; a flight of stone stairs with a rusty wrought iron rail led to the flat above. Carmel climbed the stairs slowly, her legs leaden and her breath coming in nervous gasps. Tears pricked at her eyes. She thought she was just checking the place out, exploring a possible option. But now she realised how desperately she wanted, needed Sean to be here. If he wasn't, she had no idea where to look next. And time was running out.

She walked from room to room, paused to look out of the dirty windows into the street. It was raining hard now, and seemed colder in here than outside. Carmel's heart sank. No one could live in this place! It was too cold, too dirty, had no furniture except an old wooden chair and table in the kitchen. The bathroom had ancient black and white lino, now back in fashion, a bath with lions paws – also back in fashion – and next door an old lavatory with a chain. When flushed the lavatory sounded like Niagara Falls, and caused groaning and clanking of pipes for about five minutes afterwards.

The gas fire in the living room did not work, and the electricity was off. There was no sign that anyone had been here in a long time. Carmel went into the kitchen and looked at the stained gas cooker with its filthy, greasy grill pan. There were a few old chipped mugs and dusty beer glasses in the cupboards. No food, no bread, teabags, coffee. Sean had come up here sometimes and made himself tea or coffee, sat at the table to read a paper. A white plastic kettle stood on the draining board. The windowsill was littered with dead flies and dried-out spiders trapped in their webs.

'Why aren't you here?' Carmel shouted despairingly into the silence, overwhelmed by a terrible sense of anti-climax. Tears spilled from her eyes. 'Where the hell are you?' She wiped her eyes then kicked violently at the rickety kitchen chair in an outburst of total frustration. It skittered across the floor, bashed against the store cupboard door and overturned, displacing a cardboard box containing a few old newspapers. A corner of lino sprang up.

'For fuck's *sake*!' Wearily she walked to the chair, bent and grabbed it. One of the back legs caught the curled-up corner of lino. Sean must have put the box of newspapers there to hold it down.

'Come on, you stupid ...!' Trying to set the chair upright, Carmel wrenched furiously at the leg. She felt like smashing the damn thing to pieces. More cracked, dull red lino sprang up, exposing rough grimy floorboards. She pushed the chair out of the way and stared, her anger gone. Then she knelt to get a closer look, pushing back her hair. A long-legged spider with a thick body scuttled from under the cooker.

There was something strange about the way the floorboards were nailed down. Or not nailed down, judging by the tiny holes that nails should have filled. Well, so what? This place was ancient, falling apart like her life. Now she had to endure agonies while she waited for Sean's next call, hope and pray that Anthony Maskey didn't get to him before she could do something.

'It's not good enough,' she said aloud. 'I'm sick of hoping and praying!'

Carmel suddenly realised that the floorboards had been deliberately loosened.

'Anthony! What the bloody hell's happened to you, lad?'

Standing on Mary's doorstep, filthy, frightened and trembling with exhaustion, soaked, battered and bruised, it took all his remaining strength not to start crying and collapse in a heap at her feet.

'Hello Mary,' he managed to say. 'I just need your keys to next door. I left them—'

Lying on the bottom step in the cellar before venturing into the tunnel last night. He had thought he would be trapped for ever in Joseph Williamson's labyrinth. He was hurting all over, his muscles torn as if he'd been stretched on a medieval rack. Anthony put one hand to his forehead as he swayed slightly.

'Don't stand out there in the rain, it's freezing. So are you, by the looks of things.' Mary held the door open.

'Come in, for God's sake! What the hell's happened?' she repeated, staring at him in shock.

The warm little house was perfumed with baking cakes. Mary, with her bright, anxious brown eyes, neat grey hair, multi-coloured sweater and old jeans was a comforting, motherly figure in a way his own mother had never been. He should just get the keys and go, make some excuse. But Anthony did not want to go, not yet. Waves of concern and love emanated from Mary and washed over him, making him feel warm, relaxed, safe and cared for. She wouldn't criticise or blame, ask him what trouble he'd got himself into now and whatever would his father say. Tell him he was an evil changeling who Lucifer and the bad angels would swoop down on in the middle of the night and snatch away to richly deserved hell fire. Mary loved him, like any normal parent would love a son. She had no children of her own.

'Are you all right, love?' she asked, her anxiety increasing as he stood there mute. 'Are you hurt? D'you need the doctor?'

'No!' Anthony shook his head. 'No doctor. I'm fine. I just need a rest, that's all.'

'Tell you what. Take those filthy wet overalls off, get up them stairs and run yourself a good hot bath. There's towels in the airing cupboard and one of Derek's old dressing gowns in the wardrobe. I'll do you a cup of tea and a bacon butty, then you can tell me all about it when you're ready. The last thing you need is a silly old sod like me fussing around machine-gunning you with questions.'

'You're not a silly old sod. Don't say that, Mary.'

'Go on,' she ordered. 'Get that bath going. There's loads of hot water.'

Half an hour later Anthony came downstairs, his black hair damp and shining, wearing a dark blue dressing gown with white piping around the neck, sleeves and belt, a red-and-gold coat of arms embroidered on the top pocket. The cakes were out of the oven, two perfectly cooked Victoria sandwiches cooling on a wire tray. He sank into a plush, dusky pink armchair by the television and was immediately served with two thick bacon sandwiches and a mug of steaming tea. Mary settled on the sofa and took up her knitting, some filmy angora creation in peach.

'What's that?' Anthony eyed the knitting warily. At least it wasn't crochet. And no virulent colours. I should get rid of all that crap next door, he thought. Trouble is, I can't bring myself to touch the bloody stuff.

'It's a bed jacket,' Mary explained. 'For me friend down the road. Brenda. She's going into the Women's Hospital for a hysterectomy in a couple of weeks. Thought this might cheer her up a bit. So . . .' She pointed the remote control and turned the sound down on the DIY programme. 'You feeling a bit better now? You look better.'

'Yeah. This is fantastic.' Anthony finished the sandwiches and licked his fingers, took several slugs of sweet, strong tea. 'You're bloody brilliant, you are. A lifesaver.'

'Gerroff!' She blushed. 'Fancy another butty?'

'No, thanks, I had enough. They were great. I'll have a piece of cake now.'

'They're not cold. I haven't iced them or spread the raspberry jam in the middle.'

'Doesn't matter.' He sank back in the armchair and stretched out his aching legs. The cramped stuffy room with its plush furniture and ivy-leaf wallpaper was heaven after what he'd been through last night. Anthony shuddered at the fear and desperation of it all. Mary brought him a large slice of warm cake on a flowered plate, and more tea. Then she sat down and resumed her knitting. The click of the knitting needles soothed him further. After a few minutes she paused and looked at him.

'Ready to tell me what happened, luvvie?'

'I was working in the cellar last night,' Anthony began. 'When I'd finished I decided I'd go down the road to the Bay Horse for a quick pint before closing time. While I was in the pub I realised I'd walked out of the house and left the

270

keys lying on the cellar steps. It was after eleven, a bit late to knock on your door, but I had to if I wanted to get back in and pick up my coat and car keys. I left the Bay Horse and crossed the road. I was at the bottom of Highgate Street when this white transit van stopped alongside and two guys in it asked me what time it was. They were laughing – they'd had a skinful. I didn't like the look of them.' He shrugged. 'Next thing I knew, they'd jumped out and started kicking the crap out of me.'

'God almighty!' Mary dropped her knitting and stared at him in horror.

'There was another guy in the back. He joined in. They took all the cash I had on me – about two hundred quid. And my credit cards.'

'Oh, dear God!' Mary clapped one hand to her mouth.

'I thought they'd let me go then. But they tied my hands and feet with rope and chucked me in the back. Drove off, I didn't know where. Not far though, because they stopped after a couple of minutes. They dragged me out of the van and across some waste ground into a kind of tunnel or cave. Dumped me in a shallow pit of water. It was pitch dark, I couldn't see a thing. I was terrified!' Anthony stopped and covered his eyes with his hands. His trauma was genuine, if not the story.

'Have a Scotch, love. You need it.' Mary nodded towards the bottle of Glenfiddich on the sideboard. 'Go on. Help yourself.'

'Thanks, but I'd better not. I'll have to drive home soon.' Anthony sat up and leaned forward. 'I managed to roll myself out of the water,' he went on, 'but I couldn't untie my hands and feet. I shouted for help, but of course no one heard me in there. It took me ages to undo the knots and when I'd finally managed it I tried to get out, but there was no way. There were tunnels branching off in every direction – I didn't know which one to take. I was trapped in there all night, wandering around.' His voice trembled. 'I thought I'd never get out! I was stuck there until dawn,

271

when I suddenly noticed this faint shaft of light. I followed it, came out on Smithdown Lane by the railway cutting.'

Trapped in the dark without twine or torch to guide him, unable to swim the pit and re-scale the rubble heap, and afraid he would croak it from hypothermia if he stayed where he was, there had been no choice but to press on into the unexplored depths. Anthony had tried to stay calm and work out his position in the labyrinth, keeping the image of the map firmly in his mind, knowing he was dead if he panicked. The tunnel walls and floors shook as trains to and from Lime Street rumbled through the cutting, and he knew in which direction Lime Street lay. When the rumbling ceased altogether, he knew it was past midnight.

He began to walk, if taking one tiny, tortuous step after another could be called walking, his eyes straining in the darkness, hands groping desperately at the walls as he made his faltering way along, terrified that at any second the rough floor would disappear beneath his feet. The rats were bolder without a flashing torch beam to scare them off.

On and on, hour after hour, impossible to keep accurately working out his position. Soaked, freezing cold. Stale, dusty air settling in his lungs and on his chest, making him cough. Backwards and forwards, encountering dead ends and false leads, endless rubble heaps. Exhaustion and fear, the constant fight to stop himself unravelling in panic. Finally, after all those hours, deliverance. A flight of rubble and ash-strewn steps, a draught of fresh air, glimmer of daylight. A pile of bricks to climb over, newer bricks that must have been dumped recently. He emerged from the suffocating tunnel to find himself in the middle of a building site near one of the university buildings. Anthony wondered what had previously stood on the site; old houses, probably. And he had discovered a new way in and out of the labyrinth. But he was too exhausted and terrified to be thrilled with the result of this forced expedition. He had walked back to Highgate Street and rung Mary's doorbell.

'My God!' Mary breathed, staring at him. 'You're not safe anywhere. You'd better call the police,' she advised.

'Not yet. I want to drive home, get changed and cancel those cards first. Besides,' Anthony shrugged, 'there's no point in calling the police. It was too dark for me to get a good look at those guys. And a white transit van, well, they don't exactly stick out like sore thumbs. I didn't get a chance to write down the number.'

'You've got to call the police, lad!' Mary looked indignant. 'Those bastards'll do the same to someone else if they're not caught. You could have frozen to death, trapped in that place. Mugging and attempted murder or manslaughter, that's what they want doing for. They must have dumped you in that Williamson labyrinth. I know it's supposed to be historical and part of Liverpool's heritage,' she said, 'but I think those underground tunnels and halls and whatever are nothing but a bloody menace. People been up to no good in them since the damn things were built. That, and getting hurt or killed, never being seen again. I read an article about it. What did that silly old sod want to go and build them for anyway? No wonder he was called the Mad Mole. Short of something to do, that's what he was.'

'Joseph Williamson built the tunnels so that unemployed soldiers back from the Napoleonic Wars wouldn't be short of something to do,' Anthony explained wearily.

'Served their purpose then, haven't they? They should be blocked off now. Downright dangerous, they are.' Mary knitted furiously. 'It's only those conservation people who want to keep them. Or murderers looking for somewhere to dump their victims.'

Anthony got to his feet. 'I'd better get going. Thanks for the great food, Mary. Thanks for everything.'

'You're sure you're all right now?' She heaved herself off the sofa and followed him into the tiny hall. 'You will call the police, won't you?' she said as he turned to go upstairs and change back into his wet, filthy clothes. 'You can't let those bastards get away with it.'

'Okay. I'll call the police,' he lied.

'Good. Hope this doesn't put whatshisname off.' Mary nodded at the wall that separated their two houses. 'Then again, he doesn't need to know. He seemed keen on the place. But he's right, there's a lot needs doing. Especially in the kitchen. And he had one or two other places to look at. Is he moving in, then?' she asked eagerly. 'Or hasn't he decided yet?'

Anthony stopped and stared down at her, uncomprehending. Mary was on medication for her high blood pressure, a beta-blocker called Inderal that was liable to cause drowsiness and mental confusion if taken in high enough doses. Or was he the drowsy and mentally confused party, after his night of trauma? He could barely keep his eyes open now.

'Who? What are you talking about, Mary?' He was getting a bad feeling already, but that was stupid. She must be thinking of something or somebody else.

'He came round to take a look at your mam's house, remember? The other night.' She looked up at him, smiling. 'You lent him your keys. I got a bit of a fright when I walked in and found him there. He was coming up from the cellar.'

Someone had got the keys to his mother's house too! How the fuck ...? Been in the cellar! The shock made Anthony turn sick and faint again. He felt himself blanch.

'Lovely fella,' Mary went on, unaware of the bombshell she had exploded. 'A looker too. Bet he's one for the girls. Dynamite, the pair of you out on the pull together. Wish I was forty years younger!'

Anthony could not take in her words, could not believe what he was hearing. He didn't want to believe it. There was a hissing in his ears and they felt weird, as if blocked with cotton wool.

He shook his head. 'Sorry ... what was that, Mary?'

'Your mate. What's his name? He never said.'

Chapter Twenty-two

'D'you know what "kamikaze" means, Davie?' Chief Superintendent Wilson took another stick of Juicy Fruit chewing gum from the packet on his cluttered desk. Neil knew there were at least ten more packets in the desk's top drawer.

'Yes, sir. It means "divine wind".' He glanced distastefully at the bin with its lumps of discarded gum squashed into white tissues. Pity the poor cleaning lady who had to empty that lot every day.

'Oh, you do know! Very good. Well, the way you're going you'll be back in uniform feeling the divine wind blow up from the Mersey and whistle round your arse while you direct traffic. Do you see that as the next rung on your career ladder?' Wilson unwrapped the stick of gum, rolled it up and shoved it in his mouth. 'I don't think so.'

'Sir, a neighbour who lives opposite Olivia Crane told us a man drove her home and carried her into the house on the night of her death. He must know something. We have to trace him. He could even be the murderer.'

'*The murderer.*' Wilson's thin lips pursed beneath his moustache and his thick black eyebrows shot up à la Groucho Marx. 'Still on about that, are you?'

Carmel Devine must have felt like this when she'd tried to tell him about Anthony Maskey, Neil thought. *Had* Olivia known Maskey? It was doing his head in.

'I think there's a strong possibility that DI Crane was murdered, sir,' he said firmly.

'Do you now? Well, from what I've heard of DI Crane's lifestyle – both before and after her acrimonious divorce – it appears that quite a lot of men drove her home and then had to carry her into her house. D'you think one of them suddenly got the urge to smother her with a cushion or feather pillow? There were times when I wouldn't have minded doing that to her myself.'

Neil flushed angrily. Crass bastard! 'I don't have any evidence yet, sir, but—'

'No, and you won't find it.' Wilson smacked on the chewing gum, a sound that made Neil cringe with disgust. 'Because she died of a fatal asthma attack. If those hives on her skin were caused by exposure to feathers, as you say, then where were these feathers? They didn't find any in her house or car. Or anywhere on her body.'

'She could have been exposed to them somewhere else. By the man who—'

'Shut up, Davie, I haven't finished. And the reason DI Crane died alone with her medication to hand – something else you regard as suspicious – is that she was so drunk she wouldn't have known if she'd been lying in a roomful of feathers. Her blood-alcohol level was off the scale.'

'But what about her missing mobile and address book, sir?'

'Dropped them somewhere. Lost them. That's what pissheads do, isn't it? You don't even have to be pissed. My wife loses things all the time, and she never drinks anything stronger than camomile tea.'

'Sir, the neighbour also said that the man who brought DI Crane home was driving an old, pale-coloured car, an unusual and very expensive type.'

'How nice. He or she didn't know what kind of car?'

'No, sir, she didn't. Unfortunately. But it sounds exactly like the kind of car Anthony Maskey drives – one of those old Jaguars. His is pale blue.'

'Anthony Maskey again. Another link you can't establish. Did the aforementioned insomniac manage to memorise or scribble down the licence plate number?'

'No, sir. She didn't realise it would be important.'

'And she was right. I don't intend to have this conversation again.' Wilson leaned forward and ran his hands through his thick grey hair. 'The anti-corruption squad are investigating the allegation that DI Crane stole drugs and money during that house search, kept the money and subsequently sold the drugs – plus other cases she worked on – and that's more than enough for me to be going on with at present.'

'But sir—'

'Listen, Davie, the last – the very *last* – thing we need is another corrupt copper splattered all over the media. Even if DI Crane does prove to have been less than fastidious in her working methods, it doesn't mean she was murdered. And let me give you a piece of friendly advice. I'd distance myself from all this if I were you. You worked with her. You could come under suspicion yourself.' He paused. Chew. Smack. 'I don't think you see that as a rung on your career ladder either. Do you?'

'No, sir,' Neil muttered.

'And as for this Sean Devine and Anthony Maskey business – you either get the facts and present me with a clear-cut case, or you forget the whole bloody thing. I haven't got time to hear about possibilities and useless witnesses and how you haven't got any evidence *yet* but you might have *if*. Is that understood?'

'Yes, sir.'

'Good. Now, piss off. And remember, I want facts next time, not bullshit.' Wilson glowered at him as he reached for another stick of gum. 'Anyone would think you were a fucking journalist.'

Neil went out and shut the door ultra-quietly because he really wanted to slam it so hard that Wilson would choke on his chewing gum. He stopped, closed his eyes and took a deep breath. Maybe I'm wrong, he thought. I could be making a real arse of myself over this. And it's true. I could get into a lot of trouble by aligning myself too closely with Olivia. If she had been alive she would be under suspicion following that allegation, probably suspended while the investigation took place. Why bother anyway? Olivia had let him down, betrayed him. He felt like an idiot.

Neil took the lift back down two floors, walked along the corridor and into the office. Catherine sat at her desk wearing an olive green trouser suit and looking glum.

'We can't link Sean Devine to Paula Pepper's murder,' she said as he walked in. 'And with the Gemma Geraghty murder, we've only got those hairs from his head. Nothing at all on her body. That's weird.' She looked at Neil, as if expecting him to explain it all to her. 'Whoever murdered Paula – that's if it wasn't Sean Devine – knew what they were doing.'

'Tell me something I don't know.'

'Okay,' Catherine said guardedly. 'But you're not going to like it.'

'Can't be worse than Wilson and his chewie.' Neil sank into his chair and gazed at the rain-drenched windowpane. 'Is there some sort of dick-brain gene that gets automatically activated once you reach a certain rank? Hope it doesn't happen to me. Not that I need to worry about that just now.' He glanced at Catherine, who wasn't smiling. 'Go on then,' he sighed. 'Make my day . . . even more depressing.'

'We brought Kelvin Smith in; he's been charged with stabbing that nightclub doorman.'

Neil nodded. 'He'll go down, and not before time. Him and his sister, what a pair.'

'Yeah. Colette. Gets bladdered and goes around town telling people she's Paul McCartney's daughter. And that she's sixteen, when she's pushing forty!' Catherine smiled this time. 'Harsh reality is obviously too much for her to handle.'

'I know the feeling. So what's in all this that I won't like?'

'Kelvin swears he was being blackmailed by – quote – "that dead woman copper" – unquote. Who allegedly confiscated drugs from him and sold them.' Catherine paused. 'Olivia Crane strikes again, I'm afraid.'

'Oh, no!' Neil groaned.

'My God! What *is* all this stuff?'

It was freezing in the kitchen, and rain lashed the dirty windows as Carmel knelt and peered into the dark, dusty, cobwebby space beneath the floorboards. Inside were a couple of bin liners crammed with clothes, towels, toiletries. A dark green sleeping bag, tightly rolled up and knotted with string. A supermarket carrier bag containing a thick brown envelope, some maps and papers. She lifted out the carrier bag, got up and shook the contents on to the table.

Water dripped somewhere in the silence. Carmel emptied the brown envelope and spread the folded newspaper clippings it contained over the table. There were articles about the murders of Gemma Geraghty and Paula Pepper, the same ones Carmel herself had cut out, kept and reread in the hope that they might contain some esoteric clue. More articles about herself and Sean, amongst them the 'feature' done on Carmel without her permission, the description of her as an 'attractive blonde therapist'. She stared at the photograph of herself, snapped as she struggled to shut the door on the bunch of reporters. Her features were strained with fear and anxiety, her eyes frantic, the all-important blonde hair straggled and damp with rain. She had been too angry and disgusted by the article to keep it. But Sean had kept it. She was right. Her husband had been here and he would be back. But when?

Carmel studied the rest of the carrier bag's contents. There was a map of Liverpool and its suburbs, folded to show parts of the River Mersey, the city centre and Edge Hill; the Edge Hill district was encircled with black marker and coloured in with pink. Falkner Square, the Catholic and Anglican cathedrals, and the streets around Brownlow Hill,

Mount Pleasant and Abercromby Square were also marked in pink. Smithdown Lane was underlined in black.

'Come on, Sean,' she whispered. 'What's this for? Give me a clue, for God's sake!'

She picked up the bunch of papers and flipped through them. They were printed from a website about Joseph Williamson, the so-called Mad Mole or King of Edge Hill, and his mysterious underground labyrinth. There were pages of information about Williamson and the tunnels, his life story, historical anecdotes, and photographs of explored sections of the labyrinth. A map of the tunnels, showing Mason Street and the surrounding streets, certain sections marked with pink crosses, black question marks placed along Mason Street and Smithdown Lane.

On the next page was a reproduced black and white portrait of Williamson from 1838, two years before his death at age seventy. It showed a balding man with sharp, dark eyes and arched brows, a truculent set to his mouth and jaw line. He looked intelligent, eccentric and childishly stubborn, accustomed to giving orders and having no doubt that they would be obeyed. A fascinating face, if you were in the mood to be fascinated by historical characters. Carmel was not. A sentence framed in quotation marks was written below, in royal blue ink. She recognised Sean's handwriting, and that he was probably using the Mont Blanc fountain pen she had given him last Christmas.

'Her body's hidden in a place only I know about,' she read aloud. *'Me – and a man from another century.'*

What body? Had Anthony spoken those words? Was that what Sean meant when he said he had overheard him confess to murder? The man from another century had to be Joseph Williamson.

Anthony must have murdered this girl or woman, and hidden the body somewhere in that labyrinth. Was Sean searching for her body in an attempt to prove Anthony guilty and himself innocent, prove Anthony had also murdered Gemma and Paula?

280

Carmel took a pen and notepad from her bag, sat at the table and began to copy the map of the tunnels, drawing as quickly and accurately as a trembling hand permitted. Sean must not find out she had been here – not yet, anyway – or he might not come back again. He was more frightened for her and Lisa's safety than for his own. It had taken her long enough to guess that Sean might be here, and she might not have guessed at all if it hadn't been for the keys missing from the Audi. And the spilled rice grains. She prayed again that Anthony Maskey would not guess.

When she had copied the map, complete with Sean's markings, Carmel put the clippings and other papers back in the carrier bag and carefully replaced it beneath the floorboards, making sure everything looked undisturbed. She set the box of newspapers back on top of the loose lino.

She got to her feet and glanced out of the window. When would Sean come back here? Tonight? Or did he move around, spend nights in different places? That would be sensible. She listened to the silence, longing for it to be broken by the sound of his footsteps on the stairs. Imagining the look on his face if he walked in and found her waiting for him.

'There's a long way to go before the romantic reunion,' she whispered. And she had to keep believing it would happen. In the meantime, she needed to get those bastards in the BMW off her back for a lot longer than just a couple of hours. If she was to find Sean and prove Anthony a murderer, there was only one thing to do. Carmel locked up, hurried away and took another cab from Rodney Street to the Pier Head. She went up to her office and left a message on the answering machine, ostensibly for anyone who called, giving her new mobile number and saying she would be back in a few days.

The BMW was parked near her house when the black cab dropped her off. The two men kept their ugly heads down, one hiding behind the pages of a tabloid. Carmel pretended not to notice them. Had they confessed to Anthony that they'd lost her for a while? Maybe not. He would go ballistic. She let herself into the house, ran upstairs and packed an overnight bag with clothes and toiletries. The bedside clock showed one-thirty; she had been more than an hour in Rice Street. She came down and made herself a ham sandwich and a cup of coffee. Carmel forced herself to eat the whole sandwich, a banana and a piece of shortbread. After she had eaten she scribbled a note to Rosa then called Daniel on her new mobile.

'I'm coming round to collect the stuff in about fifteen minutes,' she said tersely. 'Have it ready for me, will you?'

'Just like that?' he asked, shocked. 'Carmel, what are you up to? You can't just turn up here and collect it! Not when you're being tailed by those—'

'Don't worry, I'll get rid of them. They won't follow me.'

'For Christ's sake! You can't be sure.'

'I can. Please, Daniel, you've got to trust me.'

'But what are you going to do?'

'It's not safe to leave it with you any longer,' she said. 'We both know that. You're taking a huge risk and I don't want you in more danger. I'm going to get rid of it. I said I had an idea, remember?'

'Yeah, and you never told me what it was. Carmel, I understand you don't want to put me at risk, but I don't like this at all. Look, if you really can shake those bastards, just meet me for a coffee and we'll talk.'

'I can't, there's no time. Daniel, I promise you I know what I'm doing. Please, *please* just have it ready. I'm going away for a couple of days. I'll explain when I get back.'

'I don't suppose I'm allowed to know where?'

'It's not that I don't trust you. It's just that the less you know. Etc.'

'Okay,' he said reluctantly. 'I hope you bloody *do* know what you're doing.'

'I'll see you soon.' Carmel hung up and dialled her parents' number, dreading more explanations and excuses.

'Your dad and Lisa aren't back yet, love,' Jackie said when she answered. 'I've only just got in myself. I'll ring you when they get home, you can speak to her then.'

'No time. Mum, I just phoned to let you know I'm going away for two or three days.'

'Going away?' Jackie repeated, astonished. 'Where? What for?'

Carmel closed her eyes briefly. 'I need to get out of this city for a while. Be alone, think about everything. Get my head together. You do understand, don't you?'

'Yes . . . well, I think I do. I'm not sure Lisa will though. Where can we reach you?'

'You've got my new mobile number. I'll be driving around. I'll head for the Lake District, maybe Scotland. I'll be fine. Don't worry about me.'

'But I do, love, I'm your mother! Are you sure this is a good idea? What if something happens? There might be news about Sean.'

'Well, as I said, there's my mobile number. I'll keep it switched on.' Carmel paused. 'Can you explain to Lisa for me?'

'I'll do my best, of course. But I can tell you now, she won't be happy. Your visits are the highlight of her day.'

'Mum, don't you think I hate to leave Lisa, especially at a time like this?' Guilt pierced Carmel's heart. 'But she can't come back here for a while anyway. She's better off with you and dad at the moment.'

'Well, yes.' Jackie hesitated. 'That's true.'

Carmel sensed her mother's bewilderment and disapproval. It did sound selfish, taking off for a few days on her own at a time like this. But she couldn't put her parents at risk by telling them about Sean. And especially not Anthony Maskey.

'I've left a note for Rosa. It's difficult to get hold of her at that call centre.' Carmel felt on edge, bursting with nervous tension, longing to get on with what she had to do. 'I'll see you soon, Mum, okay? Tell Lisa I love her.'

'I will. Take care, love.' There was a tremor in Jackie's voice as she rang off.

'Oh, God!' Carmel wiped her eyes and pushed back her hair. Took a deep, slow breath as she calmed herself and gathered her thoughts. She went into the sitting room and looked out of the windows, keeping herself hidden. The BMW was parked across the street now, menacing like a poisonous spider. The bodybuilder with the moustache and black woolly hat was talking on a mobile and looking at the house.

'Fuck you,' Carmel murmured. She went back into the hall, took off her leather jacket and dropped it on top of her bag. She didn't want to look as if she was going anywhere. She slipped her house and car keys into her jeans pocket.

In the toolbox in the cloakroom cupboard she found the big hammer with the bright yellow handle, last used by Sean on New Year's Eve to nail some Catherine wheels to the trunk of the chestnut tree outside the house. Carmel remembered Lisa's screams of delight as the fireworks exploded, whizzing showers of coloured sparks into the cold night air. She stood up and gripped the hammer. She went into the yard and unbolted the door, glanced out into the alley. A few boys were playing football, with two wheelie bins as goal posts. Two men stood at one end of the alley, leaning against a red Ford Sierra. The car radio was playing as they ate their late lunch of pie and chips. They seemed busy enough. She ducked back inside.

'My God, I hope this works. Please don't let them beat the shit out of me!' Carmel walked slowly down the hall and hesitated, plagued by doubt and fear, dreading the thought of opening the big, new solid front door and going back out into the dangerous, chaotic world beyond. But Anthony had trashed this house, made it chaotic and dangerous in here too. There was no escape.

'Do it!' she hissed. She flung open the door, ran down the path and into the street, her heart pounding. She saw the shocked faces of the two men as she raced towards the

BMW. She swung the hammer and smashed the windscreen. Shattering glass collapsed inwards, showering the men. Before they had time to react she had smashed two of the side windows. The passenger door swung open and the man in the black woolly hat slid out, not daring to move too quickly in case he cut himself on the dangerous, glittering fragments.

'What d'you think you're doing, you mad bitch?' He was red-faced, mean little dark eyes furious. The driver struggled out, gasping in fright and clutching one side of his face. Blood was running from between his podgy white fingers.

'Me eye – she's fucking cut me! You drive,' he shouted to his mate, his voice hoarse with panic. 'Get me down the hospital, quick!'

'You cow!' The man clenched his fists and lunged at Carmel. She dodged away and smashed the back window. More glass showered down on to the back seats.

'This is a message for your boss,' she shouted. 'Tell him to call off his watchdogs. I'm phoning the police right now to tell them I'm being stalked. You can explain to them what you're doing here.' She gasped and jumped back out of his reach a second time. 'If you touch me I'll have you done for assault.' She waved the hammer. 'This was self-defence. Now, get out of here and don't come back.' Out of the corner of her eye she noticed a few neighbours watching. 'Help!' she screamed. 'Help me!' They did not move, just stared blankly. It didn't matter. Carmel only wanted to attract attention. There was no sign of the other men in the Ford Sierra.

The injured man stumbled around the car, dripping blood on the bonnet. He heaved himself into the passenger seat, still clutching his face. 'Go,' he shouted to his mate. 'Never mind her. Just *go!*'

'I'll fucking have you!' the bodybuilder threatened, shaking his fist at Carmel.

'Oh, yes?' she mocked. 'Personal now, is it? You sad

bastard! Just get lost and give Anthony Maskey my message!'

'Bitch!' He got into the car, swearing furiously as he brushed broken glass out of the way with his bare hands, trying not to sit on any of it. He started the engine and the BMW lurched off, tyres screeching, and disappeared around the corner. Then there was only silence, exhaust fumes and pattering rain.

Carmel looked at the shattered glass and bloodstains in the gutter. She felt strangely calm. The show over, her neighbours drifted away without question or comment. It didn't matter if anyone phoned the police; she had a feeling there wouldn't be any criminal damage or assault charges levelled against her. My God! she thought. I never imagined I could do something like that.

She ran back into the house and dropped the hammer in the toolbox, pulled on her leather jacket and slipped the little rucksack on to her shoulders. She picked up the overnight bag and took a last glance around the hall. Then she locked the front door and ran back down the path, threw her bag into the Landcruiser and drove off at speed. They would be back, of course. If not them, someone else. Maybe Anthony himself. She checked the driving mirror again. The road behind her was empty. She had done it!

Tears blurred Carmel's eyes as she thought of Lisa and Sean, and she impatiently brushed them away. No time for sentiment. Lisa was safe, would be well looked after in her absence. She had to find Sean and prove him innocent. And now she had declared open war on Anthony Maskey.

There was no going back.

Her turn to disappear.

Part Three

Chapter Twenty-three

Anthony had left her tied up all night like an animal. If he did not come back soon and release her Simona would have to relieve herself right here on the bed. She had had no food or water for eighteen hours. She wriggled her bound, swollen hands and feet as she tried to keep the circulation going, shivering in the big cold bedroom with its horrible Victorian furniture. She wore a long black T-shirt that belonged to Anthony, and nothing else. It must be midday now, although the grey, rainy light outside made it hard to guess what time of day it was.

Where was Anthony, what was he doing? If she was left in this state much longer she would die. Simona could not scream for help because of the gag. But who would hear her anyway, imprisoned in this big house surrounded by acres of garden? Of course Anthony knew no one could hear if she screamed; he just liked to gag her. It was terrible to think that beyond the locked bedroom door were telephones, a kitchen containing food and water, maybe some implement she could use to break one of the locked, double-glazed windows, but that she was trapped in here unable to reach anything.

Simona's lips were cracked and parched, and her throat was on fire. If the gag were removed now she would not be able to speak. The skin on her face was dry and tight from all the tears she had shed. She had only stopped crying when she realised with horror that if her sinuses got blocked and seized up the gag would suffocate her.

Had Anthony meant to leave her this long? He loved to tie her up in various positions with the horrible scratchy hemp rope that left red weals on her skin, then go out for hours, turned on by the fact that she lay tied and helpless, just waiting for him to come back and hurt and humiliate her any way he liked. But he had never stayed out all night and half the next day. Had something happened? Anthony was rich, a big criminal; people like him often had jealous rivals, enemies who wanted a piece of what he had got. Suppose one of them had hurt him, killed him even? That would be wonderful. But not if it meant she was left here to starve, dehydrate and choke on a gag, rot in her own filth.

Panic seized Simona again and gave her the energy to go on working at the knot she had spent countless hours trying to loosen. Her nails were broken and bleeding. She rolled clumsily on to her stomach, more pain shooting through her bound limbs. Her ankles were roped to her thighs, so she could not stretch her legs. Lying on her stomach gave her slightly more room to manoeuvre, although it restricted her breathing. She concentrated on the knot again, worming and wriggling her fingers as she tried desperately to work it loose.

Anthony had to know where Maria was, otherwise how could he have got her passport? But Simona did not believe he would allow the two sisters to be reunited. She wanted to, but couldn't. Why would Anthony do that? What was in it for him? It broke her heart to think of Maria dancing naked in some bar, being raped by different men every night. Or maybe some rich bastard had 'bought' her as a slave to abuse at his pleasure. It was hard to believe such things still happened. But they did. Everywhere, even in so-called 'civilised' countries. There were no civilised countries; only countries with greater or lesser degrees of barbarism.

The knot loosened suddenly, and hope surged inside her.

Simona worked frantically, her body covered in sweat, muffled groans coming from behind the gag as she struggled, rolling this way and that in her efforts to reach the rest of the knots. Another gave way, and another. She freed her hands, pulled off the gag and took gulps of air, crying with relief. Her fingers were swollen and her wrists had deep red indentations around them; her skin was raw from the rough hemp. She began to struggle with the rope that tied her legs. Minutes later Simona was free.

At first she could not stretch out her legs, the pain was too much. Her body felt like she had imagined it would when she was very old: stiff, twisted, bent, every tiny movement hurting like hell. What makes you think you'll get very old? she wondered. She licked her cracked lips and swallowed a few times. Pain stabbed at her, shooting through her cramped limbs and stiff muscles. Several minutes passed before she could even think about getting off the bed, but she finally managed to stand up, stagger to the adjoining bathroom and collapse on the toilet. The room whirled around her, and Simona felt very weak. She needed food. If only she could escape from the locked bedroom! She turned on the tap and drank some water, then staggered to the bedroom door and rattled the handle. She slowly knelt and peered through the keyhole.

Anthony had left the key in the lock. All the doors in the house had bolts on the inside, and locks into which long black keys fitted. What kind of people wanted locks and bolts on every single door? Simona stuck one end of a length of thin rope in the keyhole and twiddled it about until the key fell out on the floorboards. She used the rope to draw it under the door. All she could think of was to escape from this room, this house. What might happen after that was a blank.

She unlocked the door and crept slowly downstairs on her aching, swollen legs, clinging to the oak banister, shuddering at the sight of the door that led into the room of feathers where Anthony had murdered that woman. She half walked, half crawled across the hall and into the kitchen. She filled a heavy crystal glass with tap water and drank, gasping and gurgling, refilled the glass and drank again. In the fridge she found a cold, wrapped tortilla containing tomato sauce with chicken, sweetcorn, peppers and grated cheese. Simona took two bites, chewed and slowly swallowed them, but could not eat more because her throat hurt too much. She left the tortilla on the table, crept out of the kitchen and slowly made her way around the downstairs rooms. The double-glazed windows were all locked, and she could find nothing to smash one with; she did not have the strength to lift one of the heavy, ornately carved chairs and throw it. The front door was locked. She needed help to get out of here. But who would help her?

In Anthony's study at the back of the house she looked at the burgundy telephone with its many lines and meaningless symbols. Maria's passport, the pages dried and curled after being in contact with water, lay on the desk. Simona picked it up, opened it and kissed her sister's photograph, her eyes brimming with tears. She pulled the phone towards her. Simona was terrified of calling the police and putting herself at their mercy. But anything was better than being at Anthony's mercy. The police would arrest him, make him reveal Maria's whereabouts. That was the only way they would be reunited. Simona wanted to phone her parents in Romania too, but she did not know how to call from the UK, and she hadn't time to try and find out now. She dialled 999 and waited, trembling and faint, her heart pounding.

'Police,' she replied to the female inquirer. 'Hurry!'

'My name is Simona Tarnu,' she began when another woman came on the line, speaking slowly and carefully in her cracked voice, hoping her English would not let her down, 'and I am from Romania. I came to Liverpool to work, but—' She broke off, fighting the sobs that threatened to burst from her. 'I was kidnapped and forced to work as dancer . . . prostitute! My sister too. I don't know

292

where she is. Please!' she begged, her voice breaking. 'You must help me. Us.'

'All right, love. Just take it easy, okay? What did you say your name was?'

'Simona Tarnu. Please, I cannot talk more loudly, my throat hurts very much.'

'Can you spell that for me?'

'T-A-R-N-U. From Romania. I was kidnapped by a man named Anthony Maskey—'

'Who?'

'Anthony Maskey!' she repeated, beginning to sob. Panic gripped her at their slowness and stupidity. 'He keeps me prisoner here in his house. He beats me, treats me like slave, like animal. He is a big criminal. Please, I need help to get out!'

'I see.' Simona had a feeling the woman didn't. 'Where are you now, love?'

'In his house, I cannot escape. It is near Liverpool. Not in the city, I don't know exactly where. I can see trees, a big garden, high walls. You must come. Quick!'

'Calm down, love, okay? You don't have an address for us?'

'No. It's a big house, old. With many trees. I don't know where. You can trace this call, I will wait. But please hurry.'

'Right, love, we're putting a trace on it ... where's this man you say kidnapped you?'

'I don't know. He left me alone all night. If I refuse to obey him I will never see my sister again. He will kill me, he has killed someone else. A woman, she was police officer. He killed her in a room full of feathers ... no!' she moaned in anguish as the phone suddenly went dead. 'Don't go, please don't ... you wait.'

The receiver was wrenched from her grasp and banged down. Her shoulders were gripped and she was spun round and sent flying across the room. Simona crashed into the wall, hitting her head, and grabbed at one of the heavy

curtains for support as she fell, bringing it tumbling on top
of her. She lay there stunned, the breath knocked out of
her.

'Well.' Anthony's mud-encrusted boot slammed into her
left hip. 'If it isn't Dracula's daughter!'

Anthony bundled the sobbing, pleading Simona into the boot
of his car, and slammed the lid down. This was his own fault
for leaving her all night; she would have wriggled out of
those knots sooner or later. But he hadn't counted on the
bitch managing to get out of the locked bedroom. Of course
he hadn't counted on getting trapped in Joseph's labyrinth all
night either. Lucky he had come back when he did. He was
wrong about Simona, had been stupid to think she could feel
anything for him, or he for her. She had betrayed him. As did
everyone. Now he had to get her out of the way. He didn't
think she had been on to the police long enough for them to
trace the call, but he couldn't be certain.

This bitch was not his main concern though. Anthony
pressed the remote control button to close the wrought iron
gates behind him, and drove off down the narrow, tree-
lined road. The window wipers swished monotonously.
After Mary had asked him about his 'mate', he had rushed
straight back to the office to check his desk and the safe
again, terrified that something else was missing. The spare
keys to Highgate Street were still in the envelope, however,
together with the estate agent's letter and all the paperwork
for the house.

Sean must have taken the keys that night he'd got into the
warehouse, had duplicates made, then put them back. Why?
What the hell was he up to? If Sean was trying to freak
him, it was bloody well working. It had to be Sean who'd
searched the house, there was no one else it could have
been. Mary's description fitted: tall, dark, good looking, a
charmer. The bastard had charmed her all right. So now
Sean knew about the secret tunnel in the cellar. What else
did he know? Had he secretly contacted Carmel?

Fury rose in him as he thought of the two cretins who had allowed her to spot them earlier. She had gone loopy, yelling and screaming her head off, smashing the BMW windows with a bloody great hammer. The driver, Lee, was down the Royal, whingeing like some soppy kid while bits of glass were tweezered out of his face and right eye. The dozy sods round the back in the alley hadn't noticed the commotion. It freaked Anthony that Carmel was out of his sight for now. He would find her and tail the bitch himself once he'd dealt with Simona. What was the point in delegating when you couldn't rely on anyone to do the job? How the hell was he going to find and kill Sean, get his money – and his life – back? It seemed further away than ever.

He followed signs for the M62 and sped along a slip road, overtaking a couple of lorries. He hated lorries. It was hard to concentrate on driving, let alone anything else. Anthony was dropping with exhaustion now, could barely keep his eyes open. The lashing rain and swishing window wipers were dangerously hypnotic. But he couldn't sleep, not yet.

Sean Devine was after him, biding his time, waiting for the perfect moment to strike. Anthony knew it. He hadn't clocked anyone shadowing him, but it didn't matter. He sensed Sean's menacing, hate-filled presence everywhere, and it was eating away at him, shredding his nerves. He could not even search for the gold in peace, when he was so close at last, or enjoy the fact that he had fooled everyone over Olivia Crane's death, making her murder appear a tragic accident. The more he strove for control, the more it eluded him. And even though he longed for the sweet, blessed release of deep sleep, Anthony was afraid. The nightmare was more frequent when he was frightened or depressed, hitting him at his most vulnerable moments.

He switched on the radio loud and increased speed, tail-biting other drivers until they moved into the slower lanes where they belonged. Centimetres from the crash barrier on one side and a bloody great lorry with a tank full of some noxious chemical on the other, Anthony flirted deliciously with the idea of death, imagined ending it all right here and now in one huge smash and fireball. He had always believed that one day he would kill himself, and the thought comforted him. It was the ultimate act of control.

Today was just a flirtation though, his driving skills, good luck and other road users' more highly developed survival instincts allowing him to reach Manchester city centre in safety. He drove through the rainy city streets to Diane Lennox's house in Moss Side, parked the Jaguar in the garage and dragged Simona out and through a door into the main part of the rambling, three-storey house. He had tied her hands behind her back again, this time with masking tape.

'Where's Diane?' he asked two girls in the hall, both heavily made up and wearing dingy bras and knickers. One of them pointed to the kitchen door and provocatively puffed smoke in his face. Diane sat at the kitchen table reading a newspaper, drinking coffee and smoking. Anthony looked at her black leather jeans and tacky gold jewellery, her wrinkled tanned skin and her heavy breasts bulging through the tight, leopard print top. Corrupt, he thought. Pollution.

'Hello, love! Long time no see, eh? Bloody hell!' Diane exclaimed, grinning. 'You look knackered. What have you been doing? And what's this you've brought me?'

'A present,' he said, pushing Simona forward. 'Take care of it for me, will you? I'll be back to collect her in a couple of days. Don't let her out or let her talk to any of the other girls, I want her locked up in solitary. You can put her to work,' he said. 'She'll earn her keep.'

'Don't know about that.' Diane got up, stubbed out her cigarette and eyed Simona doubtfully. 'She's a bit of a mess, isn't she? I'll have to give a discount.'

'She just needs a shower and something to eat, a makeover. She'll scrub up fine.'

'Let's have a look then.' Diane pulled up the long, black T-shirt and dragged it over Simona's head so that she stood there naked. Anthony kept hold of her arms as she squirmed and trembled with fright. She had tears in her eyes. Diane inspected Simona's slim, firm body, as if she were choosing fish or a piece of steak. 'You've given her a bit of a going over,' she commented. 'Like your bondage, don't you, love?' She stroked Simona's breasts and slipped one hand between her legs. 'Hmm,' she said, her eyes gleaming. 'Not bad.'

'I'll leave you to it. Remember, don't let her out. Keep her locked up.'

'Don't worry, love.' Diane smiled lasciviously. 'She'll be safe with us.' She went to the door. 'Barry!' she called. 'Nick! Get in here, will you?'

Anthony looked into Simona's terrified eyes as she was dragged away by Diane and her two thugs. She knew it was useless to plead any more. After a couple of days subjected to Diane's tender mercies, she would think of him as a saint. He went into the garage, got into the Jag and drove back to Liverpool. The rain lessened then stopped, heavy clouds parting to reveal a pale hunter's moon and a few bright stars in the darkening sky. An autumnal chill descended; the weather lady on the radio spoke of frost and treacherous roads later in the evening. Now it was time to find Carmel Devine and sort her out.

Anthony called Carmel on his mobile, but there was no reply from her home and only the answering machine at her office. He tried Carmel's new mobile number three times: each time she hung up at the sound of his voice. Furious, he drove to Falkner Square and rang her doorbell several times. No answer. There were no lights on in the house, or none that he could see.

Where was the bitch? Anthony had a throbbing headache now, which was making him feel sick. His eyes were itchy and sore, felt like they were filled with grit. He got back in the car and drove to Southport. Carmel had probably gone to her parents to visit the clone, who was still staying with them. Maybe she had cooled down after her crazy behaviour this afternoon, and was too frightened to speak to him now. Everything was getting to her. She had lost it big time. That was good.

Anthony pulled up outside the big, square white house on the sea front and got out of the car, shivering as the icy air hit him, the smell of ozone strong in his nostrils. It was colder here on the coast. The moon shone on the calm sea, and he could make out the shape of two dredgers a couple of miles offshore. He walked up the gravel path and rang the doorbell. Feet pounded inside the hall and he heard the clone yell. A second later Lisa flung open the front door and stood staring up at him. She wore denim dungarees and a pink T-shirt and clutched a Barbie doll wearing a black jacket, red plastic high-heeled shoes and no knickers.

'Hi, Lisa!' Anthony forced himself to smile. 'I'm Anthony. Remember me?' He hesitated as her face flushed and her eyes filled with tears. 'I'd like a word with your mum,' he said. 'Is she—?'

'Mummy's gone! *You* go away!' Lisa shouted. Anthony stuck his foot in the way as she tried to slam the front door on him. 'I thought you were Daddy, but you're not. I want my daddy!' she screamed, stamping her foot. Anthony stiffened with fury.

'Lisa, go inside, love. Go into the sitting room and watch telly. Grandad'll be down in a minute.' Jackie Graham was there, her greying blonde hair swept up in a bun, pearl studs gleaming in her ears. She wore black trousers and an emerald green sweater, a plastic apron printed with herbs and flowers and their Latin names. There was a smell of food frying.

'Hello Anthony!' She looked surprised.

'Evening, Jackie.' Anthony didn't manage to smile this time. 'How are you? I just wanted a word with Carmel.'

'She isn't here, I'm afraid. Go on, love,' she repeated to Lisa, giving her a hug. The clone ran off down the hall.

298

'Not here?' Anthony echoed in alarm. 'Where is she then?'

'Carmel phoned me this afternoon and said she needed to get away for a few days. On her own. She said she wanted to think things over. I suppose I can understand that, but—'

'Where did she go?' Anthony interrupted, raising his voice. He took a step forward.

'She said she'd be driving around the Lake District,' Jackie said slowly, noting his clenched hands and furious, red-rimmed eyes. 'Maybe Scotland.' Whatever was the matter with him? She began to feel uneasy. Lisa came running back down the hall.

'I hate him!' she shouted tearfully, pointing at Anthony. 'He's not my daddy. I don't want him to come in. Where's Mummy? I want Mummy! Why didn't she take me with her? No!' she shouted as Jackie stooped and gathered her in her arms. 'Get off me.'

'It's a bit difficult right now.' Jackie shot him a pleading glance. 'If you don't mind.'

'Where's Carmel?' Infuriated, Anthony shoved the door wide open and stood over them glowering. It took every bit of his self-control not to kick the spoiled, screaming brat of a clone who had obviously never received a minute's discipline in her life. 'I need to know!' he shouted over Lisa's yells. 'It's urgent. It's about Sean.'

'Go away!' Lisa screamed, struggling in Jackie's arms. Her face was bright red.

'Sean?' Jackie gasped. 'Have you found out something?'

'Yes!' he lied. 'Where is she?'

'I told you, I don't know!' Jackie was very frightened now. 'Have you tried her new mobile number?'

'She won't talk to me.' Anthony could barely contain his rage.

'Just a second . . . darling, please!' Lisa dashed off again. Jackie got to her feet. 'Why won't she talk to you? I don't understand. What have you found out?'

'What's all this bloody commotion?' Frank Graham was

coming downstairs dressed in a virulently striped bathrobe. Anthony turned and ran out. His heart pounded with shock and fury and his head throbbed unbearably. He felt like throwing up on their fucking gravel path.

'What have you found out?' Jackie called again shrilly. 'Tell us, for God's sake!' Something was wrong. Very wrong. She watched, Frank beside her, as Anthony ran to his car, flung himself in and drove off, tyres screeching.

This couldn't be happening. He didn't understand. An invisible net was closing and tightening around him. Nausea surged in him and saliva poured into his mouth. Anthony stopped the car, ran across the dark, empty sea-front road and vomited over the rail on to the sand below.

Carmel Devine wasn't losing it. She hadn't turned into a terrified, screaming nut job who had lost the plot. That *was* the plot.

Carmel had escaped.

Chapter Twenty-four

'You should have seen the state of him, Carmel! Haggard, red-eyed, dressed like a dosser. And the look on his face when I told him you weren't here!' Jackie shuddered. 'I thought he'd hit me.'

'I'm sorry, Mum. He called me a few times, but I won't speak to him.'

'He was desperate to get in touch with you. He must have lied about Sean because he thought I didn't want to tell him where you'd gone,' Jackie said indignantly. 'What a terrible thing to do.'

'Actually, Mum, Anthony's the main reason I wanted to get away.'

'Why? What on earth is going on?'

Carmel glanced around the room, at the scuff marks on the pink carpet by the desk and the dried bloodstains on the flowered coverlet of the king-size bed. The heating vent over the door blew only cold air, and in the bathroom there was less than half a roll of loo paper. A printed note on the desk signed by someone named Julie, who described herself as the maid, hoped this four-star hotel room was cleaned to the guest's satisfaction. Carmel stood at the window gazing out over the bright lights of Manchester. A dark narrow river flowed beneath a bridge ten floors below.

'Anthony's been pressuring me to sell off Sean's share of the business,' she confessed. 'He's getting quite nasty.'

That was enough for now. She didn't want to freak her mother with the rest. Anthony must be going crazy after the cash and passports had disappeared from his safe. Maybe he thought Sean was out to get him. Good!

'He's been *what*?' Jackie was temporarily shocked into silence. 'Well!' she exclaimed eventually. 'That's friendship for you, isn't it? My God, what a ... ! I always thought he was so polite and charming. How could he even suggest such a thing! And why didn't you tell me this before, love?'

'I didn't want to worry you. Look, never mind Anthony now. How's Lisa?'

'Fine.' That wasn't entirely true, but Jackie did not want to worry Carmel either. 'I went up to check on her about five minutes ago. She was fast asleep. You should have told me what was going on,' she fretted.

'Please don't worry, Mum. I'll deal with Anthony.'

'I can't believe this! I thought they were great friends – that Anthony was as desperate as we are to find Sean. So all he cares about is taking over the business?'

'Apparently.'

'But it doesn't explain the state he was in. Surely he wouldn't be that upset because you quite properly refused to sell him Sean's share of the business? D'you think there's something else going on?'

'I really don't know,' Carmel lied. 'And I don't want to talk about him any more.' She needed to end this conversation. 'Listen, I'll say goodnight now. I won't tell you where I am in case Anthony bothers you again.'

'If he does, I'll give him a piece of my mind. Being betrayed ... pressured like that by someone you and Sean thought was a close friend. It's the last thing you need.'

'Mum, leave it, please! I told you, I'll deal with Anthony. Just take good care of Lisa, okay? Give her a big kiss and cuddle from me. Tell her I'll be back soon.'

'Of course I will. All right ... goodnight, love. You take care of yourself too.'

302

'I will. 'Night, Mum.'

Carmel laid her mobile on the bedside table, then switched off the so-called heating system. The bloodstained coverlet made her shiver more than the cold, but she did not want to draw attention to herself by complaining. Although in this dismal place a guest who didn't complain might attract attention. She had ordered coffee and sandwiches from room service earlier; a hapless-looking boy in a uniform too big for him had turned up half an hour later, bringing roast beef sandwiches instead of ham, and tea instead of coffee. But she had chosen this place because it was large and anonymous, far enough from and yet close to Liverpool. Her Landcruiser was in the long stay car park at the airport and she had hired a smaller car, a turquoise Vauxhall Astra that made her feel vulnerable after the big, powerful Landcruiser.

She sat on the sofa and picked up her inadequate map of some of the main Williamson tunnels. How much did Anthony know about the labyrinth, how far had he explored? Maybe he knew it pretty well. Carmel studied the map, feeling lonely, discouraged and full of doubt. If Sean had been searching these bloody tunnels for the past few weeks and come up with nothing, what chance did she have of finding a concealed body within days?

Williamson's house on Mason Street – or what remained of it – was ringed with steel fencing, as were other known access points. Anthony had his own secret entrances, but apart from the Highgate Street cellar tunnel she had no idea where they were. That was why she had to follow Anthony. And before she followed him into the labyrinth, there was something she had to do that terrified her even more.

'You're mad!' she whispered, trembling. 'You'll never get away with it. Just go home to Lisa.' Guilt overwhelmed her again. What must her daughter be thinking now? That she had been abandoned a second time? She could only hope that Lisa was as resilient as children were supposed to be. But all she could think of was her daughter's vulnerability. And the terrible danger she was about to put herself in.

Carmel laced her trainers and pulled a black padded jacket on over her jeans and purple sweater. She took her keys and picked up the cheap black nylon rucksack she had bought that afternoon. The missing girls' passports and the fifty grand from Anthony's safe were stuffed into it. She left the depressing room and walked down the silent, carpeted corridor. She had paid cash in advance for the room, and given a false name and address. She hurried down the ten flights of stairs to the ground floor, and passed through the door near the lifts which led to the underground car park, thereby avoiding the hotel's reception desk and front entrance.

She drove to Liverpool, headed for Edge Hill and cruised down Mason Street, wondering where any so far undiscovered entrances to Joseph Williamson's tunnels might be. She passed the house in Highgate Street. A couple of houses in nearby Shimmin Street were boarded up due to subsidence. Amazing that the entire area did not subside, if it was so riddled with caves, tunnels, underground mansions and, it was rumoured, an entire village. Carmel drove back to the centre of town and the docks, and went through the Queensway tunnel, heading for Anthony's house on the Wirral. At least this tunnel was big and well lit. Being in any tunnel scared her though; in this one the River Mersey was right over your head.

It was a frosty night and the moon and stars were out. Carmel wished again that she could give this up and go home to Lisa. She might be lying awake, wondering where her mother was, when she would see her again. She hadn't slept well since Sean's disappearance. Carmel ached with longing for Sean. Where was he tonight, what was he doing? When would he phone? He would know the answering machine message was meant for him.

Anthony's Victorian house was up a narrow, twisting road with trees crowding forward on both sides. In the darkness the road looked even more creepy, or did she think that because he lived here? Carmel turned off the road and parked the car down a dark, muddy track about one hundred metres from the house. She took a torch from the glove box, got out and slung the rucksack over her shoulders, pulled up the hood of the jacket. Walking up the road, she dodged behind a tree each time a car approached. The property was surrounded by high brick walls and the wrought iron gates were closed, a CCTV camera angled just below the stone pineapples that topped both tall gateposts.

Carmel stood on the opposite side of the road, keeping out of the camera's range. Anthony's Jaguar was parked in the drive, gleaming palely in the moonlight. The lights were on in the downstairs rooms. She didn't think she could wait for him to go out then break in and search at her leisure; as well as the cameras, there was bound to be a state-of-the-art alarm system. She stamped her feet and rubbed her cold hands together. What was Anthony doing now? Was he in for the night? What had he done with Gemma's handbag and Paula's missing earring? Carmel was certain he had kept them. Murdering psychos liked their little souvenirs.

She hid behind a massive oak as headlights appeared round the curve of the road. A white transit van slowed and stopped outside the house. The driver, a young man, got out and tried to open the gates, swore when he discovered they were locked. He pressed the bell or buzzer of the intercom set in the right-hand gatepost.

'It's Kev,' he shouted. 'Let us in, will you? Listen, mate, we had to!' he replied angrily to the indistinguishable hiss and crackle that had to be Anthony's voice. 'There's nowhere else to take them tonight. Yeah, I know, but— Okay.' He got back in the van and slammed the door. The gates swung slowly open. The van lurched forward, sped up the unlit drive and slammed to a halt by the front door steps, a few metres from Anthony's Jaguar.

The gates did not close immediately: Anthony was

obviously preoccupied with the arrival of the van and its passengers. Carmel seized her chance. She dashed across the road and slipped into the dark grounds just as the gates started to close. They swung shut behind her with a clang of finality and she stood near the high wall, concealed by trees and bushes. She was shaking with fear.

At least there were no Rottweilers or Dobermanns roaming the house and grounds, ready to give away her presence then leap on her and rip her to shreds. Anthony hated dogs, could not bear them anywhere near him. Her heart thudding, she moved slowly forward, grateful for the thick, sheltering undergrowth but terrified in case she cracked a twig underfoot. The sound would carry in the cold, frosty air. She reached the edge of the lawn opposite the front door and stopped, uncertain what to do next. How the hell could she get into the house without being spotted? Even more important, get out again.

'Come on, you lazy bitches! Move it.' A group of exhausted, dishevelled-looking girls were being manhandled out of the van by the driver and a blonde girl in jeans and a sheepskin jacket, their frightened faces pale and washed out in the moonlight. Anthony stood tensely by the open door, wearing a long, black leather coat. He frowned as the blonde girl shoved one of the other girls so hard that she tripped and fell on her hands and knees.

'Watch it, Yvonne. I don't want damaged cargo.'

'She's jealous,' the driver sniggered. 'That one's got the biggest tits.'

Yvonne rounded on him. 'Shut it, you! Sad little wanker!'

'We'll lock them in the attic rooms and give them something to keep them quiet. One night, and that's it.' Anthony turned as Yvonne shoved the last girl into the hall. 'I'm going out in a minute – got things to do. I'll help you get them settled, then you'll have to stay here while I . . .' He turned away, shutting the front door.

Carmel gasped, her heart pounding. If questioned by the

police, would those girls be too frightened and intimidated to say that they had been sold into sexual slavery? Would they swear they were backpacking tourists, waitresses, dancers, about to take up bar work? Had their passports been confiscated? She reached inside her jacket for her mobile, fingers trembling as they brushed the phone's buttons. No, she thought. Not yet. You have to do what you came here for.

Lights were appearing in rooms on the second and third floors. They must have all gone upstairs. The front door suddenly opened again, and the blonde woman came out. She got something from the van and went back inside, leaving the door ajar.

It was now or never. Carmel darted out of the undergrowth and ran lightly across the moonlit drive, crouching like an animal hunting prey. She stopped and listened at the open front door, barely able to breathe for terror. Peeked around it. The big, wood-panelled entrance hall was deserted.

How could she be so crazy as to put herself at such risk? Bit late to wonder about that now. She crept into the hall. Muffled thuds and bumps, angry voices, came from the top floor of the house. Carmel flinched and broke out in a sweat at the sound of terrified screams, followed by anguished cries and groans of pain. She had to plant the money and passports somewhere, get out quick and phone the police. Anthony would be caught red-handed and the girls rescued. That was the theory, anyway.

She looked around the hall, at open doors that led to various rooms. A flicker and glow of firelight came from the sitting room. Another room across the hall was obviously a study, with booklined walls and a big, polished antique desk. An open dark green canvas bag, like a flight bag, lay on top of the desk. Carmel was about to creep in for a look when she heard someone coming downstairs. Panicked, she glanced desperately around for somewhere to hide. She opened the door of the cupboard under the stairs and crouched inside, pulling it shut. Footsteps pounded over her head, reached the bottom of the stairs and strode across the hall into the study. Ultra-cautiously, she opened the door a crack and peered out. Anthony was moving around the study tossing things into the bag. Carmel couldn't see what.

The cupboard beneath the stairs was as good a place as any to leave the cash and passports for the police to find. She had no chance to walk around the house and select the best spot. On her knees in the dark, Carmel carefully wriggled the rucksack off her shoulders and laid it on the floor by what felt like a vacuum cleaner and some empty boxes. She pushed the rucksack into a corner behind the boxes, sweating with fear and the effort not to make any sound, then peered through the crack in the door again. Anthony was still moving around the study. The phone rang, and he let it ring several times before he picked up the receiver.

'Hello?' he said guardedly. 'Yeah?'

He was going out any minute, and she had to get back to her car ready to tail him. But how? The gates were closed and she didn't know where the remote control was. It had to be somewhere by the front door. But if Anthony found the gates open when he had closed them ... She had to get out of the house at least. Surely the entire property couldn't be surrounded by that bloody great high brick wall! There must be another way out of the grounds. Maybe even one that led near to the track where her car was parked.

Holding her breath, her eyes fixed on the study door, Carmel stepped out of the cupboard and quietly closed it. She backed away towards the front door.

'Ant!' the woman yelled from upstairs. 'Anthony!'

Anthony opened the study door as Carmel slipped outside and flattened herself against the stone wall. She suppressed a groan of terror as she heard his footsteps approaching. There was no time to run back across the open space to the safety of the undergrowth; she would be spotted if she tried. She ran to the car and tried the handle of one of the rear doors. It was unlocked. She crawled inside and closed the door, the click sounding horribly loud in the silent darkness. The Jaguar's interior smelled of leather and petrol. Carmel quickly wriggled down on the floor, merging into the blackness, and curled her body tightly, torch and mobile digging painfully into her ribs. Just in time. A shaft of yellow light hit the car windows as the front door opened wide.

'Why did you leave this fucking door open?' Anthony called angrily. The car rocked as he dumped something in the boot. Was it the canvas bag, Carmel wondered?

'All right, Ant, sorry! Don't get your thong in a twist. No harm done, is there? The gates are locked, and this place is surrounded by a bloody Berlin wall.' Yvonne followed him out. 'How long will you be?'

'Dunno. A few hours.'

'Where are you going?'

'None of your bloody business.' Anthony slammed the boot.

'I'll be dead bored, stuck here with him and those bitches. Can't I come with you?'

'No,' he replied. 'Definitely not. Remember what I said . . .' Carmel flinched as he opened the driver's door, and curled her body even tighter. 'Switch off all the lights, except for the ones in the kitchen, and keep the gates shut. Don't let anyone in, I don't care who they say they are. And the pair of you keep off my booze.' He got in, slammed the door and started the engine. The Jaguar moved off down the drive, slowed and stopped as it reached the gates. Anthony tapped his fingers impatiently on the wheel as he waited for them to open. Once outside he shot off, driving scarily fast along the twisting, narrow road.

Carmel had to dig in her feet, knees and elbows to stop her body rolling as the car swerved this way and that. Terrified, she squeezed her eyes shut and pressed one hand to her mouth. If Anthony stopped somewhere she could try to slip out unnoticed, phone the police and tell them about those girls imprisoned in his house for the night. But that wouldn't be enough to get Sean off the hook. What had Anthony put in the boot? Something he wanted to hide? She had to find out what it was.

Are you crazy? she thought. If he finds you here he'll go ballistic – he'll murder you! Strangle you, maybe, dump you with the other stiffs he's hidden in that bloody labyrinth. She lay there trembling, the torch and mobile phone lodged against her chest cavity, her cramped muscles crying out to stretch and flex. She tried not to imagine how it felt to be beaten by a strong man in a rage, to feel his hands around her throat, systematically and brutally choking her life away.

The journey took a long time. They drove back to town through the Queensway tunnel, a nightmare for Carmel because of the tunnel's bright overhead lighting. She suppressed a gasp of shock as Anthony's mobile suddenly trilled, playing *The Good, the Bad and the Ugly*. Unlike him to select a funny tune. Or maybe he didn't think it was funny.

'Okay, I'll meet you at the warehouse in an hour or so. No, I can't make it before then,' he snapped. 'I've got to get shut of some stuff first – can't drive around all night with it lying in the bloody boot, can I? If I get stopped some copper will think Christmas has come early.' There was a brief pause. 'Just shut it, will you? Get on with the search.' He hung up and dropped the mobile on the passenger seat.

What *stuff*? Incriminating evidence that Anthony had kept in his house and now wanted to get rid of in case the police came calling? Was he really afraid of that? Were they doing something at last? Carmel hadn't heard from Neil Davie again.

'I'll have you, you fucking bastard!' Anthony shouted suddenly, thumping the steering wheel and causing the Jaguar to swerve dangerously close to the rail that ran along the tunnel wall. 'You and your cunt of a wife! Car-*mel*!'

She prayed, trembling, wishing she was anywhere except in this terrible here and now. Blessed darkness closed over them as they left the tunnel and emerged by the docks. Carmel guessed Anthony was heading for the centre of town and beyond, probably Edge Hill. Who was he meeting at the warehouse? More thugs he had hired to look for Sean? Images from the violent scene in Falkner Square that afternoon flashed into her brain, the BMW driver with blood streaming from his cut eye, the other man screaming abuse at her. She was glad she had done it. The bastards deserved far worse than a shower of broken glass.

She wished she could see where they were heading. The road seemed quieter and darker now, with less traffic, and it felt like they were driving up a long hill. They were probably not far from Falkner Square. Carmel thought of her house, the wrecked rooms barely restored to rights, empty except for an anxious Rosa who would be wondering what the hell her sister was up to. Just as well she didn't know.

The car was slowing now, turning right and then left, jolting over rough ground. The orange street lights disappeared and there was only moonshine. The car slowed further and stopped. Carmel's limbs were so cramped that she felt she could barely move. But she might have to move soon – and very quickly.

Anthony switched off the engine and there was silence. She held her breath. He opened the glove compartment and rooted around in it.

'Fuck!' She caught the gleam of a pair of handcuffs as they fell on the floor, the whiteness of some kind of mint or tablet as it rolled. She didn't even want to think about why he kept handcuffs in a glove compartment. Anthony picked them up and shoved them in his pocket. Carmel stayed perfectly still, frozen with terror. She had never imagined she could be so frightened. Any second now he might discover her. He got out and the car rocked as he slammed the door. The boot flew open. He took out whatever he'd put in there, shut the boot and locked the car. A torch beam swept the rear window as his footsteps trudged away.

Carmel was still shaking uncontrollably, her body bathed

in prickly sweat. She waited for what seemed a long time then raised her head, slowly struggled to her knees and looked out of the window. It was too dark to see anything. The car was suddenly a refuge that she dreaded leaving. Nerves screaming, she squeezed the lever upwards and clicked the door open. Waited, her heart pounding, hardly daring to breathe. There was no sound, except that of distant traffic and a wailing siren. The air smelled fresh after the rain.

She pushed the door open, got out and stood up, rubbing her aching arms and legs. Took a few tentative steps forward, stopped and looked around, trying to get her bearings. She could make out the dark mass of a high wall to her left, tumbledown buildings all around. There was some sort of squat tower or chimney. Was this a demolition site? Carmel had no idea where she was. It looked like a surreal movie set of the end of the world. Or undisturbed since the blitz.

She began to walk in the direction Anthony's footsteps had gone, stumbling over broken bricks and stones, a couple of shredded types. She stopped, terrified that he might hear and come back. She dared not switch on the torch, even though it was almost impossible to see where she was going. She dreaded bumping into Anthony any second. Pressing forward, one tiny, slow, frightened step at a time, took all her remaining nerve. She passed a building that looked like an old stable block, its smashed windows gaping blacker than the night. Turned a corner and stopped. A big double brick-built arch towered above her, the entrance partially blocked by undergrowth. Rubble was strewn everywhere.

'Oh, my God,' Carmel whispered. 'The labyrinth!'

Anthony must have gone in there to hide his 'stuff'. Overwhelmed by fear, she took one step back and then another, desperate to run away. But he might hear and come after her. If only she could phone the police right now and get Anthony caught red-handed concealing murder evidence – if that's what it was – and prove Sean innocent at one stroke. Of course all that was too good to be true! Anthony knew this place and the police didn't – he might get away. She couldn't be sure it was murder evidence he wanted to hide. Catch number three – how the hell could she call the police when she couldn't even tell them where she was?

Carmel started to shake with fear again, fighting the instinct to run away screaming in panic. She hated this, dreaded it, did not think she could take any more terror.

But what was Anthony hiding in Joseph Williamson's labyrinth?

Only one way to find out.

Chapter Twenty-five

Inside the tunnel arch Carmel raised one hand and held it close to her face. She could not see it. There was no choice but to switch on the torch. Its beam swept over a roof and walls constructed of tightly packed sandstone blocks. She moved slowly forward, trying to be as quiet as possible. At the back of the arch were the entrances to two tunnels. Which one to take? The right-hand tunnel was smaller and partially blocked by rubble as far as she could see, so she chose the left. She switched off the torch and felt her way along. When the tunnel lowered and narrowed dramatically, she wondered if she had made the right choice. I could get lost in here, she thought. Trapped for ever. That thought made her switch on the torch again, despite the risk.

Carmel shivered with cold and fright as the walls pressed close, almost brushing her shoulders, making her feel as if she was walled up alive. She stopped and gasped as the tunnel suddenly opened into an enormous cavern with sandstone pillars and scorch-marked niches in the walls where candles had once burned. This was an amazing place; in different circumstances she would have been thrilled to have the chance to explore it. But where the hell was Anthony? She had to find him, not lose herself.

She switched off the torch and stood there, straining her ears for the slightest sound. Anthony could not have gone far. Then again, he probably knew this place intimately, would move through the tunnels and caverns with a lot more assurance than a newcomer terrified for her life. She switched on the torch again and looked fearfully at the tunnels branching off in all directions; which one had he taken? The silence was unnerving. She walked into the tunnel directly opposite; after a few metres it opened into another, smaller cave. One corner of the cave was heaped with rubble and there was a terrible stench that made her sick to her stomach. A dead rat, maybe. A place like this was bound to be full of them. Carmel backed out hurriedly and stumbled to the centre of the cavern, wondering where to go next. The torch's beam rested on a large round hole in the rock floor near one of the huge sandstone pillars. A few feet away was a big rusted sheet of corrugated iron.

She moved forward, crouched and looked into the hole. A steel ladder, riveted to the rock, led down a long, narrow shaft. The ladder gleamed, looked brand new. She lay flat on her stomach and peered into the shaft. There seemed to be a tunnel or passage at the bottom of the ladder. She switched off the torch and leaned down as far as she dared, hands gripping the shaft edges. Way below, a faint yellow light emanated from somewhere along the passage. Anthony was down there! She held her breath. There was a barely discernible sound of something falling, being shifted.

'Oh, God!' she whispered, panicking. 'I *can't* . . .'

She had to. Not now though, not while he was down there and might appear just as she reached the bottom of the ladder. But she had to see what Anthony was doing, where he was concealing that bag. Otherwise she could be stuck in here searching for hours, and still might not find it. The more she hesitated, the higher the risk that he would come along and catch her as she descended. Do it, she told herself. Get on with it, don't be such a sick coward! Think of Sean and Lisa.

Carmel shoved the torch inside her jacket, gripped the

top of the ladder and felt her way on to the first rung, trying not to think about making a noise, or falling and breaking her back, neck, legs, arms, pelvis. She descended the shaft in the pitch darkness, feeling her way, going as quickly and quietly as possible.

The passage at the foot of the shaft was built of brick, with tall, elegant brick arches branching off in all directions. Carmel crept along, following the glow of light and the sounds, as if something heavy was being dragged along the floor. This passage opened into a big bare room that reminded her of an antechamber in a pyramid, and the light grew stronger. The stone floor was uneven and scattered with debris. A pile of dusty old bottles made of thick glass gleamed in one corner. To her left, steps with bull-nosed edgings led up to another room, or cave. She could hear Anthony panting. Carmel edged forward and peered in.

Anthony was working hard, covering something – the canvas bag, presumably – with rocks and stones. An oil lamp in a wall niche lit his work. His leather coat lay on the floor, and his shirt sleeves were rolled up. His face was angry, glistening with sweat. He swore suddenly, picked up a broken brick and flung it against the wall instead of laying it on the pile.

'*Bastard*!' he screamed. His scream bounced off the walls and echoed along the dark passages.

Presumably he meant Sean. Carmel stepped back and flattened herself against the wall, overwhelmed with panic at being so close to him, in such danger of imminent discovery. For a second her legs refused to move. She started to creep back the way she had come. Once out of the antechamber she took a wrong turning into one of the arches, and was feeling her way down another pitch-dark passage before the ground started to slope beneath her feet and she realised her mistake. God knew where that led! She crept back, looking for the main passage, fighting the desire to run. She reached the ladder at last, and started to climb. She was covered in sweat, and her arms and legs felt weak. At the top of the ladder she breathed again.

Where to hide? Carmel concealed herself beside a pile of rubble behind one of the great sandstone pillars and sat curled up, hugging her knees, her body shaking with fright and exertion. Even from here she could smell the nauseating stench from the cave beyond the tunnel. What the hell was it? Would a dead rat smell that bad? It might be several dead rats. She swallowed hard as her dry mouth filled with saliva. This wasn't the time to throw up. She waited for what seemed like ages, so long that the chill of the subterranean cave penetrated her clothes, her skin, her bones. Her exhausted body was stiff and aching.

At last she heard Anthony's feet on the ladder. Carmel jerked her head up, gripped with terror again. He climbed out of the shaft and flashed the powerful torch around the cave, then dragged the sheet of corrugated iron across the hole and covered that with rubble. Carmel imagined trying to balance on the ladder while she tried to push that thing out of the way. No chance! She would have been trapped, perhaps fallen and been killed or seriously injured. Anthony headed down the tunnel from where the sickening stench emanated, and stayed there for some time.

Carmel thought she heard him laugh once or twice, a low, throaty sound that made her flesh creep. What the hell was he doing in there? She imagined ghouls and vampires gloating over their victims. But Anthony was no ghoul or vampire, just your average ordinary bloke who'd turned out to be a bit of a nightmare. The newspapers were full of such characters; it was almost *de rigueur* for a lady to have one in her life. Especially a blonde therapist with a seriously dodgy missing husband.

Anthony came out of the tunnel, flashing the torch around, trudged across the cave and headed for the exit. His footsteps grew fainter. Carmel stayed huddled on the ground, not daring to move in case he returned. She thought she heard the footsteps stop abruptly, as if he were listening. Waiting. A minute later they resumed. Far away a car engine started. Then silence, total and unnerving.

Carmel still did not dare to move, preferring to endure the stench and dank darkness a bit longer, rather than run outside and risk falling into Anthony's murderous arms. She felt terrified and sick to her stomach, cold and dirty, and her head ached. At last when she thought it was safe to leave she stood up, stretched and started to pick her way through the rubble towards the double-arched entrance. She knew she should look in the tunnel where Anthony had just been, but she couldn't face it. She had to get out of here.

Carmel walked faster, stumbling over rocks and bricks, crunching glass underfoot, in a terrible hurry to get outside and have the sky instead of a cave roof above her head. Be able to breathe fresh air. A minute later she was free, picking her way through the undergrowth and rubbish that surrounded and partially concealed the entrance. She walked cautiously past the tumbledown buildings, the dark tower, and back around the corner. Stopped and heaved a sigh of relief. The Jaguar was gone.

'Where in the world am I?' she whispered. She switched on the torch and carried on walking. This must be some sort of demolition site, about to be cleared ready for the construction of flats or houses. Did that mean part of the Joseph Williamson labyrinth would be lost for ever? At that moment Carmel did not give a toss.

She walked off the site and came to a quiet, very narrow road lined with workshops and derelict houses. There was a car breaker's yard opposite, with a wall of stacked lorry containers. Dogs barked out of sight; the yard owner probably had Rottweilers protecting his property. She walked down the road, nervously flashing the torch to right and left. She emerged on a main road, well lit and lined with trees, a grassy knoll across the way, behind which were blocks of flats. She realised she was near the Anglican cathedral and some of the university buildings. Falkner Square was only ten minutes' walk away.

She stood at the kerb looking around. A silver Opel Kadett with three men inside slowed as it passed and the driver blared the horn, making her jump with fright. Next thing they would stop and ask her if she wanted business. Carmel retreated to the relative safety of the road she had just come from, and pulled out her mobile.

'Police,' she said. '*Yes*, this is definitely an emergency.'

She made the call, shoved the mobile back in her pocket, then gasped and pulled it out again. The phone had been switched on all the time! She must have left it on after she had called her mother from the hotel room. It had been switched on while she was in the grounds of Anthony's house – inside his house. Travelling through the Mersey tunnel curled up on the floor of his car, following him into the terrifying labyrinth. Watching while he hid that bag under the rubble.

Carmel broke out in a cold sweat and collapsed on to a low wall, her legs shaking. She could not believe she had been so stupid. Imagine if that bloody phone had rung at any point! Suppose Anthony had called her again? She would be dead now.

She burst into tears.

'So, you actually witnessed Anthony Maskey put this here?' Neil Davie asked twenty minutes later when they were back in the subterranean cave and had pulled the canvas bag from beneath its protective rubble layer. Police officers milled around the caves and passages, flashing torches and talking in hushed voices.

'Of course I did. I told you.'

'Shame it had to be you.'

'You mean the loyal little wife who wants to prove her missing hubby is innocent of two murders?'

'Something like that.'

'For Christ's sake!' Carmel had tears of frustration in her eyes. 'How would I have even known about this place if I hadn't followed Anthony Maskey? I risked my *life*

319

tonight,' she said fiercely. 'If he'd caught me following him I'd be dead now, probably buried under this bloody rubble. He spent some time in that cave up there too.' She pointed. 'I don't know what he was doing. Why don't you send someone over to his house – I told you, he's got a group of trafficked girls locked up there. You can arrest him for that, can't you?'

Neil raised his eyebrows. 'If they have been trafficked, they might not be willing to admit it. And if they've gained illegal entry to the UK they'll face deportation.'

'Oh, brilliant! That's just great, that is. Talk about not seeing the bigger picture.' Carmel's shoulders slumped and she turned away, filled with anger and despair. 'Right,' she said. 'I've had enough. I'm leaving. You do what the hell you like.'

'Don't rush off, Mrs Devine.' Neil and one of his colleagues pulled on latex gloves. 'We'll certainly go to Maskey's house.' Especially after that phone call he'd only heard about after coming on shift this evening, the weird call which hadn't made any sense to the bewildered operator who took it. A girl, foreign, crying that she'd been kidnapped by a man named Anthony Maskey who had murdered a woman police officer in a room of feathers! There hadn't been time to trace the call and the girl couldn't give an address, so no action had been taken. Neil, furious at not being told sooner – and aware that he might not have been told at all – was arranging to go over to Maskey's house when Carmel's call had come in. 'First we'd like to find out what's in this bag.'

Carmel turned back and watched as they unzipped the bag and investigated its contents. A black quilted handbag with a gilt chain, containing condoms, lipstick, cigarettes and a tube of KY Jelly. She stiffened.

'That looks like Gemma Geraghty's missing handbag! I read about it in the paper.'

'Yeah.' Neil and his colleague glanced at one another, their faces grim. An ancient leather briefcase, papers, maps, an old shipping bill. Neil picked it up and unfolded it, shrugged. He put it down and looked into the box again. 'Hang on.' He took out a pile of passports, most of them eastern European. 'Bloody hell!'

Carmel didn't share their surprise about the passports. They would find more at Anthony's house. 'What's that?' she gasped suddenly, pointing. 'That glittering thing.' Neil picked out a diamanté earring and held it up, looking very shaken.

'Paula Pepper's earring,' the colleague murmured. 'Christ!'

Underneath the handbag, papers and passports lay a gun, a Glöck. A slim, dark green diary or address book. Neil fingered the gun, opened the address book and leafed through a few pages. 'Jesus Christ!' he breathed. He passed the book to his colleague and they stared at one another in shock.

'What is that?' Carmel asked impatiently. Neil glanced up at her.

'An address book. It belongs to Olivia Crane,' he said quietly.

'Oh God!' Carmel whispered. 'She came to my house, she was involved in the investigation against Sean. If she knew Anthony Maskey . . .!' She clapped one hand over her mouth as Neil held up a clear plastic bag. 'That's Sean's wallet! His house keys and mobile, his little red diary. I told you Anthony had done something to him.'

Neil's heart sank further as he moved aside a blue folder containing photographs of young girls and uncovered another mobile, this one blue and green. He recognised the scratch where Olivia had snagged it with the prongs of her fork while eating a lunch of steak pie and chips in the canteen one day. He got to his feet. 'Let's try this outside. Come on.'

In the yard Carmel and his colleagues crowded around as he examined the phone, switched it on and typed in the pin code, which he happened to know was Olivia's date of birth. There were only four stored numbers. His own. Olivia's mother, Alex's and a fourth number: *Anthony*.

'Anthony!' Carmel exclaimed, clutching his arm. 'I can just guess the surname! I'm pretty sure that's his mobile number,' she said. 'I tried to call him on it a few times the night Sean went missing.'

Neil's pale, latex-gloved hands, the green glow of the mobile's buttons and tiny screen looked unearthly in the darkness. Neil tried the *Anthony* number and waited, praying for all this to be a bad dream. He felt crushed with sorrow and disappointment. Olivia had played a dangerous game and lost. She had deliberately allowed a murderer to stay free, an innocent man and his family to suffer. She had lied to him and his colleagues, let everybody down big time. But most of all, Olivia had let herself down. She could have been so much better than this.

'It's ringing,' he muttered. 'But Maskey probably won't answer when he sees which number it is.'

'He may not be able to resist,' Carmel said softly. 'It'll freak him – make him wonder what the hell's happening.' She smiled. 'He might think he's going crazy.'

Neil glanced down at her. 'We'll see.'

They waited silently.

The phone went on ringing.

Chapter Twenty-six

'Who the fuck's there?' Anthony screamed into the mobile. 'Who is it? Answer me!'

There was no answer. He couldn't say the spooked feeling returned in full force, because it had never gone away since the shock of Sean Devine getting into the warehouse and then his mother's house – apparently without keys – and Carmel escaping. It was Olivia's number, but no way could it be her calling him. He'd put her mobile in the bag with the other stuff, and now it lay safely buried under rubble in Joseph's labyrinth. No one could have found it – or followed him. What the hell was going on?

'Who's there?' he shouted again, freaked. He was trembling with rage and fear. The two men standing by his desk exchanged nervous glances. The mystery caller hung up without speaking.

Anthony bashed his mobile against the desk then flung it at the far wall. The two startled men ducked out of the way. He slumped forward and leaned his aching head on the desk. He couldn't think straight, couldn't work this out. Who the fuck had got hold of Olivia's phone? *How*? He was certain he had chucked it in the bag with the rest of the stuff just before he went out. But had he? He was in a hurry, angry and nervous at the unexpected hassle of that pair turning up with a vanload of girls. Could he have left Olivia's mobile on the desk in his study? Kev or Yvonne might have picked it up and started messing about with it. But no! The phone wouldn't work unless the pin number was typed in first. There was only one person who'd know that number. And she was dead.

Anthony felt like calling Carmel Devine again, but what was the point? He didn't know where she was. All he could do was threaten – until he caught up with her. Were she and Sean working together now, trying to trick him into making a false move? They could forget it, because that wasn't going to happen. And there had been no visit from the police; they hadn't traced Simona's call. If he could just get his hands on Sean – or Carmel – everything would be solved. He had to stay cool, no matter how hard that was right now. There had to be an answer, a reason for that call.

Maybe he was so tired and freaked that he'd imagined what had just happened. It was possible. He could have mistaken the number, got it wrong. Or was he going mental, cracking under all this stress? One chaotic thought and association chased another, joined the maelstrom that whirled around his exhausted brain.

'We might as well push off. It's after midnight.' Gerry and Col glanced at each other again. 'Can we have our money now?' Col asked.

Anthony raised his head, his red-rimmed, bloodshot eyes sparking dangerously. The pair of them, undersized, scruffy and hollow-eyed, reminded him of characters in an eighteenth-century Hogarth engraving, *Gin Lane*. He drummed his fingers on the desk. 'What exactly do you two useless twats want money for?'

'The last six hours, mate!' Gerry whined. 'We've been driving all over this sodding city looking for Sean Devine, and we've had enough. We need our kip, don't we? So do you. You look more knackered than we are.'

'You get paid when there's a result.' Anthony rubbed his eyes. 'Not before.' He leaned back in his chair. 'And so far there's no result. I know you and the others lost his bitch of a wife once or twice and didn't tell me. Never mind no result, you could have fucked up everything.'

'Hey, now, listen, Ant—'

'*You* listen!' Anthony screamed, leaping to his feet. The men jumped back. 'I'm sick of the sight of you – get the fuck out of here *now*.' He pulled the gun from his coat pocket and levelled it at them, trying to stop his hands shaking. 'Or you'll never need money again!'

'Take it easy, all right?' Frightened, they backed further away. 'We're out of here.'

They were gone, muttering angrily as they went down the stairs. The warehouse door slammed. Anthony laid the gun on the desk, leaned back again and closed his eyes, let exhaustion weight his limbs and flood over him like a tidal wave. Five minutes, he thought. Just five. After that he would go back to the house and get Kev and Yvonne to take the girls away. Make sure he hadn't left Olivia's mobile in the study or safe. Sean Devine would have yet another night of freedom. Anthony heaved a long sigh as he sank into the soft leather chair and stretched out his long legs, his weary, aching body relaxing. The sensation was delicious.

He dreamed he was on a ferry crossing the Mersey towards the Liver Buildings and Cunard Building. It was raining and blowing a gale, and there was a heavy swell on the grey river. He didn't like the smoky, stuffy saloon with its unpleasant odour of damp clothes on sweaty bodies, so he decided to go up on deck and brave the weather.

He sniffed salty air and engine oil as he gazed out over the river. Needle-sharp rain stung his face, and he staggered slightly as the boat surged beneath him, grabbed the rail and looked down at the choppy waves. There was only one other person on deck, a woman sitting at the stern with her back to him, the wind whipping her long, dark red hair. Puzzled, he looked at her pale shoulders and bare arms. Why was she wearing a black strapless evening gown? She must be freezing.

He cringed suddenly. Olivia! What was she doing here

when she was dead, lying cold and blue in the room of swirling, dancing feathers? He had to get away before she turned and saw him. Anthony stepped back and stumbled as his feet caught in a coil of thick rope, bringing him crashing down on the rainwashed deck, arms flailing. He struggled to sit up and disentangle himself from the rope that coiled around his legs like a boa constrictor. He gave a cry of terror as he looked up to see Olivia standing over him holding a gun. Her Glöck. She looked like a vampire, the dark makeup around her eyes contrasting with her white face, her lips painted crimson. The ankle-length black dress was tight around her breasts and hips. Her feet were bare. She didn't seem to notice the cold wind and rain, or the lurching of the ferry.

'Where did you get that gun?' he cried, panicked. 'I stole it – hid it.'

She smiled. 'You can't hide anything from me, Anthony.'

'Get away,' he shouted, struggling to his feet. 'Leave me alone!'

'I want you to jump.' Olivia pointed the gun between his eyes. 'Go on.' The gale blew her hair across her face. 'It'll be our little secret. You like secrets, don't you?'

'No!' His back was to the cold, metal rail and there was nowhere to run. 'Don't!'

'Local businessman croaks it in freak tragic accident,' she laughed, moving closer. She licked her lips. Her teeth were stained with lipstick; it looked like blood. 'Death is soft, Anthony. Soft and warm and gentle, like goosedown. You'll love it.'

'No!' he sobbed. Olivia opened her mouth wide and started to cough. Clouds of feathers flew out and engulfed him, sticking to his face and hair, filling his nose and mouth and throat. She pushed back a strand of dark red hair and he screamed when he saw that she was wearing Paula Pepper's earring, the diamanté glittering fiercely in the dull light.

Anthony was fighting for breath, choking on feathers. The Liverpool skyline disappeared and there was only the crimson forest of his nightmare on the shore, the tree branches moving and twisting like snakes, a crimson stain spreading into the grey water. He could see Olivia's lips moving, trying to tell him something very important, but her words were blown away by the wind and the blast of a foghorn. She fired at close range, several times. The bullets hit him in the chest and knocked him backwards. He lost his balance and went overboard in a seemingly endless fall, the foghorn deafening him so that he couldn't hear his own scream.

'*No* . . . Jesus!' Anthony jerked awake, groaning aloud as he opened his eyes. To his shock he saw that it was daylight, ten past eight in the morning. The river was calm and misty. The gun lay on the desk in front of him. His body was stiff and aching, and he still had a headache. His stomach felt hollow. There seemed to be no time for eating and drinking, even if he could relax enough to do it. The hours of sleep hadn't helped, only made him feel jetlagged. Anthony leaned forward, snatched up the phone and dialled his house. There was no answer.

'Come on, he snarled, thumping his fist on the desk. 'Pick it up.' Yvonne and Kev must still be asleep. Even if they were up and about, they probably wouldn't want to answer the phone. It didn't mean anything was wrong. But he had to get over there now and get those girls away. He groaned and shook his head as he remembered the call from Olivia's mobile. Why did all this inexplicable bullshit keep happening to him? He took the gun and shoved it in his pocket.

Anthony jumped up and paused, gasping as the sudden movement sent a shaft of lightning pain coursing through his skull and down the back of his neck. He grabbed his keys and left the office. Running down the stairs, he cursed himself for stupidity. He hadn't locked the door. Then again, he hadn't planned to spend the night here. But Sean Devine could have broken in and shot him. Or whatever else he had in mind to do. Anthony was certain now that Carmel knew where Sean was, had probably known not long after he disappeared. How? Had she guessed where he was, or had Sean contacted her? He had to find her, make her talk.

He set the alarm and locked the warehouse door behind him, shivered in the cold morning air. It was really winter now, grey and raw. The shrill screams of the scavenging seagulls got on his nerves. He drove to the city centre and stopped off for a quick breakfast of coffee and a spongy, sticky lemon muffin because he was starving and dehydrated. The coffee wasn't strong enough, but at least it was hot and sweet. A few minutes later he was back in the car heading for the Queensway tunnel.

I should leave this city, he thought as he drove. Leave the bloody country. I could go anywhere I liked. But he didn't want to leave his house or the Joseph Williamson labyrinth, allow Henry Miles's gold to remain undiscovered – or worse, be found by someone else. Most of all, Anthony could not let go of his need to find Sean and kill him. Sean had to die. And soon. So did Carmel. Otherwise it didn't matter where he went or what the hell he did, because he would always be looking over his shoulder.

He slowed the Jaguar as he drove along the narrow twisting road to his house, stopped at the gates and looked up the drive. It was misty here too, silent except for the sound of gentle rain pattering on trees and bushes. The white van was parked where Kev had left it last night, the doors closed. Anthony pressed the remote control and the gates swung open. He parked behind the transit van and sat staring uneasily at the front door, tapping his fingers on the steering wheel. The place looked dead, as if it belonged to a parallel world.

'Lazy bastards,' he murmured. He would get rid of them, then lock himself in the house and sleep for the rest of the day. Go back to the tunnels tonight. The unexpected discovery of the new tunnel meant he was even closer to the gold than he had thought. One more search should do it. He was meant to find it. He got out of the Jaguar and went slowly up the wide stone steps to the front door.

The big, wood-panelled hall was silent except for the ticking of the grandfather clock. Anthony stopped and looked around. Something was wrong. He felt it.

'Kev!' he shouted up the stairs. 'Yvonne! Get down here. I want the cargo shifted.'

Nothing. He went down the dark passage to the kitchen where glasses, an empty Scotch bottle and crumpled beer cans were strewn over the table. It wasn't his booze – they must have gone out and bought their own. He'd told them to stay put. Anthony strode back to the hall and was about to run upstairs when the sitting room door opened.

Kev and Yvonne were shoved out, handcuffed and surrounded by police officers. Kev looked cowed and frightened, ready to spill everything he knew – if he hadn't already – but Yvonne was cool, her hard-faced expression intact. She looked at Anthony with hatred, silently cursing him for getting her into this mess. The group of dazed, terrified girls shuffled out, shepherded by uniformed female officers. Two of the girls were sobbing.

Anthony stood stunned and disbelieving, one hand on the smooth oak banister. The gun was heavy in his pocket. They obviously didn't know he had a gun, otherwise an armed response team would have ambushed him as he got out of his car and he would be spreadeagled face down on the drive now, their boots wedged in his vertebrae. In the swarm of people, all these people who had invaded his house, his private space, one stepped out and came towards him. Anthony recognised the smartarse detective who had questioned him at the warehouse. Neil something. Pale and red-eyed like himself, wearing crumpled jeans, a black leather jacket and the expression of the cat who had got the double cream and wild Irish smoked salmon. More officers pounded into the hall. Where had they been hiding? Round the back?'

'Anthony Maskey,' Neil began, 'I'm arresting you for—'

Anthony stood there stupefied as Neil spoke the words. Being charged with murder, attempted murder, murder of person unknown, something about trafficking in human beings. It seemed to go on for ages, and he barely listened. He shook his head and laughed as he heard the names Gemma Geraghty and Paula Higginbottom. They had no evidence, no evidence at all. It was hidden in a place they would never find. *Me and a man from another century*.

'There's no way I murdered those women,' he said, the smile playing around his lips. 'Or anyone else. It was Sean Devine – he fitted me up. His wife helped him. They want to kill me. I need protection.'

'You'll get twenty-four hours protection where you're going, no worries.' Neil's voice was cold. 'You're also being arrested in connection with the murder of Detective Inspector Olivia Crane.'

'Murder of . . .? *What*?' Anthony shouted, shock flashing through him. 'Who the hell is she? I never even knew the woman!' Several uniformed officers came forward, intending to handcuff him and probably give him a good kicking as well. Anthony jumped back and ran up a few stairs.

'So how come your mobile number is stored on her mobile? I used it last night to call you, and you answered.' Neil clenched his fists as he moved closer. 'You knew DI Crane. You murdered her. *Why*?'

The bloody call! Anthony's legs went weak. He hadn't imagined anything. He must have left Olivia's mobile here after all, and that bastard knew the pin number. He felt a flash of horror as Neil held up the phone. But they only had the phone, he thought, puzzled. Why were they arresting him for murdering Gemma Geraghty and Paula Pepper? That bitch Carmel Devine must have been telling more lies.

'We found your little bag of tricks,' Neil went on before he could say anything else. 'You were followed into the Williamson labyrinth last night.'

They'd found the bag – maybe the dead girl too! How the

hell . . .? Anthony gaped at Neil, his fevered brain desperately seeking a way out of this. He hadn't been followed last night, he was certain. Yeah, right! What was there to be certain about? Not bloody much, from where he was standing. He couldn't begin to think how or why, except that he had lost it big time.

They still couldn't prove he had murdered Olivia though. So what if he'd had her mobile? There were no witnesses to the killing. Except . . .! No. They would never find Simona. Diane would keep her until she was all used up. She might even die. Either way, Simona was finished. But so was he, if he didn't find a way out of this crap.

'I presume this is yours too. We found it in the cupboard under the stairs. Not a great hiding place, I would have thought, but that's your problem.' One of the officers handed Neil a black nylon rucksack. He unzipped it and emptied the contents on to the floor. Bundles of notes, and some passports. 'Where did this money come from? And what are you doing with these girls' passports in your possession?'

Anthony stared in shock. It must be the cash and passports that had been stolen from his safe. He shook his head, tried to speak. He couldn't think of anything to say. Three officers made a grab for him, but he was too quick. He ran up another few stairs, pulled the gun out of his pocket and levelled it at Neil's face.

'Get back!' he screamed. 'The lot of you.'

'Suspect is armed!' a hoarse, shocked voice shouted. There were screams, cries and flurries as Kev and Yvonne were dragged away and everyone scattered. Except for Neil, who stood calm and quiet, gazing up at him.

'Fucked up there, didn't you?' Anthony mocked. 'No armed response team ready and waiting to get their buzz blowing my face off. I *said*, get back!'

'Come on, Anthony!' Neil turned white. 'Be reasonable. You won't walk away from this, and you know it. Give me that gun now. Don't make things worse for yourself.'

'I'm a psycho, remember?' Anthony's finger hovered over the trigger. The gun felt heavy, almost too heavy to hold. 'I can't be expected to listen to reason or act rationally. Ask Carmel Devine.'

'No one's saying you're a psycho. Drop the gun, Anthony.' Neil raised one hand and stepped forward. 'Come on,' he said sharply. 'You won't shoot a police officer in front of witnesses.' He took another step forward, put one foot on the bottom stair. 'I know you're not that thick.'

'You don't know fucking anything!' Anthony fired twice, stunned by the noise of the gun as it went off. There were two deafening bangs, a recoil and a terrific surge of adrenalin that shook him to the core. He saw shock and amazement register on Neil's face, which seemed to crumple as he staggered and sank to his knees, clutching his stomach. Dark, arterial blood spurted from between his fingers and stained his jeans, flowed on to the shiny parquet floor. Anthony fired again at another officer who rushed in, and narrowly missed him. He turned and raced upstairs.

He knew what to do now. His time had come, as he had always known it would. He would climb to the attics and throw himself off the roof, make a glorious, spectacular exit. Take a few more of these bastards with him. He gained the first-floor landing and raced up the second and third flights of stairs, plod boots pounding after him. In the attic all the doors behind which those bitches should have been locked stood wide open, like empty cages from which birds had flown.

Anthony ran down the passage to the door behind which was the narrow flight of stairs that led up to the roof space. He flung open the door, turned and fired three more shots at the dark, menacing shapes of the powerfully built men chasing him. They jumped back out of sight, and the bullets smashed into the walls and ceiling, causing clouds of white plaster dust. Anthony raced up the narrow stairs, unbolted the green wooden door and stepped out on to the roof, slamming the door behind him. He saw dense treetops, low grey sky, the long spreading arm of the distant city and a ribbon of silver that was the River Mersey. Not such a bad sight, considering it was his last on this earth.

The plods were on the stairs now. Anthony turned, ready to fire when they burst through the little door, and suddenly realised all his bullets were used up. Never mind. He tossed the gun in a wide arc across the sky, hoping it would land on some plod's head and smash it to a bloody pulp. He ran forward and paused, smelled distant woodsmoke and shivered in the cold air. He teetered on the roof edge, looked down and saw the white plod cars with their red and blue markings. Heard shouts, saw the stupid, shocked faces staring up at him.

Anthony had never felt so calm in his life, finally at peace with this chaotic, cruel world. He had never belonged here. He smiled as he stretched out his arms, ready to fly. Looked down one last time.

'Morons,' he whispered. 'You just don't get it. You never will.'

Anthony closed his eyes.

Chapter Twenty-seven

'Carmel, you're so brave!' Rosa hugged her again.

'Crazy, more like!' Daniel looked grim. 'Scares the hell out of me to think what could have happened. We might have been putting out a television appeal for Sean to turn up at your funeral.'

'Well, you're not. So don't let's think about what could have happened.' Carmel curled up on the sofa and sipped her white wine. 'Especially as it didn't.'

'But for Christ's sake, Carmel! Hiding in Maskey's car, following him down into those tunnels – they're dangerous enough when you're not tailing a psycho.' Daniel shook his head in despair. 'You were mad to go off alone like that. The bastard could have murdered you, like he must have murdered that girl they found under the rubble in the cave.'

'I wonder who she is?' Carmel shuddered and took a gulp of wine. 'Imagine, I thought the stink was dead rats! Then again, I've never whiffed a rotting corpse.'

'We were all worried sick. And with good reason! Why didn't you tell me what you had planned?' Daniel demanded. 'You gave me the impression you were going to dump the money and passports in a safe place.'

'I did, didn't I?'

'I could have helped, like last time. I'd never have handed it over to you if I'd known you were going to try and get into his house and . . . *Jesus*!'

'Daniel, please don't go all macho on me. You're angry and I can understand that. Yes, it was a crazy risk. But I had to do it – and alone.' Carmel put down her glass of wine. 'I didn't want to endanger anyone else.' She looked at both of them. 'Remember,' she cautioned. 'There's no need for Mum and Dad to know the details.'

'Details!' Daniel snorted. 'You certainly love your understatements, don't you?' He got up and went to the sideboard. 'I'll have some more of your cognac. God knows, I bloody need it.'

'It'll only freak them out,' Carmel went on. 'All they need to know is that Anthony Maskey's activities – trafficking in women, the murders of three women, one of them unknown, the shooting of an unarmed police officer and the suspicions that he murdered another police officer – my God! – are being investigated. They've taken blood and saliva samples, and forensics people are all over his house. They've already raided several clubs in Liverpool and Manchester,' she said. 'Found some of those girls whose passports he stole. They're trying to find out who the dead girl is – *was*. His operations could stretch to Dublin and Amsterdam. Anthony had contacts in eastern Europe, mostly Romania.'

Rosa got up to close the curtains on the cold, frosty night. 'Those girls have been through hell! What happens to them now?

'I'm not sure. They might be too frightened to give evidence – that's if they even get the chance. They could simply be deported because their tourist visas have expired.' Carmel sighed. 'The blind letter of the law ... etcetera. Same old, same old.'

'But that's terrible!' Rosa came back and flopped on the sofa. 'They were bought and sold like consumer items, forced into prostitution, and *they* end up being criminalised! I suppose penalties for trafficking in human beings are much lower than for fraud or bank robbery? Stealing money, as opposed to female bodies and souls?'

Carmel nodded, her expression sombre. 'What do you

expect? It's only a few hundred years since a council of bishops met to discuss and vote on whether or not women actually had souls! The vote decided that they did – by a narrow margin.'

Rosa sat up, astonished. 'Is that true?'

'Oh, yes.'

Daniel strolled back to the sofa and sat beside Carmel, swilling the pale golden cognac around in his glass. 'The police operation on Maskey's home the other morning was a real fuck-up.' He frowned. 'That girl he murdered – Gemma – she was shot. And they found a gun in that box he hid in the cave. How come no one got the bright idea that he just might be armed?'

'It was all a bit rushed,' Carmel said. 'They raced over to his house, freed those girls and arrested the unholy pair guarding them. The man started offering to make statements before they'd even asked him anything, but the woman was a real hard case. Then they had to hide in Anthony's house and wait for him to come home.'

'That detective was damned lucky to survive two gunshot wounds in the stomach. He could have haemorrhaged to death before the paramedics got there.'

'I know. He's still in intensive care, but the doctors say he'll make it. Of course it'll be a long time before he can go back to work.' Carmel looked troubled. 'You'd never be the same again after that kind of injury, would you? Even if you didn't end up permanently disabled.'

'Makes it even worse because it was totally avoidable!' Daniel stretched out his legs and stared into the fire. 'He should never have challenged Maskey like that. Sounds as if he trained by watching cop films and series. Still,' he sighed, 'I suppose it was personal, if Maskey murdered his inspector.'

'When I think Olivia Crane must have tried to protect Anthony by obstructing any lines of inquiry that would have proved Sean innocent . . .' Carmel felt furious again. 'I just wonder why Anthony murdered her? But it's early days yet, they've only just started investigating her. Even if the anti-corruption squad dig up an entire sewage system in that police station, they won't necessarily be dying to tell me or the newspapers about it. To be honest, I don't give a damn. Let them sort their own mess.' She blinked back sudden tears. 'I just want to find Sean. Why doesn't he call me?'

Rosa and Daniel were silent, avoiding her gaze, and she knew what they were thinking. Had Anthony finally got to Sean and murdered him? Almost two days since the raid on Anthony's house, and all charges against Sean had been formally dropped. Today was Sunday, 28 November and so far there was nothing in the newspapers about him being exonerated. No reporters phoned or rang the doorbell, seeking her comments. The computer and floppy discs, all the papers the police had taken during their search, had been returned. There was talk of a formal apology, for all the good that would do. Of course the police were afraid of being sued, something Carmel did not even have the energy to think about right now.

'He probably doesn't know the charges have been dropped,' she whispered. 'He can't have been back to Rice Street and read my note. I'll go back there again later. Sean's all right – I know he is.'

She felt Daniel's strong arm slide around her shoulders and hold her tight, the wool of his navy blue sweater soft and warm against the nape of her neck. Rosa got up and handed her a tissue. Daniel swigged the rest of his cognac and looked down at Carmel, his dark eyes bitter.

'You know what really gives me the raving hump in all this?'

'Yep.' Carmel nodded. 'Same thing that gives me the raving hump.' She gazed into the firelight, tears glittering on her cheeks. 'Why the hell did those morons have to bring Anthony Maskey down in a rugby tackle before he could jump off that roof and shatter himself into a thousand pieces?'

*

337

'Thanks for coming, Mary. You shouldn't have bothered.'

'Don't be daft, lad! I phoned your house to ask how you were, and got some copper telling me you'd been arrested. Asking me my name and address and everything, saying they'd want to interview me. I had to find out what was going on. Sorry I couldn't come sooner,' she panted. 'But they wouldn't let me.'

'Don't worry about that.'

Mary pulled her dark blue duffel coat open, glanced back at the two silent police officers standing against the light green interview room wall, and lowered her voice as if she thought that would stop them eavesdropping. 'Is it true?' she asked, flushing. 'Did you really shoot that detective fella?'

'I didn't mean to. It was a terrible accident.' Anthony looked her in the eye. 'I couldn't believe Sean Devine and his wife had fitted me up – that the police thought I was to blame for those murders he committed. And I hadn't a clue what those girls were doing in my house. The police wouldn't listen to me. I panicked, lost it. I was desperate to escape and prove my innocence. Not much chance of that now, stuck in here!' He cast the officers a bitter glance.

Mary sighed. 'What were you doing with a gun, love?'

'It was Sean Devine's,' he said. 'I followed him into those Joseph Williamson tunnels. He hid it, together with some other stuff, and I found it after he'd gone. When I got home and found the police waiting, I tried to give them the gun. But they wouldn't believe it wasn't mine. They started shouting, threatening me. That's when I panicked and it went off. I hate guns. I never wanted to hurt anybody.' The police officers grimaced at one another.

'They searched your mum's house,' Mary said sadly. 'Sorry, love.' She stretched out one hand then withdrew it, remembering she wasn't supposed to touch him. 'I couldn't stop them. I wanted to go in afterwards and put things to rights, but they wouldn't let me. They still won't.' Her tired eyes filled with tears. 'I can't believe you're in this mess.' Her voice cracked. 'Accused of murder! Of keeping women for ... what they said. Blaming you for all the terrible things that fella did, that Sean whatsisname.'

'Devine. Sean Devine.'

'Yeah. Why don't they catch him?' She rooted in her handbag and pulled out a white cotton handkerchief embroidered with red roses. 'I wish I could get my hands on him, I'd—!' She bit her lip and glanced at the officers again. 'I'm just glad your mum's not here to see your trouble.' Mary sniffed and wiped her eyes. 'It'd kill her, and no mistake. She couldn't have borne it.'

'No.' Anthony was becoming irritated. Mary meant well, but she wasn't doing him any favours. Her performance made her look like the sweet, innocent, motherly old woman, tragically fooled for years by the cold-blooded murderer's lies. *What* cold-blooded murderer? He blinked and frowned, suddenly confused. He hadn't murdered anyone. It was Sean.

'I brought you these, lad,' Mary was saying. She turned to the officers. 'It's all right for him to have these, isn't it?' Anthony looked in astonishment at the ten packs of Embassy Regal she placed on the table.

'What's this?' he asked. 'You know I don't smoke.'

'I was just thinking, love ...' Mary hesitated, flushed again. 'You've got your court appearance tomorrow, haven't you? Where you give your name and address and they read out the charges and ask how you plead and you say not guilty?'

Anthony nodded. 'So what?'

'Well, those two solicitors you phoned didn't want to know. And considering what you're charged with – even though you're innocent – let's face it, you're not likely to get bail, are you? That's why I brought the ciggies. They're better than cash in prisons and remand centres.' She glanced at the officers. 'That's right, isn't it?' she asked eagerly.

'Yeah, love.' They were openly smirking now. Anthony closed his eyes in despair.

'Okay,' one of them said. 'Come on, let's move. Social call's over.'

'All right, hold your horses!' Mary snapped her handbag shut and struggled to her feet. 'Take care of yourself, love.'

'I could say the same to you,' Anthony remarked. 'Are you okay?' He looked at her with concern. 'You seem a bit breathless.'

'Never mind me, love. I'm fine. You worry about yourself. Just let me know if there's anything you want. D'you need coins for the phone?'

'He doesn't need coins to make phone calls,' one of the policemen grinned. 'In prisons and remand centres there's a special hole where you stick a ciggie.'

'Full of it, aren't you?' Mary glared at him, then turned back to Anthony. 'I'll see you in court tomorrow morning, give you a bit of moral support.' She winked, struggling not to cry. 'You'll be all right, you'll soon get out of here.' This wasn't the time to dwell on all the miscarriages of British justice that kept on coming relentlessly to light. 'That sod Sean Devine will get what he deserves. Keep your chin up, lad!'

'You're my real mother,' Anthony said suddenly. 'You know that, don't you?'

'Gerroff!' Mary was crying again as they escorted her out. The young, fair-haired detective in a grey trouser suit stuck her head round the door.

'Ready to continue our chat, Anthony?'

He hated the way they called him Anthony, as if he were a hospital patient or some demented bag of bones rotting in a retirement home.

'I've told you,' he said coldly. 'I've got nothing to say. Except that it was Sean Devine who committed those murders. Not me!' The woman sighed and disappeared.

Back in his cell Anthony sat cross-legged on the thin mattress and stared at the blue-tiled wall opposite. He felt lethargic, his mind once more shrouded in the fog that came

340

and went. It wasn't tiredness; he had caught up on his sleep in here, despite the shouts, screams, clatter and crazed laughter from prisoners in other cells. He could not think clearly. He kept losing time somehow, thinking only five or ten minutes had passed when it was actually one or two hours. Maybe they were trying to drive him crazy to get him to confess, tell them what they wanted to hear. No way. He was strong, he would not be beaten.

Anthony got up and began to perform slow yoga movements, arching and stretching his body one way and then another. But he couldn't concentrate. The floor was cold, dirty and hard, a corner by the door spattered with what looked like dried blood. He could smell the toilet and disinfectant, the depressing hospital food odour at mealtimes. As he had been put on suicide watch, his privacy was constantly disturbed. One or two police officers kept going on about Neil Davie, giving him unrequested progress reports on their beloved colleague's condition. They were obviously itching to beat the shit out of him. Anthony could handle one or two of them, no worries, but there would be a gang when it happened. As it would.

His shock and disbelief at being arrested, the anger, the satisfaction of blanking these bastards and refusing to answer their questions, especially about Olivia and the dead bitch in the tunnel, was wearing off. Anthony felt a tremendous sense of frustration and humiliation. Being locked in a police cell without belt or shoelaces, given meals at times when he didn't want to eat, endure comments and judgements from people he despised, unable to decide even when the light should go on or off, tortured and humiliated him in a way he had never thought possible. He could not face the thought that his precious, secret places in Joseph's labyrinth had been discovered and searched, that someone else might find the gold, that he would never get to kill Sean Devine.

Or Carmel. She was the one who had brought about his downfall. Anthony abandoned the Shoulderstand and sat cross-legged on the hard mattress again, squeezing his eyes tight shut in agony at the thought that Carmel had actually been watching his house, had hidden herself in his car as he drove to the labyrinth, followed him inside, waited for him to leave and then called the police.

Was it true what they told him, or was all this a wind-up? Venting their spite because he wouldn't co-operate? Surely Carmel Devine would not have had the bottle to do that! But how else could they have found the bag and the girl's body? Was it Carmel who'd stolen the money and passports from his safe and planted them in his house? He still didn't really understand how she'd done it. Anthony also didn't want to think about it too much right now, because he had the terrifying feeling that if he did he would become crazy, raving, end up drugged and straitjacketed in Broadmoor or nearby Park Lane. Park Lane had a new name now, but he couldn't remember it. He had to keep his head, concentrate, stop losing time. Otherwise he was finished.

Anthony longed to regain that wonderful sense of total peace and freedom he had experienced just before he had been about to jump off the roof. It was like he imagined *samadhi*, the joyful state of altered consciousness that he had tried and failed to achieve through meditation. Total peace, awareness, the sense of oneness, unity with all things. Enlightenment. Why was there only one person in this world who loved him? he suddenly wondered. Would Mary still love him if she knew the truth about him and his life?

Scientists in labs were doing tests on his DNA, matching it with samples found at the crime scene. *Scenes*. Anthony did not feel remotely connected to the murders they accused him of. It was as if they were talking about someone else. At times he felt confused and frightened, almost panicking. At this moment the whole thing just bored him. He needed to be free from all this shit. And that didn't mean being banged up for the next thirty years.

More images flickered behind his tightly closed eyelids, emerging and receding. One particular image took shape and form, banishing the others; the face of Carmel Devine. He saw her long, thick, blonde hair, those split ends that irritated him because she didn't get them chopped off often enough. The striking, cornflower-blue eyes, the straight, slim brows that sometimes made her look as if she was frowning. Carmel was not frowning now though, she was smiling. Mocking, triumphant. Celebrating a victory.

A dark cloud formed around her head, pressing down. The cloud was his hatred, the simmering anger that was building, massing beneath his apparently calm exterior until sometimes it felt like his head would burst. Anthony opened his eyes and stared at the pale blue wall.

'I'm not done with you,' he whispered. His hands were clenched, so rigid that they had become stiff and painful. He relaxed them, flexing his slender fingers.

He had been ready to die the other day, had longed for death. He had been dragged back from the brink, brutally pinned down by fists and boots and curses, forced to remain bound and imprisoned in the world he so desperately wanted to fly out of. He had lost it then, had kicked and screamed and fought his captors, cursed them back. He accepted what had happened now though, realised the time wasn't right. The police were surprised and relieved at his apparent docility. Good.

Anthony lay on his back and stretched out, stared up at the blackness beyond the barred window. He wished he could be out in that darkness, smell the earth and the river, look up at the moon and stars. Go back to Joseph's labyrinth. The bright light in the cell hurt his eyes.

One day he would experience that sense of perfect peace and freedom again. When he was done. When he was ready.

Not yet.

Carmel parked the Landcruiser in Rodney Street, got out

and headed quickly towards the corner with Rice Street. Once she would have been scared to walk alone in the city at night, but Anthony Maskey's arrest and incarceration gave her a wonderful sense of freedom and safety. Although she was worried about his court appearance tomorrow morning. Was it possible he would get bail? The police said 'highly unlikely' and 'almost certainly not', considering what Anthony was charged with, but that was as far as they were prepared to go. You couldn't always tell, they said, with magistrates and rules of evidence, what was and was not admissible. Of course they would strongly oppose the granting of bail.

Anthony had money – a lot of money. Most of it was the proceeds of crime, and his bank accounts would no doubt be frozen at some point. But when? Not for weeks, months maybe. Carmel dreaded the thought that Anthony might be able to buy himself temporary freedom. It could take up to a year or even longer before his case came to trial. She had no doubt that he hated her now, wanted to kill her even more than he wanted to kill Sean.

What had made Anthony that way? Carmel believed everyone was born with their personality intact, and that life events served to either accentuate or suppress various character traits. Some people simply had less resistance to crime, for one reason or another. Nevertheless, murdering another human being was always a choice. Carmel stopped, stunned by a sudden feeling of deep sadness and dread. It was as if she could look into Anthony's soul and see the darkness, pain and misery, the terrible loneliness. He had tried to commit suicide. Did he wish he was dead now? The police said he refused to talk to them about anything. She shivered as she imagined him alone in a cell, silent and endlessly brooding.

'Get over it!' she muttered, feeling in her jacket pocket for the keys. 'You won't feel sorry for him if he walks out of court tomorrow!' She hurried along, pulling up her collar against the cold night air, her heartbeat quickening as

344

she turned the corner into Rice Street and looked up at the flat's dark windows. Would Sean be there tonight? Had he been back since her last visit?

'Sean!' she called hopefully into the silent darkness as she walked into the garage. 'It's me, Carmel! Are you there?'

She waited, her heart thudding. No joyful answering shout, no footsteps on the stairs. She didn't put the lights on in case he came back while she was there and thought it was someone else. Anthony, maybe. In the kitchen Carmel picked up the note she had left on the table and read it again by the pale orange street light.

> *Darling Sean,*
> *I know you've been here, and this is to tell you you're safe now. Anthony has been arrested for murder and trafficking in women, and he's in custody. All charges against you have been dropped. Come Home!*
> *I love you!*
> *Carmel XXXXXXXXXXXXXXXX*

Tears came into her eyes as she reread the words. She put the note down again, securing it with a mug, and peered out into the street. Two men strode past, muffled up against the cold. One of them laughed, threw down a cigarette and trod on it.

Carmel did not know where else to look. This place was her only hope. Sean would come back here sooner or later. He had to! She moved the chair and took up the floorboards again, shining the torch into the space below. Nothing seemed to have been touched.

She switched off the torch and struggled to her feet, went into the sitting room and unrolled the sleeping bag she had left in a corner by the fireplace. Climbed inside and zipped it up, sat leaning against the wall. Listening to sounds of cars, dogs, people. Longing to hear a key being stuck in the lock. Sean's feet on the stairs. Thinking how she missed him. Wanted him to come home. Talk, cuddle, laugh, make love. Wake up together. All the things she had never quite dared take for granted in case she lost them. So why the hell should she be punished now?

Waiting, waiting.

Chapter Twenty-eight

'Bloody hell, that was cosmic! D'you enjoy that as much as me, love?'

The man rolled off Simona, his pale sweaty flesh squelching away from hers, and lay on his back panting as though he'd run for a bus. He had so much dark hair on his face, neck, chest, shoulders and back that he looked barely human, more like a wild beast that belonged in the forest. Except wild beasts didn't wobble with fat and stink of cigarettes and hamburgers with ketchup. He raised himself on one elbow and grinned down at her. Simona looked away.

'You're bloody lovely, you are!' He fondled her breasts. 'Not like the other bow-wows in here. You look like my daughter. She's about your age.'

'Did you fuck her too?' Simona sat up and began to peel off her only item of clothing, the lacy black stockings that made her legs itch and caused red indentations around the tops of her thighs. She didn't wonder how he could ask if she had enjoyed it. She had given up wondering how anyone who handed over money in order to impose their sexual desires on another person's body could seriously imagine that person would enjoy the experience. But they did.

'Hey!' His watery, bloodshot brown eyes narrowed. 'Watch it, you little bitch! That's not funny.'

'I know it isn't.' She looked at him. 'I am someone's daughter.'

'If you start that shit again I won't come here no more. Don't try and take advantage because you know I like you.' He got up and began pulling on soiled white underpants and greasy, baggy blue jeans. It's only because you remind me of my Chloe that I don't do—' He looked away. 'Other things.' He put on a black T-shirt and sweater, his denim jacket. Leaned over and kissed her. 'See you next time, Beautiful! Take care.'

When he had gone and she was locked in again, Simona pulled on her thin pink silky robe, hurried to the window and stuck her fingers between the blinds. Dawn was coming up, dark blue around the horizon, and a few stars glittered. An aircraft passed overhead. She yawned and shivered. The house was quiet now, no more shouts and screams, or drunken manic laughter. Take care, he said. What the hell did that mean under these circumstances?

Simona went back and sat on the bed hugging herself, wondering how many more tricks she would have to service before she was allowed to go back upstairs to sleep through most of this coming day. She refused to think of the men as 'clients', pretend that each violation of her body and spirit was nothing more than a straightforward business transaction. They bought her body and didn't think of her as a person; she was just a whore, slag, cow, bitch, cunt, all the epithets applied to human beings who were not considered human. They didn't care about anything as long as they handed over their money and got to fuck her. Even that pig with the daughter who said he liked her. He probably really believed that. What did he imagine this kind of life was for any woman? A solution to unemployment?

Simona had never imagined she would be glad to see Anthony again, but now she couldn't wait for him to come back and get her. She did not dare think what would happen after that, could not think beyond trying to survive each day in this hell. But where was Anthony, what was he doing? She had expected him back before now; Diane was beginning to grumble about how much it cost to feed her. Simona knew she was earning the woman a lot more money than whatever her food cost.

What did Anthony want from her? There was no chance he would trust her again, not after her escape attempt. There was no chance to escape from here. She was locked up all the time and only allowed out to go to the bathroom, or downstairs to this plush room where she spent her nights servicing tricks while one of Diane's bouncers stood guard outside and took the money. There were other girls and women in the house, although Simona had only seen one on the first day, a young blonde girl in black lingerie. Did they work here voluntarily, or had they too been kidnapped and raped?

She jumped and gasped with fear as the door was flung open. Barry marched in, gripped her arm and dragged her to her feet. He was stockily built, stubble-headed, and stank of cigarettes. His arms and what she could see of his neck and chest were covered with tattooes of snakes, daggers and muscled hands brandishing flaming, deep blue torches. He boasted about having been in the army, said he had killed people in the Balkans. Simona believed him. She did not resist as he dragged her up two flights of narrow, red-carpeted stairs, pushed her into the bare attic room and locked the door.

There was a silvery can of fizzy orange on the floor, gone flat after being opened hours ago. Simona picked it up and drank, then lay on the stained mattress and covered herself with the scratchy grey blanket. She could not look out of this window, which had black cloth nailed over it. Like that nightmare room in the first house where she had been beaten and raped by the four men.

Simona was sore and bruised inside and out; all her muscles ached. She was shivering so much that she wondered if she was coming down with flu or some kind of fever. If she got sick would they let her rest for a few days? Suppose she needed medical treatment? She could not imagine Diane letting her see a doctor. Don't get sick! she told herself. She curled up and closed her eyes, thought again how she had not had a period since setting foot in the UK. That didn't worry her unduly, because she had once read that periods often stopped if a girl or woman was subjected to great stress and trauma. It was a kind of defence mechanism, the body shutting down. But Simona was terrified she might get pregnant or be infected with some sexually transmitted disease, maybe even the HIV virus. Condoms gave protection, but not complete safety. It was too awful to contemplate what might happen then.

It was pointless to try to relax, let alone sleep. The room was cold and her brain filled with too many images. Maria, her family, her old life, walking in the fields around the village in happier times, not realising how many people in the world didn't wish you well, only wanted to use and hurt you until you were finished. It upset Simona to think how naïve, how stupid and trusting she had been.

Suppose she somehow managed to escape this life and go home? Would she dare tell her family what had happened to her? Would she even be believed? How could she bring herself to trust a man again, any man? Talk with him, laugh, let him touch her? Perform an act that was supposed to be about desire, sensual pleasure, fulfilment, mutual passion, sometimes love, but which she associated only with violence, pain and powerlessness? She could never marry, Simona thought, never have children. Especially not girls.

The phone rang downstairs in the hall and she heard Diane answer it, give a loud, shocked exclamation. Footsteps climbed the stairs and halted on the landing. Low voices, Diane's and Barry's, some other man's. The voices and footsteps moved closer and stopped outside her door. Moved away again. Simona sat up, tense and frightened in the cold darkness, the blanket wrapped tightly around her, staring at the yellow chink of light beneath the door.

'No!' she whispered. 'No more. Twelve hours – they have to let me rest now!' She would die or go crazy if this went on. But what did they care? She clapped one hand

350

over her mouth to stop herself moaning out loud. Cigarette smoke drifted under the door. Of course they were smoking. Always, always smoking. Simona listened, desperate to hear what they were saying. They believed she could barely speak or understand English, and it suited her to let them go on thinking that.

'If he's been nicked,' Barry said hoarsely, 'what the fuck do we do with *her*?'

'Dunno.' Diane coughed. 'She can't stay here, but we can't let her go either. They might be looking for her. She could land us all in the shit. How could Anthony be so thick, letting himself get arrested? Stupid bastard!'

'He could be out tomorrow morning, Di. Get bail.'

'What, when he's charged with murder and kidnapping? Shooting a copper? And that's only the half of it. Have a day off, will you!'

'You never know. Ant's loaded. And remember he used to boast about having some high-ranking copper in his pocket? He could walk.'

'Maybe. But I want rid of that bitch. Tonight. You can do it, Barry.'

'I'll do it, no problem. But shouldn't we wait a bit? Anthony'll go ballistic if . . .'

They moved away, leaving Simona crying and shivering with fright. Anthony was in prison, accused of murder! Shooting a policeman. He wouldn't be coming back now. She would never escape, would never see Maria or her family again.

The darkness in the room pressed down on her, choking, suffocating, making her feel as if she was buried alive. She could not stand it any longer. Simona got off the bed, stumbled across the room and pounded on the door in panic, tears pouring down her face.

'Let me go!' she shouted. She banged on the door, hurting her fists, and began to scream, terrified, tortured screams that reverberated throughout the silent house. 'Let me go, let me out of here! Please! Help! *Help* me!'

But there would be no help. Not now.

They would kill her.

Carmel woke up, dazzled by the morning sunlight that had started to slant across the dirty white walls and bare floor-boards, and had now got around to her face. She groaned and shifted, her back and neck aching with the hardness of the floor. Eyes closed against the sun, she recalled the dream that had just woken her.

She had been climbing out of the sitting room window in her parents' house, trying to escape from Anthony. Her parents were frightened, bewildered, asking what was going on. She screamed at them to call the police, get Lisa, just do it. She was in the dark garden, hiding behind the sycamore tree by the shed, being so quiet and still. Waiting, waiting, until she was sure Anthony must have given up and gone away. Cautiously she stepped out from behind the tree and gave a horrified gasp at the sight of the tall, dark, menacing figure not far away, standing on the path that wound through the rose bushes. He started to walk towards her, his feet making no sound on the gravel. He raised the gun. She couldn't escape.

Carmel opened her eyes and slowly sat up, squinting in the sunshine. The dream's fear, its strong sense of evil, was still with her. She had to remind herself that Anthony was locked in a police cell with a stack of evidence mounting against him, that he was no longer capable of hurting Sean, Lisa, or anyone else she loved.

She unzipped the sleeping bag and left it open to air, stood up and slowly stretched. She was a mass of aches and pains. The dark thought crept back – was it possible that Anthony had found and killed Sean before his arrest? Just as well the evidence was mounting, because Anthony refused to co-operate with the police, still would not answer a single question after days of interrogation and being repeatedly informed that the less he co-operated the longer the stretch. Anything else she or the police wanted to know, they were going to have to find out for themselves. Maybe Anthony would even refuse to acknowledge his name, address and date of birth at his court appearance this morning.

Carmel decided not to go to that. She hated to admit it, but she was frightened. She did not want to see him standing motionless in the dock, his eyes locked on her, filled with hatred and the desire for vengeance. Or filled with nothing. She glanced at her watch and smiled slightly; it was almost ten-thirty. Wouldn't it be over by now? Anthony would be in a police van, handcuffed and on his way to the remand centre. Or ...? She thought about bail.

'No!' she hissed, impatient with herself. 'There's no way – don't worry about *that*, for God's sake!'

She glanced at the note on the kitchen table before she left, checking that it was secured by the old blue rose Spode mug and could not be blown off by a draught and go unnoticed by Sean when he came back. She ignored her irrational desire to plaster the note to the table with sticky tape. She went slowly down the stairs, through the garage and back yard, and out into the cold, bright morning. On Rodney Street she got a shock as a tall male figure in a dark coat turned a corner and strode towards her. It wasn't Sean. Carmel stopped briefly and shut her eyes, felt the hollowness in her stomach that didn't come only from lack of food and the need for a caffeine fix. I can't take much more of this, she thought. But what choice do I have?

At home she picked up the phone, gas and electricity bills lying on the mat and tossed them unopened on the hall table. She went upstairs and took a long, hot shower, blowdried her hair and selected a stretchy turquoise top and a pair of black trousers. She put on some makeup for the first time in days; red lipstick, blusher, mascara and pale gold eyeshadow. Sprayed herself with perfume. The clothes and makeup gave a welcome illusion of efficient normality, being in control of her destiny. She took Sean's giftwrapped package out of her handbag and studied it, turning it over in her hands.

Carmel dismissed a sudden image of herself as a grey-haired old lady, standing in this same spot still holding the unopened birthday gift, her eyes full of tears as she listened to the distant shouts and laughter of her and Sean's grandchildren. She put the package back and closed her bag.

Down in the kitchen she made coffee and forced herself to eat an apple and a slice of toast with butter and apricot jam. The silence in the house no longer felt peaceful and welcoming, but threatening, as if some other terrible thing was about to happen. The people who should be here, safe and happy, were not. Unnerved, Carmel switched on the radio for company. Madonna's latest, followed by something from a band called Coldplay about living in a beautiful world. Then the brief hourly news bulletin. Carmel drank the hot, sweet coffee and poured another cup. Might as well head for the office, she decided. I'll go crazy if I just sit around here. She sighed, running her hands through her soft, newly washed hair. The tension was unbearable. She got up to switch off the radio, then stopped.

'A man is appearing at Liverpool Magistrates Court this morning, charged with the murders of local prostitute Gemma Geraghty and nightclub singer Paula ...'

She gasped and knocked over her coffee cup. Dark brown liquid spilled over the table and dripped on to the floor. Carmel stood there, her hands clenched, trying to take in what the self-important female voice was saying: Anthony Maskey's name, where he lived, that he was a local businessman. And ...

'Oh, God!' she whispered.

'... Maskey is also strongly suspected of being involved in the disappearance of his business partner, Sean Devine, against whom all charges have now been dropped. And now the weather. Cold and frosty, with temperatures later expected to drop below freezing ...'

Carmel switched off the radio and stood there, one hand

to her mouth. Seconds later the phone rang. She stared at it, then snatched up the receiver.

'Carmel, it's Rosa. Did you hear the news?'

'Yes,' she replied.

'I'm on my break. This is bound to be in the papers as well. It'll all come out now. Everyone will know Sean is innocent. Are you okay?' she asked. 'Carmel, talk to me!'

'I'm shaking. I'm okay though. It just feels unreal, hearing it on the radio like that.' Carmel sniffed, and swallowed hard. 'I hope Sean was listening somewhere. I hope . . .' She paused, fighting for control. 'I hope it's not too late and that he's not lying buried somewhere in that fucking labyrinth!'

'Oh, Carmel!' Rosa's voice was anguished. 'Don't think that, *please*.'

'I don't want to. But Anthony won't tell the police anything – I might never see Sean again, never find out what happened. Every Christmas, every birthday, every time the phone rings or the doorbell goes, I'll get that awful rush of hope and longing for it to be Sean. And it won't be!' She wiped her eyes, ruining the carefully applied mascara and dark gold shadow. 'I just had a vision of myself as an old lady, with Lisa's children running around. Still not knowing what had happened.'

'Carmel, listen. Don't go anywhere. I'll take the rest of the day off and come home.'

'No, Rosa! You'll get the sack if you take any more time off. I'm all right, really.'

'You don't sound it.'

'I am. It was just the shock of that news bulletin.' Carmel reached for a tissue and blew her nose. 'I'll go to the office now. Make some calls, get a few things sorted.'

'That can wait. You must have had a terrible night in Rice Street. Why don't you get some rest?'

'Because I'd go crazy. And I just flooded my bloodstream with caffeine and adrenalin. I'm all right now, Rosa, I promise.'

'You've been freaked about Anthony's court appearance too. Well, we all have. But there's no chance he'll get bail. That's impossible.'

'Yeah,' Carmel sighed. 'I just won't be happy until I know the magistrates have said – "Wot, bail? You 'avin a larf, mate?" Listen, I'll see you later, okay?'

'Are you sure you're all right?'

'I'm fine. I'll go shopping after the office. Might make us a cottage pie for dinner.'

'Lovely. When are you picking up Lisa?'

'Tomorrow evening. It'll be great to have her back again.'

'I know. I've certainly missed her. Listen, I've changed my shifts.' Rose lowered her voice. 'You can still go out at night and look for Sean. I'll stay with Lisa.'

Carmel was silent for a few seconds. 'What would I do without you?'

'Hey – we're *family*, as they say in all the best soaps. See you at cottage pie time.'

Carmel was amazed at the amount of e-mails, faxes and phone messages that awaited her at the office. Consultants and former clients were happy to associate with her again now that they knew she wasn't the wife of a man wanted for murdering prostitutes and nightclub singers. She shook her head in disgust at the hypocrisy of some messages.

'So you want to be best bosomy mates again,' she murmured, deleting e-mails and ripping up faxes. 'I'll take your dirty money, you bastards, but I won't forget ... what's this?' She clicked on another e-mail. 'Even Lady Jane wants to come back! No chance, Janie. I'm sure you'll understand you don't fit my profile of the loyal little secretary girl.' There was no message from Sean.

She left the office at lunchtime, after answering most of the messages and setting up a few appointments for later that week. Before getting into the Landcruiser she paused to look at the cold blue sky and the sunlit River Mersey, smell the air. She realised she had not thought about Anthony Maskey for more than an hour.

She would phone the new liaison officer when she got home, and ask what had happened. Which remand centre would Anthony be sent to? Risley? Conditions there would come as a severe shock to someone who had lived in a squat on a rundown inner city estate, never mind a beautifully restored, early Victorian house on the Wirral. Would Sean be back with her and Lisa by the time Anthony's case came to trial? Carmel wondered. They would probably both have to give evidence.

The liaison officer was not available, and it seemed that no one else at the police station could give her any information about Anthony Maskey. They promised to call back. Carmel was in the kitchen putting away a load of groceries when the doorbell rang. She gasped with fright and dropped the lump of Cheddar she had been about to store in the fridge. Her heart began to pound, felt as if it was expanding and filling her chest cavity so that she could barely breathe.

'For God's sake!' she whispered. 'Take it easy – you'll make yourself ill.' She ran down the hall and flung open the front door, bit back a howl of outrage and disappointment. Nikki Harris, one of her neighbours, stood there, her trademark dangly silver fish earrings and bleached blonde spikes flashing in the sunlight. She wore an acrylic sweater in a virulent salmon pink shade, and pale blue shiny tracksuit pants with a white stripe.

'Hi, Carmel!' Nikki shivered, her round shoulders hunched. 'God, it's freezing out here, isn't it? I heard the news,' she said, looking sheepish. 'About Sean being innocent and everything. Terrible, isn't it, that his own business partner . . .!'

'Can I help you with something?' Nikki had blanked her for the past few weeks, had stood outside her house laughing the night Les Higginbottom had smashed the windows. But Carmel wasn't interested in recrimination or reconciliation. She just wasn't interested, period. The surge of adrenalin drained away, leaving her weak and very depressed.

'Well—' Nikki folded her arms and looked down at her dirty trainers. 'We used to be good mates before ... you know.' She blushed. Carmel waited. She didn't feel like helping Nikki out.

'I'd like us to be mates again.'

'Sure,' Carmel said coldly. 'I'll lend you a cup of sugar any time.' Let's just be mates again, like nothing happened. Forget it, she thought. She stepped back, ready to close the door. 'If you don't mind, I'm a bit busy right now.'

'How are you doing?' Nikki asked in a rush. 'And how's Lisa? I haven't seen her around the square lately. Megan says she's not in school either.'

'Lisa and I are fine.' Carmel glanced beyond Nikki's round, salmon-pink shoulder and stiffened. A police car was turning into Falkner Square, coming to a slow stop outside her house. She recognised the new liaison officer who was supposed to keep her informed of any developments in the search for Sean, DS John Edwards, driven by a uniformed constable. Her heart jumped with terror again. Nikki turned, following her gaze.

'Oh!' she exclaimed nervously, watching the officers get out of the car and slam doors. 'You've got visitors. Some news about Sean, maybe.' She turned back to Carmel. 'Are you okay? Is anyone else home? Would you like me to be with you?'

'No.' Carmel's blue eyes were hostile. 'Actually, I would like you to go away.'

Nikki blushed again and backed down the path. She turned and collided bosom-first with the uniformed constable. John Edwards walked past them and nodded gravely to Carmel. He was tall and dark, dressed in jeans, sweater and bitter-chocolate-brown leather jacket.

'Hi there. How are you?'

All this concern! 'I'm okay.' Carmel folded her arms. 'What's happened?'

He glanced back. 'Could we go inside?'

She led them into the sitting room, her heart thudding. Her hands felt cold, the palms sweaty. She looked at the empty spot on the mantelpiece where Lisa's photo should have been, then turned and faced them.

'I'm afraid we've got some bad news.' John Edwards's voice was gentle.

'Sean?' Carmel gasped, feeling as if she was about to collapse into a black void.

'No, no,' he said hastily, realising her terror. 'There are no new developments concerning your husband. This is about Anthony Maskey. You know he was due to appear in court this morning?'

'How could I forget!' Carmel moved to the sofa and sat down because her legs were shaking. She stared at them. Both officers looked awkward and embarrassed, would not meet her eye. 'He got bail, didn't he?'

'No. The bail application was denied because of the seriousness of the charges – and the fact Maskey continues to refuse to answer any questions put to him by the investigating officers.'

Carmel took a deep breath and wiped her sweating hands on her trousers. 'Then what . . .?'

The officers exchanged nervous glances again. 'Well, this was the magistrates court,' John Edwards began, haltingly. 'The security's not as good as in the—'

'*What's happened?*'

'He kicked open a door in the dock and ran out of court before anyone could stop him.' John Edwards finally looked her in the eye. 'We've come to warn you, Mrs Devine. You and your family. I'm afraid Anthony Maskey has escaped.'

Chapter Twenty-nine

Once the initial euphoria of his escape had subsided, Anthony felt horribly vulnerable without cash, credit cards, a gun and his Jaguar. What had they done with his beloved car? It must be languishing in some police pound – or maybe it had been nicked. He might never see it again. He couldn't go back to his house or the office either. Most important of all, how could he get his hands on some money? Sean Devine still had his sixty grand, the bastard. Or what was left of it. Well, Anthony intended to have something that belonged to Sean. Something Sean would do anything to get back. I'm not finished yet, he thought. No fucking way.

He raced through the city streets away from the court building, slowing to merge with crowds of shuffling, dull-eyed shoppers, most of whom looked as if they started the day with a breakfast of Special K horse tranquilliser. He wore a suit and black coat; his jailers assumed he would want to make a good impression on the grim, self-important lady magistrates, not do a runner. Anthony was quiet, docile, slow and relaxed in his movements. They hadn't cuffed him. That didn't always happen in the magistrates court anyway.

The escape was easier than he had anticipated, laughably easy. He had heard on the news about prisoners escaping from court, slipping away or running out, and found it incredible – until he tried it himself. People just stood there shocked, wide-eyed and paralysed by inaction, too frightened to show initiative and make a move to tackle him. They could not believe what was happening, and did not want to. What must not be cannot be!

No one gave Anthony a second glance as he crossed the busy intersection, strode down Victoria Street and hurried through quiet, secluded Temple Court. In Whitechapel he was about to hail a black cab to drop him near Lime Street station when he remembered the drivers were cynical bastards who kept the doors locked until they arrived at the passenger's destination and got paid. There was nothing for it but to walk. That took fifteen minutes. At Lime Street he managed to slip through the barrier and hop on an ancient, noisy, smelly diesel destined for Manchester Piccadilly.

The landscape between the two cities looked dull and depressing even in the sunlight. Once Anthony had to get off to avoid an approaching ticket collector and wait on an old deserted station with rusted iron colonnades, and weeds growing knee-high out of the platform flags. Britain was a badly maintained museum, he thought. Everything looked knackered.

At Manchester Piccadilly he found a white minicab in which the seatbelts didn't work and whose driver didn't keep his doors locked. He gave an address near Diane's house and jumped out a few streets away. The driver thumped the wheel and screamed abuse, but did not even attempt to give chase as Anthony sprinted across the road past a group of children playing around a burnt-out car. They laughed with delight, jeering at the infuriated cab driver. He ran down another road where most of the houses were boarded up and sprayed with graffiti, and young overweight women wearing leggings and short black leather coats pushed babies and toddlers in prams. He staggered across a patch of grass and stopped to catch his breath. The ground was littered with aerosol cans, crumpled beer cans, turds – dog, and human, for all he knew – empty cigarette packs and used needles. Young trees recently planted were torn up by their roots and scattered, fragile branches snapped off and broken. Short of something to do, Mary would have said. He arrived at Diane's house and burst into the kitchen through the garage door.

She was alone, sitting at the table drinking white wine and smoking a cigarette, a local paper spread out in front of her. She wore black leather jeans, same as last time, and her favourite leopard skin top, her wrinkled, sunbed-tanned neck hung with tacky gold chains. Bleached hair, brutal eye makeup. It wasn't often that someone looked exactly what they were, Anthony thought.

'Jesus Christ!' Diane leapt up and stared at him. 'What the hell ...? I thought you were banged up for the next millennium!'

'I got bail,' Anthony lied, hoping it was too soon for his escape to have made the news. It probably was, but he didn't have much time.

'You *what*?' Diane choked on her cigarette, coughed and started to laugh. 'With all this lot?' She slapped her beringed hand down on the paper, and Anthony glanced at the headline: *Liverpool Businessman Arrested for Murders of Prostitute and Nightclub Singer*. There was a long feature underneath, which he had not the remotest desire to read. 'You're famous, darlin',' Diane said nervously. Barry waddled into the kitchen and stiffened when he saw Anthony.

'All right? You walked then.' Barry nodded at Diane. 'Told you he would, didn't I?'

'I need money,' Anthony said, ignoring him. 'Wheels. And the package I asked you to look after for me. Upstairs, is it?'

'Yeah, Go'n get her, will you, Barry? We had a bit of trouble with her last night.'

Anthony glanced at Barry. 'Put some clothes on her.'

'She was in a right state – started screaming the place

362

down around four this morning. We had to ...' Barry paused, grinning. '*Restrain* her.'

'I'll come up with you.' Anthony turned to follow.

'Why d'you need money?' Diane stubbed out her cigarette. Anthony paused and glared at her.

'They took my cards and all the cash I had on me. That was a mistake, it'll be sorted in a day or two.'

'But didn't they give you them back when you got bail?'

'No! I told you, there's been a mistake. What is this, Question Time? You owe me,' he warned.

'Sure, love. I know that. No problem. I'll give you the cash and Barry'll go and get you a motor when he comes down.'

'Oh, and I'll need to borrow your gun.'

'What? I haven't got a—'

Anthony stepped forward and grabbed her arm, twisting it behind her so that Diane cried out in pain. 'It's a war zone out there – in here most nights, too. Where is it?'

'In the drawer,' she gasped. 'Over there.'

'A Glöck 17,' Anthony remarked as he opened a drawer of cutlery and took out the weapon. 'You girls seem to like them.' Glöcks were only seventeen per cent plastic, despite what most people thought. The barrel and internal works were constructed of solid steel.

He shoved her against the wall and checked the weapon. Diane sat down, nursing her injured arm and shoulder. She picked up her glass of wine and drank. Anthony put the gun in his coat pocket and ran up the three flights of stairs. Simona lay on the bed in the bare attic room wearing a silky pink robe, her ankles and wrists tied with red nylon rope. Her face was bruised and tearstained, and there was a dazed, frightened look at her eyes. Anthony untied her and pulled out the black stocking that was gagging her. Simona sat up, threw her arms around his neck and burst into a storm of tears. She smelled of sweat and noxious perfume, but underneath all that was her own sweet smell, her essence.

Something flickered inside Anthony, gave him a weird feeling. Another human being was glad to see him, even this girl he had kidnapped and abused. Before he realised what he was doing he was hugging her tight, his chin pressed against the top of her head. He stroked her black, silky hair wonderingly.

'Ahh! See that,' Barry laughed. 'Gets you right here, dunnit?' He thumped his broad chest. 'Looks like she's really missed you, mate.'

'Get the clothes,' Anthony said abruptly. Barry sloped out, still laughing.

'He drugged and raped me,' Simona sobbed. 'So did that woman. They hurt me, they—' She started gabbling in Romanian.

'Speak English.' Anthony tried to prise her off. 'Better still, don't speak.' He stroked her smooth bare thigh, saw the tiny mark that Yvonne's brutal injection technique had caused. 'Stop crying,' he whispered. 'I'm going to let you go in a couple of days, take you to your sister. You want to see Maria again, don't you?'

'How is this possible?' Simona gulped. 'I thought you were in prison.'

'They let me out. It was all a mistake.' That made him smile, for some reason.

'Where is Maria?'

'In Dublin,' he lied. Of course Simona would never see the Emerald Isle. Any more than her precious sister had.

She clutched at his coat lapels. 'They thought you would not come back. They planned to kill me. I heard them talking.' She burst out sobbing again.

Anthony pulled her to her feet as Barry came in and tossed some clothes on the bed. 'Come on, get dressed. Hurry up.'

It was too cold outside for the skimpy black top, short denim jacket, tight red jeans and high-heeled gold mules. Simona shivered as Anthony led her to the black Renault Megane Barry parked in the garage for him. He took the keys out of the ignition and locked Simona in the car.

'I'll just be a minute. Don't try anything stupid,' he warned. 'Because it won't work. And then you'll never see you sister.' She nodded, her eyes frightened. He went back into the kitchen. The house was quiet because most of the girls slept until late afternoon. Diane and Barry were murmuring together in the kitchen. They stopped when he appeared. Barry turned away and got a can of Heineken from the fridge.

'Talking about me behind my back?' Anthony took the envelope of notes Diane handed him, and riffled through them. 'Two grand?' He looked at her. 'This won't buy the baby a new frock.' He didn't know why that old expression of his mother's suddenly came to him.

'It's all I've got now, I swear. I'll have more by tonight.' She and Barry carefully avoided looking at each other. 'Come back then, love, okay? Around eleven.'

Anthony realised what the plan was. 'Walk into an ambush? No thanks.' He was a threat to them now, might grass Diane up in exchange for a lighter stretch. Or so they reasoned. Did it occur to them that worked both ways? His visit had taken them by surprise, and Diane had no choice but to give him what he wanted now. It would be a different story if he came back.

'An ambush? Come off it, love!' Diane forced a laugh and raised her plucked, pencilled eyebrows, attempting to look amazed. She pulled a cigarette from the pack and lit it, her fingers trembling. Barry took several swigs of beer and wiped his mouth with the back of his hand. 'You know me better than that, love,' she said gravely, shaking her head. 'We go back a long way.'

'Yeah.' Anthony stroked the seventeen per cent plastic. 'Too bloody long.'

He pointed the gun and squeezed the trigger so quickly that they had no time to look shocked, disbelieving or terrified. The roar in the enclosed space of the kitchen, the gun's recoil, and an incredible surge of adrenalin made his body shake uncontrollably. His ears were ringing. One bullet made a horrific mess of Diane's face – or improved it, depending on your point of view. Another two bullets went into her heart, that atrophied organ. Barry's brain – another atrophied organ, along with his dick – spattered on to the greasy, eggshell-blue wall. He fell heavily and sprawled on the floor, pale yellow frothy Heineken mingling with his blood, his stony little eyes frozen in death.

Anthony fled back to the garage and collapsed into the car. He gunned the engine, put his foot down and reversed, crashing through the doors. Simona cried out in fear, then went quiet as he sped down the road. She was frightened, but no longer in a panic. Anthony had a feeling she wouldn't be sorry to know that her tormentors had choked their last gasp.

'They're gone now, that scum and vermin.' He swung the Megane round a corner in a tight turn, causing a scared young woman with a pram to pull back sharply. 'Just something to be thrown away one particular day.'

He was still shaking, still high on adrenalin. The shootings were as much of a shock to him as to Diane and Barry. Incredible to think he had awoken and breakfasted in a police cell only that morning, ostensibly facing an indeterminate stretch in a remand centre and then prison. This afternoon he was free again, in control of his destiny. He had killed two people – if they could be called *people*. He glanced at Simona. 'Do you believe in an afterlife?'

'I don't think so.' She shrugged her thin shoulders, staring at the road ahead. 'But if there is and it's beautiful, I can't see why we have to go through this one.'

'To learn lessons.' He slowed the car briefly then picked up speed again as they turned on to a dual carriageway, heading for the M62 and Liverpool. 'That's why.'

'I don't want to learn any more lessons!' Simona's lustrous dark eyes filled with tears. 'I'm sick of it!' She turned to him. 'Will you really let me see Maria again?'

'Oh, yes.' Anthony nodded. 'I promised, didn't I?'

'But I don't understand why you would do this.'

'I've told you before. I like you. And I'm not a complete bastard. I've been good to you sometimes, haven't I?' They drove along the busy flyover, past UMIST. 'You were happy to see me.' He glanced at her again. 'Go on. Admit it.'

'All right. Yes, I was ... happy.'

'We'll get you some better clothes. A nice, hot shower. Something good to eat. I bet you're hungry, aren't you?'

'Where are we going?' Simona wiped her eyes. 'Please tell me, Anthony – what do you want from me?'

Traffic lights turned red, and Anthony glided the Megane to a smooth stop behind an articulated lorry with 'fuck off' written in the dirt on the back door. He turned and stroked Simona's face and slender neck, looked at the curve and swell of her breasts outlined by the tight black top. He slid one finger between her lips and held it there, enjoying her vulnerability, the feel of her warm, wet tongue. Simona submitted to his touch, although her body stiffened. Then he pushed his hands inside her top, kneading her breasts and pinching the nipples. She moaned, low in her throat. He forced her head back and kissed her savagely, opening her mouth wide. There was blood on Simona's lips when he drew away.

'I need you to help me find a friend,' Anthony said softly.

'So that's the story.' Carmel closed the book. 'And now it's time for you to go to sleep, young lady. Back to school tomorrow.'

Lisa frowned as she snuggled under the quilt. 'I don't want to go back.'

'Now come on, we've talked about this. School will be fine again, you'll like it just as much as you used to. It's been on the news and in the papers about Daddy. We knew all along that he hadn't done anything bad, but now

367

everybody else knows. They'll be nice to you, don't worry. People feel sorry about what happened, they want to help us. Be friends.'

Carmel hoped that was true. She put the book on the chest of drawers, switched off the toadstool lamp and went to the window to draw the curtains. The moon rose high above the trees. Now that most of their leaves had fallen, she could see further into the park. A few dark figures were grouped around the pagoda, and she caught the red glow of cigarettes. Kids, probably. Or dossers. It was a bone-freezing night; huddled in the pagoda, they would get little or no sleep. But Carmel forgot about the dossers as she stared into the park.

Sean still hadn't called. And Anthony Maskey was out there somewhere. He had no cash or plastic on him, the police said, and wouldn't dare go back to his house or office. Or her house. He wouldn't get far, she was assured. They expected to have him back in custody within twenty-four, forty-eight hours at the most. She and her family should be careful until then, of course, but there was no great cause for concern. Anthony's priorities would be to find a safe hiding place, maybe even get hold of a false passport and try to flee the country. Although how he could do that without money was anybody's guess.

They didn't know him at all, Carmel thought. She believed he wanted revenge, couldn't let go of that need. Anthony might be close by, right now, watching her at the window. She shivered. A police car turned into the square and cruised past, stopped briefly outside the house and moved on. They did that every couple of hours. Big help.

'Mummy?' Lisa's sleepy voice broke into her thoughts.

'What is it, Gorgeous?' Carmel turned and walked back, sat on the bed.

'I was thinking about Daddy.' Lisa's face was in shadow and her pale blonde hair gleamed faintly. 'It's nearly December. I think Daddy will come home for Christmas. Don't you?'

Carmel swallowed. 'I hope he'll be home long before that.' She leaned forward and kissed her daughter. 'Stop thinking and go to sleep,' she whispered. 'D'you like the way we've done your room?'

'Yes. But it still stinks.'

'It doesn't stink!' Carmel smiled down at her in the darkness. 'It only *smells* a bit. The paint smell will be gone in a day or so, and then your smell will take over.'

Lisa giggled. 'I don't smell!'

'Only of sticky sweets, strawberry bubble bath and minty toothpaste. Now, go to sleep. It's nearly nine.'

'Don't go yet.' She felt Lisa's small, soft, warm hand slide into hers and grasp it. 'Wait until I'm asleep, Mummy.' There was a note of fear in the child's voice.

'I will, babe.' Carmel sat there in the darkness until she felt Lisa's grasp slacken, heard her breath slow and deepen. She leaned over and kissed her again. 'I love you,' she whispered. 'So does Daddy.' She stood up and tiptoed out of the room, closing the door softly.

Carmel smelled fresh ground coffee as she went downstairs. In the kitchen Rosa poured her a cup and pushed it across the table. She wore her red dressing gown, and her light brown hair was damp from the shower.

'Thought you might like this before you set out on your nocturnal journey.' She sat down and drummed her fingers on the table. 'Do you think it's a good idea to go out tonight, with Anthony Maskey on the loose? Maybe you should stay home until the police have picked him up.'

'We don't know when they'll pick him up. *If* they'll pick him up. In the meantime, I've got things to do.'

'D'you think he might come here?' Rosa looked frightened. 'The police said he wouldn't, but I'm not so sure.'

'He'd be crazy to turn up here.' Carmel sat down and stirred sugar into her coffee. 'He's not that thick,' she said, trying to reassure herself as much as her sister. 'Lock up after I've gone, okay? Don't answer the door. Phone the police if there's anything suspicious.' She sipped her coffee. 'They're keeping an eye on the place – I just saw them cruise past – and Anthony must guess we've been warned. What's the point anyway? It's too late to shut me up – the damage is done. He's finished.'

'But he might want to stop you – and Sean – giving evidence at his trial.'

Carmel smiled. 'I don't believe that's even crossed his mind. Being recaptured and put on trial won't be part of the plan.' What *was* his plan? she wondered nervously.

Rosa frowned and shook her head. 'How the hell could he just kick open the dock door and run out like that? It's crazy, unbelievable!'

'Prisoners have escaped from court a couple of times this year,' Carmel said grimly. 'One guy was recaptured, but the other is still free.'

'Always the bloody same, isn't it?' Rosa got up and began to pace. 'If either of us nicked a packet of chocolate digestives from Tesco we'd probably be strip-searched, cuffed and put under surveillance twenty-four hours a day. For God's sake, can't those morons get anything right? Screwing up all the time, accusing Sean, putting you in danger. And when they finally get the bastard who's responsible for all this trauma and misery and murder, what do they do then? Let him escape!'

Carmel leaned her elbows on the table. 'Right now I'm beyond anger,' she sighed. 'All I care about is to find Sean. Things will be okay then. Not immediately, of course. But eventually.'

Rosa turned away, tears spilling from her eyes. 'Don't go out tonight.' Her voice was choked. 'Please, Carmel, I'll be worried sick.'

Carmel got up and hugged her. 'You can worry, but not make yourself sick. If I sit around here waiting for news I'll go apeshit. You can understand that, can't you?'

'I suppose.' Rosa wiped her eyes. 'At least get Daniel to go with you. He wants to help more, but you won't let him.'

'Daniel's done enough. I won't put anyone else at risk,

Rosa, and that's final. I couldn't live with myself if anything happened.' Carmel turned, pulled on her black jacket and drank the rest of her coffee. 'Got to go.'

Rosa scrubbed her eyes with a tissue and blew her nose. 'Be careful, for Christ's sake! When will you be home?'

'Don't know. About two in the morning, I expect.'

'You can't keep this up, not now that you've got some work again.'

'I'll keep it up as long as I have to.'

'Well, at least have a lie-in tomorrow morning. I'll get Lisa off to school.'

'Thanks, that'd be great.' Carmel grabbed her torch and keys. 'Okay, I'll see you. Take care.' She walked down the hall, opened the door and went out into dark Falkner Square. She glanced around nervously, looked through the trees into the park. Andy came out, his retriever dawdling behind. He saw her and waved. She waved back, got into the Landcruiser and drove off, checking that no one was following her. It was horrible to have to worry about that again. She remembered her dream, and the strong sense of evil, the fear, flooded back. Good thing she didn't believe in premonitions.

She parked in Rodney Street near the derelict church, got out and walked around the corner to Rice Street. She shivered, yawning widely with cold and tiredness. Rosa was right, she couldn't keep this up. It would be freezing in the flat; she was liable to end up with pneumonia if she spent another night there.

Carmel stopped and glanced back, thinking she heard a footfall, as if someone had jumped behind a wall out of sight. There was nobody. Her terror of Anthony had enlarged and dominated her thoughts so that he now appeared all-seeing and all-knowing, an evil monster shadowing her every move, ready to strike when she was at her most vulnerable. She unlocked the garage doors and relocked them behind her, stood in the dark, cold, empty space breathing the still, musty air.

'Sean?' she called, looking towards the door that led to the stairs. No answer.

Was it possible he'd lost the keys, and that was why he didn't come back? That still didn't explain why he hadn't phoned. I can't do this any more, Carmel thought suddenly. I'll drive myself crazy if I keep coming here, waiting and hoping. Especially with Anthony on the loose. He could be anywhere. Go home, try to get some sleep.

But she didn't go home. She went upstairs and wrapped herself in the sleeping bag, sitting in the dark with her back to the wall. She raised her arm and looked at her watch by the faint light from the street lamp. Ten minutes to midnight. Would somebody hide Anthony, give him money? Help him get away somewhere? Carmel blinked and closed her eyes, surrendering to the tiredness that weighted her body. No, she thought, drifting off. Anthony never had any friends. Except Sean. Only Sean. She gasped and jerked upright as a motorbike roared through the tiny street. After that there was only silence. And cold. She nodded off.

There was a distant scratching sound, like mice, that went on and on. It didn't matter. Carmel wasn't scared of mice. How stupid was it to go crazy at the sight of such tiny, harmless creatures, even if their bare, flesh-coloured tails were a bit yukky? And of course you didn't want them sharing your home. The scratching noise got louder and came nearer, as if the mice were scuffling about on the stairs. Feet came slowly up the stairs, dragging slightly with each step. The mice scattered as someone shooed them away, cursing under his breath.

Someone tall and dark, whose face Carmel could not see. His breath came in gasps, as if he'd been running. She recalled the dream, Anthony's dark figure standing in her parents' garden. He knew where she was, he had followed her here! He would kill her now. Slowly, imaginatively, with a knife. He had planned how he would kill her during his empty days and nights in the police cell. Lovingly. Gloatingly.

372

Carmel turned her head and whimpered with fear. The whimpering awoke her. She was trembling and sweating, despite the coldness in the room. Aching all over.

'Oh, God!' she groaned. Couldn't she sleep without Anthony invading her dreams? She opened her eyes, blinked and stared into the darkness. A split second later she froze.

The figure was there, really there, outlined in the doorway. She wasn't dreaming! He swayed slightly, clenched his fists, took a step forward. It *was* Anthony! How the hell had he got in when she had locked the doors? And what did that matter anyway? He would murder her now. She would never see Sean or Lisa again. This was the end.

Carmel screamed.

Chapter Thirty

'Carmel, stop! Please, it's okay. You're safe. It's *me* . . . Sean!'

She stopped screaming and struggling, and he relaxed his grip on her shoulders. She stared at him, hunched over her in the darkness. Sean was trembling, with cold or emotion, and the sleeves and lapels of his coat were damp, beads of moisture shining in the faint light. Carmel put up one hand and touched his face, tracing the outline of nose and chin, the roughness of several days' growth of beard. His dark, curly hair had grown; it was matted and dirty. The vein in his temple pulsed against her fingers.

'*Sean*?' Her voice was a cracked whisper of incredulity, catching in her throat. She tried to speak, ask him all those terribly important questions, but she did not even know where to start. And suddenly they were not important any more. Carmel had tried to imagine her reaction if and when she saw her husband again: tears, outpourings of joy, love, relief. She had not imagined being shocked, stunned. Empty. 'It's really you? I can't believe . . .!'

'Yes. *Yes*.' Sean gripped her shoulders again. He had tears in his eyes. 'How did you guess I'd come here? Are you all right? How's Lisa?' His voice trembled with the emotion Carmel could not feel. Until he asked that question. She was totally unprepared for the fury that gripped her then.

'How do you fucking think Lisa is?' she shouted, making him flinch. Before she realised what she was doing she was hitting out at Sean, slapping him, pounding his arms and shoulders with her fists. Pushing him away. She heard him grunt, gasp with shock and pain.

'Where the hell have you *been*?' she cried. 'You selfish bastard!' Carmel scrambled to her feet. 'Why didn't you call me, like you promised? Do you have any idea what you've put me through?' She was shaking and sobbing, her eyes streaming. 'I was terrified that Anthony might have got to you – murdered you! Why didn't you *call*?'

'Listen!' Sean interrupted, his voice harsh. 'It hasn't exactly been a picnic for me either. I got lost in those fucking tunnels and then injured. I've been trapped in there for days. That's why I couldn't call. Don't have a go at me, Carmel. Save your anger for the bastard who caused all this shit.'

There was a silence, broken only by Carmel's sobbing gasps. Sean stepped forward and the streetlight slanted across his face and shoulders. He looked pale, gaunt and washed out, his dark eyes full of shock and hurt.

'I'm sorry,' Carmel's anger died and she felt guilt-stricken. 'I'm sorry, I'm sorry!'

'No.' They were in each other's arms, clinging so tightly that they could barely breathe. '*I'm* sorry.' Sean stroked Carmel's hair and kissed her, his tears mingling with hers. 'Of course you've gone through hell—'

'You don't know about Anthony!' Carmel ran into the kitchen and came back with the note. 'Look, I left you this. He was arrested – charged with the murders of those two women – and another one whose body he'd hidden in that labyrinth. Maybe the one you overheard him confess to murdering.'

'They found her?' Sean burst out. 'How?' He snatched the note and moved to the window, held it up so that he could read it by the light of the street lamp.

'That's a long story, I'll tell you later.' Carmel hugged

him. 'But all the charges against you have been dropped. Anthony was also charged with trafficking in women. He was in custody—'

'*Was* in custody?' Sean let the note flutter to the floor.

'He appeared in court this morning.' Carmel stared up at him in dismay. 'He escaped. Kicked his way out of the dock and ran off.'

'But how the fuck . . .?'

'God knows.' She wiped her tears. 'The police are searching for him now. They say he can't have got far and he'll be recaptured soon. Of course they would say that. But don't worry,' she said urgently, hugging Sean tight, terrified that he might suddenly disappear again. 'Anthony can't hurt us any more. There's no point in him trying to silence us now that the police know all about him. And he's got no money, nothing. Oh God, Sean!' she wept, brushing away more tears. 'I can't believe you're here, that we're really together again. I'd practically given up hope. How did you live without money? Where did you hide – apart from here? What happened the night of my birthday?'

Joy was blossoming inside her after the weeks of terror and despair. So was anxiety. She had found Sean and he was safe, although they would not be really safe until Anthony was recaptured. She and Sean were reunited, and that was all she cared about. Unfortunately she couldn't write the ending to this story. Not yet.

'I'll tell you everything. Just give me a minute.' Sean held her face in his hands and kissed her hungrily. 'I missed you so much!' His voice was choked. 'I love you, Carmel. I don't think I can stand to let you or Lisa out of my sight again, not even for five minutes at a stretch.'

'*You* can't stand to let *us* . . .!' Carmel broke down again and sobbed on his shoulder. 'I'm sorry I shouted at you,' she wept. 'I was terrified, I thought it was Anthony come back to kill me. I just couldn't believe it when I saw it was really you.'

'I know. Forget it. It's okay.' Sean turned and drew her

gently towards the door, his arms tight around her. He paused at the top of the stairs, and they kissed again.

'Let's go home,' he whispered.

'No Anthony! Please, I cannot stay in this terrible place!' Simona wept with fear as Anthony dragged her along the narrow passage, torchlight flashing over the tunnel's brick walls and sandstone roof. 'Why do you bring me here?'

'Its safer. For tonight, at least.'

'Safer? Why? I don't understand.' She pulled back, digging in her heels. He stopped and turned, his features twisted with anger.

'You don't need to understand! Haven't you got your head round that yet?' He hit her across the face and Simona reeled from the blow, collapsed sobbing and whimpering against the dank, moss-covered tunnel wall. 'Does that help your claustrophobia?' he shouted. 'Now, come on!'

He pulled her to her feet and dragged her further into the bowels of the labyrinth. She could barely walk in the stupid, high-heeled mules, let alone run. Anthony had her new clothes in a plastic carrier bag, together with a length of rope. She didn't know why he had made her buy the dark-brown, close-fitting pinstriped trouser suit and the shiny, dark-brown ankle boots. He had pointed to the suit in the window of a shop called Kookai and shoved her a handful of notes, waited outside watching her through the window as she made the purchase. After that she had gone into the shoe shop next door and bought the boots. It felt very strange to buy something instead of being bought. Both times Simona had longed to ask the shop staff for help, but her nerve and her English had died on her.

Even if the staff had called the police and they had arrived before Anthony could drag her away, what then? What proof did she have to back up her story? She didn't know what Anthony had done with the body of the woman he had murdered. The police might refuse to believe her, throw her in jail until she could be deported. She would never find Maria then. Her only chance now was to stay with Anthony, do what he wanted, hope he would honour his promise to reunite her with her sister. Hope he would not kill her. It wasn't good enough, of course, no way. But she had no choice.

Anthony still had not told her what he wanted her to do, which made Simona even more frightened because she knew it was something terrible. That was why he wanted her to wear those clothes tomorrow. So that she would look respectable. Not like a woman whose body had been bought and fucked more times than she could remember – or wanted to remember. Simona felt dirty and damaged and stained, polluted to the depths of her body and soul. Nothing would ever wash away the stain. If she survived.

What was this horrible place, all these underground tunnels, caves and passages? Sometimes the torch beam picked out the glow of red eyes, belonging to large grey rats which immediately scurried away into the darkness. Anthony stopped suddenly, catching his breath as the torch-light fell on a jagged, gaping hole in the debris-strewn floor.

'What the fuck . . .?' He shone the torch into the hole and Simona peered down, clutching at his arm. There was an oily black pool a few metres below, poison-green scum and a dead rat, stiff and swollen, floating on the water. Damp walls with crumbling brickwork. We have to go back, she thought. It's too dangerous. God only knew what lay ahead. Anthony turned to her, pulling his arm free.

'Jump.' He threw the carrier bag across the hole. 'Go on, it's not far. I'll follow.'

'I can't!' she gasped, terror-stuck. She screamed as he grabbed her by the hair and forced her to her knees, holding her head out over the gap. Her long hair tumbled down, hanging in the dark space. A chunk of stone crumbled and fell, splashed into the turgid water. The rat corpse bobbed.

378

'You either jump now, or you drown like that rat. I won't waste a bullet on you, you bitch! Do you want to see your sister again?' Anthony forced her head further down. '*Do you?*'

'Yes!' she sobbed. 'Yes, yes! Let me go, please!'

'Get up. Take those shoes off.'

Simona stumbled to her feet and slipped off the gold mules. Anthony picked them up and threw them across the gap, hitting the carrier bag. 'Right.' He turned back to her, breathing hard. 'Do it. *Now.*'

Don't look down, she told herself, her heart pounding. She imagined herself flailing in the cold, filthy water, swallowing mouthfuls as she gasped for air, the dead rat touching her face. She took a running jump and leapt, caught a glimpse of torchlight flashing on oily water as she landed on the other side, her bare feet slapping painfully on to the stone floor. She crouched, hugging herself, stared at Anthony as he prepared to follow. Suppose he missed, fell into that water? She could not rescue him. She would be trapped in here, wandering around until she dropped dead from exhaustion. She closed her eyes as he jumped. A second later Anthony had picked up the carrier bag and was dragging her towards an elaborate brick arch that led to a smaller, narrower tunnel.

'My shoes . . .'

'Fuck your shoes.' They had to stoop as they entered the tunnel. At the end was another arch, blocked with rubble. Anthony turned left into another tunnel, stopped and flashed the torch over the walls and ceiling. A long rusted chain hung from an iron grating in the ceiling. Anthony dropped the carrier bag and pulled hard on the chain, testing its strength.

'Yep,' he muttered. 'That'll hold.' He pushed Simona to the ground and tied her wrists with rope, tied the other end of the rope securely to the chain. She crouched, shivering with cold and terror, her bound wrists raised in front of her. Anthony picked up the torch and paused, admiring his handiwork. 'Not too tight, is it?'

'No,' she said dully, knowing he didn't ask out of concern for her well being.

'Good. I'll be back in a few hours. Get some rest.'

He was going to leave her here? Alone, in the dark? A wave of panic welled up inside Simona, and for a second her mind went blank. No, she thought. Keep control. Anthony shone the torch in her face, and she knew he was enjoying her terror, feeding off it, waiting for that panicked reaction. He wanted her to beg and plead with him some more. She forced herself not to. When the back of his hand came down hard across the side of her head she knew she had won that little psychological tussle. It suddenly felt very important to her.

'I should strip you.' His voice was angry. 'Let the rats nibble your tits.' Simona turned her head away, bit her lip and kept silent. Anthony grabbed her hair. 'Look at me!' She obeyed, gasping with pain.

'When I come back,' he said slowly. 'I'll give you your instructions for tomorrow. I want you to listen very carefully, and do exactly what I tell you. Because if you don't, if you fuck up in *any* way – I'll kill you. And I'll have Maria killed. So her life as well as yours depends on your co-operation tomorrow.' He let go of her hair and stood up. 'Think about that while I'm gone. Think about it a lot.'

Simona controlled herself as Anthony walked out of the tunnel and turned right, shining the torch ahead of him. The glow of precious, beautiful light remained for a few seconds. She heard him jump back over the gap in the tunnel floor. The last of the light died and she could no longer hear Anthony's footsteps. When she knew she was alone in the cold darkness, a live, breathing being trapped in a tomb, Simona bowed her head and started to cry.

Very softly, as if she was afraid someone might hear.

Carmel Devine imagined she had suffered these past few

weeks, Anthony thought as he went back down the tunnel. That was a woolly and unrealistic perception which was about to be blasted out of the water. She also imagined she had him stitched up, that he would be recaptured any minute and thrown back in the slammer before you could say 'cognitive dissonance'. Wrong again.

'One thing at a time,' he muttered. 'Hold your horses.' Another expression of his mother's. He paused as he reached the space where a passage led downwards and a flight of steps with bull-nosed edgings led to one of the upper levels. Anthony had the map and its markings fixed in his head, but soon he would be into unexplored territory. He had to make sure he found the correct tunnel this time, the one parallel to the tiny tunnel where the gold lay hidden.

Searching for the gold had been a great thrill – but his future depended on it now that he could no longer gain access to his money. Anthony also could not count on Sean Devine having much of his sixty grand left. Henry and Alice's gold was his only hope. It was a godsend, finding that new tunnel entrance – or exit – after his night of terror. Simona didn't know she had only one or two days at most to live, or that she would never be reunited with her sister. Not in this world anyway. But he would spare her that knowledge, of course. Until her final moment.

Anthony walked slowly down the passage that led to the lower levels. In this part of the labyrinth he was much closer to the gold. According to the map. He could bypass the tunnels he had been searching from Mason Street, the lord mayor's stable yard and his mother's house. But what might have changed since the map was drawn? More tons of rubble, subsidence, flooding? Victorian tomb robbers? Anthony stopped, puzzled, flashing the torch over the sandstone walls and roof. Since when had he thought of this place as a tomb?

Alice's letter to her sister mentioned several short journeys to move the contents of the chest of gold down into the tunnel. How much gold was there, and would he be able to move it all at once by himself? Maybe not. Then again, Alice had been a small, weak Victorian female, more than likely suffering from iron-deficiency anaemia, or some other malnutrition and childbearing-induced medical condition. Anthony stopped again, breathing hard. He was getting close now. Very close.

Zen-like concentration was needed to make sure he didn't get lost again. Sweat dripped off the end of his nose. The walls and floor trembled as a train to or from Lime Street rumbled through the distant cutting on Smithdown Lane. That was good, confirmed he was in the right place. Excitement rose in him, making him forget about Diane and Barry, the police, Carmel and Sean. He was alone with his quest, the hero of an adventure story.

He could hear water dripping, and the sandstone walls were slimy. The roof gradually sloped, so low that he had to stoop, and the walls closed in on him. Anthony was used to that, but it still gave him an unpleasant fluttering in his stomach. The tunnel forked left. He was doubling back now, towards Mason Street and Shimmin Street. He did not dare follow the tunnel that led to his mother's house of course, or contact Mary, even though he believed she would still be willing to help him. He wondered if the police had explored the tunnel running from his mother's house.

He came to another even tinier passage which forked sharply right, but he ignored it. He was on the correct path now, had to keep going left. What a warren! Joseph Williamson certainly was a Mad Mole. The labyrinth had started as one of the first work experience schemes, and become an awesome creation that had got mind-blowingly out of hand.

Anthony was glad to note the absence of rubble here. Apart from the fact that it saved him a lot of digging with his bare hands, it meant that most people hadn't penetrated far enough to dump their junk. Or nose about. He walked slowly on, keeping the map fixed in his brain. There should be another tunnel soon. Or possibly two, one of them a keyhole shape. He had to take the keyhole tunnel.

Anthony shivered and coughed. It was even colder down here and the air was musty, as if it was the same air that Williamson and his workers had breathed. He imagined he could smell their sweat, the smoke from their candles. He paused to touch the wall. It was damp. A chunk of sandstone crumbled and broke off in his hand. He dropped it and carried on. The rest of the tunnel sloped further downwards and the torchlight showed that it was blocked and partially flooded. Anthony stopped, gave an exclamation of dismay. Not now, not when he he'd come this far! He breathed again; the keyhole tunnel was just to his left. He had almost missed the small black gap in the wall. Dirty water pooled around his feet.

Anthony stooped and entered the tunnel. He was suddenly frightened, trembling with nervous anticipation. What if the gold wasn't here? He could hear his own breathing, feel his heart throwing itself against his ribcage. On and on, further down. The water was up to his ankles now. He gave a hoarse cry as the torchlight picked out a solid object on the tunnel floor, shoved against the wall, what looked like a bundle of sodden rags lying next to it. He caught the white glint of a thigh bone, a leering skull with most of the teeth missing.

'Jesus Christ!' His right foot knocked something. He shone the torch downwards, then bent and picked up a rusted dagger. Was he looking at a two-hundred-odd-year-old murder victim and murder weapon? What the hell had gone on here? Had someone followed Alice Miles as she moved the gold, and got more than they'd bargained for? He would never know, but he didn't care any more. He shone the torch on to a chest with a crumbling, rusted iron padlock, and gave a yell.

'Yes! *Yes*!' Charged with energy and excitement, he kicked furiously at the lock until it gave away. The chest lid was stuck down – probably due to damp – but several more vicious kicks got that loosened too. Anthony was laughing wildly as he pulled the lid up and looked at the contents, bags of some sort of coarse dark brown cloth, now mildewed and falling apart. He wedged the torch between his knees and tore at the material, seized handfuls of dully glinting, roughly shaped gold nuggets. Henry's fortune from the Australian goldfields. At last!

Alice Miles and the unknown corpse had been the last people in this tunnel. Alice had gone from here back to her house in Mason Street. The next stop had been prison and the law court in St George's Hall, finally the death cell in Walton Jail. Anthony imagined Alice as small, fragile and deceptively submissive looking, with a slender white neck snapped easily by the cruel rope. The chest was stuffed with gold coins, nuggets and bars. He could not stop laughing. This was a dream, the fulfilment of an amazing adventure. And after all he had been through lately! It filled him with joy and confidence, swept away all vestiges of doubt and depression. He could do anything now. He stuffed his suit and coat pockets, cramming them with nuggets and minted coins, a few bars. The gold weighed a ton!

Anthony closed the chest lid and sat down to try and calm himself, shining the torch on the opposite wall. He felt like he'd been drinking. Did he really want Carmel and Sean now? Whatever was left of his stolen sixty grand? Wouldn't that just be asking for more trouble? Anthony loved risk and danger, but he wasn't thick. On the other hand, if he'd wanted a quiet life he wouldn't be in this glorious situation now. He smiled as he recalled the gorgeous surge of adrenalin he'd experienced when he shot the police officer, that bastard Davie. Diane and Barry. Gemma. He wanted, needed to feel that again.

Anthony hated Carmel more than Sean now. She had turned Sean against him in the first place, changed Sean from a loyal friend – his only friend – into the cold, critical, suspicious bastard who had stolen his money and betrayed him. It was all her fault. Scratch a rage, find a woman. He could forget that money, now that he had the gold. But Anthony realised he didn't want to forget it. Didn't want to let Sean or Carmel's betrayal go.

Didn't want to let anything go.

Chapter Thirty-one

'Anthony had become a problem. A *big* problem. He was aggressive, secretive—'

'Exactly what he accused *you* of!' Carmel broke in angrily.

'Yeah. We argued a lot because I hated his ideas for expanding the business.' Sean took a gulp of coffee. 'The last argument was on the afternoon of your birthday – he wanted to sell clapped out X-ray machines and CAT scanners to Russia and Romania. I thought that was bad enough. But until that night, I didn't have a clue what he was really up to.'

'So when you called in to see me – you'd decided to break up the partnership?'

He nodded. 'I'd had all I was going to take from Anthony Maskey. I planned to phone the solicitors the following Monday morning, get things started. Then tell you. I hadn't told you what was going on sooner because I didn't want to worry you. You'd only recently gone into practice on your own, Lisa had just started school – you had more than enough on your plate. Of course, I'd totally underestimated how serious the situation with Anthony was.' Sean's arm tightened around her shoulder, and his face was grim in the lamplight. 'When I heard him talking to that woman, it all made sense – the money, the trips to eastern Europe. The weird behaviour.' He took another gulp of coffee, leaned down and put the mug on the floor. 'I'd only nipped back to the warehouse to collect your birthday present. Thought I'd be in and out, home within ten minutes. He caught me on the stairs. His little pal, that bloody cat, gave me away.'

They sat curled up on the sofa in the television room at the back of the house, Lisa's books and toys scattered around. Carmel's glass of white wine stood on a pile of books topped by *The Princess and the Pea*. The blinds were drawn and only one lamp was switched on. Sean wore his dark blue bathrobe and his hair was damp; he hadn't bothered to shave off his beard. The house was silent, Rosa and Lisa asleep. Carmel and Sean needed to be alone for a while, relish the joy, relief and comfort of being reunited at last.

'I wanted to go straight to the police with that sixty grand.' Sean pulled her closer and she slipped her arms around his neck. 'I'd been shot, for Christ's sake! I was obviously the injured party. But it was still my word against Anthony's about what had happened between us. And I didn't know where he'd dumped that girl's body, so I couldn't prove he'd murdered her. I couldn't even prove the cash wasn't mine. Okay, why would I hand it over if it was? But he would have lied, twisted everything. He was desperate. Anthony wanted to kill me, and I knew he'd kill you and Lisa too, if I went home. Or if he thought you suspected him.' Sean stroked her hair and twisted a curl around one finger. 'I could only protect you by staying away.'

Carmel nodded. 'I guessed that – eventually. But what did you do then?'

'I was bleeding, panicked, scared to death. I needed medical help, but I knew hospitals report gunshot wounds to the police. I decided the best thing was to get out of Liverpool, so I headed for Manchester. My arm, shoulder and hip were hurting like hell – don't know how I managed to drive. I staggered into an A&E department in a hospital there, gave a false name and address and collapsed on to a trolley. I thought they'd treat me before they called the police, and that's what happened. The doctors were going on about how lucky it was that the bullets had missed major organs, blood vessels etc. But I was weak, I'd lost some blood and I was in shock. Then the pain kicked in. I wanted to leave, but at that point I wasn't in a fit state to go anywhere. I kept thinking about you and Lisa, how freaked you'd be. But I didn't dare contact you then. Two coppers turned up to interview me, and it was obvious they were suspicious. The doctor told them to go, said I needed rest and had to be taken up to a ward for the night. They said they'd be back in the morning, and in the meantime they'd send a constable to wait by my bed. I had to get out then. I was in a cubicle by myself. I got my clothes, nicked some dressings and slipped out before the copper arrived.' Sean shook his head. 'I don't know how I made it, Carmel. I could barely walk.'

'Oh, Sean!' She had tears in her eyes.

'I checked into a hotel for the night. Gave another false name, paid for the room with Anthony's cash. I had no money of my own, he'd taken my keys and wallet when he had me at gunpoint in the office.'

So that was how Anthony and his men had got in that night, Carmel thought. She hadn't told Sean about the assault on her and Rosa. It could wait for now.

'Next morning I left the Audi in the hotel car park. I knew Anthony would have people looking for it – for me. I used more of the money to buy a secondhand Cortina from a Manchester dealer.'

'A Cortina?' Carmel smiled slightly and raised her eyebrows. 'Not exactly *you*.'

'No, well, I didn't fancy being noticed. All the time I was wondering what to do, trying to think how I could prove Anthony was a murderer and get him banged up. How to keep you and Lisa out of danger. What he'd said to that woman kept going through my mind, about the girl's body being hidden in a place only he and a man from another century knew about. Then I remembered Anthony was obsessed with that Joseph Williamson labyrinth, how he used to say the place had fascinated him since he was a kid. I decided to find out more about it and start looking. But I was too ill to do anything. And I needed somewhere to hole up. I thought of Rice Street. I'd checked the glove box before I abandoned the Audi, put the keys in my pocket without even thinking. It seemed perfect, the last place anyone would expect me to hide. Including Anthony.'

'He never knew about Rice Street at all?'

'I think I mentioned it to him once or twice – years ago – but he never went there. He didn't know the address, and I was pretty sure he wouldn't remember it existed.'

'I wondered about that.' Carmel shivered. 'I was terrified he *would*!'

'I thought you'd have forgotten about it because you hadn't been there for years. So I got some stuff, went there – and collapsed again before I could do anything else. My temperature went up, I got a fever and a terrible headache. I was afraid the wounds were infected, but they seemed okay. I still don't know what it was. Shock, trauma, maybe. I just lay there for a couple of days, drinking water and changing dressings. On my next trip to the outside world I saw a newspaper and realised I'd been set up for two murders.'

'I knew you'd been set up.' Carmel wiped her eyes. 'I just couldn't think how or why.'

'The bastard didn't hang around, did he? Stitched me up good and proper.' Sean lifted her chin and looked into her eyes. 'I was going through all the torments of hell, and I knew it had to be even worse for you. But I couldn't call you at home in case the police had tapped the phone. Or Anthony had managed to bug it. We dealt in security products – he could have come round to see you and planted it then. There was no point phoning you at the office, because I knew you wouldn't go back there for a while. Christ!' he muttered, brushing away a tear. 'I didn't know what to—'

'It's all right,' she said softly. 'Sean, don't blame yourself for anything, *please*. None of this is our fault.'

'Of course you still thought Anthony was your friend . . . our friend. I'm not surprised he told you all that bullshit, twisted everything. That was typical.'

'I had moments of doubt,' Carmel admitted reluctantly. 'About why you'd disappeared, I mean. There were times when I wondered about our marriage, if things had really been that good between us. Because there were no clues. Anthony fooled me completely.' She shuddered. 'For a while.'

Sean kissed her lightly on the lips. 'Must have been even worse for you because the last time we saw each other you guessed something was wrong. I should have told you what was bothering me then. I really fucked up!'

'No, you didn't! You couldn't possibly have known what would happen. Anthony was angry with you for refusing to go along with his horrible ideas for expanding the business – he looked on you as a pain and a threat. Who's to say he wouldn't have tried to kill you anyway at some point? Picked a time when you'd have had no warning, no chance to escape.'

'Yeah, you're right. He would have done something sooner or later.' Sean hugged her again. 'Once I'd recovered a bit and had a chance to think, I decided my only chance was to search those tunnels, find that girl's body and expose Anthony for what he was. I went to a library and got some info about Joseph Williamson and the labyrinth. I realised what I was looking at – it'd be easier to locate a phone number in a warehouse stuffed with directories. Besides, Anthony knew the labyrinth a lot better than I could ever hope to do. He might have discovered parts of it that no one else knew about. But I had to try.'

'We both came to the same conclusion,' Carmel sighed. 'Eventually.'

Sean reached down and picked up his empty mug, one of

a pair that Lisa had made in pottery class. It was thick and uneven with wild blue, red and green swirls, and *Daddy* etched into the clay. A few little fingerprints were visible. Sean smiled. 'It's good to see this again,' he said softly. He started to get up. 'Is there any coffee left?'

'I'll get it. You stay here and relax.' Carmel went into the kitchen, poured more coffee and returned. 'Have you had enough to eat?' she asked, handing him the mug. 'I could do you another couple of ham and cheese sandwiches.'

'No, thanks. I'm fine.' She settled on the sofa and Sean sipped the hot coffee. 'That tastes great,' he breathed. 'Fantastic.'

'You look so pale and thin!' Carmel stroked his face. 'You've got more grey hairs. And I noticed you were limping a bit. Did you hurt your leg?'

'Yeah. When I got trapped in the labyrinth.'

'Oh, my God! How did . . .?'

Sean kissed her again. 'I'm coming to that. I didn't stay in Rice Street every night,' he went on. 'I had to keep moving, stay alert, not develop a routine. Sometimes I'd get out of the city, drive along motorways, stay in travel lodges. That day I called you, I was in Cheshire. I'd been trying your office for days, hoping you'd be there. I wanted to tell you I was alive. But I couldn't say where I was or what I was doing.'

Carmel nodded. 'You don't know what a relief it was to hear your voice again! Of course I was still worried sick about you.'

'I tried to take care of myself, not to eat junk all the time. But it's not easy in those circumstances. And I was still weak, still in pain. I caught a terrible cold. I was sneezing and coughing my guts up. I was afraid it'd turn into a chest infection, even pneumonia. I couldn't exactly stroll into the nearest GP's surgery and ask for a course of antibiotics. All the time I was terrified of being arrested and banged up for two murders I hadn't committed. I'd grown a beard, but I was still shit scared of being recognised. Thought I'd end up on *Crimewatch* or something.'

'How did you hurt your leg – get trapped in the labyrinth?'

Sean hesitated, as if wondering how much to tell her. 'I went back there one night to have another look for that girl's body. I got lost. Then I had a fall.'

'My God!'

'That place is a fucking death trap, Carmel!' Sean shook his head, his expression grim and frightened. 'I went in and I thought I knew where I was, but I lost my bearings. I was wandering around for hours until I nearly dropped with exhaustion. I lay down and fell asleep. When I woke up I started walking again, searching for a way out, trying to remember which way I'd come. But it was hopeless. It went on for ages, it was a bloody nightmare. I started to think I'd end up trapped for ever. Or bump into Anthony and get shot again. I had no idea if it was day or night on the outside. I had a bottle of water, that kept me going. It was hard not to panic, lose hope.' Sean stared at her, hugging her close. 'You took a crazy risk going in there,' he whispered, tears in his eyes. 'You might have ended up . . .' He couldn't finish.

'I had to do it.' Carmel kissed him. 'What happened then?'

'I was walking along this passage when part of the floor just gave way beneath me. I thought, this is it! I've really had it now. I dropped the torch and fell into a pit of freezing water. Luckily it wasn't too deep. I managed to crawl out. But then I fainted. I was soaked and freezing. When I came round I had a blinding headache and my right ankle was blowing up, hurting like hell. I thought I'd broken it in the fall, but it was only badly twisted. I couldn't move though. I was too weak from everything, in a lot of pain. I just lay there, passing in and out of consciousness . . . don't know for how long. I think I got delirious at one point. I had a dream about you, it was incredibly vivid. I really

392

thought you were there with me. I could smell your perfume.'

'Oh, Sean!' Carmel was crying again, thinking of the times she had imagined him lying somewhere hurt, in need of help that didn't come.

'Ssh!' he whispered, kissing her. 'I'm here now. I'm all right. It was that dream did it – I knew I had to get out of that place, get back to you and Lisa. I couldn't let Anthony win. But I was trapped in the pitch dark, didn't dare go back or forward in case there were other hazards. I decided the best way was to get back on the upper level, through the hole I'd fallen down. There was rubble and bricks lying everywhere. It took me ages, but I managed to build a pile against the wall, big enough to climb on and pull myself up.' He shivered, shook his head again. 'God knows how I managed it! To cut a long story short, I took a different route and came across this great long steel ladder. I climbed it – that took me about twenty minutes – and came up into this big cave with tunnels branching off in all directions. I tried a few and eventually found a way out. I was on some derelict ground with demolished houses, not far from the Anglican cathedral. Nowhere near where I'd gone in. I walked back to Rice Street and ...' Sean's voice choked and his eyes filled with tears again. 'You were waiting for me!'

They clung together, their bodies trembling. 'You don't know how great it feels to hold you again,' Sean said shakily, his face buried in her hair. 'I've missed you so much. Sometimes I thought I'd never see you again. I thought of Lisa growing up without me around. I wondered what would happen to her, if she'd think I'd deserted her and be traumatised about it for the rest of her life. I told myself I was a stupid bastard who'd fucked up everything. I felt like I'd let her down. Let you down.' His voice trembled. 'I still feel that.'

'Why?' Carmel kissed him again as they drew apart slightly. 'Because you didn't realise Anthony was a murderer who trafficked in women? He's intelligent, cunning, manipulative. And you didn't fuck up! You were going to break with him. How the hell were you supposed to know what he really was until you accidentally got in his way? Actually, I don't feel too clever myself,' she said glumly. 'A psychologist, specialising in rational emotive behaviour therapy – I wasn't very rational, was I? Until it was almost too late. Listen to us now.' Her blue eyes sparkled with anger. 'Sitting here blaming ourselves for not being psychic!'

'Yeah.' Sean sighed. 'You're right.' He took her hand and kissed it.

'Let's not talk any more now,' Carmel whispered. 'It's very late, and you're exhausted. Come to bed.'

'My own bed!' He turned her hand over, softly kissing the palm. 'With you in it. I've missed *that* like you can't imagine!'

'Shall we take another look at Lisa first?'

'Yeah.' Sean smiled. 'I won't disturb her. She'll have a big day tomorrow. More than enough excitement.'

Lisa was deeply asleep, her breathing soft and slow. They stood in the moonlit bedroom, their arms wrapped around one another. Carmel felt Sean's chest heave with emotion as he gazed down at his sleeping daughter. He leaned over and kissed Lisa very gently on the forehead, lightly stroked one little hand that clutched a corner of the pillow. Then they tiptoed out.

'Rosa will get the shock of her life when she sees you,' Carmel whispered, smiling up at him. 'She's been great. So have Mum and Daniel. I don't know how I would have managed without them.' Her smile faded. 'I suppose we should call the police, let them know you're home. They'll want to question you about Anthony.'

'Sod the police.' Sean opened their bedroom door and drew her inside. 'They can wait until the morning. So can everybody else.' He shut the door quietly and leaned her against it, kissing her hard. She responded, loving the feel of his body against hers. Sean unzipped her jeans, unhooked her bra and pushed her sweater up. Carmel groaned, a rush of desire mingling with all the other emotions, sweeping over her as she felt his hands on her bare skin. She thought of all the long, lonely nights when she had lain awake wondering where Sean was, the agonising pain and grief of missing him, not knowing if he was alive or dead. Missing his presence, his touch. They collapsed on to the bed and lay still for a minute, gazing into each other's eyes.

'I love you,' she whispered.

'And I love you.' Sean kissed her. 'Tonight's just for us!'

'Move it, you dozy bitch! Come on, it's eight in the bloody morning.'

There was no morning down here, only endless night. Simona blinked and groaned, shivering with cold. She turned her head to avoid the torchlight Anthony shone in her eyes. Torture to wake up again and find the nightmare still going on. She felt the hardness of the stone floor, her tired, aching body, especially her arms, the soreness of her wrists after being chafed by the rope for hours. Her mouth was dry and she hated to breathe the dank musty air. The walls were thickly covered with green mould; she imagined breathing its spores deep into her lungs, where they might cause an infection. But that was the least of her worries. Anthony untied the rope and dragged her to her feet.

'Strip,' he ordered. 'Hurry up.'

Simona gasped and shrank from him. 'Why . . .?'

'So you can change into these,' he said impatiently, pulling the boots and trouser suit out of the carrier bag. 'I'm not going to hurt you. Get a move on.'

She stripped off her clothes and stood naked and trembling. Anthony handed her the stretchy bitter-chocolate-brown top, the trousers, boots and jacket. He hadn't thought to let her buy tights, bra and underpants, but that didn't matter. When she was dressed he flashed the torch over her again.

'Looks good.' He nodded. 'Fits perfectly. Your hair needs combing. We'll do that in the car. Pity you've got no makeup, but it's too late now.' He grabbed her wrist and pulled her towards him. 'You remember everything I told you? What you have to do?'

'Yes,' Simona whispered, hanging her head. How could she forget! What Anthony wanted was worse than anything she had imagined, and she had no idea how she was going to go through with it. Anthony let go of her wrist and grasped her chin.

'Are you ready?' His flinty eyes bored into hers, searching for signs of reluctance, refusal, any dangerous independence of spirit. 'Because if you're not ...' He reached into his coat pocket and pulled out the gun, held it to the pulsing artery in her throat. 'Tell me now. And I'll tell Maria she had to die because you bottled out.'

Simona wondered why her heart did not jump with terror again, or her legs turn weak. She bore the gun's pressure patiently. Did she want Anthony to just pull that trigger once or twice and relieve her of the misery, fear and suffering, the horrific rape scenes that replayed themselves in her brain until she thought – hoped – she would go crazy? He could pull that trigger and blast away the oily, sticky, filthy stain that covered her soul, had turned it from a tiny, golden, glowing sun to a black coal inside her head. She imagined all that horror flowing out along with her blood, leaving her at peace for ever. How wonderful that would be. Then she thought of Maria again, was overwhelmed with love and remorse. She was being selfish. She couldn't give up now. Later, maybe.

'I'm ready.' She raised her eyes and looked at Anthony. Not too challengingly, in case he hit her again. She was sick and tired of being hit. Being on her back or on her knees instead of standing tall, without some man pressing her head down.

'Good.' Anthony sounded relieved. 'Right. Let's go.' He lowered the gun and glanced at his watch by the light of the torch.

Anthony had no respect or empathy, Simona thought. No compassion for any living soul. He did not think in terms of living souls. Only commodities, and how much money their suffering would bring him. He led her back through the dark, dangerous warren of tunnels, caves and passages, and they emerged, blinking and shielding their eyes from the sunlight. It was a cold morning and the autumnal air smelled of traffic fumes and the sea, woodsmoke from distant fields. Simona looked longingly at the blue sky.

Then she started to pray.

'This is a miracle,' Sean murmured. 'To wake up with you in our own bed. Even the sun's shining. What a night!' He kissed her breasts. 'What a morning!'

Carmel arched her back, stretching luxuriously. 'I actually feel relaxed.' She hugged him, pressing her body against his. 'Lazy. It's unbelievable.' She smiled. 'Let's go and surprise Lisa now, shall we? I can't wait to see her face!'

'Yeah.' Sean smiled back, let go of her and sat up. Carmel scrambled out of bed and pulled on her robe, shook back her long hair.

'Oh, *damn*!' she exclaimed, catching sight of the bedside clock. 'We've overslept – it's after nine.' She looked at Sean, dismayed. 'Rosa will have taken her to school. I remember now, last night before I went out she told me to have a lie-in.' She opened the bedroom door and hurried across the landing. Her daughter's room was empty, the quilt flung back. Lisa's pink comb lay on the floor, next to the jar of glittery gel. Sean joined her, tying the belt of his robe.

'So we'll have to wait until this afternoon?' he asked, disappointed. He took her in his arms and kissed her. 'Listen, we'll go out and buy some stuff, make her a special

397

tea. Collect her from school together later. Okay?'

Carmel smiled. 'Good idea. Why don't you go back to bed?' she suggested. 'The police can wait a bit longer. You look tired, I'm worried about you. Maybe we should get the doctor to check you over. Your ankle's hurt, and you kept passing out after you fell in that tunnel. You could be concussed.'

Sean shook his head. 'I'm all right,' he said firmly. 'I don't need a doctor. I'm back with my wife and daughter at last. That's all that matters. I just need to be with you. Get plenty of rest and good grub. And of course see Anthony Maskey put away for the next thirty years. I hope to Christ they pick him up soon.' He frowned. 'I suppose we'll have to give evidence at the bastard's trial, whenever it comes up.'

'Don't let's talk about that now.' Carmel kissed and hugged him. 'Or even think about it. We're not going to let him spoil your homecoming. Go back to bed,' she repeated. 'We'll phone the police when you're ready. I'll bring you coffee, fresh orange juice, toast and scrambled eggs. You can sleep some more, then take a nice long bath. How does that sound?'

'Pretty damn perfect.' Sean gently pulled open her robe and slipped it off her shoulders. His eyes darkened and his breath quickened as he stared down at her naked body. 'I'll go back to bed if you come with me,' he whispered. He kissed her and lightly stroked her breasts, watched the nipples harden. 'No more lost time.'

'No more lost time!' Carmel breathed. She closed her eyes, loving the feel of his mouth on hers. Desire overwhelmed her again, another great rush of emotion. 'I missed you so much!' she cried, clinging to him.

Later on she went down to the kitchen, took coffee beans from the freezer and whizzed them in the grinder. It felt cold, despite the sunshine. Carmel turned the thermostat a few degrees higher, resisted the irrational urge to run back upstairs and check that Sean was still lying asleep in bed.

The delicious coffee smell filled the kitchen. She took half a dozen eggs from the fridge, broke them into a cream china bowl, and reached for a whisk. Sliced bread and laid it on the grill pan.

Her happiness was tempered by anxiety. When would Anthony be recaptured? When would she and Sean and Lisa be able to feel normal again? Lisa would be overjoyed to see her father later today, but the traumatic weeks of his absence would not be easily and quickly forgotten. Then again, children were resilient. They all had to try to live a normal life again. But it would take a long time to feel safe. Carmel paused as tears filled her eyes.

'Bloody hell,' she muttered, brushing them away. 'I'm more fragile than these eggshells.' She knew she would cry again each time she broke the news about Sean's homecoming. I have to call Mum and Dad soon, she thought. Rosa, Daniel. She gasped as she suddenly remembered two client appointments that morning. The first one would be knocking on her office door in about ten minutes. She rushed to the phone and called them, cancelled her appointments for the rest of the week and rescheduled, scribbling furiously on the telephone pad. She needed to find a new, part-time secretary soon.

Back in the kitchen, Carmel poured herself a cup of coffee and sipped it while she arranged Sean's breakfast tray. She shivered with horror again as she thought of him trapped in the Joseph Williamson labyrinth all that time, lying injured and delirious. It could so easily have ended in her worst nightmare.

'But it didn't,' she whispered, closing her eyes. 'It *didn't*.'

She picked up the tray and turned to leave the kitchen, sighed with irritation as the phone started ringing. She didn't feel like answering it. But it might be important. Maybe the police to tell her Anthony Maskey was back behind bars. That would certainly help the fragile feeling. She put the tray on the table and picked up the receiver.

'*Mummy*!' Lisa's voice was high-pitched, raw with panic. '*Mummy*!' She was sobbing uncontrollably, gulping for breath.

'Darling?' Carmel turned faint and icy cold. 'What's happened, what's wrong? Have you hurt yourself, have you had an accident?' Terror gripped her.

'*Mum-m-yyy!*'

'Lisa, darling! Try and calm down, please talk to me. Don't cry, it's all right!' But Carmel was crying herself. 'Why are you phoning from school?' No answer. Lisa's terrified crying grew louder.

'Is there a teacher with you?' Carmel asked desperately, in a cold sweat of horror and fear at the thought of her child being so terrified, maybe hurt. 'Who's there? Darling, I need to know what's happened. Please, calm down. Let me—' Lisa's terrified, gulping sobs receded into the background as someone took the phone away from her.

'What's going on?' Carmel cried. No, she thought. Oh, please God, *no*! 'Who is that? Who's there?' But she knew.

'Not the teacher, I'm afraid. Although I'm a kind of teacher. Lisa darling isn't phoning from school,' Anthony Maskey said. 'I've given her the day off.'

Chapter Thirty-two

'Be quiet, Lisa, please! Stop crying. We will not hurt you, I promise!'

Could she guarantee that? Simona was close to break-down herself as she fought to control the hysterical little girl in the dark blue school uniform who struggled in her arms. Lisa's face was bright red and streaked with tears, her blonde hair tumbling over her shoulders and down her back, sticky with a glittery gel of tiny gold stars.

'Let me go!' Lisa wailed. 'I want to go home, let me go to my mummy!'

Simona could only too vividly empathise with the child's fear and anguish, the terror and panic of her poor mother to whom Anthony was speaking at that moment. She was stunned with horror and pity for their plight. Sick with shame that she had helped cause their anguish. Was Anthony capable of killing this child? Why would he do that, and how could she stop him? Where would all this end?

Simona did not know how she had steeled herself to walk into that school and tell the friendly woman teacher in the tortoiseshell spectacles and rumpled black suit that she was new to the area, thinking of sending her son there, and could he start before the autumn term ended? Anthony had timed it perfectly: she had grabbed Lisa Devine as the children were filing into the playground for their morning break, seeking her out and recognising her from the newspaper photo Anthony had made her study. He had only the photo, torn from the page. No headline, no story. She had given Lisa Devine Anthony's terrible message: 'Your daddy's outside in a car. He wants to see you.'

A frown of doubt, puzzlement, caution and finally joyful incredulity had flitted across the child's open, friendly face in quick succession. Caution lost, big time. The school gates had remained unlocked since Simona had entered. She and Lisa raced out before the teacher following the group of children could do anything. A small Asian boy and two girls had run after them, yelling Lisa's name and asking her where she was going. Simona had turned, shouted at them to get back; they halted in fear and bewilderment at the school gates. One of the girls started to cry. The children did not understand exactly what was happening. Only that it was bad.

I am as evil as Anthony, Simona thought. Worse. I made this child trust me, and then I broke her trust. She grabbed Lisa's flailing arms and pinioned them by her sides, shot a look of hatred at Anthony.

'Please,' she begged, 'be quiet now, Lisa.'

'I want my mummy! She's upset, she's crying. I want to go home. I don't want to be here, why do I have to be in this horrible place?' Lisa looked at the crumbling walls and rubbish-strewn stone floor of the derelict railway hut. Across a patch of stony ground was the concealed entrance to the tunnel, down a flight of sandstone steps. Then she looked at Anthony. 'I know him,' she sobbed. 'I don't like him. I want my mummy and daddy.'

'You can go home later. See your mummy and daddy then. I promise.'

Simona despised herself for saying that. Another lie, another promise she was in absolutely no position to make or keep. Before going to Lisa's school she had robbed a man of his mobile phone, on Anthony's orders. They had cruised the streets around the university buildings and student flats, Anthony on the lookout for a suitable victim. At last he had found one, driven around a corner out of sight and stopped, leaving the engine running. Simona had raced up to the bespectacled middle-aged man wearing a dark overcoat and carrying a briefcase, and breathlessly begged him to let her borrow his phone to call an ambulance because her friend had had a terrible fall and was lying unconscious.

She was distraught and well dressed enough to be utterly convincing. The man cut short his conversation and offered to call the ambulance for her. She snatched the phone, dashed back around the corner and jumped into the car. They drove off leaving the man shouting and gesticulating furiously. Anthony laughed and said they made a good team, that she had a natural talent for deception and robbery. Simona was learning terrible things about herself and what she was capable of, things that made her sick to her stained soul.

'Where's my dad?' Lisa screamed. She freed her arms and pummelled Simona with her little fists. 'You said he wanted to see me. That was a lie, wasn't it?'

'Yes. I'm sorry!' Simona grabbed her arms again. 'Be still, please, Lisa.' She glanced at Anthony. She was afraid he would hurt the child if she did not calm down soon. He had encouraged her to cry on the phone to her mother, but Simona could not imagine him tolerating this noise level much longer.

'I want my sixty grand back,' Anthony was saying into the phone. 'Make sure you replace every penny of it. And absolutely no police. I don't need to tell you what'll happen to Lisa darling then.' He had to raise his voice. He did not seem angry, Simona thought, not yet. He had a big smile on his face, as if he had played his trump card and won at last. Which of course he had. That poor mother would do anything to get her daughter back. Who was the woman, Simona wondered? What did Anthony want? To kill her as well as the others? What had *she* done to offend him?

403

'Come to think of it, I *do* need to tell you what'll happen.' Anthony looked at Lisa as he continued talking, his eyes cold. 'There's a huge demand for little blonde clones like her. Especially in countries that even the Brit Foreign Office can be arsed to warn people not to visit. She's pretty – the long blonde locks and big baby blue eyes are very appealing. And of course she's a virgin. She'll fetch a great price on the open market.' He smiled at the scream that came out of the phone. 'You'll never see her again. But don't worry, she won't suffer long. They don't last more than a few months.'

'*No*!' Simona gasped. She stared at him, horror struck. Lisa couldn't be more than two or three years older than her own niece. 'She is just a child! You can't ...!' There was another wail of anguish on the other end of the phone, then a man's voice shouting, furious and desperate. Lisa suddenly stopped struggling in her arms and went quiet, her eyes wide with shock.

'That's my daddy!' she whimpered, staring at the phone. Her tears rolled down, dripped on to the stone floor. 'I just heard him! Where is he?'

'You can't do this!' Simona screamed at Anthony, beside herself with shock and outrage. 'Not to her, not to a *child*!' She flew at him and lashed out, her ragged nails raking his face. He gasped with pain and surprise as the long scratches tore his skin and drew blood. She felt savage triumph that at last she could hurt him. Triumph was shortlived.

'Don't fucking tell me what I can and can't do!' Anthony dropped the phone, grabbed her shoulders and pushed her against the wall, banging her head. He punched her in the stomach and face, knocked her to the ground and kicked her over and over as she lay there, grunting with fury. Simona tried to curl up and protect herself as his foot slammed into her hip, back, stomach, head. Her hands shielding her face were covered with blood that poured from her nose and mouth. Dimly she saw Lisa crouched in a corner, shaking and whimpering, blue eyes dazed with

404

terror. Anthony strode back to where he'd dropped the
phone. He picked it up and dusted it, held it to his ear.

'You still there? Good.' He touched his cheek, glanced
disgustedly at the blood that came off on his fingers. 'My
old friend Sean's there too, I hear. I knew all along you
were in contact with him, you bitch! The pair of you plot-
ting to bring me down. But I didn't realise he'd actually
come home. Fooled me, didn't you? Bet you don't feel too
clever now. Right, this is what I want you to do. No fuck-
ups, or your darling daughter gets sold to the highest
bidder. And remember, no police there tonight. The second
I spot one, she's . . .'

Simona must have passed out because she did not hear
the rest of what Anthony said. When she opened her eyes,
she found herself still lying curled on the dirty ground, her
teeth sticky with blood. Her lower lip was split and bleeding, she hurt all over and her ears were ringing. Her head
ached and she felt sick and dazed. Lisa still crouched
sobbing in the corner. Anthony stood there pointing a gun
at them. Simona remembered where he had got it. It was
Diane's gun, and Anthony had used it to murder her and
Barry.

'I have done what you wanted,' she whispered through
bloodied, swelling lips. There was a sharp pain on the right
side of her face; had he broken her cheekbone? 'Can I see
my sister now? Please! I want to go to Maria.' She was torn
with anguish for Lisa's plight, for her distraught parents.
But what could she do, how could she help them? She was
in enough danger herself, she had her own family to worry
about.

'You never learn, do you?' Anthony's foot slammed into
her thigh, and Simona flinched, whimpering with pain.
'Never stop making demands. If you want to see your
sister,' he said brutally, 'you'll have to go to a morgue.
Check out the chilled stiffs. Won't mind that, will you? Of
course I know your family prefer them still warm.'

'What do you . . .?'

'I *mean*, your sister's dead.' He laughed. 'Or undead, I should say! Months ago. She was a demanding, betraying bitch too. Runs in the family, doesn't it?' Anthony squatted beside her. 'I killed Maria because she kept trying to run away. Hid her body in these tunnels. I was going to show you her final resting place. But the police fucked that up. They took her away.'

'No!' Simona whispered. Tears spilled from her eyes, trickled sideways and mingled with the blood on the ground. 'Maria... oh, no!' She lay there battered, bruised and shivering, the fight gone out of her. All the hope. Hope was what had kept her going. But it had also blinded her. How could she have thought Anthony would let her go, let her see Maria again? She was stupid, crazy, an imbecile. And now she was guilty of kidnapping this crying child in the corner, whose fate would be even more terrible than her own.

The mental anguish was worse than her physical pain. Simona groaned and shut her eyes as she was gripped by the raw, agonising, inconsolable pain of a devastating loss, the awful knowledge that Maria was dead and she would never see her beloved sister again. Her suffering, her stupid hope, had all been for nothing. She thought of her parents. How would they cope? Lily, growing up without her mother.

'And as far as I'm concerned ...' Anthony jammed the gun to her left temple. 'You're already on borrowed time.'

'We need a few moments alone,' Carmel said to the group of sombre police officers standing around the sitting room. They glanced at one another and nodded. She and Sean went out, closed the door behind them and walked down the hall to the kitchen. They couldn't go into the television room and see Lisa's toys and books scattered about, the things she should have been home playing with by now. Carmel was experiencing a hideous *déja vu* of the emotions she had suffered when Sean disappeared. She hadn't

406

believed anything could be worse. Until now. She had imagined Sean being at Anthony's mercy, or herself, and that was bad enough. But not Lisa. Never Lisa.

'If that bastard hurts her, I'll kill him!' Sean strode to the window, anguished and white-faced, his eyes full of tears. 'What am I talking about, *if*? He's hurt her already, she'll be terrified. I'll kill him anyway. Jesus Christ, where's he taken her, *where*?' He chewed his lip, raked his hands through his untidy dark hair. He had thrown on jeans and trainers, a black cashmere sweater. 'Must be those tunnels, I can't think of anywhere else he'd go. But there's miles of them, we could be searching for ever. Oh God, *Lisa!*' He stared out into the back yard, at the silver birch tree, the green plants in their big terracotta pots, and the empty swing seat. They could hear children shouting and laughing in the alley, unaware of the drama that was unfolding behind the bolted wooden door in the wall. Sean turned away from the window and sat down, buried his head in his hands. 'This is my fault,' he groaned. 'All of it's my stupid, bloody fault!'

'Sean, please don't talk like that.' Carmel put her arms around him. 'It's Anthony's fault, he's the one who . . . did this.' She could not bring herself to say it: *kidnapped*, *abducted*. She straightened up and began to pace. It was impossible to keep still.

'How can he say "no police"?' she fretted. 'He must realise the school called them the minute it happened. And this girl with him – she sounds exactly like his description of the one he tried to get me to believe you'd run off with. The police say Anthony took her from that brothel in Manchester where he shot the madam, or whatever they call them now, with her own gun. And that bouncer. I wonder why he murdered them? Who the hell *is* that girl? Did she go with him willingly, or did he force her? It sounded like they were arguing at some point.'

'Christ knows.' Sean rubbed his eyes. 'He's lost it, hasn't he? He's a nut job, he's off his fucking head!' He looked up at her. 'I don't care what that lot in there say. I'm going alone tonight. With his precious sixty grand. It's me he really wants.'

'No!' Carmel stiffened. 'Anthony said I was to go too.'

'Forget it.' Sean clenched his fists. 'No *way*, Carmel. He'll kill you.'

'We've got to do exactly what he wants. Go along with it for now – or appear to. Like the police say.'

'Oh yeah, the police!' Sean smiled bitterly. 'We're supposed to put our trust – Lisa's *life* – in the hands of a bunch of dickbrains who charged me with two murders, harassed you, trashed our house and even put a corrupt inspector in Anthony Maskey's pay in charge of the bloody investigation. She gets stiffed, they finally get the right guy – who, incidentally, turns out to have murdered this inspector for God knows what reason – and they discover all this thanks to *you*, not their own less than meticulous detective work. And what happens then? They let him escape from the bloody courtroom!' Sean's voice rose, cracking with rage. 'He murders two more people, and now the bastard's got my daughter! He might have already—' He broke off and looked away, covering his eyes with one hand.

'No!' Carmel cried. 'She's not . . . he hasn't killed her! What would be the point?'

'What's the bloody point of anything that nut job does?'

Carmel sniffed and wiped her eyes. 'Sean, we can't handle this ourselves, even if we had that option. There'll be an armed response team. They're highly trained, they're used to dealing with this kind of situation.'

'Are they? Well, great! That makes me feel better already. A bunch of gum-chewing macho wankers get to play Dirty Harry – with our daughter caught in the cross-fire. I suppose it'll make a nice change for them from blowing away sad pissheads, or schizophrenics who forgot to take their medication.'

'It won't be like that.' Carmel was trying to convince

herself as much as him. 'Anthony won't see them until it's too late. They won't do anything that puts Lisa in more danger. And there's that girl. We don't know why she's with him.'

'Fuck *her*.' Sean thumped his fist on the table. 'She snatched our daughter. She's helping him, she's as guilty as he is.'

'But Anthony might have forced her. You heard them arguing. I think he hit her.'

'And that's our problem because *what*? Maybe she wanted more money for snatching our daughter and he got the raving hump.' Sean turned on her, his blue-grey eyes dark with fury. 'What the hell is this, Carmel? Are you telling me you feel sorry for that bitch?'

'No.' Carmel lowered her eyes. 'I'm just hoping ...' Her voice wavered. 'Just hoping that maybe she'll help Lisa. Be on her side, be kind to her.' More tears slid down her cheeks, and her lower lip trembled. 'That's all.'

Sean grabbed her and pulled her close and they cried with fear and panic, holding on to one another. 'I can't bear to lose her,' he sobbed, his body shaking. 'Our little girl! Can't bear to think what she must be going through right now. She'll be so frightened without us. She doesn't even know I'm home. The bastard ruined that for her too.'

'We won't lose Lisa. She'll see you again.' Carmel made a big effort to stop crying. She hugged Sean tighter. 'I don't want them to rearrest him,' she whispered, leaning against his shoulder. 'I want them to blow his fucking head off!'

'If they don't, I will.' They drew apart. Sean picked up a cup of cold coffee and took a gulp. 'Wonder why he wants to meet outside the warehouse? At eleven.'

Carmel wiped her tears and smoothed back her hair. 'It's a good idea – from his point of view. You've got the river all around, and that empty stretch of land those developers bought recently. It's going to be difficult for the police marksmen to hide.'

'Listen to me.' Sean took her in his arms again and

looked into her eyes. 'Once I've handed over the money . . . Anthony will shoot me.' He swallowed. 'He wants me dead, Carmel. You have to concentrate on Lisa. Get her away, no matter what happens. Don't try to save me.' He kissed her. 'Promise me you'll protect Lisa?'

'We're not going to lose Lisa,' Carmel said slowly, her voice trembling. 'And I'm bloody well not going to lose you either, certainly not after we've gone through all this shit.'

'Promise me!' His voice was fierce. 'About Lisa.'

'All right,' she whispered. 'I promise.'

Sean kissed her again, holding her tight. 'I love you. Never forget that.'

'I love you too.' Carmel stared up at him, her eyes wet. 'And of course I won't forget. Because you'll be here to tell me, and I'll be able to tell you. Every day for at least the next forty years.'

They turned as they sensed a presence. John Edwards, the liaison officer, stood there, hands in his coat pockets. His dark eyes were sombre.

'Are you ready?' he asked awkwardly. 'There's not much time, and we've got a lot to get through before tonight.'

He hated their distress and felt personally responsible for it, even though he was not. To have their young daughter snatched by Anthony Maskey, just when they thought the nightmare was over . . . Neil Davie, just out of intensive care, would recover in time. Unfortunately, he could not guarantee a happy ending for Carmel, Sean and Lisa Devine. Especially Lisa. There was a strong possibility that Maskey had already murdered the child. They just had to hope he hadn't.

Carmel and Sean looked at each other again. Sean reached for her hand, and held on to it.

'We're ready,' Carmel whispered.

Chapter Thirty-three

'It's not supposed to rain,' Anthony murmured, glancing at the leaden orange-grey sky as he slid the Renault Megane to a stop outside the dark bulk of the warehouse. He left the engine running. He couldn't see any police marksmen in the orange-grey gloom, but the good news was that they wouldn't see him either. On the other hand, they might have those infra-red vision things. They were around, they had to be. But there was no problem as long as he kept his cool. He felt excited and nervous, but not afraid. There was nothing to be afraid of. He had the gold, he had Carmel and Sean at his mercy. Mercy, what mercy?

He smiled as he got out of the car. Tonight was the beginning of a new phase in his life. He would take Henry and Alice's gold and start again. Somewhere far away. Anthony fancied Australia. He would get a false passport. He could get anything he wanted now. He liked the idea of the gold being shipped back to where it had come from more than one hundred and sixty years ago, this time in the cargo hold of a 747 instead of the White Star Line's clipper ship *Shalimar*. The wheel would have turned full circle then. It was as if it was meant to happen.

He turned up his coat collar as cold rain fell on his head and dripped off his nose and chin, rolled down the back of his neck. It was throwing it down, straight like needles. The river was still, the foghorn sounding at intervals. He shivered and gripped the gun in his pocket as he peered across the dark misty patch of ground from which he expected Carmel and Sean to appear. Surely they didn't think it was cool to be late?

Anthony drew in his breath as they emerged from the darkness, walking slowly, hand in hand. Sean wore jeans, trainers and a black sweater, a leather jacket. He carried the aluminium briefcase with the sixty grand. Carmel wore jeans, ankle boots and a short padded jacket, zipped up. Her blonde hair was loose around her shoulders. Anthony's smile broadened. They both looked pale and terrified, sick with anxiety about the little blonde clone. Wondering if she was still alive.

'Nasty night,' he commented as they drew near. He got out the gun and pointed it at them. 'You've lost weight, Sean. You're all peaky and hollow-eyed. A changed man. I've missed you. Missed us working together.'

Sean, obviously struggling to hold on to his self-control, looked as if he wanted to say a lot to that. But he kept silent. He slowly and carefully put the briefcase on the muddy ground and edged it forward with his foot.

'Sixty grand.' He shot Anthony a look of hatred. 'It's all there.'

'Thanks a lot. I'll trust you. I know you're not stupid.' Anthony glanced around in the darkness, wishing he had infra-red vision. He could practically feel the police rifles trained on him. At the same time he felt excited, wanted to laugh. The adrenalin was flowing. Chasing away the nightmares, the bad stuff, making him feel on top of the world. 'How much did you spend during your time away from home sweet home?' He wanted to play with them first. The rain poured down. Anthony wiped the gun on his coat sleeve, and levelled it again.

'Nearly two grand.'

'Hm. Reasonably frugal. Didn't blow it all on gentlemen's entertainment then?'

Sean clenched his fists. 'That's your thing, you sad bastard! Not mine.'

'Please, Anthony!' Carmel cried, shivering. 'Where's Lisa? Is she in the car?'

'I'd listen to your wife if I were you, Sean. Politeness always opens door. No, I didn't bring Lisa darling. Come on!' Anthony said as Carmel gave a sob. 'You didn't seriously imagine I'd drive her here, hand her over, wait patiently to get my head blown off and you all live happy ever after?'

'Where is she?' Carmel was weeping. 'Let me see my daughter! *Please!*'

'What would you do?' Anthony asked, interested. 'How far would you go? Did you really take that money and the passports from my safe and plant it in my house?' He looked at her. 'I suppose you think you're one cool bitch. How did you . . .?'

'We want our daughter!' Sean stepped forward. 'If you've hurt her . . .'

'You'll what?' Anthony's playful mood disappeared and he felt angry.

'I'll kill you, that's fucking *what!*'

Carmel grabbed his arm. 'Sean, don't!'

'She's right, you know.' Anthony's finger brushed the trigger. 'If you want to see the clone again—'

'Stop calling Lisa that!'

'– this really isn't the best way.'

'Anthony! Anthony, lad.' The voice came out of the darkness, somewhere behind Sean and Carmel. Anthony nearly dropped the gun in shock. What was this, some kind of trick?

'Mary?' he gasped.

'Yeah. It's me.'

'What the hell are you doing here?' Of course he knew. The plods were trying to get psychological. He was shocked and unnerved nevertheless.

'Came to see you, didn't I? Put the gun down, there's a good lad.' She emerged from the darkness, a tiny figure in her dark blue duffel coat. 'Come on.' She held out a gloved

413

hand. 'This is just daft, you know it is. Tell us where that little girl is, let her go back to her mam and dad. Think how frightened she must be.' Carmel bowed her head and gave another sob.

'I don't know what they've told you.' Anthony swallowed. 'But you don't understand.'

'Look, love, you're in trouble and I want to help.' Mary came closer, her face earnest. She seemed to have aged, Anthony thought, shrunk into herself. That was his fault. He felt a twinge of guilt.

'Let her go,' Mary pleaded. 'Stop this now. Please, love! You're not doing yourself any favours. Don't be a lost soul.'

He was already lost. Anthony suddenly felt panicked, hemmed in, surrounded by hundreds of unseen eyes. He had to get away from here. Now. He backed away, waved the gun at Carmel and Sean.

'In the car!' he shouted. He glanced at Carmel. 'You drive. I'll give you directions. Make sure you lose *them*,' he pointed into the darkness, 'for the clone's sake. Move!' he barked as they stood there terrified and uncertain. 'Listen! We can fight and maybe you'll get this gun off me, have me arrested or shot. I don't give a fuck. You'll never see Lisa darling again. It's up to you.'

Carmel and Sean glanced at each other. Then Carmel got behind the wheel and Sean sat next to her, slamming the door. The police had no choice but to let them go, Anthony thought, even if they did try to follow. It was all working out. Except for Mary being here. That wasn't supposed to happen. Carmel and Sean would pay for that. Even if it hadn't been their idea, they had gone along with it.

He hesitated, gripping the door handle. He did not want to leave Mary like this, standing in the cold rainy darkness looking at him with pity and concern. He could promise to write, phone, send money, come back to see her one day. But he knew this was the last time they would set eyes on one another. Mary knew everything now, and she hadn't wavered. She still cared about him.

'I'm sorry,' he said. 'For everything. I let you down.'

'You've never let me down. And you won't now, because you're going to let that little girl go. For me.' She stared at him, her eyes bright. 'Will you do that, Anthony?'

He opened the door. 'I've got to go.'

'Don't hurt her,' Mary called. 'Or anyone else. You can stop this now. It's up to you, Anthony. You can do it.'

'Goodbye, Mary.'

The car drove off at speed, bumping over the wet, greasy cobblestones. A group of armed police officers ran forward. John Edwards joined her. Another officer was talking urgently, relaying instructions to the pilot of the helicopter which suddenly swept into view, lights blazing low overhead. Mary stared at John Edwards, her expression grim and frightened.

'Thanks.' He patted her shoulder. 'Very brave of you.'

'No.' Mary shook her head, wiped away a tear. 'I tried,' she muttered. 'Did me best. It's in God's hands now.'

'Left here. *Left*. Jesus Christ, women drivers!'

'It's not so much my gender as the fact that you're holding a gun to my head.' Carmel slammed the Renault Megane to a stop, wrenched the gears and swerved left into the narrow road of terraced houses and closely parked cars. The window wipers swished back and forth, barely coping with the drenching rain.

'Faster,' Anthony urged, glancing back. 'Come on, give it welly!'

'I can't,' she cried. 'Someone might be crossing the road.'

'That's their fucking problem. Put your foot down.'

Carmel increased speed as much as she dared. She glanced in the driving mirror again, looked into Anthony's angry eyes. They had lost the police car chasing them – or so it appeared. But the helicopter was overhead somewhere. How could Anthony think he was going to get away? He was impatient with her driving, but didn't seem unduly nervous. The fact that he wasn't nervous made her more frightened. What the hell was he planning? They had driven up Brownlow Hill past the Roman Catholic cathedral, and were now heading for Edge Hill. Surprise, surprise. Carmel slowed as they approached an intersection.

'Turn right. Up Crown Street.'

'But the lights!' The traffic lights were orange, about to turn red.

'*Fuck the lights!*'

Carmel gasped in terror as Anthony jammed the gun against the back of her neck. She put her foot down and the car shot forward, the wheels swishing spray. She swung round in a tight turn, brushing past a cyclist who wobbled perilously for a couple of seconds then fell off, collapsing against some railings. Anthony laughed loudly.

'Dickhead! Serves you right.' He sat back and lowered the gun slightly. 'That's a very versatile word, isn't it?' he said conversationally. 'Fuck, I mean. It can be used as an adverb or adjective or—' He laughed again. 'D'you know what the last words of the captain of the *Titanic* were? No? "Full speed ahead and fuck the icebergs!" And the mayor of Hiroshima? "What the fuck was that?"'

'Hilarious,' Sean said grimly, staring at the wet stretch of tarmac ahead. 'D'you mind if I ask where we're going?'

'Shut up. Down this little road to the right.' Carmel obeyed. They were near a railway line. 'And now down here.' A narrow dirt track sloped into the darkness between barbed-wire fences. There were garages and workshops all around, a railway bridge and a row of boarded-up houses.

Carmel hesitated. 'It says "no entry".'

'What a law-abiding little citizen you are. They should give you a medal.' The gun was pressed to the nape of her neck again. 'But maybe you'd prefer a bullet? *Drive.*'

She drove down an embankment, the headlights picking out grassy tracks where railway lines had once been, an old signals hut, bricks, stones, piles of rubbish. People probably dumped toxic chemicals and God knew what else here. Carmel was freaked to think of Lisa being in such a place. But *where* was she?

'Okay, stop. Switch off the engine and lights.'

Carmel did as he said, and they sat in the silent darkness. Rain drummed on the roof and bonnet.

'Turn around, both of you.' Anthony kept the gun levelled at them. Carmel and Sean twisted round in their seats. 'Right,' he said, 'we're going on a little journey. Underground.'

'Oh, my God!' Carmel gasped, tears starting to her eyes. There must be another entrance to the labyrinth nearby. 'You didn't take Lisa down *there*? She'll be so frightened, she'll—'

'She's fine. Shut up and listen. I'll take you to her now. You won't find her without me, so if you try anything she'll be trapped down there for ever. I've got my money, now you can have her. Your only problem is that you'll have to find your own way back. I'll get out via a different route, where I've got another car waiting. I nicked it this afternoon,' he said, 'in case you're interested. So – you'd better concentrate on remembering the way, rather than trying to find the perfect moment to jump me.' Anthony looked at them in turn, searching their faces. 'Understand?'

Sean cleared his throat. 'Got it.'

'Yes.' Carmel's fear increased. Anthony wasn't going to let them go, despite what he said. She knew Sean was thinking the same thing. Once they were down in those pitch-dark, dangerous tunnels they were lost. In every way. They could jump Anthony and get the gun off him, but what then? He wasn't going to show them the way out. There was no choice now, though, but to follow him. They had to bide their time and hope that perfect moment came. Maybe it would not come. Carmel felt suffocated with terror at the thought of doing down into the tunnels again. This was a different entrance. How many did Anthony know about?

'Let's go. Take it slowly.' Anthony opened the car door. He took a torch from the boot, put the briefcase in a large canvas bag and slipped the straps over his right shoulder. Sean put one arm around Carmel and hugged her, touched his cold lips to her cheek.

'Be all right,' he whispered in her ear. 'I love you.'

'Hey!' Anthony flashed the torch in their faces, dazzling them. 'None of that. You don't want to piss off the empty-hearted psycho even more, do you?'

They stumbled across the rough ground to the blackened stone wall near the mouth of the tunnel, cold, sharp rain soaking them. Anthony stooped and moved aside some planks and a heavy wet sheet of tarpaulin, uncovered a hole with sandstone steps leading steeply downwards. Carmel tried to conquer her panic at the thought of going into it. But Lisa was down there. She had to. She gasped as Anthony grabbed her arm.

'You first.' His dark hair was soaked and his angry face glistened with raindrops.

'I'll go first,' Sean shouted. 'Don't touch her.'

As they picked their way down the steps Carmel thought she heard the helicopter approaching. Would the police be able to find the tunnel entrance, follow them? Would they be in time to help? At the bottom of the steps was a large chamber with crumbling sandstone walls. Faint light came from a square hole in the floor. Carmel and Sean looked down. A long wooden ladder led to another room below. A tall, thick red candle flickered and dripped in a scorched wall niche.

'I left that there to welcome you,' Anthony said. 'Pretty, isn't it? Go on.'

The ladder rungs were not that steady. Carmel climbed carefully down, terrified in case she fell and broke her neck, wondering if she and Sean would get the chance to climb back up again. She prayed that Lisa really was here. The walls were damp and she could hear water dripping in the silence. Then a distant roar started and grew louder, made the ground shake beneath her feet. It sounded like an earthquake or subsidence. Sean joined her at the foot of the ladder.

'It's okay.' He reached for her hand and squeezed it. 'It's just a train.'

They were not far from Lime Street, Central and Moorfields stations. There must be a warren of railway tunnels around here, used and unused. Many of them abandoned years ago. Carmel remembered reading about how Robert Stephenson's workers had dug the tunnel to Lime Street during the 1830s. A hole had opened up beneath them and they had found themselves staring down at Joseph Williamson's men, who were digging their own tunnel. The shocked railway workers had fled, terrified that they had dug right down to the devil's kingdom.

'Move!' Anthony ordered. 'We haven't got all bloody night.'

They went along a tiny passage, walking a few feet ahead of him. Water slopped around their feet.

'It's dangerous down here,' Sean called back. 'Getting flooded.'

'Just keep moving. If you want to see Lisa darling.' They went along more passages and came to a sharp bend where the walls narrowed. Further on, Carmel collided with Sean as he stopped suddenly.

'Get back!' His voice was harsh with shock. 'There's a bloody great hole in the floor. A pool of water down below, with a—' He stopped. Carmel didn't need to know about the rat. At least the thing was dead, bobbing about with its paws in the air.

'I wondered if you'd spot that in time.' Anthony came up behind them. 'You'll have to jump. I did it, your daughter did it. So can you.'

Sean did not hesitate. He took a running jump, and Carmel followed. She landed on the other side, shivering with cold and fright, imagining how terrified Lisa must have been. How much further? She could remember the way up to now, but not if they went on for much longer. The torchlight flashed over the sandstone walls, and their shadows loomed large. As she rounded another corner, Carmel thought she heard faint crying.

'Lisa?' she called, her heart leaping. '*Lisa*!'

'Mummy!' a small voice wailed. 'Mummy, help me.'

'I'm coming!' Carmel shouted. 'Daddy's here too. Don't be frightened, we're coming to get you!' She pushed past Sean, ran forward and stopped. 'Where are you?'

'Carmel!' he hissed. 'Wait, for Christ's sake! It's dangerous, you can't see—'

'In here, Mummy!' Lisa's voice was louder now, coming from her left. Carmel turned and ducked into a tiny tunnel or room; it was too dark to see.

'Lisa?'

'Here, Mummy, over here!'

Carmel stumbled forward in the pitch dark and fell on her knees. A second later Lisa was in her arms, her small body trembling.

'Oh, darling!' she wept. 'It's okay, you're safe now. I've got you.' Carmel clutched the child to her, kissing her face, smelling her hair. Lisa's hair felt sticky and gritty. The gel! 'Lisa, are you hurt?' she gasped, hugging her.

'No, Mummy. But I'm frightened. I hate it here, I want to get out.'

'We will. Darling, Daddy's here. He came home. We're all together again.'

'Daddy?' Lisa's voice was high-pitched, breathless with fear and uncertainty. 'Is it really Daddy?'

'Certainly is, babe!' Sean edged his way forward, knelt and hugged his wife and daughter to him. 'Come here. That's right, hold on to me. You're safe now.'

'Daddy, where have you been? Did Mummy find you?'

Anthony's torch flashed on to them as they huddled together. 'What a touching little scene,' he remarked. 'The joyfully reunited family, beloved theme of fiction writers and film directors. I really hate to interrupt. Almost makes me wish I'd got married and bred a clone.'

'You bastard!' Sean said fiercely, clutching Lisa and Carmel to him. 'How could you leave her all alone in the dark?'

'Did the candle go out? These sudden cold draughts down here are a bugger. Sometimes I think this place is haunted.' Anthony stooped and struck a match. A candle flame rose, wavered, then burned steadily. The candle was red, like the one in the wall niche by the ladder, standing on a broken brick.

'And she's not alone.' Anthony foot rested on what looked like a bundle of clothes lying against the wall. 'My little helper's not been doing a very good job of looking after her, though, I'm afraid.' He kicked the bundle, which whimpered and stirred slightly. 'Sit up. Useless bitch!'

Carmel and Sean stared in horror as Simona, groaning with pain, slowly uncurled her body and sat leaning against the wall, breathing heavily. Her face in the candlelight was battered and bruised, covered in dark, dried blood, her hair caked with dust. Her clenched hands were bloody too, her clothes filthy. She coughed, groaned and clutched her ribs with the pain. Blood trickled from one side of her mouth. She opened her swollen eyes and looked at them.

'I'm sorry,' she whispered. 'He forced me.' She gave a sob. 'He murdered my sister.'

'That's enough from you.' Anthony dropped the rope and briefcase and kicked her in the hip. Simona cried out and slumped sideways. Lisa whimpered and clung to her mother and father.

'It's all right,' Carmel whispered, hugging her and stroking her hair. 'It's okay, baby, Mummy's here. So's Daddy.' She looked at Anthony with hatred. 'You've got your money, you've got your escape route. Let us go!'

The perfect moment hadn't come. They were trapped now. She still wouldn't give up though, she would fight to her last breath for her daughter. But what could she do? Carmel's heart sank.

421

'Yeah.' Sean got to his feet and faced Anthony. 'Let us go.'

'Here you are in my sights again.' Anthony raised the gun and levelled it at Sean's face. The candle flickered. 'You don't think I'm going to let you go this time.' He smiled. 'Do you?'

Chapter Thirty-four

'Who gets to die first?' Anthony stepped back, keeping the gun trained on Sean. 'Is it going to be a case of love triumphing over self-interest, or will everyone fight like rats to save themselves? Let's ask the psychologist.' He glanced at Carmel, crouched against the wall hugging her daughter. The child's arms were tight around her neck, her face hidden in her mother's shoulder. 'What do you think?'

Just do it, Anthony told himself. Stiff the lot of them and get out. He had heard the police helicopter before entering the tunnel; they were closing in. What was stopping him? Why couldn't he just pull the trigger? He was nervous, afraid, unsure of himself suddenly. He couldn't lose it now.

'Nobody has to die,' Carmel said, struggling to stay calm for Lisa's sake.

Candlelight flickered over her blonde hair, shone in her frightened eyes. 'This is all totally unnecessary, you know it is. Just let us go, Anthony,' she pleaded. 'Let us walk out of here now. You don't have to kill anybody else.'

The gold was waiting, piled in the boot of the white Omega he had gone out and nicked earlier that day after leaving Lisa and Simona imprisoned in the dark cave. He had avoided the busy streets; he felt like Public Enemy Number One, and was shit scared of being recognised. But most people were dozy, unobservant, totally preoccupied with themselves and their own concerns. No one had taken the slightest notice of him. Anthony did not know whether to feel relieved or disappointed.

'Think of Mary.' He flinched as he heard Carmel's soft voice speak the name. 'You're everything to her. You know she doesn't want you to do this. She'll be terribly hurt. She loved you, Anthony. She was there for you all those years when your parents didn't want to know, didn't care who you were or what you were about. She'll never desert you. Don't do this to her now.' Carmel kissed Lisa's head, smoothed back a strand of hair. 'She's had a terrible shock – she can't take much more.'

'What makes you think I give a shit? Get back!' he screamed as Sean made a sudden small movement. 'Hands up!' Sean obeyed and he relaxed slightly, took a breath. He put the torch on the floor, held the gun with both hands. 'What makes you think I can feel guilt or love?'

'You're a human being. I know you get depressed a lot.' The soft voice went on, relentless. 'Unhappy, unsure of yourself. You can't focus, can't centre yourself. I know how that feels.'

'You don't know how anything feels.' Pull the trigger, an inner voice urged. Get out. *Now*. Anthony wanted to, but he couldn't. 'It's more simple than you like to think.' Welcome anger rose in him again. 'I want money, power, I like fucking people over because it makes me feel good. Killing makes me feel good. That's the truth. It gives me a buzz like you couldn't even imagine.' So pull the fucking trigger, the inner voice shouted. 'I hate the pair of you!' He glanced at Sean. 'Your life, the clone, your stupid, smug, self-satisfied delusions. We were friends once, Sean. But you changed. Thought you were better than me. Now I'm going to destroy you. No one gets in my way.' He stretched out his arms, holding the gun in both hands. Sean flinched and backed away, looked wildly around the candlelit cave. His back touched the wall. There was nowhere to go.

'For Christ's sake!' he hissed. 'This is between us. Let Carmel and Lisa go.'

424

'I'll spare the clone,' Anthony lied, smiling. Of course he couldn't take her with him now. 'I've got plans for her.'

'*No!*' Carmel cried. Her eyes were filled with fear and hatred. 'I was wrong.' She cradled her daughter in her arms. 'You're not human. Why the hell did they stop you throwing yourself off that roof?'

'Now we come to it. You do think you're better than me.'

'Anybody's better than *you*!'

'Stand up,' he ordered. 'Let go of the clone.'

'I won't let Lisa go!' Carmel's voice was low and fierce. 'I've got my daughter back and I won't let her go. Ever again. *You* can go to hell, where you belong!'

Anthony shook with rage at her defiance and contempt, the utter refusal to co-operate. But he still didn't relish the idea of shooting a woman with a child in her arms, even when that woman was Carmel Devine. Mary's face floated before his eyes, and he heard her voice again: '*Don't be a lost soul.*'

Suddenly Anthony felt suffocated. No! he thought. Don't let the bad stuff take over. Not when it's going right for you at last. He coughed, shook his head, stepped back and levelled the gun again. He would do Sean first. He curled his finger over the trigger, started to squeeze. It seemed to happen incredibly slowly.

A sudden sensation of heat at his ankle made him gasp and glance down. Simona lay there, holding the burning candle to his leg. She must have held it for a few seconds because a flame was taking hold, burning the hem of his trouser leg. The flame gathered strength, licked higher and seared his skin. Anthony's brain registered what was happening a fraction of a second before his nerve endings kicked in. He screamed in agony and pulled away. Out of the corner of his eye he saw Sean throw himself sideways. He fired at him and missed. The noise of the gun was deafening. The bullet smacked into the ceiling and brought clouds of choking dust showering down on them all. There

425

was a loud, menacing rumble of something shifting, subsiding.

Lisa screamed and cried. Sean leapt on him, grunting with fury, grabbed his right arm and bashed Anthony's hand holding the gun against the stone floor. The candle went out and the torch was kicked around as the two men fought, its light flashing on walls, white dust, terrified faces, looming shadows. A charred smell hung in the air.

'Sean, watch out!' Carmel screamed. 'Watch out for the gun!' She prised off the clinging, crying child. 'Darling, stay down, stay out of the way!'

'Lisa!' Simona gasped. 'Come here, take my hand.'

Anthony still had the gun. He tried to bring his arm up and squeeze the trigger again, right in Sean's face this time, but Carmel was hitting at his hand with a broken brick. His hand, his fingers, had no power in them. He shouted in pain and let go; the gun skittered away in the darkness. Sean punched him around the head and face, grunting with the effort.

'Bastard!' he panted. 'Fucking, psycho *bastard*!'

One punch broke Anthony's nose and started it bleeding. He tasted blood at the back of his throat, in his mouth, felt it spurt out and run down his chin and neck. There was an agonising pain between his eyes, which were streaming with tears. He had to hope it wasn't a serious bleed. If he could just get away from Sean and hide somewhere quiet, he might be able to staunch it. Where the hell was the bloody gun? Desperate, he brought up one leg and managed to knee Sean hard in the stomach. Winded, Sean toppled sideways, coughing and spitting.

'Sean!' Carmel grabbed the torch and shone it on them. Anthony struggled panting to his feet, half blinded, blood streaming from his nose. She swung her arm and hit him over the head, several times.

'Get away!' she screamed, her eyes blazing. 'Leave us alone!' The canvas straps slipped from Anthony's shoulder as he sank to his knees, and the briefcase fell on the floor.

426

'Where's the gun?' Sean gasped, holding his stomach. 'Don't let him get the—'

There was a second deafening roar that knocked Anthony off his feet and hurled him back against the wall. He collapsed, screaming in pain and clutching his shattered right shoulder. Carmel swung round and the torchlight hit Simona, who was sitting against the wall, the gun shaking in her outstretched hands. Lisa clung to her, hiding her face. Simona dropped the gun and put her arms around Lisa.

'Come on!' Carmel shouted, panicked. She grabbed Lisa and hauled her to her feet. 'Let's get of here! Sean, are you okay?'

'Yeah.' Sean got up and walked to Simona, stooped and picked up the gun. He also picked up the briefcase in its canvas bag and slung it over his shoulder. Then he looked at Anthony, a look of pure, murderous hatred.

'No!' Carmel gasped, guessing what he was thinking. 'You're not going to dirty your hands on *him*,' she said fiercely. 'Don't do it, Sean, don't lower yourself. Not like this, not in front of Lisa.'

'You're right.' He put the gun in his pocket and hugged them both. 'Give me the torch. I'll go first, you follow. I think I can remember the way out. Do you?'

'Yes.' Carmel nodded. 'And dump that gun somewhere. We have to hurry,' she gasped. 'Did you hear that rumbling? I don't think it was trains this time.' She glanced back at Simona. 'Can you walk?'

'I think . . .' Simona was on her knees, swaying. 'Not so good.'

'Come on. I'll help you.' Sean lifted her to her feet and put one arm around her. Carmel handed him the torch.

'You're not going to steal my money and leave me bleeding to death alone in the pitch dark?' Anthony watched helplessly as the four of them left the cave, heading back towards the main tunnel. 'Come on, help me out here!' Panic rose in him as the torchlight faded. 'You're better people than I am,' he shouted sarcastically.

427

'We've got a child and an injured girl to look after,' Carmel called back. 'You can wait for the police. And that money's not yours. It belongs to your victims.'

'Don't leave me here!' he screamed. 'I'm in terrible pain. And I don't like the dark!'

'Neither does my daughter!'

The torchlight disappeared and their footsteps grew faint. Anthony could hear his breath rasping, feel blood pouring from his nose and pumping from the bullet wound in his shoulder. The burn on his lower leg throbbed and stung like crazy. He leaned his head back, but that made no difference to the nosebleed. How long before he started to feel weak, passed out? He couldn't stay here. If he could just get out, get to his car. He still had a chance. But he needed to move quickly.

He took the matches out of his pocket and groped around for the candle. Its wick was bent and twisted, crushed in a pool of hot wax which immediately turned the tiny flame blue and killed it. Anthony swore.

'Come on, you ... *light*!'

He struck three matches and they all burned down. His fingers were slippery, sticky with blood. It was no use, the candle wick was too damaged. He had to find his way out of here by the light of approximately twenty matches. Anthony rolled over and crawled on all fours, feeling his way back into the tunnel. He was panting and sweating despite the damp, bone-chilling cold, in agony from his bullet-shattered shoulder. Water was dripping everywhere, the drips coming faster and faster. It seemed to be pissing rain down here as much as it was above ground.

Why the hell had he kidnapped the clone? He had been too greedy, overreached himself. Anthony did not feel angry or full of hate any more, just frightened and terribly alone. He did not even begrudge Simona the bullet in his shoulder. His right arm was stiff and very painful, swelling rapidly, and the pain in two of his fingers made him think they might be broken. He crawled on as fast

428

as possible, gasping and groaning, leaving a trail of blood.

Choking dust engulfed him as part of a wall or tunnel collapsed. Had the bullets, the roar of the gun, dislodged something? Anthony gave a hoarse cry of horror as a swarm of squeaking rats disturbed by the subsidence scurried past, their bodies brushing against him, long tails flicking over his hands. He had to light a match. He paused, coughing, slowly lifted his left arm and wiped his forehead. He was covered in sweat.

Blood flowed relentlessly from his nose and shoulder; Anthony wondered how much he had lost. More than when Sean Devine had chucked the plant in his face? How had it come to this? From a chance meeting in a pub to a life or death confrontation in a secret labyrinth! He struggled to his feet and clumsily struck a match. His legs were weak and trembling. Anthony leaned against the wall, holding the burning match aloft. Which way now? He couldn't think.

'Shit!' he gasped, breaking out in a fresh sweat. This was worse than his nightmare. Any nightmare. He blinked and stared into the darkness. Mary was walking towards him, smiling, her hands outstretched.

'You're all right now, love!' she called. 'I'll help you. I'm your real mother, aren't I?'

There was a figure behind her, a small, stocky man in Victorian dress, scruffy and balding but with a haughty air, obviously accustomed to giving orders, being his own boss. It was Joseph Williamson, the architect of the devil's kingdom! Anthony realised he was hallucinating. His heart thudded, banging around his diaphragm like a panicked, trapped animal. He dropped the match as it burned down, and hurriedly struck another. A smell of charcoal, like a barbecue, hung in the air.

He struggled on, cursing the weakness in his legs. He longed to lie down and rest, but if he did that he would never get up again. He knew the way now. It wasn't far. Anthony imagined himself coming out on the other side, getting into the car full of gold and driving away. The image gave him hope. He lit another match and plunged on into the darkness, going faster now. More rumbling started, came closer. The ground shook beneath him. What the hell was happening? Surely a couple of gunshots couldn't have caused this?

A cold draught hit his face and blew out the match. Anthony swore, but he was glad nevertheless. The tunnel was slanting upwards and the draught must mean he was near the surface. He carried on a few steps. Stepped into air.

In that fraction of a second when he knew what was happening before it actually happened, Anthony tried to stop himself and pull back. But it was too late. He fell, down and down through several tiers, and landed with a great thud and splash in a pit of ice-cold, filthy water. The water was only inches deep, though, and the fall broke his back. Rat corpses disturbed by the impact bobbed crazily around, nudging his broken, twisted body.

Anthony lay there in the freezing, wet blackness, barely conscious. He couldn't seem to breathe. Dimly, from above, the rumbling grew louder and came closer, until it was on top of him. Bricks and stones rained down, splashing into the water around him, striking his face and body. He could not move, could not protect himself from the missiles.

Anthony knew what this was. Death. But it wasn't like it had been in his fantasies. He wasn't free, he wasn't flying. There was no joyful calm, no peace. Only helpless, suffocating terror, and the awful knowledge that it was too late. His father's beloved Proverbs 16:25 came into his mind again: 'There is a way that seemeth right unto a man, but the end thereof are the ways of death.'

He didn't think much of the grammar. And typical how all that childhood bullshit stayed with you. Even at the end. He groaned, tried and failed to turn his head. A ton of earth and rocks fell, choking him, clogging his mouth and nose. Burying him deep in the labyrinth.

Anthony didn't want death now. Not here, not this way. Not like this.

'Did you dump the gun?' Carmel shouted to Sean as they climbed the ladder. The place was collapsing around their ears and she couldn't think how they had got this far, especially with Sean having to carry Simona most of the way.

'Chucked it in that hole we jumped across,' Sean shouted back. He reached the top of the ladder and let the exhausted Simona slide to the floor in the stone chamber. He leaned down and lifted Lisa, then helped Carmel. They clung together for a second. 'Come on,' he gasped. 'Up the steps.'

Carmel grabbed Lisa's hand and they ran forward. Sean followed, half carrying Simona. She groaned and whimpered in pain, on the verge of unconsciousness. They climbed the steep steps and came up into the rainy night. Carmel coughed, ridding her lungs of the stale air of the labyrinth. The city air had never smelled so fresh. As they came up the steps there was more deep rumbling from below. She trembled and held on to Lisa as she thought she heard the ladder crash down. They had made it just in time. Anthony would surely be dead now, either from massive blood loss or being buried alive. She shivered with horror.

Policemen ran towards them shouting; she recognised John Edwards. Police cars were parked all around, their lights blazing, and the helicopter had landed some distance away. The Renault Megane was being searched, its doors and boot flung open. Paramedics were waiting. Carmel knelt and clutched Lisa to her.

'It's okay now, babe,' she breathed, kissing her. 'You're safe. Everything's going to be all right.' Sean wrapped his arms around them and they stayed there, huddled together while the paramedics attended to Simona. 'We're getting soaked!' Carmel gasped after a minute. 'We have to move.'

'Yeah.' Sean lifted Lisa, cradling her in his arms. 'I've had enough of this place.'

'So have I, Daddy.' She clung to him. 'I told Mummy you'd be home for Christmas.'

'And you were right.' Sean looked at Carmel and smiled. 'Let's go home.' They walked towards the waiting police cars.

'You sure you're going to be okay to do this, love?' The policewoman looked at Simona with concern. 'You don't look all that well to me.' That was an understatement. The girl was deathly pale where she wasn't bruised, hollow-eyed, and not too steady on her feet. But she had insisted on dragging herself out of her hospital bed this morning to come here. Grey light filtered into the tiled room, rain lashing the windowpanes. Outside was a view of flat wet roofs and a distant flyover crawling with traffic.

'Thank you, but I am all right. I must identify my sister.' Simona sat on the hard chair. Her heart was pounding and she tried to steady her breathing. Her hands were cold, clammy. She felt weak and faint, hurting all over. She wore dark blue denim jeans, a purple sweater and a soft, black leather jacket, all borrowed from Carmel Devine. The brown leather boots Anthony had made her buy, only yesterday. It seemed like a century ago. Simona had had to turn up the jeans; Carmel was taller than she was.

She looked fearfully at the closed mortuary doors. It was hard to believe Maria was lying in there, that the police had discovered her body in those tunnels. Anthony had murdered Maria, lied about her being still alive. The police were very kind, and they wanted to know everything that had happened to her since she entered the United Kingdom. When she was feeling better, of course. It was going to be hard, telling them all that. Simona could still barely take it in herself. It was difficult to believe she was safe now. She felt she would never be safe in this world. She could not imagine living a so-called normal life again.

'You ready, love?' the policewoman asked as a small,

432

dark man with a moustache pushed through the swing doors and beckoned to them. They followed him into the mortuary.

More tiles, pale blue here. All the stainless steel, just like in films. The man was talking, explaining something, but Simona could not hear and did not care what he was saying. He slowly opened one of the stainless steel doors and pulled out the white-sheeted body. Glanced warily at her. He lifted the sheet and uncovered the head.

The dark shiny hair looked just like Maria's. The face was blue and mottled, bloated with death, partially eaten away by God only knew what. Simona cried out and her stomach heaved. She turned away, hands clutched over her mouth.

'D'you want to go out, love?' the policewoman asked.

'No!' Simona gasped. 'No, I must look.' She turned and forced herself to look at the dead face of the young woman, really study it. It was still recognisable. To somebody. But not to her. The policewoman gently took hold of her arm.

'So, is this the—?'

'No!' Simona turned to her, tears spilling from her dark eyes. 'That is not my sister. That is not Maria!'

She fainted.

Epilogue

'So what did you think of the party?'

Sean walked to the bedroom window and looked out into Falkner Square. It as an icy December night, frost glittering on the pavements and on the roofs of parked cars. The trees had lost all their leaves, and he could clearly see the houses on the opposite side of the park.

'I hated it.' Carmel sat at the dressing table taking off her makeup. She wore a tight, black, sleeveless dress. 'It was even more of an ordeal than I'd imagined.'

'Yeah.' Sean sighed. 'For me too.'

'I couldn't stop thinking about what happened the last time we had a party.'

'Neither could I.' Sean looked at her. 'You put on a great act, but I knew you were having a hard time.' He drew the curtains. 'Seems nice and quiet out there,' he commented. 'No creeps spying on us from parked cars.'

'I even wore the same dress I had on the night you disappeared. Just put it on without thinking. I only realised half way through the evening. I spilled some wine on it so I'd have an excuse to change. Talk about macabre.' Carmel shuddered. 'Why the hell did we bother with a bloody party?'

'Exorcising demons. So we could prove to ourselves that we're back to normal.' Sean stood behind her, lifted a strand of her blonde hair and let it fall. 'And Lisa wanted to celebrate. She was up for a party.'

'Wasn't she just!' Carmel smiled suddenly. 'She was in her element tonight. Incredible to think it's only a month since ...' She looked down, biting her lip. Sean's warm hands stroked her shoulders and smooth bare arms.

'Kids bounce back quickly.' He moved her hair aside, kissed the nape of her neck.

'Do they?' Carmel looked at him in the mirror. 'I hope Lisa really has bounced back. I hope we do soon. Did you check on her?' she asked anxiously. 'Is she okay?'

'She's fine. Fast asleep.' Sean's voice was gentle. 'We should get some sleep too. She'll be up at dawn, all ready for her visit to the Maritime Museum. And fudge shop.'

'Amazing about that gold they found in Anthony's stolen car.' Carmel picked up her comb. 'Of course now it's Crown property. Treasure trove. The Crown will end up getting all Anthony's property, seeing as he died intestate and has no living relatives. Relatives wouldn't be allowed to profit from his crimes anyway.'

'No. Only the state.' Sean straightened up and turned away. 'I really don't give a fuck.' His voice hardened. 'I don't suppose any of that money will be used to help trafficked women and children.' He sat on the bed, unbuttoning his blue shirt. 'Mary was devastated to find out what her precious Anthony was really like. She didn't believe it at first, but once he kidnapped Lisa ... that was it. She told me she'd pray for his soul, but couldn't bring herself to go to his funeral.'

'Who could? I'm sorry for her,' Carmel sighed. 'But more sorry for us. For Lisa. And those women Anthony murdered.' She stood up and unzipped her dress. 'I'm glad they managed to recover his body. I knew he had to be dead, but otherwise I wouldn't have been able to really believe it. That part of the labyrinth was even more dangerous, and those gunshots must have set off the subsidence. I read in the paper that the labyrinth will be cleared, fully explored and eventually opened to the public. There's talk of a European development grant.'

'Won't get any further than talk, I bet. But again ...'

Sean pulled off his shirt and threw it on the floor. 'I don't give a toss. Christ!' he sighed. 'What an evening! You're right, it was macabre. It was bloody bizarre. Everyone trying their best to pretend nothing happened. At least no one told us we were *lucky*. Suppose I should be grateful for that! And the newspapers and local telly seem to have given up pestering us for interviews.'

Carmel stepped out of her dress. 'Thank goodness Simona's been reunited with her sister.' She looked at him, her face brightening. 'Isn't it wonderful that Maria wasn't dead after all? To think she really was in Dublin!'

'Terrible about Maria's cousin though, the girl Anthony murdered and buried in the tunnel. There was a family resemblance, he must have got the two girls mixed up. Ironic, isn't it?' Sean shook his head grimly. 'All the time he believed he was lying to Simona, he was actually telling the truth. And crazy that Simona and her sister will still be deported, despite the fact that they were victims of traffickers. As usual, the law is an arsehole.'

'I don't think they'll mind leaving this country though, do you?' Carmel's blue eyes were sombre. 'Not after what they've suffered. I just hope they get the help and support they need back home.' She dropped the dress on the stool and slipped off her black bra and pants. Sean's eyes darkened as he stared at her slender, naked body.

'You look gorgeous,' he whispered. 'Come here!'

She hesitated. 'I think . . . I'll check on Lisa first.'

'I just did that.' There was a slight edge to his voice.

'I know.' Carmel nodded, swallowed. She was being over-protective, of course. But she couldn't help it. 'I'll only be a minute.' She pulled on her robe, went out and hurried across the landing to her daughter's bedroom.

Lisa's sleep seemed deep and peaceful. Moonlight slanted through the partially open curtains. Carmel sat on the bed and kissed her gently, listened to the child's quiet breathing. Thought about the traumatic events that had shaken them all to the core.

People were said to learn from traumatic experiences and become stronger, but Carmel thought that was bullshit. She didn't feel stronger, and neither did Sean. How was that supposed to happen? And what had they learned? That people were more vulnerable than they realised, that lives could be destroyed or turned upside down on someone's evil whim. That bad things happened simply because some people chose to behave in an evil manner, and you had to try to ensure you didn't fall victim to them. She was more anxious, scared and worried now, could hardly bear to let Sean or Lisa out of her sight. They felt the same about her.

Carmel was relieved that Anthony Maskey was dead, happy that Simona was free now and reunited with her sister. But she felt a tremendous sadness for all that had happened. Anger that their lives had almost been destroyed, and fear that they could so easily not have survived. It would never again be easy for her to trust, to believe anyone was really what they seemed. A lot of people did not wish you well, had bad intentions. That was what she had learned. Simona Tarnu had learned that too. Carmel stood up and tiptoed out.

Sean was in bed. He looked handsome and relaxed, lying there in the lamplight.

'This evening doesn't have to be a total disaster,' he remarked, gazing at her as she slipped off her robe. 'We can still get a lot of pleasure out of it.' He smiled, and Carmel smiled back. She got into bed and threw herself into his arms.

'I found this,' he said, holding up the tiny blue-and-gold wrapped package. 'At the back of my drawer. Forgot all about it.'

'Oh!' Carmel stared at the package. 'I made a vow not to open that until you came home,' she whispered, her eyes wet.

'Well, now I am home. Thanks to you.' Sean leaned over and took her in his arms. He kissed her and stroked her breasts. 'You never gave up on me,' he murmured. 'I love you!'

437

'I love you, Sean,' Carmel looked into his eyes. 'And I want you. Right now.'

'Fine by me.' Sean kissed her again and ran his hands over her body. He grinned.

'But open your damn present first!'